A
SWIFT
PASSAGE

OTHER WORK BY BARBARA HENNING

POETRY
A Slow Curve (Monkey Puzzle Press, 2012)
Cities and Memory (Chax Press 2010)
My Autobiography (United Artists, 2007)
Detective Sentences (Spuyten Duyvil, 2001)
In between (Spectacular Diseases, 2000)
Me and My Dog (Poetry New York, 1999)
Love Makes Thinking Dark (United Artists, 1995)
The Passion of Signs (Leave Books, 1994)
Smoking in the Twilight Bar (United Artists, 1988)

FICTION
Thirty Miles to Rosebud (BlazeVOX, 2009)
You, Me and the Insects (Spuyten Duyvil, 2005)
Black Lace (Spuyten Duyvil, 2001)

NON-FICTION
The Selected Prose of Bobbie Louise Hawkins (BlazeVOX, 2012)
Looking Up Harryette Mullen: Interviews on Sleeping With the
Dictionary *and Other Works* (Belladonna, 2011)

COLLABORATIONS
How to Read and Write in the Dark (with Miranda Maher, 1996)
Words and Pictures (with Sally Young 1996).

A
SWIFT
PASSAGE

Stories & Poems by

Barbara Henning

QUALE PRESS

Poems and stories in this collection have been published by *Press1, Poets for Living Waters, Downtown Brooklyn, Quill Puddle, Peep/Show: A Taxonomic Exercise in Textual and Visual Seriality, Brooklyn Paramount, Anthology of New Writing from the Upper Peninsula (WSU Press), Bone Bouquet, Sun Skeleton* and *Talisman*. *The Dinner* and *Twelve Green Rooms* were also published as limited edition artist books by *Long News*, and *A Slow Curve* was published as a chapbook by Monkey Puzzle Press.

Much gratitude and love for the friends and editors who have helped put these poems and stories into the world: Gian Lombardo, Dumisani Kambi-Shamba, Krystal Languell, Martine Bellen, Lewis Warsh, Miranda Maher, Bobbie Louise Hawkins, Anne Waldman, Phyllis Wat, Valerie Fox, Nicole Kline, Amy King, Heidi Lynn Staples, Wayne Berninger, James Hart, Emily Brent, Lynn Behrendt, Anne Gorrick, Sarah Wallen, Lisa Rogel, Ron Reiki, Tony Iantosco, Dan Owen, Ed Foster, Nate Jordan and Jordan Antonucci.

Most of the poems and short-short stories in this collection blend fiction and autobiography. The two full-length stories, "Hegira" and "The Dinner" are both works of fiction; any resemblance to actual events or persons or stories is entirely coincidental. Revised by author June 2015.

Cover Photo by Miranda Maher
Author Photo by Martine Bellen

ISBN: 978-1-935835-10-3
LCCN: 2013943137

Quale Press
www.quale.com

CONTENTS

A Slow Curve

TWELVE GREEN ROOMS

Third Street, Tucson

The light is white today and the oranges are glistening with rain water. Orange trees were brought here by the Spaniards, along with the Jesuit missions. Today the birds are quieter than usual. Maybe when they sing a lot, it's because they are thirsty. The Santa Cruz used to flow year round, but then ranchers gold miners farmers   population   suburban   water   drain   sprawl On Third Street, a young man comes out of a seven-bedroom house to smoke on the porch. I pass under a big sparse tree with low branches, so old and just standing there, one of the tallest trees in the neighborhood. It appears deciduous, but in fact it's a low pine, an aleppo, an ancient tree from the Mediterranean. The estimated appraisal value is well over $20,000. Brought to Tucson as seedlings by a gas station as a gimmick 70 years ago   too much   too little   water flows from the Colorado River to the Gulf of California and Tucson gardens   overflow downpour perennial springs   irrigation   tree-lined   rivulet   monsoon riverbed   barren   run dry   Stein says that the work of man is not in harmony with the landscape, it opposes it and it is just that that is the basis of cubism. Peddling along, I look down at my blue socks, one higher than the other. No city money for street repair this year, but instead an incredible pattern of intersecting cracks and potholes.

Blue Beard Cafe

My dad sent me an email saying I wasn't particularly mistreated, that he had spent the same amount of money on each of us. The Caspian Sea region in Iran has potentially the world's largest oil reserves. *He beat me, yeah, but not unnecessarily. When he found out he shouldn't do that, well he just said, he had never beat me over anything I didn't deserve. He would accuse me of something and if I admitted, I got half a beating.* There were nuclear projects in Iraq, somewhere. Well it was good thing to do anyhow, wasn't it? *Now he's on a poor little old me thing. He threw the pressure cooker at my mom's head once and broke the pane window. Little Joey was sitting on the floor, watching.* The history and residue of eons past. So old and just sitting there surge gush disperse dissolve scatter *And he doesn't think anything of it . . . Excuse me Miss, could you bring me more coffee? Yeah, this is fine. . . . My first memory was shutting a door and hiding. You had those stripes, too, didn't you? I had them all over my back. You were shot, too? Yeah? And then they kept you hour after hour and picked it out themselves. I know.* Black sludge is drifting over the U.S. shores. Greed Stupidity   Collateral damage   Quiet   Low   Along   *I read something and then I realized that's why I can't have a relationship with anyone. I had to cry* surge   spilt   trickle   rush forward   *But to tell you the truth, no matter what, I'm a happy little*   surge   spilt trickle   rush forward

Nonstop Las Vegas

A woman tries on a pink veil and a guy in the back has his computer open to a porno site, a naked man with an erect penis. Some other folks in back are playing poker. Everyone is chattering   up above   the thunderstorm   I order a cup of tea   cloudburst down below   betrayal   bayou   abundance   five thousand dolphins, drum fish, jelly fish, northern gamut, man o'war, sea turtles, dragon flies and the laughing gulls are the hardest hit. It costs $15,000 to clean the oil from one pelican and return it to its environment. The order of pelecaniformes, ancient symbol of heavy rain   hurricane   down below darkness   Then the lights dim and I fall asleep and dream I'm walking past a dark body of choppy water, wandering out to the outer edge of a peninsula, the tiny band between us, shaped like a long finger with water thrown wildly about. When the sun comes out the slicks of brown and green oil start to boil   sentient beings sold down the water way   sway that baby sway   In Nigeria, thousands of corroding pipelines   600 plus million barrels Spilt   Brutal   Shock   Throat   Money   Shut up   Suddenly from around the corner a female lion charges toward me. I stand absolutely still, stare her down until she disappears, then I open one of my eyelids, just to make sure

Bayport, Long Island

A shock of black hair, little cleft chin, round face, little feet like a fish. Pelican. Pelican. Pelican. Two weeks later he is more than one-third larger. One day he'll be over six feet. With a ten-foot wing span and a layer of webbed fibers. Throat pouches full of water   fish   oceanic   ripple   spill   sentient   brim over   full over   The terns are fragile little birds, one dive into the oily water and they don't resurface. I take the baby into the kitchen, and then in the red glow of the night light, we sway that baby sway. Pelecaniformes, ancient symbol of   spill out   spill over   Later I come down the stairs for a glass of water. In the dark, the TV is on with no sound and Greg is stretched out in the chair, his big linebacker body and the infant curled up in his armpit, both sound asleep. Half a mile south, the Atlantic laps against the shore.

Little Green Rooms

Cacti are growing tall in the yard and as I walk through, one collapses and then the other crashes down. We untwist the big one and prop it back up. Now it has a network of walls inside, little green rooms with no ceilings. I'm standing inside when water and fluids start rushing in   torrent   squall   spill over   gushing welling   Up the cactus goes again, towering overhead. Now it's my childhood house, and my aunt and uncle are there and the house is overgrown and   decaying. The infant is curled up in his father's armpit. I beg them not to sell the house. But someone has stolen the water spigot. And all the trees are dead. There are spider webs with black widows in every corner and crevice. We could fix it, I say, by each taking one room. We could get jobs and save our money, put in a wood floor. We could have running water and lawns watered with recycled rain water. We could have a filter system installed for clean drinking water   rushing   torrent   squall   spill over   gushing welling   We could still watch television and drink ice tea without a worry. We could each have our own electric car and mini computer, and a garbage disposal, solar heating—we could have our organic groceries delivered to our doorstep. A special room for meditation and working out. We could have our own stationary bicycles. Lots of books, of course. We could enjoy ourselves. I'm too old for all this, my aunt says, and so are you. Let's not get carried away again. All I need is one little room and a mat to sleep on. A good blanket. Water we need some water. And a little burner, a cup and a plate. And some vegetables and fruits. That's all, Barbara. That's all.

Lake St. Clair

I'm surrounded by photos and knick-knacks, corn dolls with turquoise eyes. A bust of a pink plastic lady, eyes closed, a crown of plastic flowers mounted on her head. Eons ago tiny plants and animals sank to the bottom of a body of water and then clay sand silt pressure decay sewage spills subarctic slow dissipation petrochemicals ethylene propylene butadiene I fall asleep on an inflatable bed and dream that my friend Marsha is standing in front of me with a black eye and wearing tinted sunglasses. How'd you get that I say? She smiles and raises one eyelid. You should write a book about all your black eyes. And I'll write a book about you writing a book about your black eyes. Then I'm in a doctor's office with a Doctor Cortázar. Are you related to the writer Cortázar? I ask. The elevator in the old Williamsburg Bank Building stops abruptly between the floors, and uh-oh, then it starts speeding down clay sand silt pressure decay absolutely still and now the ceiling is collapsing floating belly up 600 plus million barrels Split Brutal Shut up And here I am this morning on my knees in Marie's flower garden in St. Clair Shores, Michigan, scraping old paint off a cement swordfish and then painting it white up to the snout where no water shoots out anymore.

Barrett Avenue

Linnée sits cross-legged on the sofa nursing the baby. Little Luke starts zipping and unzipping my vest. I put his two little stuffed rabbits inside my vest and zip them in. I'm pregnant I say. I'm pink. His eyes light up and then unzip—two babies! He looks at Né nursing Logan, and then back at me. I unzip his pjs and put the babies in there. Luke is pregnant. Where is Luke? I play it on the piano. Full of glee, he's shaking, laughing and running in circles. Come outside and help me plant these flowers. It's windy. The wind is lifting his curls. He picks the hyacinth up by the stem, breaking off the roots and then he walks across the yard, holding the purple flower. Yesterday, nearly 60 pelican chicks washed onto an island in coastal Louisiana, fragile, wading into oily puddles or smeared by oil from their parents' feathers   floating   too much   too little   down to the ocean   A crown of plastic flowers for British Petroleum   In the park, an old woman holds a string and a bat kite flying high up in the sky. Her daughter says—she keeps everything. It was mine when I was a child. Oil is used to make plastic, preservatives, food packaging, hair curlers, telephones, televisions, balloons, ammonia, insect repellent, heart valves, trash bags, body bags, but not paper kites and cotton string. Luke runs out into the center of the field, watching it waver back and forth   eons   oh   sand   oh   pressure   oh my sword oh the tempest   squall   hurricane   oceanic   subaquatic At dusk, Luke takes me by my hand and we walk slowly down the street under the big maple trees.

Deepwater Horizon

Unable to fly, float, escape or find food—irritation, vomiting, diarrhea, oil aspiration, ulceration, skin death, confusion, vertigo, tremors, seizures, cardiac arrest, hemolytic anemia, liver and kidney damage, sudden death, chemical pneumonitis, choking, coughing, gagging, swelling, bronchospasms, bleeding, fever. For long-haired animals and birds it is worse. The chemical dispersants break the oil into tiny droplets, causing irritation, inflammation, headaches, genetic damage and mutations, difficulty breathing, vomiting, kidney and liver damage. *Baby turtles leave their sandy nests and head straight for the sea knowing everything a turtle needs to know*   wavering back and forth   spread out   spill over   brim over   The largest fish on earth are four miles from the leaking wellhead. From Belize to Honduras to Alabama. *They filter plankton and tiny fish from the water through sieve-like mechanisms in their mouths.* Each animal particular. Like a fingerprint. When the whale shark dies it disappears, sinking to the bottom of the sea   plastic   lifting   too much   too little   wavering back and forth   When one animal is extinct another proliferates. Biodiversity. The bristle worm is churning up the bacteria on the sea floor. The fishermen will die or relocate. And beach houses in Texas keep tar sandals as regular guest items, the oil just a nuisance, after all BP has been good to them, pouring money into their economy, and so they vote, yes, yes, yes.

B & H Dairy / Kabul

Josephine's face is more wrinkled, but of course—she's 70 years old now and she's been working with   battered   imprisoned homeless   from the wellhead mother and baby   We're sitting in B & H on Second Avenue. The man is wiping down the counter, and she's talking about driving a car across the dry dusty mountains outside Kabul to help set up a new shelter. The men in the car were surprised. They had never seen a woman drive before. And Josephine can be a wild driver, directed but kind of unpredictable   perennial   recurrent   permanent   continuing   precipitation   When one animal is extinct another proliferates. The falcon is the fastest bird on earth. Afghanistan used to be a migratory thoroughfare, but the birds are not flying that way anymore. 10,000 villages destroyed   unsafe water infrastructure leaks   bacterial contamination   landfills   I ask her if she wears a shawl on her head. No I hate something on my head. Do you ever see any women outside with their heads uncovered. Never. Not one? Not one. Just you? Aren't you worried you will excite someone's anger? I'm here aren't I? Well you can only die once. Well then I will, I'm not covering my head.

Seventh Street and Avenue B

At one A.M. I am preparing to take my bath when I realize that my cell phone is in the car. I put on my sweat clothes and go down to Avenue B, past some folks smoking and consulting on the corner by the Horseshoe Bar. When I come back, the medical examiner is parked in front of our building. And up from the basement, two men carry a stretcher with a black body bag zipped shut. I climb the stairs to my apartment and lie still wondering who died. How come. Why. I can hear the click clacking of shoes down below on the sidewalk and above me the clickity-click from the toenails of somebody's dog. The next day I'm in my car double parked waiting for alternate side parking. On the phone I tell my stepmother about it and she says, That happens more there. Death? No, seeing body bags. Three people are talking outside the front door. I get out and ask if anyone knows who died. The guy who lived in the basement apartment. A heart attack, the young man says. Patrick was only forty years old or so. I feel guilty. I told him it was probably just heart burn. Well, a woman says, I told him to get to the emergency room right away. He said maybe tomorrow. He didn't have health insurance. He didn't have a lobbyist. 1,750 companies and organizations hired 4,525 lobbyists. 2,000 plus pages. Health Scare. Anytime. Loopholes. High premiums and penalties. It starts raining and then all four of us commiserate our loss of Patrick and the absence of health insurance in our lives. The common good. Meanwhile politicians, pharmaceutical companies, insurance companies, physicians, hospitals, and medical equipment companies lobby up. Cover up. Lock 'em out. Think about it. Well then I will, but I'm not covering my head. No matter what. Today as more and more tar balls wash up on shore along with dead birds, turtles and fish, oil industry contributions flood Washington D.C. In your pocket. Think tank. Cover up. The animals. The poets. The artists. Us. Cover up. Let us think for you.

Between the Sound
and the Atlantic

The criminals have been found and law and order and the stars and actors are passing in front of the screen as their mortality is documented. I'm in the rocker with a newspaper on my lap remembering this and that and then I remember my grandmother sitting in her chair weeping about her dead friends as we were chasing each other around the house, passing her by, six, nine, eleven, and twelve. Then she'd sit up, start yodeling—yo-dli-oh-laa-haa-dee—and she'd take a newspaper and reach out and whack us as we passed her by. Ecstatic. Static. Wet. Rivulet. Inlet. Droplet. We keep going until the last word and then someone else finishes the sentence and starts another. Maybe tomorrow. I pick up the newspaper and start reading about the oil spill, a photo of a dead baby pelican on the front page. Maybe tomorrow. Lolo can't walk yet but he stands next to the sofa, sways, claps and hums to music. That's the way children's language takes shape, I think, as a shadow that slowly gains detail and then the sun goes behind a cloud, and I drift off for a moment, coasting over the deepwater horizon and then slipping into a hot oil slick. When the man leans over the bird, carefully wiping off the oil, she turns her head to the side. Then from the shadow another sound emerges   a   squawk   gush   surge   2100   get to   well I will   As the ice cap melts and the sea level rises   squawk well I will   perhaps the pelicans will   multiply   20 million years   pelicanus   squawk   gush surge   flying   *well I will* clumsy   graceful   ungainly   and their ancestors will   majestically fly   too much   too little   over our flooded shores and cities

Second Avenue

An old woman crosses Eleventh Street, pushing a walker on wheels. Shrunken with her frame bent forward, wearing little heels and a tweedy old coat—she stops for a moment and lifts up her foot to kick some stone or dirt off the wheel. She does this three times. Then she starts rolling steadily, one foot stepping carefully in front of the other. As she passes my bench, a taxi pulls up and the door opens. Two women climb out, one about forty and the other near sixty. Both are wearing black sunglasses, carrying canes for the blind, and holding on to each other. They stumble a little over the curb and then bump right into the old woman. The younger woman says with a questioning lilt, UPS? The old woman stops rolling, looks at them and points to the UPS store, but then she looks at them again, realizing that they can't see. She says something else, maybe—Hold on to my arm—because then they lean against her as she steers them over toward the store. The door is too heavy. Before I can stand up to help, the clerk opens it. And our mortality is documented, the shadow slowly gaining detail. One of the women leans out the door and yells thank-you-god-bless-you.   Ecstatic.   Static.   Wet.   Inlet.   Rivulet.   Let us meet at the river in silence   with the gliding sliding PCB fish   Down the street the old woman goes, lifting her left hand slightly, as if to say don't even think about it twice. And just then at that moment, as the woman makes a left onto Tenth Street, there is a cloudburst and it is raining.

A
SWIFT
PASSAGE

On Avenue A

The police cut the chains on two motor scooters parked on the sidewalk. I see them parked like this all over the East Village. Away they go on a flatbed. Across the street, the pigeons are in a perfect V formation high over the park and then they swoop down, settling on the roof and an electric wire to briefly rest and then a swift passage outward and back into a V again. At the entrance to the park, an old man is strumming his guitar as the clouds gather grey overhead   a triangle   presence   arriving holding   for a moment

Tompkins Square

Once a swamp, once a military parade ground, once surrounded by shanties, then six- to seven-story tenements, sweatshops, Eastern European, Puerto Rican, the site of many demonstrations and riots—Charlie Parker lived across the street—heroin culture, chanting love, Hare Krishna, the punks camped on the southwest side, once a tent city where the homeless staked a space, then property values climbed, and so a curfew and a wall of armed police tore the city down   desertion   *égress*   *salida*   August 6, 1989 and we were sitting in Lucy's when the police cavalry charged up Avenue A   agitate   rouse   excite Then the park bench was redesigned with a bar in the middle. The thinning of trees. Now closed after midnight except for the tulips, daisies, pigeons, rats and squirrels   the weeds in the cracks   get away going along   goodbye for now   Birds of prey migrate into the city for easy feeding. At noon, a hawk perches in the giant elm with the bird house in the middle, its thick branches snaking over the park. Following the curving iron rails that separate grass from cement, I clasp my hands behind me and hum—*Summertime and your mama's good looking*. Words and bird sounds on the breeze . . . The guy across the way is pounding a beat on his hip. All night, all right. A woman on a bike with big speakers on the back greets her friends at the circle where the public stage used to be, electric, the center of, the birds are on, the amps are on, the rain is holding off and we are wearing clown makeup. Anything can happen here   into a V again   at any moment   off we go

Single on a Stem

My right lung is sore. The air inside and outside. Along the park, the green points of the tulips push up out of the ground. Bike over to Chinatown to buy a wedding gift. Downhill Avenue A to Third Street, uphill to Broadway and then downtown downhill, the clouds hiding the sun, sometimes for many days. Lewis won't be there tonight   you are caught in the drift   the outside of his heart inflamed. They removed the problem with a needle. Now, he says, there is a cardiologist in my life.

Humidity

In a cafe on First Avenue, Julie Patton and I eat gazpacho and
then we ramble through the park, standing in the dark under an
ancient elm tree   *trees make the best poets   they draw in the sky*
See that window with the half curtains and the lights on, I say,
that's where I live   for the time being   *the animal anima alpha-
bet*   Julie lives around the corner and back and forth to Cleveland for the time being   *where everything is   see   come-here
look*   Your cough, she says, sounds like my mother's, and a doctor helped her with acupuncture. Not long after, I'm sitting across
from him, and unexpectedly I fall under Nina Simone's spell
distant or near   the things you do   My lungs compressed. I
should have loosened my clothes, but now I'm woven with
needles. So I ask him, like one yogi would another, if he could
unhook it   unfasten   and release   *the hinges of my wings
and put them in a corner*   He reaches under me, fumbling, and
then he says, I'm a little out of practice.

On Highway 23

On Highway 23, heading north toward the Upper Peninsula of Michigan. It's raining beautiful rain, pine trees, deciduous, now pine, now foggy and the little trailers and trucks leave a trail behind them of smoke and water, the wipers going back and forth, pretty continual the rain today, but a lightness in the northern sky   constant   incessant   perennial   Over the Mackinac Bridge, I pass a big truck with logs on the back, the sky still grey, and the ethereal span of the bridge, white and green pillars, delicate and tall, reminding me of Genny Kapular's yoga instruction: lift your diaphragm, like delicately lifting a lady's handkerchief on two pillars   dividing north from south   freestanding   Half way over, the rain stops. I grew up around water, I think, as I turn into the Welcome Center. Sitting on a picnic table, I read a brochure. Michigan didn't want the UP, but to become a state they were forced to take it. Too cold, too rough, only a place Indians would like. Give it to Canada, the folks in the lower peninsula said. I'm speeding through farmland with giant sprinklers on wheels slowly progressing across the fields, water and something that grows very low for August, maybe a root of some sort. Then a sign for a disaster kit and I start imagining invaders coming in tanks, but now if anyone takes over, it will be through ownership. Just then on the right, a chain fence with a sign, HALLIBURTON, and a parking lot full of trucks and machinery. Monumental government contracts. Work for the locals. War. Profit. Greed   *only a bird will wonder*   Surrounded by miles of Michigan timber.

Nelson Creek

Allen's ashes are buried somewhere on the back slope of Nelson Creek, a tributary from the Chocolay River. After a couple of big storms with trees collapsing, the creek now has two branches divide   disconnect   bifurcate   I wade half way in, between sharp slippery rocks and the water moving along quickly, higher than I've ever seen it before, just above my knees. I stand still and look into the forest. Then I close my eyes. I want to take you with me, Allen. If you are wandering around here   come with me take leave   come along   *so light is the urging   so ordered*   I follow my sister back into the house. Once inside, she starts to cry *the word that flies in the night*   She puts a hunting knife and a stack of photographs on the table for her ex-husband, on top a photo of their family when their children were young. Leaning over the dining room table, she picks up a photo of her ex and his girlfriend. I've never seen the woman before and I don't want to like her, but in the photo she has a rather ordinary face. We walk around the yard, lamenting that the flower beds have been untended and the house is shabby. The piano mover says to me— That piano looks like it belongs here. Nice house. I hope I can have something like this for my family some time. I tell him how they built it twenty-five years ago, but then their marriage fell apart. He says that never would happen to him because his wife is an angel. Then he gets into the empty truck with his partner and we get into our car and head back to town where Patti is moving again.

Almost Everything

The movers took away almost everything. Now the dogs are gone too and the house is very quiet   the clicking of the computer keys   I'm upstairs writing and it's windy outside   *caressing and addressing a noun*   I hear a noise and when I look around, I see a moving shadow. Quietly I stand up and edge my way over to the door. The wind is unrolling the toilet paper and it is willowing into the hallway, swaying and creating a shadow dance on the wall.

Turn Right

After you pass Orchard Restaurant, turn right on Sandling. Straight up you'll see a clearing and an old brown broken-down barn. Turn there, the directions say, and then go past the house and turn left, park, and walk another fifty feet to a little broken-down shack and behind it there's another newer looking cabin with a tin roof. One room with a big stove in the middle, old furniture, table, cabinet, no running water, no toilet, but on the other side of the drive an outhouse and in the main farmhouse, Susan can take showers every few days. She's collecting rain water for washing and hauling drinking water from the farm. I look out over the meadows. Stein says that civilization began with a rose is a   Quiet, the way the trees blow in the wind, the rustling of leaves, the wind bending the long grass   distance   solitude stillness   We hike around the meadow and stoop down to look at little fungi growing in different colors and shapes on the edges of the path. Some are white and look like carved and feathered radishes and another is yellow with little buttons on top. We stop and pick raspberries and later I eat so many that I'm no longer interested in raspberries. There are a few things I want to ask Susan but for one reason or another I don't think of them until I am driving downstate, like why she is living on $400 a month, and how does she plan to stay in this uninsulated cabin in the winter when there is a three-foot snow cover for months on end solitude   stillness   distance

Traverse City

Katie's hair is almost white now. I met her in '72 and for a number of years we lived with the Cass Corridor community in Detroit. After a while, she married Allen's close friend, Joe, and they moved up here and Allen and I moved to New York City. There's a drawing of Joe, David, Allen and Tony on my living room wall. All those guys are dead now, from too much smack and too much alcohol   departed   outward bound   evacuate   Sometimes I weep because I miss them, but today I'm traveling. I kiss Katie and I'm back on the road. Driving along, I start thinking—if I had not decided to go back to college in '72, and to drive downtown one day and pick up a *South End* to start looking at apartments, I wouldn't have become Betty's roommate and Betty was a close friend of Katie's. Then I wouldn't have walked down Willis Avenue and met Allen when he was bartending at Cobb's. If I hadn't have met Allen, Katie probably wouldn't have met Joe and maybe they'd never have moved to Traverse City. And if Katie didn't help Betty get her apartment, I'd have found another roommate on the other side of campus and I wouldn't have gone into Cobb's Corner Bar at all. And when Betty went down to Colombia, she wouldn't have looked up Alex in prison as a favor to Allen. And maybe he'd still be sitting there in Bogotá just for buying some marijuana. And my children and grandchildren would not be alive, and I wouldn't be here years later writing these words. Sometimes it seems as if you are caught in the drift—And yet everything, every act is impregnated with possibility fragility   runaround   sidestepping   It makes me want to crawl inside my tent and just lie still and listen to the rain.

I Like Camping

I like climbing out of the car all sweaty and dirty and putting up a tent. I like pounding in the stakes and then climbing into it and sleeping while the air is flowing through the screens. I like the sound of rain on the tent when I'm inside and somewhat dry. And in the morning, I like getting up and pulling up the stakes, standing there under the trees in the early A.M. fog, rolling everything up and driving off. I like doing this all alone. Today, I follow an arrow for camping, off the highway, down a back road, where I discover a farm house converted into a campground, pristine with manicured lawns, no showers or toilets, fine for RVs, but a little odd for pup tenters. A spigot for water and an outhouse. Sweeping the dust off her porch, a short squat grey-haired woman looks at me over her glasses. Is there cell phone reception here? She nods her head and squints—as if to say, what are *you* doing here? I'm tired and it's late so I put up my tent in the middle of the lawn. Her husband is driving a tractor around the grounds. For some reason I start to feel uneasy. These rather ordinary people send me off on Alfred Hitchcock and *Psycho*. Alfred probably put a lot of mom and pop motels out of business. When I get in the tent to go to sleep, one room is still lit up in the house on the hill. And I lie there awake for a good part of the night, with my finger poised on the alarm switch on my car key. But we are too far away for anyone to hear anyhow. And all the other RVs are empty. Just me and the old couple. In the morning when I am tearing down, she is standing at the window watching me.

Livonia, Michigan

I meet up with an old friend at a Thai restaurant next to the drug-store. Roberta talks about a guy in her neighborhood that she is seeing. I tell her I'm in love with someone I met right before leaving town. Thirty-five years ago for a few months, my friend and I were lovers. She was tall and slim, long brown hair, the mother of three, and she wore cowboy boots and challenged any too pushy guy in the Song Shop Bar. For an hour or so, I felt protected. In the parking lot now, we stand between our cars. Hers is turquoise, the same shape as my little orange car. Indian colors. And we both like driving across country. A passerby, a woman with a little child in a shopping cart agrees to take our photo. I glance over the cars at the scattered cumulus clouds   drifting over the horizon   *you are lifted   in the crisp sand   that drives the wind*   gradually   carried along   in a body.

Hegira 1

My father and my stepmother moved to St. Clair Shores after we were grown, leaving behind our old cinderblock house for this slightly more upscale place near the lake. The blinds are drawn and the house is dusty and full of knick-knacks, clocks, photographs, magazines and the accumulation of a life of saving everything. Marie walks through the house, holding onto tables and walls. Her knees are shot and she is overweight, making it even worse.

How do you get down these stairs to the basement?

I take my time, she says.

Do you want me to vacuum?

No, I'm fine. I can take care of it. Don't worry.

She sits back in her recliner watching a station where a woman is selling jewelry, a closeup on a jade stone dangling from a gold chain. Marie has always loved shopping. When I lived in Detroit, I used to take her to Kmart and follow her around for hours. Often she wouldn't buy anything. Now she can't get around the store without a wheelchair. She is cutting a paragraph out of a flier, the clippings falling to the top of a little pile on the floor.

Sometimes Marie looks at me, narrowing her eyes and I can feel the slit of anger that ignited my teenage rebellion—like the time when she wouldn't let me shave my legs and I shaved all the way up to my crotch and bleached my hair blonde. I'm not sure what the exact problem is today, but she definitely doesn't like me to volunteer to clean anything, and it might have something to do with my vacuuming while she was at a meeting. I couldn't help it. The floor was filthy and she has so much trouble moving around. I wanted to help. When I go out to a cafe to pick up the internet, though, and come back later in the evening, she is cheerful again. Even though she's always in pain, she's usually cheerful.

It's midnight, and again we are watching a shopping station.

Did you get that postcard from your friend? It's on the mantle.

All is well, Nawal and Latifah together again. Love, Tamar. There's a picture of Niagara Falls on the Canadian side of the falls.

Who's Tamar? Marie asks.

Don't you remember her? She was at Emily's wedding. You know the tall woman who was very elegantly dressed in a black suit, short grey hair. She's a photographer, and I think she was sitting right next to you at the reception. I remember you talked together for quite some time.

Maybe I remember her. I'm not sure.

The last few years, Tamar's been working in Afghanistan. Back and forth from New York to there. She's had photos published in *The Times* and *National Geographic*, lots of places. The woman she mentions in the postcard, well, Tamar saved that woman's life, and I'm not exaggerating. Latifah's husband was going to take her daughter away from her. He'd already snatched her son when he was seven years old. She was walking down the street with both children on their way to school when he pulled over to the side of the road and jumped out of his car and grabbed the little boy. Latifah was screaming and crying and she has never seen him since.

She should call the police.

That won't do any good in Afghanistan. A divorced mother can only have her children until they reach the age of seven for a boy and nine for a girl, then the father has permanent custody, and she has no more rights to them. Latifah would have killed herself if she lost her daughter, too, and her husband would have killed her if she resisted.

Do you remember Peggy from the DAV? Her granddaughter had to get an order of protection against her husband. He's terrible. They don't know where he is now. . . . Later I'll show you a photograph and you'll remember her. I'll show you tomorrow. Are your friends in New York now? Marie tears a page out of the middle of a magazine and starts clipping out something.

No, this was in Kabul, a big city in Afghanistan.

I mean, is she in New York *now*? The card says everything is ok. Marie holds up a narrow clipping with a daisy on top and some text underneath. A perfect book mark. She leans over, picks up a romance novel from the stack next to the chair and inserts the clipping. This is the one I'm reading next.

Now I'm not sure if I really want to tell Marie the story. She doesn't seem that interested.

So what happened? Marie sets the novel down in her lap, crosses her arms and leans back in her recliner. You and your father are both such storytellers. I used to sit here all night and listen to him telling jokes and stories. Now I'm alone, so go on, Barbara. What happened?

Well, if you're sure you don't want to read now. I hesitate and then begin. It's a long story. Tamar has a lot of energy for a woman her age.

You have a lot of energy, driving all over like you do with all that unloading and loading. I can't imagine.

Tamar's a little older than me and way more energetic. I'm just kind of wandering, but she's very directed and once she makes up her mind, she can't be stopped.

My friend Isabelle is ninety-one and she still drives. Every week she picks me up to go to bingo.

Ninety-one? I hope she can see well enough.

Isabelle? She's a card, very funny and a good driver, too. She goes very slowly, taking the back streets.

In Afghanistan very few women are allowed to drive, and they can put a woman in prison for things like running away from a violent husband or father, refusing to marry someone, whatever, and the young children go to prison with her. Latifah used to volunteer to teach children in one of these prisons, and Tamar was doing a photo shoot there. That's how they met. Sometime later when Tamar came back to the States, Latifah sent her an email, saying she had miraculously gotten a temporary visa to the U.S. to attend a conference and another for her daughter in a program to help with some medical problem. When they got here, the plan was for Tamar to take them to the Canadian border where they would claim political asylum. Canada at the time was very friendly to Afghans who needed asylum, and Latifah had friends in Montreal. Many people come here to the U.S. and Canada to find a safe haven from political repression and violence—but they don't all get it. There was a Salvadorean man the U.S. sent back last month. He was afraid of some gang violence against him, but the U.S. didn't recognize that type of violence as political and so they didn't let him stay here. When he went back to El Salvador, within a week he was murdered.

I keep the doors and windows closed and the curtains drawn. And I don't watch crime shows on television either. They make me nervous. There are a lot of teenagers who hang around Jack's Party Store. If they look across the street and see me passing in the window, I might have trouble like last summer when they broke in and stole my television . . . Let me get a cup of tea before you go on, dear. Do you want some? Grimacing, she pulls herself out of the chair.

No, I've had enough tea for tonight.

I follow her into the kitchen talking as she methodically moves from the counter to the table, holding on to relieve the pressure in her knees.

Well, we can't let everybody in, she says. What about the terrorists?

Of course, they have to check out those who are crossing the border. If Latifah had stayed in Afghanistan, she would have refused to give her daughter to her husband, and he would have killed her and it would have been ok with the law there. She has scars all over her body. Once he struck her with a hot poker.

Marie shakes her head, sitting down again, groaning and rubbing her right knee.

Did you want to try some arnica cream I have in my suitcase?

No, Zinny is giving me a shot tomorrow.

I go into the bedroom. Maybe this will help for tonight. I toss the tube over to her, and she sets it on the table.

When Latifah arrived in New York, Tamar drove her to Denver to pick up her little girl. On the way back, they got a call from an immigration lawyer in Canada, saying that the Canadians had just recently—only a week before—changed the law, and now Latifah could not go to Canada. They couldn't walk across the border anymore. They had to declare asylum in the country where they first landed, and for Latifah that was the U.S. So here she and her daughter were in New York City without enough money to live there.

Latifah thought it might be possible to take a boat from Niagara Falls or an airplane. She was talking to friends in Canada and Afghanistan, and at one point she even considered hiring some guy to hide her and her daughter in a truck for $12,000, but her parents didn't have that kind of money, and Tamar tried to tell her how dangerous that would be. She showed her articles in the news about people crossing the border who were tricked and killed. But if she were to stay in the U.S., her future would have been pretty grim. She could have moved in with some friend of Tamar's who lived in rural Pennsylvania, a place where she wouldn't find work, she wouldn't have been able to drive, and she would have had to live there in poverty, with no Afghan friends. Latifah was pretty depressed about this possibility. In Afghanistan, she had had a fairly decent job as a director in a girls' school, with an ok salary, and she had never lived with poverty. There was a list of requirements for people to get into Canada, and Latifah didn't fulfill any of them. She didn't have family there, she didn't have a business or money, and she couldn't work there. There was absolutely no way to get her in.

I stop talking and look over at Marie. Her eyes are closed and her tea is untouched. Then she opens her eyes and looks at me.— Go on, dear. I'm awake and I'm listening, I'm just resting my eyes.

The last person who said that to me was driving me from Bangalore to Mysore in a cab. He scared me to death and every time his eyelids drifted closed, I'd scream at him.

Well, I'm just here in my chair and I'm not falling asleep. Go on.

Ok ... Well Tamar thought about trying to find some guy to marry her in the U.S. and that way she'd be a U.S. citizen and qualify for welfare and other assistance.

That's just what I was thinking. Why didn't she marry someone? My cousin was visiting here from Poland and she married this guy who worked at the Chrysler Plant on Jefferson. No problem.

But Latifah was adamant. She *never* wanted to get married again. Once was enough. Then Latifah read something about how gay marriage is recognized in Canada. Maybe she and Tamar should get married, she joked. They both laughed about this. It was a wild idea. But then Tamar thought maybe if they got a marriage license in Vermont—you know women can marry each other in some states—maybe they'd let them into Canada for the wedding. At one point Tamar started thinking that maybe they *should* in fact get married, but then she discovered that even if Vermont recognizes gay marriages, that still wouldn't make her a U.S. citizen, and you have to be a U.S. citizen to cross the border.

Marie squints her eyebrows in a slightly disapproving gesture, but then she shrugs her shoulders and throws out her hands—as if to say, well the world is changing. Then she smiles. You know my family didn't like it when I married your father, a Protestant, but finally they gave in.

They sort of gave in, right, but continued to be mean to him. Remember how horrible Dad was to Allen just because he was Jewish. He turned his back to him every time he came into the house. That went on for a long time. Don't you remember?

Marie's eyes widen and then narrow. There is a gleam. He had his ways, she says.

Yeah, we all have our ways. Tamar is gay, but Latifah isn't and she probably didn't even know about Tamar. If Latifah were to marry a woman and then return to Afghanistan, if anyone knew about it, she would have been killed. She was concerned about that, but they weren't going to really get married, they were just going to get a license. Perhaps this would be a way to get over the border. They both thought this idea was hilarious. So they drove to Vermont first to get the license and then to upstate New York where they tried to go through a small crossing, telling the border patrol that they had family in Canada and wanted to be married there. But the guy wouldn't hear of it. He left them sitting in the car for a long time, maybe an hour, and then he leaned over and stuck his fat face in the window of the car, and snarled, Don't try this trick again. Or we'll arrest you. I'm alerting all the other border crossings. Latifah was very frightened, but Tamar tried to explain to her that the border was 7,000 miles long and he couldn't possibly contact all of them.

Marie shakes her head. But you know she wasn't a Canadian citizen, not really.

Yeah, ok, but you're not a Canadian citizen and you can cross the border into Canada. Do you see what I mean? So they found a motel and Tamar stayed up all night studying the maps of the border and eating donuts. She must have had a sugar high. She told me that little by little she became more and more determined until her mind was finally set. She was going to get Latifah into Canada, one way or the other, no matter what.

The guy at the border had said something odd and Tamar kept playing it over in her mind. He asked if she had a dying relative in Canada. Was he trying to give them a clue? Was it a secret message? They didn't say yes because they didn't know if he would ask for a hospital and a name. And Latifah had given up. She was afraid of losing her daughter so she shut down. Tamar kept telling her to call her friends in Canada and see if anyone was dying in a hospital or even for the name of a hospital. But she refused. She said they wouldn't want to get involved. No. Absolutely not.

While sitting in the office of the motel, drinking coffee, Tamar was pretty sure the two guys at the desk were gay so she approached them and told them the story. Had they ever heard of anyone getting across to get married? Had they ever heard about the dying relative clause? No, but they thought she might be able to get into Canada on a ferry from Maine. But Tamar knew they'd never let Latifah on the ferry without a visa. Tamar called every hospital she could find and asked for patients with common Afghan names—Nawabi, Sherap, Hamibi, Asafe. None, no Afghans in the hospitals with any of the names she could come up with.

In the morning Latifah was crying. She wanted to go back to New York City immediately. She didn't want to take a chance on losing her daughter. She'd go to Pennsylvania, she said. So she'd be poor.

Fine, but how will you find the $5,000 to pay a lawyer for your immigration case? Tamar asked.

She'd figure something out.

They'll end up sending you back to Afghanistan, Latifah. You'll be an illegal, Tamar insisted. She had been up all night studying maps and now she was determined. No. I'm going to get you through somehow. She started driving over the speed limit.

We're going through a busy checkpoint and you are going to say that you are an American citizen. Hide your papers under the seat. Tell them you were born in Brooklyn at Brooklyn Jewish

Hospital. And if they ask for ID, start hunting for it and then pretend you've lost it. Maybe they'll just flag us in. It's a busy holiday weekend.

As they drove along, suddenly Tamar changed her mind and started cutting down little roads and heading in the direction she thought was north, toward the border. After a while, the road curved around so much that she was confused about where she was—north, south, east or west. She stopped in some wooded area and put her cameras and a rubber boat she used for camping on her back. They started hiking through the woods. If she were stopped, her plan was to tell them she was writing a piece about the border and Latifah was her assistant. After a while, they decided to turn around because she wasn't sure if she was near the border and she was afraid they might get lost in the forest. And Latifah was complaining. I can't do this, Tamar. I can't.

Tamar continued driving down one dirt road after another. After a while she looked over to her left and through a lightly wooded area she could see a rail and every so often a car would go by so she started heading toward that rail.

What are you doing? Where are you going? Latifah asked. It was a rural area with very few houses, with fields of dry corn, some abandoned fields now sprouting various weeds, and a few farm houses here and there.

Finally the road ended and there was another dirt road with an old abandoned barn at the end. Tamar pulled the car behind the barn, very tightly wedging it in between the barn and some shacks, hiding it behind some piles of rubbish.

You stay here, lock the door, she told Latifah. And if anyone comes by to ask you what you are doing there, say that your friend is out looking at the property because she's interested in buying it.

Is this a true story or are you making it up as you go along? Marie asks.

Marie, this is exactly as Tamar told me. I stand up and start pacing back and forth behind the cocktail table in the living room.

Tamar was pretty sure no one could see the car unless they were in a low-flying plane. She started hiking through the woods and when she got to the other side of the trees, she could hear water rushing. Then there was a deep embankment and down below a narrow river, maybe it was a stream, and on the other side she could see the rail. So she slid down this embankment—she's fairly agile and even if her legs hurt her sometimes, like I said before, when she sets her mind to something, she does it. So she rolled up her jeans, the water was shallow, not quite up to her shins, but it was extremely slippery. She fell down once and dropped her glasses somewhere and couldn't find them. Her heart was pounding and she was too excited to stop and look. When she got to the other side, she grabbed hold of the branches and pulled herself up. It was about one hundred feet deep. When she got over the top, there was a road, but no cars and in the distance there were a couple of houses, but no one seemed to be at home, no cars anywhere. So she walked along the road, hoping a vehicle would go by so she could see their plates and figure out where she was. Was she in Canada? Or was she still in New York? She didn't know, and she wished she had brought a compass with her. She saw a mailbox in front of one of the houses. What if someone had looked out the window and seen her climb over the embankment? Maybe they were calling the police right then. But everything was quiet so she walked up to the mailbox and opened it. There was no mail, but there were a couple of fliers. She took them out and turned them over. They were in French! She *was* in Canada. She was ecstatically happy. Tamar turned around, hoping no one was watching her, and then she went right back down the embankment and crossed the river. On her way back, she saw a Canadian marker, a granite obelisk with the word *Canada* engraved in it. She stepped cautiously from one rock to the next until she found her glasses on a rock, and then she pulled herself back up to the other side. Running toward the car, she opened the door and flung herself inside. She was panting from running so fast.

Where have you been? Latifah asked.

And she screamed, Canada. I've been in Canada! Latifah, take some money, your jacket and no ID. Leave everything else in the car. Come now. I'm taking you to Canada.

They hiked back through the woods, climbed down the ravine and then Tamar pointed to a globe of shrubs. See those bushes over there. Latifah, you climb in there and stay hidden until I honk. It might take an hour. It might take two hours, but I'll get here.

Then Tamar went back to the car and drove to another busier checkpoint and showed them her driver's license, talking about how she had never been in Canada before and wanted to see the country, to do some sight seeing. They flagged her in. No problem. After all she had no record and she was a U.S. citizen. At first she couldn't figure out how to get to the place where Latifah was hiding, but after an hour or so, she found the road, pulled up by the bushes and honked. Latifah came running out.

Tamar is really something, isn't she? Marie says. This definitely sounds like a movie. Just a minute, I have to go to the bathroom.

I follow her to the door. This really happened, Marie. I'm telling you. You read the postcard, didn't you?

Then she is back in her chair, shuffling her papers.

Tamar drove along until she came to a small convenience store and restaurant and she left Latifah there while she went back across the border and back to the motel to get their luggage. She told the border patrol that she had left her cell phone in the motel and had to go back for it. When she got back to the motel, one of the guys was at the desk and he asked, Where is Latifah? When Tamar told him she was in Canada, waiting for her in a coffee shop, he came around the desk and swept Tamar off her feet. You did it. Hurray, for you. He brought out a bottle of brandy and offered her a drink. And he never asked where or how.

Why didn't he ask?

Probably he knew she had to keep that a secret. Like the underground railroad, the string of secret houses and people who would help slaves escape north to New York and to Canada. They never tell the exact story.

Is this the truth what you are telling me?

The truth that I know.

Tamar had no trouble crossing back into Canada again. She picked up Latifah at the coffee shop a few hours later and they drove straight to Montreal where friends were waiting. When Tamar got back to New York, for six weeks she had to take care of Nawal until she was finally able to bring her legally to her mother in Canada. That's what this postcard was about. She was worried whether everything would go smoothly at the border. Or would she have to smuggle Nawal in, too? No problems, I guess. In Canada now they will be safe. Her husband can't come there and take Nawal away. And she'll get some job training so she can find work. In the U.S., this wouldn't have happened.

It's a movie. That's what it sounds like.

I'm thinking about writing a story.

I think it could be a movie. It sounds more like a movie.

Tamar wants the U.S. military to stay in Afghanistan to help protect the women. So the Taliban don't take over again. If that happens, she's sure the women will lose all of their rights and many of those who have spoken out and helped each other would then be killed. I think that as long as there is money to be made for the big corporations, like those that provide security and supplies, the U.S. will stay. Still both Tamar and I both wish there was a more peaceful way to help the women, working more with other countries, you know . . .

I don't know, Marie says, shrugging her shoulders. I only know about my life. I don't know about that. You know so many people, Barbara. Aren't you tired? You must need a glass of water. Are you going to bed?

I guess so. I want to wake up early and do my yoga practice before I leave.

Isabelle is picking me up at eleven tomorrow and we're going to a lunch at the Eagles Club. Then, later, Zinny's coming over.

I lie down on the blow-up bed on the back porch with the windows open. My father used to sleep in the room next door when he became ill and we would have birthday parties on the screened porch where I am now resting. It is swampy hot and the crickets are singing loud and thick, chirping, rubbing their forewings together, traveling in packs, devouring and singing, a mass migration in search of protein and salt. My grandmother and grandfather migrated here for work, for well-being. Like a lot of working-class Americans, my father was afraid of people who were different from him, a kind of ignorance, a protect-what's-mine mentality. So we close our borders and police them. He was afraid to visit me when I lived downtown Detroit. Every car that backfired in his mind was a black man with a gun. As he grew older, he rarely left his neighborhood and community of friends. In 1983, I took my children and moved to New York City   *a suitable & preferable environment   leading always to a new center the migration which filled America*   Just as I'm falling asleep, I notice in the middle of one stack of books in the corner of the sofa, my high school typing book and an old unread book club collection of Montaigne's essays with prints by Salvador Dalí. I wonder how that book got here.

Five Hundred Miles

At dusk, I'm swerving down a pine-forested highway to Hickory Run State Park. So quiet I can hear the wind blowing through the pine trees. Then I take a shower and crawl into the tent. With my flashlight, I begin to read the pamphlet the ranger gave me. *Be aware of black bears. They are wild animals and are stronger and faster than people . . . they can become aggressive when people get between them and food.* Just as I am drifting off to sleep, a car pulls into the space next door and a couple starts talking loudly, bickering with each other. *I did not . . . Yes God Damn it you did . . .* Then they build a big fire flashing light and smoke into my tent, along with the smell of burning hotdogs. My nose starts running and I get up to pee in the bushes in the darkness *indeed a rose is a rose and it makes a pretty plate a rose is a* Finally I drift off. At 4:30 A.M., the sound of wind on the tent and I think I hear someone snoring. A clutter of empty beer bottles on the picnic table next door, then a rustle in the dark forest. I shine the flashlight in that direction. Is it a bear or a squirrel? Maybe it's just the wind. The handout says bears like the smell of personal hair products and soaps, and I just stupidly brushed my teeth by the picnic table. I am apprehensive, standing there for a few moments under the trees in the early A.M. fog. Then I get into the car, lock the door and make a fast U turn out of the campground. Five hours later I pull in front of my building on Seventh Street where an empty parking space is waiting for me.

Second Ave

My acupuncturist moves around me putting needles into my wrists, ankles, chest. I lie there in the dark   *as bodies of earth turn* intermittently dreaming about dancing with him, my arms around him, swaying, and then my nose starts to itch on the left side. It itches so much that my eyes start to water and then it moves to the right side, and then it stops and I start dreaming again, thinking about Allen and how much I loved him, and I get teary and my right nostril starts crying out for a scratch. I call out but no one can hear me. I look down at my arm, there's no needle near my elbow, so I bend it carefully, the two needles in my wrist dangling and I touch my nose with my thumb and it stops, lay it back down again, off into my dance   on air   whirling   *as bodies of earth turn*   I cough once and my chest hurts where the needle is. So I relax every muscle in my body. Then he's back, turning on the light and taking out the needles. Get those tests to me next week. Ok see you then   decamp   vamoose   skip out   On my bike peddling down Second Ave, I remember him saying, You will watch yourself die. Everyone watches themselves die. Well, some of us have been searching for a suitable and preferable environment for a very long time.

August Rent

Michah's sore throat isn't letting up and he can't go to work. His landlord has torn out sections of the floor in the living room and bath and there's no toilet or running water and Mook's afraid to leave the apartment untended   descent   into the cavity   no need to   *here are the roses—three opening*   Reading Williams's "Descent of Winter" and I feel his lived life in the cavity of my chest. *On hot days, the sewing machine whirling*   no need to explain or compare   Across from me in the cafe, a father and his young son are quietly reading their books. They are both wearing glasses and Billie Holiday's singing, *I'm like a song without words*. In Michigan, the crickets rub their forewings together. Outside it's misty and grey and August.

On My Way

On my way upstate, after making an impulsive turn, driving the way I follow recipes, a little of this, a little of that, oh I wonder where this road will take me, Sprain Brook Parkway. On and off, the rain thick and misty. When I pull up the dirt road to Lucinda's, the rain has stopped. I lie down on the wooden walkway, looking up at the trees and the grey sky   for a long time the crickets   I've been doing this since I was a girl. That's an oak. That's a sycamore. That's a tree of heaven. Then I hear a car come up the dirt driveway, the crunching of wheels over leaves and little branches. When we go inside, Lucinda points to the pond and hands me some binoculars. Look there. See him on the rock. A giant snapping turtle glides off the rock, deliberately slipping down and disappearing under the glassy water. Seven years untended and the turtles take over.

The Living Theater

Sometimes I don't remember what I've written, but it's in my handwriting unfamiliar   perhaps wistful   and then slanting Diane di Prima hooks an oxygen cord around her ears. You sleep and then you wake up and write, she says. I was just lucky to be in that cafe and listening to Miles in 1953 with no cover.

Hegira 2

At an outside table at a cafe on Seventh Avenue in Brooklyn, I watch Tamar coming down the street. She's wearing a little tweedy blazer over tight jeans, her hair now shoulder length grey. You are looking terrific, I say.

You're looking good, too.

Are you ready to order? the waiter asks.

I want the hummus with one piece of pita and a glass of white wine. What kind of wine do you have? That's fine. I'll have that.

I'd like the hijiki salad with avocado instead of goat cheese. And just a glass of water.

So what's new with you?

I'm in love with my acupuncturist.

Tell me about him. She leans over the table.

Well, one night last summer, I ran into a friend on the street and she gave me his phone number. Just think if I didn't have this cough, I never would have met him. As soon as I walked into his office he started flirting with me. So I flirted back. Then he kept inviting me to invite him. So we started seeing each other. My friend, Kristin, was concerned that he was my doctor and it wasn't ethical, but if we think like that, we'll never meet anyone.

Yeah, that's silly.

I didn't feel as if he had some power over me. No, the thing is we have a lot in common. We're close in age, leftist politics, we're both vegan, he's a healer and he has a spiritual life similar to yoga. He's been involved with an African American group that combines Eastern philosophies with Egyptian mysticism.

So what's the negative? There's always something . . .

He has a young child a few days out of the week. I thought I was done with that, my children raised already, but I like the boy.

I tried to break it off when I found out about his child, but you know, I liked him so much that I couldn't stop seeing him.

You better be careful Barbara.

Well, what could happen?

You could have your heart broken, that's what. I don't want you to get hurt.

Tamar, this is different. I think I'm going to be with him for the rest of my life.

I hope you're right. After Denise, I'm not interested anymore. It's too draining. She looked straight into my face and straight out lied to me.

Well, I don't think he lies. He talks openly about everything, kind of like I do.

Good for you, Barb. I'm so busy that if I meet a woman in the middle of this, well then it will happen. Otherwise, I'm happy as a lark.

I wasn't even looking for anyone. It just happened. Have you heard from Latifah and Nawal? That was courageous what you did for them, climbing down that ravine and all at your age. I want to write a story about it.

Well, you just do what's necessary at the time. Right? They're fine. They love Montreal. They have moved out of the shelter and have their own apartment now. Nawal calls me on the telephone and says that she misses me. I'm surprised when she says this, though, because she was so unhappy and difficult when she was with me. I thought I was going to go crazy. She wouldn't get dressed in the morning. I had to physically dress her while she lay stiff like a board on the bed. She hated day camp. She hated everything I cooked for her. It was a nightmare.

She must have been extremely anxious about her mother being in Canada and then being in Brooklyn with you.

Yes, I'm sure that was part of it.

And you've never raised any children. They are difficult for their parents, let alone a babysitter and she's only eight years old.

Think of how children treat substitute teachers. You were a substitute mother with no training.

I had to put her in a day camp so I could get some work done, and every day she came home, she said that she hated it, but the counselor said she was doing fine. I had to get her vaccinations, a health examination, everything. Then she stuck a Q-tip in her ear and she couldn't hear so I took her to the emergency room. She was ok, but they are still sending astronomical bills. We didn't even see a doctor. It was a physician's assistant and the bill for five minutes was $600. The total bill was $2,000. What a scam. And remember when Bush was saying that anyone could go to the emergency room. That's such crap.

I remember when Emily was little and I used to have to get her dressed for school before she went to sleep or she would refuse in the morning and we'd never get there on time. Children go through things like this.

When she first came, I got out my mother's old waffle maker and I made waffles. At first she loved them, but after a week, she refused to eat anything. She liked grilled cheese sandwiches and then she hated grilled cheese.

Maybe she wanted Afghan food.

Well, I couldn't make that food. I'm not much of a cook anyway. I tell you there was only one thing she wanted—McDonald's. And I said you are not going to live on McDonald's for four weeks. That's out of the question. I'll take you there once a week. So I said I'll make you a great hamburger. I bought chopped sirloin and hamburger rolls and the whole business and she wouldn't touch it.

And every night I couldn't get her to go to sleep. I had to go to sleep with her. She would not go in the bedroom unless I was there, so I agreed to do this, but then I was going to bed at 9 P.M. and I wasn't getting any work done. She'd snuggle up with me in bed. Those were the only pleasant moments.

I think she was traumatized.

As the weeks passed, I was extremely nervous that the papers wouldn't come through. I was afraid there would be some kind of screw up. But when we got to the border, everything was in order. I almost didn't recognize Latifah. She had on tight jeans and a ski jacket with a little woolen hat. Very stylish, totally different from the woman in Afghanistan. And they were thrilled to see each other.

You did a good thing, Tamar. By the way, where did you get those glasses?

They're the same ones I lost in the river. I was worried when I dropped them, you know why—not because I couldn't see, I had an extra pair in the glove box—but because they cost me $400, that's why. Have some wine. Let me buy you a glass of wine.

Ok, red. I guess one little glass won't hurt me.

Suddenly, it starts raining, pouring down. Anything can happen here, I say, putting on my sweater. It wasn't supposed to rain and I didn't bring an umbrella. It's a good thing we are under the awning. We sit there sipping wine and looking at the rain fill up the street and the gutters. An old man rushes by holding a newspaper over his head.

What's the name of that tree over there, Tamar asks.

It's a gingko. Aren't they beautiful? Brought here from Asia. They are all over the world now. That tree can live to be a thousand years old well, maybe not here though, with all the pollution. But it will definitely outlive us. It's one of my favorite trees, very sturdy, but it looks delicate, the way the branches curve upward.

Just the Kind of Day

It looks like rain so I buy an umbrella in the cigar store, go across the street to see if the Second Avenue bus goes near Church Street. It doesn't. I feel around in my bag for my new umbrella. It was there a few minutes ago and now it's gone. There was only one guy waiting for the bus. He must have snatched it out of my sack. Back I go across the street to buy another one. Then Michah calls. His throat is worse and now he's running a high fever. He's on his way to the clinic at Gouveneur. Ok, I'll meet you there, I say. I take a cab and find him on the corner, standing in the rain. The clinic is closed. We head up to Bellevue, a room full of people in rows of plastic chairs and a line with standing sick people waiting for triage. No one tells us where to go and the woman at the desk won't give us the time of day. Finally another patient, an old woman wearing a stained turquoise sweater, gets out of her chair, and walks toward us, telling Michah where to stand. Three hours later, the doctor arrives   ta-dah   a most agreeable surprise One doctor, says the guard to the crowd, and fifty of you waiting. It's because you are poor. Down the street at NYU those with money and insurance go right in. This is the United States in 2010.

Good Men and Women

Spent all day reading and thinking about the Puritan forest as the place of temptation, the wilderness slated to become paradise as they routed out everything wild and unfamiliar. Tempted, Goodman Brown easily gives in, and then he hates himself, hates the world around him, and especially hates his young wife, Faith who's tempted, but undisturbed. Then I fall asleep and find myself running down a path with a big lake on both sides. I stop and look around, water everywhere. At the edge of a swamp, I turn to go back, but the path has disappeared. Have I been running through a swamp all along? Then I'm on Second Avenue, watching a man lean over his cell, texting someone. Then we are in the church   *my dreams lifted me right out of bed*   We stand on the sidewalk, touching our fingertips. Someday soon   *with an infinity of time*   but tonight we nod goodbye to Peter Orlovsky. *Tryambakam Yajamahe.* As we walk along, the wind blows scraps of paper down the street.

Billie Holiday Sings

One never knows does one, when love will come along. Then so suddenly life turns out to be a song. I'm a little out of practice, he says and then he laughs. That's a joke. Lying on my belly with what feels like thirty needles in my spine. Out the window in the rain yellow locust leaves are scattered over the grey world of cement and cars. This is enough   with a tendency   gradually carried along in a body   arriving   holding for a moment   and then a swift passage outward   and back into a V again

A
SLOW
CURVE

for Bobbie Louise Hawkins

If You Walk Faster,
It Strolls Faster

Just be yourself, says a woman on the radio while I'm following a big grey truck perhaps full of perfume with a sexy woman painted on the back door. *Intimacy in even the slightest stripping.* She's wearing a pink bra and a furry pink shawl and her lips are open as if she could suck you into her mouth and wrap you up in her pink fur. *We went over the falls in a mindless rush.* Along the roadside, tall thin trees with no leaves, looking very brown and parched, but also feathery and delicate.

The Center of
Christian Think Radio

We recycle plastics. I'm for that. Don't you agree, Ched? *All right. I guess.* I'm for recycling anything. I don't want to be accused of being hostile to the universe. So sure I take my plastic milk jugs out to the curb. It only makes sense from a conservative point of view. Don't you agree, Ched? His partner is skeptical   break a fall   a belly flop   *We'll talk about this in just a minute, Jim.* Ched's next topic: *Why do you think President Obama don't make that birth certificate public?*

To Be Reckoned With

Red-winged blackbirds are falling from the sky, dead, thousands dead. I thought maybe they were sucked into a thunderstorm, the man says on the radio. But I was wrong. There was an eye witness in Beebe City and he said there were blackbirds perched in trees in big numbers. They can't see well at night so they couldn't have flown into a storm. After the cannon went off a few times, my friend went outside and he could hear the sounds of wings flying low, flying into trees. This was just before midnight on New Year's Eve. Maybe it was the fireworks. Or lightning or hail or something. *Porpoises lower their voices to the range of their captors.* Blackbirds falling from the sky, a western sky, blue with big splashes of white, the weather just warm enough to open the window.

Or Lightning or Hail
or Something

A man and woman are standing beside their car, a wreck, duct tape and cardboard covering the side windows. Across the gas island, the man tells me they need money to get to El Paso. She's pregnant and heavy. Some mother to tell. Can you help? It's starting to get dark. I give them $5.00. There is the strong smell of oil in the air. The stars that were so vivid not long ago are now hidden behind a thick mist of dust.

And He Was Taken Into the Story

On the way back from a rest stop, a big old guy moves to the side so I can pass—I mean he might be my age, but he's in terrible shape, big stomach, scowling, and he looks at me with a look that always scares me, the way, for some reason, some rough redneck men look at me, when I'm just passing through their space, with a combination of desire and hatred, as if they'd like to force me to have sex and then shoot me. *Looking back with her little eyes the moon was a definite and vivid crescent*

The Back of the Front

Once when Mook and I were hiking in Dharmasala, he brushed against a plant and his ankle instantly swelled up. A few minutes later, a travel guide happened by. He looked at Mook's ankle, picked some leaves from another plant and rubbed them into his skin. Miraculously, the itching stopped. There's always an antidote nearby, he said, and then he disappeared around the bend with his entourage. There's a yoga sutra—when you are stressed or fixed on a negative thought, think the opposite. It's always nearby, one thought next to another, and it helps to see more clearly. Through the dust and the glare from the setting sun, a sign for Midland College. I put my mind elsewhere, adjacent. Crawling along on the service drive, I can't see more than a few feet, just following the car in front of me and then, oops, back on the highway again, the sun sinking with oil fields all around.

The Philadelphia Eagles Fall to the Dallas Cowboys

Hovering above the horizon, a yellow half circle, with a narrow red outline. Miles and miles of scrubby fields with oil pumps excavating ancestor plants and animals. I fill up the engine and speed past monstrous refineries, horrifying like Zug Island with its steel and iron mills outside of Detroit, miles of sprawling tanks and towers, pipes and pistons. No wonder they want to have their guns. Mega war material, oil refineries, greedy politicians. Big money takes the table. Even the clouds are dark and ominous. They spread a shadow over Texas Gas and Crude oil. On my right, a military base. The word *unit* and the word *correction* stand out in the misty dust. A hard consonant. Red lines shoot across the skyline, the dust and the smell of oil so thick it seems like the end of the world. A capitalist nightmare. *Or a state of domestic felicity.* Just past dusk, when I leave the oil fields, there is a clarity of vision, so that even an exit sign stands out as a relief.

There Was *That*

A few weeks ago, I went up to Herald Square just after the big snow storm. Many days with no sunlight. The snow was melting and was covered with sooty black smoke and urine from passing dogs and men. You have to be careful you don't kill yourself on a day like this, slip off the curb and fall into a big icy puddle in the middle of a crowd of Christmas bargain hunters. That's why I left New York City in 2005, I tell my accountant Howie. But then I have to remind myself, it's mostly the way I'm seeing, just a reflection of my mind today. *These boots are as good as any.* But it is what it is, too. Mind and reality interact with each other. One hundred miles past El Paso and heading west like the gold miners, like Dorothy and Toto   but with speed   side by side   moving with the wind   miles of open land in every direction. A double-decker train on the right and mountains far into the distance. The horizon   *a slow curve into the sky*   Yes there was *that* and there is *this*, too.

Visual Transmission

Tucson is usually somewhat peaceful, but today a boy buys a semi-automatic handgun and goes on a shooting spree in a shopping center parking lot. I prop my cellular connection up on the counter and talk to my lover while he's cooking in his kitchen in Long Island and I'm doing dishes in Tucson. Then I am on the floor collating books and doing yoga and he's lying in his bed, talking and watching me   to move together among the clutter from one room to the next   then outside without losing reception to see the saguaro, the mountains and the bright blue sky. My shoes are dusty from the dry ground. Missing you, dear. From Tucson Airport to LaGuardia. Gliding, not falling. Your little boy between us on the sofa. Then he falls fast asleep and you carry him upstairs to bed. We watch the rest of Harry Potter, but become involved in our skin and drift off into the bedroom. *Later I slip into the front room*. Tactile reception has its limits. Outside the window, Long Island is covered with a thick layer of snow.

Only Then Will
Success Be Possible

Protests in Tunisia, Cairo, Yemen, Libya, Bahrain, Iraq, Algeria, Morocco, Jordan, Oman. I drink a glass of water and wonder if I should live with my lover. Instability. Strife. Hundreds of thousands fleeing, oil prices climbing. The thought of living in the suburbs, so far from the city makes me anxious. I generally rely on my own sense of things, but today I go to his counsel, the *I Ching* and read: Do not press forward, be gradual and gentle. Things that accord in tone, vibrate together. Only then will success be possible. *Or the rhythm of a motor that won't catch.*

For About Ten Minutes, the House Is Rattling

Probably it was an earthquake, a woman says the next morning while we do dishes in the ashram kitchen in San Francisco, nonchalantly, as if she is referring to a thunderstorm. After meditation, I check my email. Panic. Suffocation. Heartache. In her sleep last night, Akilah Oliver died. She wasn't sick. It was a surprise. Turn over to look at the clock, and then roll flat and then . . . A few weeks earlier, we sat at the same table. We *are* at the same table. I find an email from her. See you soon at the Mullen talk. Hope it's much warmer there than here. . . . Fall asleep and then turn over to look at the clock and then . . . Some years ago her son, her only child, a very young man, died a sudden death after being denied emergency care in an LA hospital. I am weak and broken. Just like that, gone. The mother and the son. See you soon   What you said   What you didn't   The river is flowing down to the sea. Mother carry me, down to the sea.

The Sloping Petals
of an Iris Blossom

You must see this, Norma Cole says, as we leave the cafe and walk down the block. Norma moves very slowly, using a cane after paralysis from a stroke. Behind us, old warehouses, one of them refurbished as a post-modern hotel. Around the corner, Norma points with her cane. See that, she says, making *a slow curve into the sky*, passing over a row of angular pastel three-story buildings, Swiss new age and behind them a towering row of poplar trees, winter brown and wavering in the wind.

If You'dda Talked to Me

Steve Katz and I read together at Moe's Bookstore. Despite his aging fragility, he picks up my heavy suitcase and carries it up the highest flight of subway steps I've seen since Moscow, the BART in Berkeley. In the train, we observe the passengers. It's much quieter than in the New York subways. Suddenly a man screams at a young woman for talking on her cell phone. She stands up and moves to the other side of the car. Then a robust Latina stands in front of him and says, You're waco Mister and if you'dda talked to me like that, I'dda knocked your head off. Behind her a row of quiet folks, watching *Buildings smashed flat by war* When we are ready to go, Steve stands up, pulls up his pants, shifts his weight and barrels off the train.

Seattle to Eugene to Portland

It's raining in Seattle and it's raining in Eugene. The windshield wipers only work on fast and this big automatic rental car seems to automatically make a U turn in bus-only lanes. Pitch dark and not knowing which direction I am driving. In Portland when I finally climb into the back seat of an old car full of young poets heading out to the Way Post, it's still raining. After the reading, a young woman tells me she is a hula hoop dancer, revolving fire and light and that she almost started crying when I was reading a poem about Detroit. Detroiters always miss home, she says.

Women, Naked Light Bulbs and Linoleum

In letter after letter Jane Bowles goes over the most insignificant issues, unable to come to a decision, constantly overwhelmed by multiple possibilities. Impact closer, wiser not. Her characters make U turns and zigzags. She ridicules her own suffering and indecision. She loves women, naked light bulbs and linoleum, and she constantly nods to Paul. His writing comes first and she's very insecure about her own. But her writing is so splendid. To decline. To be less than needed. To fall short. After she dies, the doctor says, For her it was fatal, the early life of pleasure, the drinking, the excitement, given her sensibility. After a while, her friends became embarrassed that she might lose control. When she was a grown woman, trying to hold on to her sanity, her mother called her my little princess, asking if she had candled her ears. There are some benefits, I think, of economic necessity and *a sooty bit of cemented yard.* On I-10, the big trucks and the trains go by, and on every side of me, far distant horizon and jagged mountains.

There Are Some Benefits

In Macy's on 34th Street, my friend is checking out the price of shoes and searching for sales. I'm in Texas, passing a group of motorcyclists on Harleys, wearing sneakers instead of black Hell's Angel boots. The wide open treeless desert, I tell him, it's like driving on a two-lane highway on the moon. The mountains seem like big piles of sand that the wind has blown into shapes. Then traffic slows to a standstill. Lines of trucks waiting for inspection and men in uniforms stopping cars. I turn off the phone and put it in my bag. Seven cars pulled over to the side, one guy on one side of a truck and another on the other while a big German shepherd circles the vehicle, sniffing. A guy climbs up on the cab to talk to the driver. They don't open the truck, they just depend on the dog. There are many ways to fall. On the cab side, we move into the against. Then the truck pulls out and the man looks at me. Are you a U.S. citizen? . . . Ok, go. I guess I look safe, with my white face, brown hair and glasses. Little do they know.

We'll Come, Omnipotence

The magic bus from Quebec on tour disappears and then reappears, swerving with the wind. I stop at a rest area and then back on the road, and they're ahead of me again. The land is flatter now, the mountains far off in the distance. It gets this way, I think, right before the oil fields, coming in from the west this time, nine miles to Pecos. Water tanks. Dust and dirty air. Some huge smooth mounds of some kind of shale, must be those big chunky black spots on the aerial maps. A lot of trucks on the road now. In the heat of the afternoon, a butterfly and a flock of birds, black birds of some sort. A big plant or refinery, HALLIBURTON says the sign. I pull into visitor parking to take some photos. Odessa, home of George Bush senior and now the Haliburtons, too. Between them, a matter of money. I imagine living here. How long would it be before the oil runs out? What are you going to do when it's gone, George? Enjoy one's darkening? *Well, when it's gone, we'll go elsewhere. It ain't gone yet.*

It Gets This Way, I Think

What looks so horrific at dusk in the middle of a dust storm when the western setting sun is glaring in your eyes, what looks horrifying then, doesn't look that bad in the light of day. I stop and watch *the sun in the leaves*. Still monstrous wealth, and kind of hellish looking, but around the bend, *a slow curve into the sky* and hundreds of white windmills. On the other side of the road, an oil field with jack-pumps going up and down amongst an orchard of uniformly planted small pecan trees. You can smell the oil as the turbines majestically revolve. It's possible to live in one spot and grow our own food, but we are zigzagging across the earth, horizontally with the desire to go faster and faster. Then prairie land, open space, horses grazing, the color green appears, and *we blossom into an enormous round*. Austin is like Ann Arbor in the desert, an oasis with mega health food stores and a university. Take from the land and the air and multiply. We mean to do it right this time. I read poetry in Dale and Hoa's lovely house on the side of a hill. Very graceful, the woman and the space, with a poetry salon, folding chairs, and poets listening and buying books. It is warmer here. Poetic culture all over the U.S.A., even in Texas.

Coming Down Down Down

Less than one hundred miles to go. The sky is pale blue with a rose-colored sunset and purplish clouds here and there. Almost all the trees are bare. A beautiful night to drive into the city. Not much traffic through New Jersey. Heading steadily downward toward sea level, from the idyllic country, so serene, gliding over a newly tarred highway, swooping down between trees with wiry brown fur, a month before greenery, up ahead the crux of the V. The clouds lie over the horizon. It's not a western sky, but still immense. Coming down down down and then the street widens into ten lanes and zoom all roads merge together, gliding into the city under the clouds, now heavy and dark and then the city with its lights spreading out. I text you. Lower and lower. You text me. Pay a toll and then lower yet into the Holland Tunnel and then I emerge inside an amazing gigantic throbbing city with thousands of toilets flushing at the same time. On Second Avenue a man is standing in front of his office building, looking into his cell phone. He smiles when he sees me and then he climbs into the car. My lover.

I'll Put Them All in a
Story By and By

Out on the island, we go shopping for garden plants and then to the beach together. Naked inside our clothes, I am cold so he holds me inside his jacket. I like your skin. I like your skin, too. As we walk along the shore, he talks about when he was a boy and there was a separate beach for African Americans. Their side was very crowded and small. He would look over through the gate at the other people, the whites with their luxurious space   in the depths of the ship   his mother's skin was whiter than mine. Her father was a Jewish guy, he says, and she only saw him once. She was afraid of him. Even long afterwards there continues to be the feeling.

*

With burning sage, Honorable Spirits of Yi please reveal our destiny. By the nightlight reading a story by Dylan Thomas and it is as if I am in a dream, the words highlighted and then disappearing into the prose.

What Mattered Was
the Entirety

Who he was, where he was. Sitting on a park bench I'm worried but succumb   yield   bow down   to be above intent   *in the cool of the afternoon*   the trees are thick with leaves and birds. The traffic sounds pre-empt more rain, like the world making a low roar before the storm. Don't worry, It's just me. My chair tilts and crashes to the floor. And then we are in bed again. You would stick out, the only one, he says. His little boy pokes me—Can you count by fives? by sixes? backwards? In the middle of a circle made with tire tracks, we blow bubbles. Not just disappointment, something else has occurred, something like empty holes burrowed into our thinking mind and emotional body.

As If to Conclude an Inch

Twelve noon in New York City, I'm sitting in the car waiting for the street cleaner to pull up behind me. Then I cut out into the center and quickly angle in behind him, cutting off any cut takers. Listening to Peter Thompson talk about his book, *Wars of Afghanistan*. Very complicated tribal wars carried over centuries. We are involved too much, he says, in a reconciliation of conflicts we don't understand. *It is a hurricane*, I rush to conclude. But today the air is clear, except for a little wind making it difficult to bike uphill, legs heavy, the wheels turning so slowly. A trucker passes, yelling, Maybe you can go slower, Lady. At a light I pass him and yell into his cab, The turtle wins. Then I hit the top of the tiny slope on Manhattan Island and coast downhill, my wheels spinning, my hair blowing in the wind.

Yes, I'd Like a Soft Chair

No feeling of sacred privacy anymore in a public park, Louise says, as she blows the smoke away from me. You are my only non-lawyer friend, she says, and when Roberto was in the third grade, he told me that I was the weirdest mother in the whole third grade. Our little wild ones. Then one day, he came home and said, I wasn't the weirdest mother, but his friend Michah's mother, she was definitely the weirdest one.

As If We Have Finally Arrived

When little Luke is sitting quietly looking at a book, the afternoon light sifts through the blinds onto his skin and his soft and smooth new limbs. *In all likelihood, there's no real danger.*

*

An old woman just walked past wearing a low red top hat, yellow short sleeve blouse, white Jamaica shorts, a little hot dog on a leash. She has henna red hair and big yellow framed glasses and buck teeth. She stops, looks in the window at me for a moment and smiles. The East Village. I imagine her years back, jaunting along this same avenue on her way to some underground club.

When It Starts Pouring

It's like living in a lake. When I look up and through the locust leaves there is a light in the sky   *a soft grey glimmer*   My salad is deep green and light green with half circles of radish red. Thunder. And then water comes through the screen and rolls off the aloe leaves. When it stops, I take a walk. Kneel down with a woman named Denise to look at a big green bug with beautiful variegated wings, stuck in fear on the door grating. We both take cell phone shots. I break off a locust twig and lift him away. He spins his wings and slowly magically propels himself across the street. More insects, Denise says, now that they have stopped putting rat poison in the park. The red-tailed hawks do a fine job. When my etymologist friend looks at the photo, she tells me, it's a green lime hawk moth.

The Flowers Gust
Into the Wind

Dramatic music and muffled conversations coming from the direction of the park. It sounds like a film. I go out to mail a letter. *His voice comes down through the ceiling*   *who he was, where he was*   not so many people on the street in August. There's a film in the public circle with hundreds of quiet people, sitting and reclining on the ground. Subtitles. Sounds like Goddard. *Contempt*. Yes, a couple arguing and making up. Lots of slow bodies, panning out and then up close posturing. A film about a film. Walk past an ambulance inside the park, doors closed, lights flashing. Across the street and all is well. I take my lover's name out of my poems and turn the books about Taoist sexuality around so I can't see the spines. Looking down at the floor, I notice a little black curl. I wet my baby finger, pick it up, study it, and then flick it into the breeze. With personal drama, sometimes we tend to forget the rest of the world.

At Montauk

At Montauk, Martine and I are both in lawn chairs, reading. Little children, women and men parade in front of us with varying body sizes and colors. The tide comes up suddenly and laps right over our knees. In a damp moment, I grab my bag and lift it up high, just in time. As I hand Martine HD's *Vision and Meditation,* I say, I don't think I actually read this book today, but I did look at each word. We laugh   *to look askance*   the mind and the meditative moment may never visit each other. Is it this? Is it that? Well, it just is.

14
X
14
X
14

for Dumisani Kambi-Shamba

May 9, 2011

The locust trees are under constant revision. The passersby are
wearing hats. These things seem innocuous, but when he says
that my body feels like home, a chair falls on my head, an omen
three years short of Medicare and my heart racing like
a teenager. A drummer on Astor Place catches the beat. Crouched
in a doorway on Avenue A, my hand over my left ear, listening
to Cleveland in my right. Trucks, motorcycles and buses blowing
smoke. At home a check from the Poet's House and the sound
of birds and muffled voices in the park. My neighbor's dog barks
for an hour while I fold towels into small rectangles, the branches
swaying high over Tompkins Square. Politicians want, politicians
want to privatize education, kill Medicare, log the forests, 15,000
species cut off, cut out. Verizon and AT&T donate to the Tea Party.
Sign here. Quiet. Distant traffic rushing in and out like the sea.

May 10, 2011

To sleep is beautiful with spring morning light. Our paths
cross for a reason they say, but then sometimes they run
parallel for years and years. Outside the Christians pontificate
with loudspeakers over the food line on the edge of the park,
three times as many people this year waiting for a sandwich.
The lord loves you and gives you this sandwich and this apple.
Bernadette asks me on the phone, Are you still eating only grapes?
I know you used to. There are fourteen joints in the human hand.
Yod dalet, fourteen, is also the Hebrew word for *hand*
and fourteen pieces of the body of Ausar shape all the forces.
My cards keep coming up one short, Hebrew through marriage,
African ancestors more distant. All of us related and yet—
in Bahrain, a woman can be horsewhipped for driving a car.
This afternoon a tree asked him to hug it, so he did.

May 11, 2011

A little bird is sitting on the window ledge, singing.
A man meditates in a chair with needles in his body.
The garbage truck lowers its tray, gears up and moves
forward. Folded back at my knee joints, reclining, I remember
Allen. Then I curl into a child's cry. Dying, his penis disappeared
inside his groin. Try not to force anything. Biking, I lean
forward into the wind. First Joe Brainard remembered,
then Perec, now I'm forgetting. Henya Drescher posted,
Erica Hunt sent you, Kristi Maxwell wants to be,
Andrew T wants to be, Sally Silvers invited. The sounds
of people talking and traffic. He used a music score
to write a narrative. It's not public knowledge so
please don't tell anyone I told you that he held me
inside his jacket as the ocean winds whipped around us.

May 12, 2011

Why didn't I notice the bird sounds this morning?
Busy mind with wide awake losses. Bike over to Second
Avenue to bring a friend some lunch. Can this lover become
a friend? Coasting along. That girl is pretty isn't she?
Michael Lally told me once that I looked like Barbara Guest.
I looked at a photo of her youthful beauty and said—
that's hard to hold on to, isn't it? Maybe now with automated
investigations and with a little nudge to the rectilinear
a swerve back into, what is this heart ache anyhow? Madame
regent opens the drapes and the trucks and cars crawl
along and uneventfully merge. Hi Gramma, the little voice says
over the telephone, I really really want you to find Mr Tickle
for me. One more book and we sink into the soft sofa
with a flashlight and streaks of light that flash beyond.

May 13, 2011

Martin Luther said that girls begin to talk and stand on their feet
sooner than boys because weeds always grow up more quickly
than good crops. Today I was the troll under the bridge, the evil
fairy on the slide, under the Long Island sun, a robin red breast
posing in the Blue Point Library with a swarm of mothers
and toddlers. At noon, Luke's asleep in the chair and Logan's
bouncing in his crib to James Brown. I'm dozing off while a wise pig
mother on TV is planting a garden. I happen to like weeds,
not valuable enough to be harvested, but hearty and prolific.
Five o'clock and I follow the digital line, pay $6.50 to avoid the BQE
then the aggressive search and swerve to find a spot. On the elevator
three single women with grocery bags. Broccoli, green beans
and two books. As the dishes pile up, the character, the man
and the idea takes hold again—the romance of our bodies.

May 14, 2011

A crane dangles a pillar high over twenty-five stories
and thousands of pedestrians. Squawk. I love you.
Put your body beside mine. That means something.
Only sixteen stamps and look at that, we're saving
the environment. Bernadette says her mind has
become digital. *Synonym is a sino—damn I can't
pronounce it.* And she used to think that Aristotle
was an asshole. Walking with Cynthia MacAdams
and her little dog on Second Street. Each dot
with its own squawk box, messing up the impervious
nirvana winds. In this novel, the characters suffer
in stiff Victorian ways. In my dream, I kiss my lover
but he doesn't kiss back. When I ask him if he received
my message, he says no. That must mean something.

May 15, 2011

Wake up looking at locust leaves and the misty sky.
Write an email, a thank you and then stretch out.
A siren and the trees swish in the wind, hesitate,
then swish again. Aloe leaves at the Korean bodega.
Hurray for more grey sky and my downstairs neighbor's
rolling rising falling scales and the faint voices
of screaming children in the park. Summering
is a word the very well-off use. When Jacqueline plays
I float out the window frame. This is a Coney Island
bound Q train. The next stop could be charmed except
when a door in the hallway slams. We seem to have
forgotten that the *I Ching* gave a positive prediction.
For a very long time, we love our skin, too. What a
crazy world we live in, entropy and megaentropy.

May 16, 2011

The locust leaves are like wet green lace, twinkling
in the breeze. We walk over to Broadway in our raincoats,
my shoes swelling up with water, socks soaking wet,
buy bowls and black rubber boots. Five lines behind
fourteen at most. Lee Ann asked me to ask Harry
if he could write a goedesic dome, what form would
the poem take? How about coming to my house on
Tuesday night? Want to stop by. Pin you down.
Dream of you. You're in love and then you're not
in love. You can't be in love with someone who isn't
in love with you. We'll just see how the time shakes out.
Nothing about you. It's me. Suddenly I remember
my grandson's face and I ache to be near him.
Want to come to my house and walk on the beach?

May 17, 2011

Sometimes it's not possible to resist the fall in one's
heart, an alternative movement, opposite side turning
left then right, find your balance. Run into Brenda
in Alphabets, looking at skirts. Then I'm sitting
on a stoop on Fourteenth Street, talking on the cell
with Michah, moments of affection and affinity,
an intersection between essay and fiction. By the time
I wrote down the fourth word, *staccato*, I was exhausted.
They just end like that. Soon you would realize,
the poet says that in our faculty meetings there's
always someone whose rank we don't quite
understand. And they are always there, looking at us.
I miss you, dear, texting me, the words appearing inside
bubbles, possibly possible and then a little more.

May 18, 2011

Sleepy but with a quick dash of water on my face,
I bike over to Wooster St. Arm balances and forward bends.
Everyone is quiet. A passenger in a yellow cab swings open
his door into the bike lane and I squeeze around him.
Open your eyes mister. Sweeping the floor, I pick up
a paper clip. A student sends me extra work to critique
and the class is over. Should we become more organized
or continue with this chaos? What I love most about this room
is the window in the middle of the largest city, a green rain forest
In the subway car, a skinny guy with bare tattooed arms
and a blue baseball hat, four-day-old beard, soaked boots,
and a wooden cross around his neck is writing meticulous
prose, tiny narrow rows filling up the page. And then
he nods out, leaving a blob of black ink in the middle.

May 19, 2011

I'm resting my head on HD's *Helen of Egypt*.
The cantaloupe was not quite ripe enough.
The SUV with Pennsylvania plates took one
and a half spaces. Are you new in the building?
Well sort of, a visitor for two weeks, blonde hair,
black sunglasses, and he looks like a young
Todd Colby. Maca, maca, maca, buffered C and chocolate,
First Avenue to the L to the Q to DeKalb Avenue.
A woman with two little girls and a child in a stroller
apologizes. It stops raining and I'm in the classroom.
The young people write about their relationships
and their pain. My cell phone jingles. Salsa dancing
in Spanish Harlem, Do you want me to come over?
What now? Spooning my body into his, yours, ours.

May 20, 2011

Down Avenue A, over Third Street, through
the garage and across Houston. Chain up my bike
squeeze knees against upper arms and lift up
feet and diaphragm like a mosquito in the rain,
gliding over Bleeker, Bowery, Fourth Street
to Avenue A. In the rain, in the rain, in the rain,
it never stops raining. Do your brakes work in the rain?
Does your bladder stay healthy as you age or
do you let echo photos invade and shut down your
computer? Bloody nose and food poisoning interrupt
my daily accomplishments. Starksnet is a super saboteur
with a digital code that looks legitimate, a little like
Typhoid Mary speeding at the speed of sound.
I climb under the blankets and drift off down the alley way.

May 21, 2011

There is a lightness in the sky and the rain has stopped.
So have all our dreams of wrong turns. I'm as distressed
as you are, but things were spinning too rapidly and
someone is using all of the washers in the basement.
When I opened the door from the airport, I could smell
and hear a stomach virus, lost in a maze of narrow streets
as a rickshaw driver helped me look for oatmeal. Drumming,
relentless drumming, vibrating trees and people, vibrating
virus. Stay home and lose myself in Conrad's distraught
and dark heart. Three naps later reformat a long document
with jpgs. Memories that I can't remember recording.
Even though it's drizzling, I can hear the birds. Hungry
but it's not wise to eat after eight P.M. and chocolate is always
nice as I gear up for midnight writing and reading.

May 22, 2011

Light flickers through the leaves. Another overcast morning.
My first shower was with my first lover on Brooks Street.
My first car was a Ford Maverick and I got two tickets
in the first week. Do I remember or do I remember remembering?
Under billing, do you see a five-digit zip code or are there nine?
Before the man retired he was a supervisor of software
designers. Now he checks out groceries for Trader Joe's,
part-time at $12 an hour. Gramma, I'm over here. Get me.
Get me. I'm an evil princess or a fairy cat woman and
they always get away. Two hours earlier than East Village
nightlife, easily I slide into a parking space. People often
say things that they don't really mean, sometimes they say
them hundreds of times, like, I'll never leave you
and we're going to be together for a very long time.

THE
DINNER

a novella

(1)

"Where are you?"

"In the study," Emily hollers. She's sitting cross-legged on a wooden chair, rapidly striking the typewriter keys. There are stacks of smooth white paper on the table and many crumpled sheets scattered on the floor with scribbling in the margin.

"These keys are so stiff," she complains.

"Why didn't you answer the phone?"

"Sorry, I forgot to turn it on. . . . Jack, let's order Chinese tonight. I don't feel like cooking, do you?" She keeps typing.

And then the sound of the cathedral bells across the park. Jack stands there silently for a few minutes looking out the window. "Why do you insist on using the typewriter? The computer is so much easier."

"The words just don't come out the same way, that's why."

Emily takes the sheet out of the typewriter and puts it in the second stack. Outside the window the bare tree looks almost too human, with arms reaching up, the trunk anchored at an angle between the sidewalk and the curb. A golden locust. A policeman walks by the window, his stick in the palm of his hand. Then a policeman appears in her story, too. *Sometimes with too much security, there's a volcanic undermurmur. And that's when the thief grabbed the young woman's iPhone.*

Jack makes a phone call for carryout and then he leans over the kitchen table, holding a plum in his hand, studying it. "Round, smooth, visceral, sweet and organic, grown in California."

Emily is listening to him talk about the plum as she types, trying not to put a plum into the story, but then there it appears on the ground rolling away from the crime, part of the girl's lunch. Emily struggling against too much clarity, but nonetheless the sentences follow one after another like a locomotive that barely disguises the evening's sadness. And then a sentence about the evening's sadness.

The doorbell rings and when Jack hands him fifteen dollars and a three-dollar tip, the teenager says, "Thanks man." In the middle of the table there is a glass vase that the previous tenant left behind, five daffodils and an inscription, DONALD ZALINSKI, 1922–1983. Like many other nights, the couple prepares to sit down with their big white bowls and begin to eat spicy vegetables with cashews.

(2)

With the flat of his hand, the delivery man slapped the thief in the face and knocked him on the floor. Then he graciously handed the girl in the tight black coat, her pink iPhone. By the end of the week, all contradictions were resolved. Then I hesitated. I wondered where this incident had come from—something I had overheard or was it an episode of Law and Order? *The thief was impoverished, his father a prisoner of Mao, and so he spent his days holding up delivery men from Chinese restaurants.* I remember getting caught up in the madness of composing this mystery night after night until the Friday night when Jack slapped me. For me, or perhaps I'm talking about my character, marital love may be impossible. Then I threw my notebook and my laptop in a bag with some clothes and I took off. "Such a sweet man," my friend Lally said. Oh, yeah. You weren't there when he called me a skinny cow, but I am no longer bellowing, right now I'm traveling on a train speeding across the plains.

After endless cups of coffee in the cafe car, my limbs are crossed over each other and tucked under brown blankets, stretched out in the seat, the circle of my belly quiet, even though the test was inconclusive and right now perhaps cells are doubling in amniotic fluid, like the bright colors of the autumn fields, orange, red and yellow, accumulating. The ongoing even-paced lines on the page, too. The yellow bruise on my cheek. Forty-two years old, but still there is a possibility. I was going to tell him about the test after we finished eating. It was just one moment exploding out of many calm hours together. Then I fled.

The sun is slowly setting in the west. Art does not have to pay me, and art does not have to slay me either. If I could just stop working and spend a little more time with him. That's what Jack said. He wanted me to be there because he couldn't write anymore. But I'm alone with my own world when I'm writing and I like entering into and transforming the city of my childhood, not forgettable, but lost, like living in a house full of what could you have and what could you not have.

Just as Jack put the bags on the table, the delivery man in my story slapped the thief, and I stood up and told Jack I had a lover. I didn't get to finish my sentence when he slapped me. But I was inside my story. That's all.

In the dark when I lean back in the train seat and close my eyes, drifting off, Jack's thigh rubs against mine and the tiny music starts up again, those hands of his always adjusting the engine of my havoc.

(3)

An uninvited flute makes disharmonious sounds and the sound floats into the cavernous Mexican church where I am quietly kneeling down beside an unknown man, a German guy that I met on the bus from Mexico City. I tell him to leave and he gives me his card and says, "Emily, I am your friend. Call me if you ever need help." I sit up extending my spine, feeling each vertebra. Michelangelo could do it with marble. So why not me? That little curve in my thoracic spine and the cramp from hours of leaning over a typewriter. I look over at the German. He refuses to leave, and he's wearing a grey fedora even though it's hot in here.

In 1988 some wild obscure gossip about some rock stars sent Jack and me to Lincoln City in a Volkswagen bus with a couple of other teenagers. We didn't know each other when we left but we were engaged when we returned home. The grateful ones were already gone by then. On the way back we stopped at a farm in Colorado. Come on. Come in. At last the door opened to the barn and crowds of people were trying to fit through a tiny opening with an increasing crescendo of despair. Inside, a dead man was frozen in a block of ice, preserved for another era. One was pushing the other. We took some acid. And then female dwarves started to dance in a circle outside the barn. I wasn't intoxicated. You may think I was, I whisper to the German, but I wasn't. I saw them clearly in the early morning light. They came out at night, wearing swishy skirts and when the sun started to rise they disappeared into the forest. I'll dedicate my next story to the Female Combination. It takes two to make a combination. Her ears will ring and her mouth will talk in great sentences with rumors of divine pink. The problem was with the present participle, it kept ringing and ringing and ringing in my journal. Let's pluck her off a shelf and set her there, all alone. Not where I come from. Rung up and dry. I take out my notebook and jot down a few words so I'll remember them later. Then I slip away from my new friend, move two pews back and drop down on the wooden floor, pretending I am my maternal grandmother who used to pray for hours on her knees in the Presbyterian church on Mack Avenue. Outside the wide-open sky is littered with violet clouds. The winds are tame and the idea of my family of two stretched over 3,000 miles, a photographic memory in an imaginary album. Michelangelo had no family crest, but perhaps some crusty conclusions were made about his heritage. All of Europe and then add in Russia. That's me, not Michelangelo.

Be quiet I tell my chattering mind. My knees are a little tight from sitting in the bus for so long, but after a few minutes they relax and I enter into a prayer trance.

(4)

At the corner of Second Avenue and Ninth Street, two policemen are sitting in their car, drinking coffee. I pass them again on another corner. From across the park, I see someone coming out of our front door. I circle across the street and around the block, like a minnow following the radius of a circular aquarium. Some fireworks explode over the East River. When I get closer, I recognize Emily's friend Monica, carrying a box, her keys dangling on the side of her Euphrates hip, each one like a soft pillow on a Broadway stage. When she turns around and sees me, she hugs the box to her chest and calls me every swear word she knows. God damn. I almost charge her, like a bull, but then I pull back and stand still. "How could you?" she says. "You hit her."

"Look what she did to me." I point at the scratch on my cheek and the bruise on my forehead. "She's in love with someone else."

"She's in love with you, you idiot."

"She said she had a lover."

"Millions, but you are the one, aren't you?"

Monica is making me nervous. She always makes me nervous with her accusations and straight-to-the-point answers. "What's in the box, Monica? Are you taking something out of the apartment?"

"None of your business," she says setting it down on the stoop.

Then just as I am ready to go inside, a cab pulls up and Professor Tower gets out, and suggests that we celebrate the recent election in his department. Everything is still except for a few leaves floating through the air. October in New York. Monica looks at Tower and then she looks at me and she picks up her box and says, "See you guys later."

Tower doesn't dream anymore, he explains, because too often his partner bawls him out at night and then he falls asleep exhausted. Some people never dream when the night is too cool. I am determined to get a good night's sleep even though I feel so melancholic. So I have a drink and listen to Tower's suggestions for marital bliss. "Jack, tell her you love her, and do what she wants. If you do what she wants, you'll get what you want," he says. "It's as simple as that." He hesitates, "Unless she is involved with someone else."

I try calling Emily again, but her cell phone isn't on, and when I send an email, her vacation notice instantly pops into my inbox. I'll look in the cafes again in the morning, I mutter to myself as I walk back home, every so often kicking some leaves into the gutter.

(5)

Anachronistic dreaming. Aren't all dreams anachronistic, time and space as we know them, scrambled and rearranged? A tattoo on my forehead. After the attack, the girl in my novel could have had a little flower put on her forehead. I can feel a tattoo on the inside of my skin, a little residue left over from the dream. It says, Dummy. Dumb, dumb, dumb. Go home. The night is dying. The morning is awake and sunlight is streaming in the windows. Seventy percent of twenty-four is daylight here. And it reappears, the great big blue, grey or white reappear every day. It is very windy outside, and all I can say to myself about Jack is—Nope, not that, not that, not him, no more. And then I waver, thinking well, maybe it was really all my fault.

I take a walk down some side streets and around the block and then from across the cobble stone street, a truck driver yells to a guy across the street, "*Hola Juan—Mira esas chicas atrás del camión.*"

Two young Mexican girls in halter tops, tight jeans and long flowing black hair.

Whistle and two smiles.

I bend down to pick up a little leaf and then lean against a banyan tree, pretending to be examining it, but really I, too, am admiring their beauty. The banyan tree wraps around the host, strangling it and then it goes on to grow heartily.

A group of children are running and yelling while a little girl stands on the sidewalk, counting and holding a handkerchief over her eyes. She feels around for the door to the hotel and then goes inside, leaving it open a few inches.

I follow her. After all, this is where I am staying. The lobby has a fairly large open chamber, but the hallway is dark. The little girl goes outside again, but I feel my way around to the next door and the bed and then I lie down and fall deeply asleep.

Eventually time and space collapse and in deepest sleep the end of my marriage seems like a trifle, like the result of a mistake I made one day when I just turned the corner and there was a terrible unrelated explosion that changed everything.

When I wake up Oskar is sitting in the chair in the corner. When I tell him about the dream, he says, "You are a funny lady. The way you twist and turn your narratives, first forward, then to the left, to the right and finally at an angle. I adore you. Let's go for a swim."

(6)

It is dark in the park and I hear some steps behind me. Almost midnight and a group of Tibetan monks pass by my bench. The full moon is up above and a street light shines on a newly planted little oak tree. They don't pay any attention to me as I sit there with my flashlight reading, *The Savage Detectives*. The visceral realists are throwing apples at a poet they don't like. I salvage what words I can from the air and copy them into the inside cover—page, monk, oak leaf, tree trunk, apples, garbage, branch, the lights from the Empire State Building—and then I take myself down the street to the bodega on Avenue A to buy apples, coffee, and there is one more item on my list but I can't remember what it was. As I walk, I twirl the dangling plastic bag in a figure eight. I pass a friend on the street, an artist who makes his living by cutting mats and glass. We nod. A passerby says into his cell phone,

"Catherine, that sex was good." Good is to do good. A newspaper headline—buy gold and silver. Maybe I should buy gold to help protect us. The gold bars were unharmed by the financial crash, in fact they gained value, still sitting somewhere even though they are no longer the security that holds the system in place.

When I walk into our apartment, I hear the sound of the refrigerator. When one is accustomed to coming home and saying, "Hi, Emily," but then no one is there, the space feels awkwardly different, ominous, and yet it is the same.

As I copy the words into my notebook, one on each page, outside an eighteen-wheeler pulls over to set up for a movie shoot in the morning, the engine rumbling. In the morning, stars will be all over Seventh Street. Whitman, you and me, we are all stars and yet still mourning for the lost one. Is the echo of loss, the sound of my typewriter, the return exactly minus one?

(7)

Oskar once visited Omsk, a city in Siberia, the spot where the Russians stored their gold. In the winter it can go down to 40 degrees below zero. That's cold. The sound of ice shattering. I gently touch the bougainvillea drooping over the side of a wall on a side street in the barrio. Soon the flowers will die. And then new ones will reappear. In Mexico a few blocks from the Pacific where Corso traveled extensively, the sign says WATCH OUT FOR FALLING BOULDERS. Does it get any better? The sky and the mountains and the soft breeze. At mid-afternoon, we seek shade under an umbrella outside the hotel bar. Oskar is still wearing his fedora.

"When will you return to your husband? After all, darling, who is the real guilty one?"

It is mid-afternoon, and I am with a stranger sitting under a palm tree, gazing out at the ocean. I turn on my laptop and search around for some old tune on CKLW from Detroit where I grew up. Nostalgia for a new beginning and an old ending. My character dials up her go-for-broke-husband and when he doesn't answer, she eats bunched-up acrid green stalks of celery. Celery is a natural source of salt. I'm looking out at the ocean when Oskar puts his arm around me. "It's so lucky we met in the bus. My wife would like you very much." I look at him like he is crazy or something and then I go back to my laptop: *The delivery man could have been rehabilitated if he wasn't sent to Spofford. But at Spofford, he was brutally raped. And so he went on with his career as a criminal.* A young man carrying a surf board walks into the sea, the sunlight glistening on his wet body.

"It was subtle, the arc made into woman," Oskar says.

"I want you to leave now, Oskar. Please go." I try to be polite. A storm is brewing in the west and the tide is coming in very strong. An admonition. Blame me and blame me. I am irritable and guilty.

But the German philosopher keeps talking, "You might say more. You might say, a wo/man could never change me, or a wo/man can never change him/herself. Both are lies."

I get up, wander a little bit down the beach, and try to call Jack, but before he answers, I hang up. And then my phone rings and rings.

(8)

On the television, the woman pulls a trigger and the gun explodes. Her husband lies dead on the yellow linoleum, some dark blood pooling under his head. Bernhardt goes on acting for a few minutes, groaning and rolling his eyes.

My relationship with Emily shifted a bit in the last few years. I started watching television and she kept going into the back room and writing and babbling about her characters. It seemed as if the heat in her body was dimming, for me at least.

I was writing a novel when we met, then short stories, then sonnets, then haiku and finally one-word poems. And back then she admired me. Then I began to count the c's and r's on every page and just keep lists of numbers. I started cutting out numbers from magazines and pasting them into notebooks. She was in the bedroom clicking away. The rabbit laid out, snared in the rush. That's how I felt.

"Hey, Red, I said—I loved your red hair when we first met— why don't we go out for a film?"

She was too busy, her narrator was eloping with a teenager. He's sitting high up in the mountains now, she said, meditating.

Now she is somewhere, I don't know where. I write a word on a paper. *Mimosa.* I open up a bottle and take a drink. Then I write a sentence. *He hiked up the mountain with those bottles in his backpack.* My narrator is on Emily's mountain! *And he perched up there in the intolerable August heat.* These are the first sentences I have written in a long time. I'll put a box up there, too, I think. What was in that damn box Monica had? *Some one left it here, he thinks. Maybe an alien. He opens it and finds a note. Dear Jack and then the words disappear. One word starting with a V flies off over the horizon. Very. Very much love for you. And when he looks inside the box, there's a tiny set of wings and a little toy soldier.*

Nonsense. I wake up on the sofa, turn off the television, pick up a piece of paper, glance at it, and then crumple it up and throw it in the wastebasket.

(9)

I was in a rush to get dressed and then I fled out the door wearing an old pink sweat jacket. It was suddenly simple: leave. The color orange and the palest of blue—that's what I saw when I looked outside. And I said. Ok, I'm not with you any longer. You crossed over, Jack.

A messenger boy flits by like a bat on a bicycle.

We had promised each other to be there no matter what happened. That promise we all say with such assurance and then break so quickly. But it didn't work that way. Last February, a telegram arrived from Tokyo, warning Jack to be more productive. He was translating a technical book on the composition of computer chips, but the last few months he was translating only one phrase a day, sometimes only a word. They became impatient for the manuscript.

Then Jack knocked over my grandmother's teapot and it broke into a pile of green chips.

I walked into the room and screamed at him. "What the fuck is going on with you?"

He was sitting there tapping his pen on the table.

Months later on a cloudy day, I said, "I'm in love with someone else. That's what's going on with me."

Jack stepped over our cat Lulu and smacked me in the face.

The second time, I stepped out of the way just in time. Then I threw a book at him and went into the bedroom, locked the door and packed. Lulu was scratching on the door.

When I left, he was sitting at the kitchen table with his sleeves rolled up to his elbows. "Let's talk," he said, but I just walked past him. "We're married, for God's sake, Emily."

I didn't want to talk about the details of my transgressions. The country's full of folks like me, wanderers, just slam the door and go somewhere else.

Today my narrator waves goodbye to Daedalus who is standing on the edge of the cliff cheering him on. And then he climbs back down the mountain to find his secret lover, his tenth grade teacher, Miss Ariadne. I close my computer, put it into my bag and then I wade out into a little cove in the Pacific, dive underwater, gliding and watching the schools of minnows collect and disperse.

(10)

At twenty Emily was a beauty. Five feet eleven inches. And the sun, the moon, the earth, the little earthworm, too. They all contain a multiplicity of metaphors.

Leggy, all legs. I met her on a minibus, with a group of friends. She was a cousin of my friend Lewis. She brought her little chihuahua with her. Her long red hair was in a thick braid. Brown eyes and a long classical nose. And then those freckles. She was wearing a tight black jacket and a pair of tight jeans with rhinestones down the sides.

When I looked at her, I thought to myself, I could almost put my hands around your waist, you're so tiny.

When we stopped at a campground, I walked along beside her while giving her dog little bits of my sandwich. "You're so generous," she said, laughing.

Misstinguett didn't have anything on Emily.

I was finished with college, but she was a sophomore. I was working on my first novel about those who live across the flattened landscape pretending to be freedom fighters, weirdos and winos. I was melancholic back then and dreamy, too. A reviewer said it was really about my brother who was publicly so righteous, a journalist who later died in the Gulf War.

Emily wanted to know everything about how I wrote. You work in the morning? For how many hours? Do you work late at night, too? She was taking notes in a little notebook with a picture of Einstein on the cover.

On the second night, we crawled into my pup tent together. And her little dog, Cheekie, kept jumping on us and crying to get in between. For two days just sex, wine, ice tea and peanut butter sandwiches.

Someplace in Colorado we started telling each other stories. She could go on and on. I think it was about a frozen man on a space ship. I said, you've got to write a novel. You're a natural. And so we got married.

(11)

My story just got out of control, flying boxes and mythological figures. Mostly I like writing noir-like city mysteries, but my emotions are up and down lately and I can't sit still for long enough to develop anything.

Monica called and woke me up last night. She shipped the box of notebooks to me. They should be here in a day or two. And she told me that Jack was a mess, drinking, his clothing was rumpled and he was wandering around the East Village looking for me. Each word she said was like a sharp piece of shattered glass. When the lights go out, no one, nobody. And yet I walked out on him. He heard the key turning, he must have when he walked across the room.

He knew about my grandmother on my father's side and how she said over and over to me, "Never let a man hit you." She didn't say anything to me about forgiveness. She was a funny woman near the end, sitting there in her arm chair with her rheumatism and her stroke, mumbling about all her friends who had passed away, and her five husbands. "Never let a man hit you." She'd just take their money and go to the next husband.

I look over at Oskar sunbathing on a big Mexican blanket. He has a big muscular body with some softness here and there. A lady passes by with some beads strung up and dangling on a rack. *Se vende.* Her shadow crosses over Oskar's big white back. I am so warm and dry in the sun. And then an old lady walks by in a black bikini, her after-many-birth-stretch marks glistening in the sun. She is encircled by a group of young men. Her pancreas seems a little enlarged. I start writing about her in my notebook. Her pancreas. I touch my belly, swollen from the sudden rush of blood. No minnows in amniotic fluid, not in this lifetime. After all, I wasn't meant to be a mother. Maybe I'm too self involved for that anyhow. Derrida calls it a kind of logic that asserts itself and then denies itself, and then backs into itself again, retracing, dispersing.

Oskar reappears at my table under the umbrella. "My wife Isabelle will arrive tomorrow. She will love to meet you. She is a wonderful photographer. I want her to photograph you. She will love your skin. So smooth."

I look at my cell. "Missed call." I hit "View" and see Jack's number.

"Doesn't that get to you?" Oskar asks. "You just keep opening and shutting your phone. Why don't you answer? The sun is burning my back like a razor." He puts his white shirt over his now red skin and sits down to order a piña colada.

(12)

He climbs up the mountain huffing and puffing, his asthmatic bronchial tubes closing from the pressure of the altitude. Strength is not the issue. He is a stocky strong man. But his lungs don't function well here. The cabin is at the top of the path, an outpost from the monastery. He must get to the top, he thinks, and there he will learn something new. As he climbs he slows down his pace and inhales smoothly through his nose and then slowly, very slowly exhaling through his mouth. He hesitates at the bottom of the exhale and then lets the thin air float into his nose. On the table in the cabin, he finds a big wooden bowl, filled with thick noodles and green beans. Even though he is dizzy, he eats and then takes off his checkered suit and lies down on a mat on the floor. Two weeks of absolute silence with his dinner and breakfast delivered to his door. He takes a buddha seat outside and watches the sun go down. También este es sustancia.

The words and sentences are flowing as Jack sits at the computer. With Emily gone he's sad, and yes, there's a hole in his day without a doubt, but he's moving into and through this darkness with this story. In between pages, he glances out the window, thinking maybe she will come around the bend. He takes out the camera and photographs the corner. Nothing but a digital flash of light on the screen. Then typing again—*Japanese houses are in Japan. In the Rockies, there are secret cabins for those who need to reconnect with the earth and sky. Phil jumps up from his chair, thinking, Joe Hill never really died. Democracy comes from below.* What does Joe Hill have to do with this character? So he googles him. They were both friendless. Joe refused to speak and his narrator goes off into silence to find direction. Joe dies for not speaking. He protects the woman. And his character? Is there a woman here, too? There must be a woman. There must be a problem.

Jack goes outside for a break, walking toward the East River, crossing the freeway on a little bridge, down the steps, standing by the river, across the lights on Long Island, so many Brooklyn-Queens lights. Tonight there are even some glimmers of stars in the sky. Under a streetlight, a young gymnast is twirling her baton, a type of wholesomeness, cart-wheeling across the parking lot. Her skirt turns upside down, and there's her crotch. Sixteen at most. And then up above the fluttering yellow elm leaves.

Perhaps the guy in his story is a prominent conceptual poet with an academic post, the words tumbling out of him this way and that way. No, he's a construction worker, like Jack's father, something concrete. The cheerleader is sitting on a bench now, hunched over and looking at her feet. How could those endorphins have settled so quickly, Jack wonders. Sometimes Emily used to hunch over and cry at night for her mother who died when she was eight years old. But Jack hardly ever cries. Instead, he has a drink and that's what he's going to do now, reach into his pocket and pull out a pint.

(13)

Three weeks after Emily disappeared, I wake up to an insistent doorbell. I stick my head out the window and look down. A guy with a fedora and a blonde woman with a big backpack. They certainly aren't the proselytizing religious peddlers that I expected at this time in the morning. I buzz them in. Then I dash into the bathroom and comb my hair. "Fair Greek, though art." I grab a few liquor bottles and throw them in the garbage bag, and then open the door and look through the chain. "Yeah?" The guy says with a thick German accent, "I'm here to talk to you about your wife, Jack."

"Emily?" I open the door quickly and let the couple in. "Sorry for the mess. Sit down." I scoop up the old clothes on the sofa and throw them into a pile on the floor.

We sit looking at each other. I'm suddenly afraid to say anything. They look so serious. Did anything happen to Emily? Why are they here?

"I know where your wife is, Jack. She is confused right now, but she still loves you. We left her in her room in a hotel in Puerto Vallarta." And then he trails off into silence with his sooty brown eyes looking straight ahead.

"She may not want me to come."

"She needs you to come."

The woman who looked so young from up above is in fact a fifty-year-old woman with a strong body and bleached hair. She sits there shaking her head up and down. "Your wife is ok. I saw her only briefly. But she is not eating properly. Mimosa and coconut, only. She is watching movies in the hotel room and swimming at night. You should go—besides that, Puerto Vallarta is a great place now, the beach, the rolling tide, and at night in the mountains hundreds of thousands of free-tailed bats."

"Free-tailed bats?"

"Forgive me, my wife is, how do they say it in English, umm, a birder. She photographs birds. She was so excited about the birds in Mexico. And she didn't really want to come to New York."

"Well there are lots of pigeons here. Check out the park," I say, slightly irritated.

I pick up a piece of paper from the floor and then dig down into the back of the sofa for a pencil. "What's the name of the hotel where she's at?" Oskar reaches into his jacket pocket and pulls out a card. "I wanted to send you an email, but Emily would not give me your address and I had some business in New York on our way to Germany so I decided to stop by and intervene. Buttinski—that's what my wife's mother would call me."

I just sit there, staring at him and holding the card. Mexico? When they leave, I look down at the street and watch them walking away arm in arm, the man with his briefcase and the woman carrying everything else on her back.

(14)

The notebooks arrived yesterday. I have been reading them, one after another, intermittent journal entries from the first year after we were married. Jack with his readings and his students. I was going to creative writing classes at the community college. Throughout the day I would copy down words in the left margin of every other page, a word I'd hear or see on the street, a word that would come to me when I closed my eyes. *Manu was right.* I copied that phrase in the middle of the page. Where did it come from? Of course, Manu had to be right. Emanuel was our super and he had a spiritual side to him. Whenever we would complain about something, anything, the sound of the pipes rattling at night, for example, he would look at the positive side. "You know you have heat when you hear that banging. It reminds you that you are alive."

"Ok, Manu, ok, but fix them."

Some of the other words I wrote were *tunnel of rage, ready-made, radical reforming* and *rush to power.* Then I went on in the opposite column to analyze Jack. Yes, a radical reformation is needed. Yes, he loves to sit at the dinner table and brag about his literary successes. His voice breaks when he tries to be humble. I hardly ever analyzed myself. But now, I'm starting to realize that I was extraordinarily competitive with him.

Then I describe the dark shadow of the pine trees in the campground in the Smoky Mountains where we stayed for a week after we got married. That's the place I told myself I'd always remember. I had drawn a sketch of the mountain in my journal. And the cliff over the river. And then I forgot about our promise. It was as if we were traveling on a fast ramp and my mind was spinning along the freeway like a moving lamp. And Jack makes the sound track with a series of eccentric electric guitar moves.

I reach into my bag and take out a pile of change. It clinks and rolls over the table. I make stacks of paper money and coins—five centavos, ten centavos, twenty, fifty, and the pesos, too. Collecting coins and words on little white cards.

The hotel housekeeper, Patsy—an older Anglo hippie—is cleaning the bathroom, and I'm packing things up. I can't stay here and hibernate. *Blue.* My face might turn blue like the sky. *Picturesque.* Patsy comes out with a scrap of his hair jutting picturesquely across his face. He wasn't cleaning. He was preening in front of the mirror. He struts by me and winks. *Submerge.*

He reminds me of my father when he would catch my mother in the shower. Parents and children with ties so submerged. Remember darling your chin should be at shoulder level and then you dip down and up. That was my father, teaching me how to dance.

And I write some more words in my notebook—*breaking, butterflies, my stamps, my old shoes, shifting, bourbon.* Patsy tucks his tip into his back pocket, and then I put my hair into braids and go out to swim before dusk turns into evening and evening into dawn.

(15)

Professor Tower calls a cab over. "I loved the book you wrote about the post Gulf War syndrome, Jack. You must get back to that time with your writing. And quit putting your face into the mattress. All this poetry and this global muttering. You say you don't care but you do care. That student in your novel who walked around with photographs of piles of bodies alongside the road. His inability to make sense of his experience. Enough haiku, Jack."

"Thanks for the advice Prof. Bring on the king. The book has begun." I look back out the window of the cab and on the sidewalk Tower gets smaller and smaller. And all I can say is "Kings have fallen over and over and we continue to put our hopes on the ashes."

The driver is humming some tune inside his plastic box. I lean over and ask him, "Are you a Native American? What tribe?"

"Montauks."

"Your grandfather kept his teepee on the move?"

"Yeah, all over Long Island. Like I drive this cab, Mister."

"I wonder . . . "

"Mister you have a tendency to begin sentences with, I wonder, don't you?"

What a smart ass, I'm thinking. "And you end yours with what-will-happen-now, don't you?"

At JFK, I've had about enough sparring for a while. I get out with my suitcases, give the guy a $5 tip and head toward the Aeromexico counter.

Two men in front of me are arguing. One of them claims that Ezekiel was a visionary and the other says, no, he was epileptic. Two points of view, two porcelain slabs and a hook. Ezekiel suffered but he raised those boys from the dead. One of them turns around and asks me what I think.

All I can say is, "Life is cruel and then there is the religion of being, being right or being wrong. Like at night when you realize you can't drink alcohol and eat steaks like that every night. Eventually your organs begin to weaken. Then you will begin to consider the benefit of salads."

They look at me blankly and then head down the corridor to the plane.

I get a window seat, put on my head set, take out a photo of Emily. She's wearing black sunglasses. I try to remember her green eyes and the little brown speckles. The plane is climbing and heading toward Phoenix. Aretha Franklin sings about prayers and forever and ever. The clouds are all misty and blocking the world from my view. Darling believe me. Please believe me.

(16)

A pair of white seagulls / Sidelong Sidewhite Sunlight / Oh Dear oh dear me oh my.

The guy in the video store scowls at me, "*Mujeres,*" he says when I claim to have forgotten my ticket. "You are two days late."

"I don't have any Mexican money. *No tengo ningún dinero mexicano o americano. No tengo dinero.*"

I paid that guy enough. "Arrest me," I say.

And then I give him a sidelong graze with the edge of my hip, I pick up my suitcase and stroll down the boardwalk.

A group of women tourists arguing under big white sun hats. Negativism everywhere. "I met him in 1965. I tell you it was 1965, Claudia."

Oh, I miss the comfort of reading those Victorian novels, all shelved together at home—Dickens, Austin and the Brontës. Too many words though. I want to stop this endless flow of language and worry.

Jack used to like me to wear that lemon-colored blouse. Unbutton it slowly he said as I stood in front of the mirror. Being a couple was at times like moving in a cloud back and forth from the kitchen to the bed. At other times it was heavy and loud. When we are together, I want privacy. When I am alone walking down the beach with my suitcase, I want to be with him.

Why did I give that blouse to the Salvation Army?

Last month when we were arguing, I came out into the living room and he rolled off the couch and stood up, unshaven, without his shirt, without his pants. He stood there naked and scowling.

Yes, the conditions of our privacy were quite untenable. I sit on a mound of sand and open my journal. I write down one word, *untenable*. And I helped create that lack of ease with our co-tenancy.

Then I get up and walk a little further down the beach. Miles and miles of sand. I'll catch a cab I think. Then I climb up over a gigantic barrier of rocks and sit down in front of the big ugly yellow Sheraton. The global hotels invade the Mexican beaches. I write down another word. *Rage*. The rocks are ragged and sharp here. I move back a little further from the ocean, sit down and watch the tide come crashing in and then pulling back. Two old men, wearing khaki bermudas sit under an umbrella, reading magazines.

I was in a rage for a while. I really needed to do something besides writing stories. That's when I made the decision to go to work for the call center. Desperate teenagers dialing for help.

"I'm going to kill myself. Some guy took my iPhone and my mother is going to kill me. It's her phone."

A sense of purpose comes into my life when I am helping others. "You will have many cell phones in your life. It seems like this is the only one, Jenny, but you will have many. Did you call the police?"

"Yes, but I can't tell my mother because I wasn't supposed to be out at night. I'd just left my boyfriend in the pizzeria."

"I think you will have to tell your mother."

And so we went on and Jenny didn't kill herself, as far as I know, I never really heard. When I called back, someone else answered and said that she had borrowed his phone, but she had taken off running down the street.

Then I'd come home and write a story. The woman whose child died and she was home alone in her room while her husband was working and she was so unhappy. "Get a job I told her. Volunteer somewhere. Get out in the world. Everything passes, changes, transforms. We have to accept our losses and our joys." And she was weeping.

When I came home and thought about her and how I didn't have a child, the locust tree outside our window began to take on an artificial shade of purple.

I am lying in the sand now with my eyes closed, thinking about that tree and how I miss it. Home isn't just your suitcase and your papers. It's the people who live there too and the trees and the animals. And then I start laughing at myself. Maybe I will go home. Maybe Jack will have me back.

(17)

Just before the plane lands, I take the material out of the seat pocket and shuffle through it. In big red letters, a card says, "Eat the body of the lamb, not the body of Christ." Who put this here? Some joker. Why do we eat bodies? That's what Emily would say anyhow. No animal flesh. No human flesh. And then she would nibble on my earlobe. Silly. Sometimes we are so close I forget who thought what first.

I take the card for the hotel out of my breast pocket. Hotel Villa del Mar. I try to pronounce it in Spanish for the cab driver, but the old man turns around and speaks to me in English, "But you don't say it like that." "Otell beeya del mar." Nevertheless, he takes me there, driving for blocks on rough cobblestone streets. Inside, I try to speak to the woman at the desk. It is dark. She doesn't understand English. I write down Emily's name on a sheet of paper.

She nods her head.

"What room?" I ask.

She shakes her head and points to the door.

"What?" I am distraught. "Gone. *Vaya?*"

"*Si, Señor, ella fue por la mañana.*"

Somehow I negotiate a room. A boy takes me across the street and I discover that I have rented an apartment rather than a room. This afternoon at three there will be an eclipse, the moon moving in front of the sun.

I set out to find someone who can speak English and Spanish to help me talk to the hotel clerk. As I go out the door I step on a squishy rope in the street. When I kick it over, I discover that it is an old worn and wet child's ragdoll. Not gonna ever forget about you baby, I keep saying over and over. And on I go, carrying the tattered ragdoll with me. I am going to forget, I promise myself, all the other little abnormalities and irritations.

And then in a bodega on the corner I ask if someone speaks English. A tall skinny blonde guy behind me volunteers and I ask him to please come back and help me.

He says to me, in a German accent. "Do you want to see the movie, *Night of the Iguana* with Elizabeth Taylor and Richard Burton?"

I look at him quizzically.

"They filmed it here, sir. Yes. Beautiful movie. On the Malecon tonight. I will take you to the Malecon." He smiles at me and winks.

There must be a lot of Germans here, I think. "First the hotel," I say, "please come. I think I saw a sign that they are showing the film in the hotel, too."

The man and the hotel clerk chatter away in Spanish and then he turns to me and says. "Your wife was here for two weeks, but she just left around 11:30 this morning. She was walking down toward the beach with two suitcases. Maybe she caught a cab."

Why doesn't she answer her cell phone? Shit. I beg the man to come with me and help me find her. We head down the street. I have the photo of Emily with me and I show it to shopkeepers as we go by. When we get near the beach, a waiter remembers her. "She was sitting here for a long while," he says, "just looking out at the water, and then she headed down that direction, stomping through the sand with those two suitcases."

I take off then with the German guy running beside me. After a while, we come to a big barrier.

"What is this doing here?" I ask.

"The hotel likes to keep the vendors and beggars out so they put all these rocks over here. There is a path around them over here."

I am standing looking at the endless shore when suddenly I see a woman at the water's edge with two suitcases. I slow down and watch her, afraid that if I close my eyes, she might blend into the environment. Here and then gone, this erratic over-swinging pendulum.

I squat down, take out my notebooks and write a few words to describe the sky and the ocean, the shades of blue almost merging with a slight change in tone. And then Emily turns and starts walking away, and I jump up and start jogging toward her.

(18)

In the kitchen Jack makes a list of words while Emily is cutting up vegetables for a salad to go along with the pizza.

At the dining room table, Monica argues with Tower. "You shouldn't quit your job at the university to go traipsing across the country, Tower. So you collect a bunch of stories about border crossings. Can't you just take a leave of absence? You are the only one of us who has a stable job and now you're giving it up."

Emily comes in with the salad. "Hey, Monica, he has to follow his passion. This is an important project."

Jack sits down. "Ok, here's the first question, Do words carry a glimmer of light?"

Tower jumps up. "The shifting light carries us to the other side of time, inside, outside. And I'm going to follow it. I can't work in a dungeon any longer. I want to do something useful rather than teaching Clifford Gertz for the rest of my life, or like Tony writing those little treatises on Heidegger."

"A dungeon," Monica says—"you go into the office two days a week. And you have a big bright office and a salary and health insurance. Such a dungeon we all should have."

"Well, you don't know what it's like having to talk to those people about their little tenure issues."

"Yes," Emily says, "the never-ending hunt as we pony up. Did I tell you I'm going to start a new series?"

"No," Monica says, "you didn't tell us. A magazine? More words of wisdom from post-war present-war America's most gifted?"

"I'm going to ask fifty-five poets to collect and/or write as many twitters as they can about the war in Afghanistan and then translate the sound of birds in the park into weird text or symbols and intermix the twitters with the sound of the birds. And other city wildlife, too. Then I'm going to make these into tiny little Japanese folding books and drop them from the Empire State Building."

"Emily, that's ridiculous," Jack says. "They'll arrest you for dropping things over the edge."

"They'll fall down like little flags over the city, Jack. It'll be amazing."

"And people complain that life is too short."

"You better go up there and check it out first. They might not even have holes big enough. You'll have to sneak one at a time. One lonely little flag flittering down. Please stop the war in Afghanistan."

"Well," Tower says, "that's interesting. Little flags. Little protests. I want to leave the university now before the semester is up. With this new law, allowing border patrols to stop anyone who looks suspicious; i.e,. any Mexican . . . I have a friend who lives in Patagonia and I'm going to stay there and then camp close to the border with my tape recorder and my camera."

"You better bring some water with you, Tower. It's pretty hot and dry out there. Maybe you should take a gun, too."

"I have news," Monica says. "I got a new job working for La Mama making stage scenery. And it's union."

"Cool. So there's your stability. The union. So, Jack, what is the list of words you want us to work on?"

"*Pencil.*"

"Pen-*cil*?"

"The proper way to hold a pencil is between your index finger and your middle finger."

"So is *proper* another word we should entertain?"

"Ok, Tower we got that. . . You're the professor."

"That's what the man said while he was writing names down in his notebook for the deportation camps. I'm the professor. I'm in charge."

"Do you have the tape recorder on, Emily?"

"Yeah, I'm getting it all. What about *happiness*?"

"Oh, that's a word that doesn't have much of a string connecting it to anything concrete, happiness and/or tenure."

"Where is the pizza?"

"Well pizza is salty and tomato-y and it goes in your gut like cement. But it tastes good in your mouth."

"Something more interesting. Like the doorbell ringing. Are you going to get it, Emily? It's the pizza."

"We don't have a character yet."

"There's always the pizza delivery man. You get it, Jack. Let's let Monica add something to the list."

"*Golden.*"

"The golden locust tree that grows outside your window. Completely stark in the winter and slowly it becomes feathery with those flag-like leaves. And then it drops down its seeds on the sidewalk. The composer of the forest. Ok, ok, we'll put *golden* on the list."

"Are you going to Arizona on your own, Tower, or is Tony going with you?" Jack asks as he opens up the box of pizza— "White cheese and spinach, yum . . ."

"We're through. I'm going on my own. Tony moved out last week."

"Oh, that's what this about. Heartache."

"Yes and no. I've been wanting to do this anyhow. I bought an old Ford pickup truck. I guess we're all on the move always, aren't we? Are you working on a new novel, Jack?"

"Nah, I'm in one of those lulls right now. Maybe this tape will inspire me."

"Hey, pass that salad down here, Emily. It's pretty good. What's in that dressing?"

"Oh, things like tumeric and tahini and lemon and agave. Combined, it's an aphrodisiac."

"That's a word for our list." Jack gets up and puts on a CD of Billie Holiday singing summertime and my ma is so super good looking. He's humming.

And then Emily starts singing along, too. "Oh your daddy's rich and your ma is good looking so hush little baby don't you cry. . . . Did you ever hear Larry Adler do this on the harmonica? It's amazing."

"You got a phone book anywhere?" Monica stands up.

Emily points in the corner.

"What happened to this phone book? All the white pages are stuck together."

"Now it is an art object," Jack says. "I shellacked it. We don't need it anymore with the computer you know. I'm going to set it up on that stand there as a relic of time past. You have to keep looking ahead, down the roads and avenues as those lines and colors blend and merge. But you can't forget the past."

"Yeah, you certainly do. Speaking of the past—What's Oskar up to? Do you still hear from him, Emily?"

"Well, I haven't heard from him six or seven months and then just a few weeks ago he sent me an email. He's going to Mexico again, Puerto Vallarta."

"Touristville, Mexico. Almost like an outpost of the U.S."

"Or maybe Germany."

"Oskar wants me to meet him there. His wife is birding in Sub-Sahara Africa for a month."

"Emily, you're not going to Mexico again are you? Come on, baby."

"Well I'm *thinking* about it, Jack, that's all. I haven't gone anywhere besides the supermarket for months. And I want to do a photographic study of the Mexican sea shore, documenting how the foreign countries are taking over Mexico. The drug lords may have the interior but the foreigners have the shores. And they'll have to get rid of the cartel if they want to continue colonizing the shore. Oskar will be my escort. And this will give you time to start your new novel, Jack."

"Oskar, dear old Oskar. Let's talk about this later." Jack shifts around and straightens out the lilacs in the vase in the middle of the table.

"Come on, you guys," Monica says. "Enough is enough. What are the last words on your list?"

Jack turns over the page and says, "*Domelight . . . dashlight . . . limelight.*" And then everyone is quiet for a few seconds, thinking and Mama Holiday's singing, "No regrets . . . I know our love will linger when the other love forgets, so I say goodbye with no regrets."

And then the four friends start to eat their pizza and talk about the various etymological twists and turns for the words *golden* and *limelight*. And who among them moves energetically toward one word or the other.

Notes on This Collection

Twelve Green Rooms. After excerpting vignettes from my journal, editing them until I liked the way time and space were woven, then cracking apart the narratives, splicing in words and phrases from research about the oil spill, water pollution, shortages and the effects on animals—after all this, I excerpted words in the shape of a W from each piece and then wove them into the next one. I am now calling this process *sequential quilting*. Written in 2009–2010, the final quilting took place in summer 2010 in Marquette, Michigan, next to Lake Superior, one of the largest freshwater lakes in the world. The water on earth and in our animal human bodies plants lands air is the same water that was here when the dinosaurs were lumbering   water   sound   earth ether   moving   reassembling   to destroy   re story   call forth   again   *om nama shivaya*

A Swift Passage. When writing this poem, I was thinking and living with migration, migrating words and phrases, migrating people and animals, the capital M, from one prose block to another, many writers and friends migrating in and away, including Charles Olson, Gertrude Stein, HD, William Butler Yeats, Emily Dickinson, William Blake, Peter Orlovsky, Julie Patton, Lewis Carroll, Herman Hesse, William Shakespeare and Ezra Pound

A Slow Curve. I drove out west in the winter of 2011. Twice I passed through the oil fields in Texas, once at dusk and once at noon. Later that summer when I was teaching at Naropa, I read Bobbie Louise Hawkins's book *One Small Saga*, the story of her life with her first husband. In this novel, she is traveling. In my poem, I'm traveling. Both of us are moving through love and space. I designed a process of extracting phrases and words from

One Small Saga, and then quilting these floating words and phrases into "A Slow Curve."

14 x 14 x 14. One May day, I was talking with Martine Bellen about possible poetic projects and writing constraints. I suggested working with the sonnet form—write one line an hour for fourteen hours for fourteen days. Then I noticed a 4 x 6 index card on my desk, and there were exactly 14 lines on each card, perfect for the project. So I carried a stack of cards around with me for fourteen days, collecting.

The Dinner. Initially, this story was inspired by a list of words and passages taken from some of my reading in 2008–2009, approximately two hundred books. There was an exact method used for extracting the phrases, but then the story evolved by improvising, inventing and transforming. When I scan the text, all that remains *sometimes* is a word or a tiny phrase. For example, the first lines of the novella started from a few words from Kobo Abe's *The Secret Rendezvous:* "concerned the whereabouts of my wife." After rewriting, the phrase disappeared, but the story unfolded.

Many thanks to the writers who inspired or contributed unknowingly to this text, among many others—Kobo Abe, Kathy Acker, Stanley Aronowitz, Martine Bellen, Roberto Bolaño, Jorge Luis Borges, Paul Bowles, Gaudier Brzeska, Pam Brown, Paul Buck, Reed Bye, Jack Collum, Julia Conner, Julio Cortázar, Brenda Coultas, Robert Creeley, Katie Degentesh, Edward Dorn, Ed Friedman, Michael Friedman, Gloria Frym, Cliff Fyman, Michael Gizzi, Anselm Hollo, Jeanne Hueving, Kenneth Koch, Berel Lang, Kimberly Lyons, Stephanie Marlis, Harry Mathews, Bernadette Mayer, Rosemary Mayer, Cormac McCarthy, Michael McClure, Myung Mi Kim, Stephen Paul Miller, Marianne Moore, Hilda Morley, Sheila Murphy, Eileen Myles, Alice Notley, Frank O'Hara, Michael Ondaatje, Maureen Owen, Frank

Parker, Michael Pelias, Georges Perec, Simon Pettet, Tim Peterson, Ian Record, Joan Retallack, Kit Robinson, Jerome Rothenberg, Michael Rothenberg, Sappho, W.G. Sebald, Eleni Sikelianos, Juliana Spahr, Jack Spicer, Alfred Stieglitz, Gertrude Stein, Lorenzo Thomas, Lynne Tillman, George Tysh, Anne Waldman, Lewis Warsh, Jo Ann Wasserman, Hannah Weiner, Philip Whalen, Tyrone Williams, Jeff Wright, Laura Wright and Lila Zemborain.

quale [kwa-lay]: *Eng. n* 1. A property (such as hardness) considered apart from things that have that property. 2. A property that is experienced as distinct from any source it may have in a physical object. *Ital. pron.a.* 1. Which, what. 2. Who. 3. Some. 4. As, just as.

CPSIA information can be obtained
at www.ICGtesting.com
Printed in the USA
BVHW031406100120
569191BV00001B/221/P

Graded examples in

Negative Numbers and Graphs

M. R. Heylings M.A., M.Sc.

Schofield & Sims Limited   Huddersfield

0 7217 2333 0

First printed 1984
Reprinted 1986

Acknowledgements
The drawings on page 35 by Sir D'Arcy Thompson,
On Growth and Form, are reproduced by permission
of Cambridge University Press.
The 1:50 000 map extract on page 42 is reproduced
from the Ordnance Survey map with the permission
of the Controller of Her Majesty's Stationery Office.
Crown copyright reserved.

The series **Graded examples in mathematics**
comprises:

Fractions and Decimals	0 7217 2323 3
Answer Book	0 7217 2324 1
Algebra	0 7217 2325 x
Answer Book	0 7217 2326 8
Area and Volume	0 7217 2327 6
Answer Book	0 7217 2328 4
General Arithmetic	0 7217 2329 2
Answer Book	0 7217 2330 6
Geometry and Trigonometry	0 7217 2331 4
Answer Book	0 7217 2332 2
Negative Numbers and Graphs	0 7217 2333 0
Answer Book	0 7217 2334 9
Matrices and Transformations	0 7217 2335 7
Answer Book	0 7217 2336 5
Sets, Probability and Statistics	0 7217 2337 3
Answer Book	0 7217 2338 1

In preparation:

Revision of Topics	0 7217 2339 x
Answer Book	0 7217 2340 3

Designed by Graphic Art Concepts, Leeds
Printed in England by Pindar Print Limited, Scarborough, North Yorkshire

Author's Note

This series has been written and produced in the form of eight topic books, each offering a wealth of graded examples for pupils in the 11–16 age range; plus a further book of revision examples for fifth formers.

There are no teaching points in the series. The intention is to meet the often heard request from teachers for a wide choice of graded examples to support their own class teaching. The contents are clearly labelled for easy use in conjunction with an existing course book; but the books can also be used as the chief source of material, in which case the restrictions imposed by the traditional type of mathematics course book are removed and the teacher is free to organise year-by-year courses to suit the school. Used in this way, the topic-book approach offers an unusual and useful continuity of work for the class-room, for homework or for revision purposes.

The material has been tested over many years in classes ranging from mixed ability 11-year-olds to fifth formers taking public examinations. Some sections are useful for pupils of above average ability while other sections suit the needs of the less able, though it is for the middle range of ability that the series is primarily intended.

Contents

Inequalities

Further Topics

Symbols

=	is equal to
≠	is not equal to
≃	is approximately equal to
<	is less than
⩽	is less than or equal to
≮	is not less than
>	is greater than
⩾	is greater than or equal to
≯	is not greater than
⇒	implies
⇐	is implied by
→	maps onto
∈	is a member of
∉	is not a member of
⊂	is a subset of
⊄	is not a subset of
∩	intersection (or overlap)
∪	union
A'	the complement (or outside) of set A
$\mathscr{E}$	The Universal set
∅ or { }	the empty set
(x, y)	the co-ordinates of a point
$\begin{pmatrix} x \\ y \end{pmatrix}$	the components of a vector

The Greek alphabet

A	α	alpha
B	β	beta
Γ	γ	gamma
Δ	δ	delta
E	ε	epsilon
Z	ζ	zeta
H	η	eta
Θ	θ	theta
I	ι	iota
K	κ	kappa
Λ	λ	lambda
M	μ	mu
N	ν	nu
Ξ	ξ	xi
O	o	omicron
Π	π	pi
P	ρ	rho
Σ	σ, ς	sigma
T	τ	tau
Y	υ	upsilon
Φ	ϕ, φ	phi
X	χ	chi
Ψ	ψ	psi
Ω	ω	omega

Directed Numbers

Number lines
Directed numbers
Combining numbers

Number lines

Part 1   Introduction

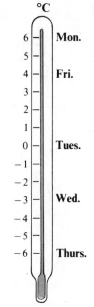

°C

1   Every morning before breakfast, Diana reads a thermometer in the garden.

These are the results on five days in winter.

What is the difference between the temperatures on
a   Monday and Friday
b   Monday and Tuesday
c   Tuesday and Wednesday
d   Tuesday and Thursday
e   Friday and Wednesday
f   Monday and Thursday?

2   When I got up this morning, the temperature was −3°C. By 10 o'clock it was 4°C. How many degrees had the temperature risen?

3   At sunset the temperature was 2°C and at midnight it was −7°C. How many degrees had the temperature fallen?

4   Room temperature is 12°C and the temperature outside is −2°C. What is the difference between these two temperatures?

5   The thermometer read −5°C one frosty morning, but by lunchtime it had risen by 8 degrees. What was the temperature then?

6   Inside Mrs Chidswell's fridge, the temperature is −3°C. To defrost it, she lets the temperature rise by 7 degrees. What will be the temperature then?

7   It is 4°C outside, and the forecast says it will fall by 12 degrees. What will the temperature be then?

8   When the temperature in London was −2°C, it was −13°C in Edinburgh. What is the difference between these temperatures?

9   The temperature in Inverness on Christmas Day was −15°C; but by the following day it had risen by 7 degrees. What was the temperature then?

10   The coldest recorded temperature is −88°C which occurred on 24th August 1960 at Vostok in Antarctica. The highest shade temperature was recorded at 58°C on 13th September 1922 at Al' Aziziyah in Libya. What is the difference between these two temperatures?

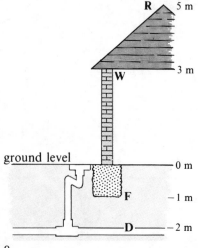

11   A bungalow is being built with walls W 3 metres and a roof R 5 metres *above* ground level. The foundations F are 1 metre and the drains D 2 metres *below* ground level.

Find the difference in height between
a   R and W
b   W and F
c   W and D
d   R and F
e   R and D
f   F and D.

12   The restaurant in a department store is 12 metres above ground level, and the basement is 5 metres below ground level. How high is the restaurant above the basement?

Number lines

13 A bridge carries a road 6 metres above the surface of a river, and the river is 4 metres deep. How high is the road above the river bed?

14 A diver is working 14 metres below sea-level, and the deck of his supply ship is 5 metres above sea-level. How far is the diver below the level of the deck?

15 An archaeologist finds some broken pottery 2 metres below ground level and some pieces of wood $3\frac{1}{2}$ metres below ground level. How far apart were the pottery and the wood?

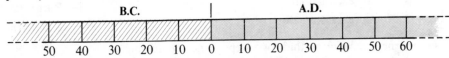

16 Fabius Maximus was born in the year 20 BC and he died in the year AD 35. How long did he live?

17 His wife, Augusta, was born in 14 BC. If she died in AD 40, how long did she live?

18 Marcus Sextus died in the year 6 BC. If he was born in 58 BC, how many years did he live?

19 Rome was founded in 753 BC, and in AD 455 the Vandals destroyed the city. How many years separated these events?

20 Julius Caesar invaded Britain in 55 BC, and William of Normandy invaded in AD 1066. How many years separate these two invasions?

Part 2 Bus-stops

A bus service from Edinburgh to Dundee passes through the places listed, and there is a stop outside your home. Your journeys start from HOME each time.

A positive sign (+) indicates a journey *up* the list.
A negative sign (−) indicates a journey *down* the list.

Find where you are after the two stages of these journeys.

1 + 5 − 3	11 + 5 − 7
2 + 6 − 2	12 + 7 − 1
3 + 7 − 4	13 + 2 + 3
4 + 6 − 1	14 + 4 + 5
5 + 8 − 5	15 + 1 + 6
6 + 2 − 5	16 + 1 + 4
7 + 4 − 7	17 − 2 − 3
8 + 2 − 4	18 − 4 − 5
9 + 1 − 6	19 − 2 − 4
10 + 2 − 7	20 − 5 − 1

Three steps are needed for these journeys.

21 + 2 + 4 − 7	26 + 4 + 1 − 5
22 + 5 + 2 − 6	27 − 1 − 7 + 8
23 − 5 + 3 − 2	28 − 5 − 1 + 4
24 − 2 − 1 + 7	29 + 7 − 10 + 3
25 + 4 − 6 − 2	30 − 5 − 3 + 9

Edinburgh
Blackhall
Dalmeny
Queensferry
Rosyth
Aberdour
Burntisland
Kinghorn
Kirkcaldy
Glenrothes
HOME
Kettlebridge
Pitlessie
Cupar
Dairsiemuir
St. Andrews
Leuchars
Tayport
Newport
Dundee

9

Number lines

Remembering to start at HOME each time, find the missing steps in these journeys if they are to end at the places given.

31 + 2 ? to reach Rosyth
32 + 5 ? to reach Queensferry
33 − 5 ? to reach Dundee
34 − 3 ? to reach St. Andrews
35 + 4 ? to reach Cupar
36 − 2 ? to reach Rosyth

These journeys have more than two steps. Find the missing steps.

37 + 6 − 1 ? to reach Kirkcaldy
38 − 7 + 2 ? to reach HOME
39 − 1 − 3 ? to reach Glenrothes
40 + 3 − 1 ? to reach Edinburgh
41 + 1 + 2 + 3 ? to reach Kettlebridge
42 − 2 + 3 − 4 ? to reach Dundee

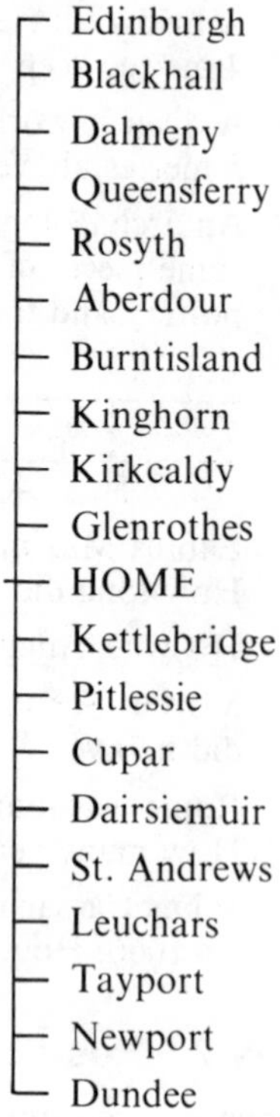
Edinburgh
Blackhall
Dalmeny
Queensferry
Rosyth
Aberdour
Burntisland
Kinghorn
Kirkcaldy
Glenrothes
HOME
Kettlebridge
Pitlessie
Cupar
Dairsiemuir
St. Andrews
Leuchars
Tayport
Newport
Dundee

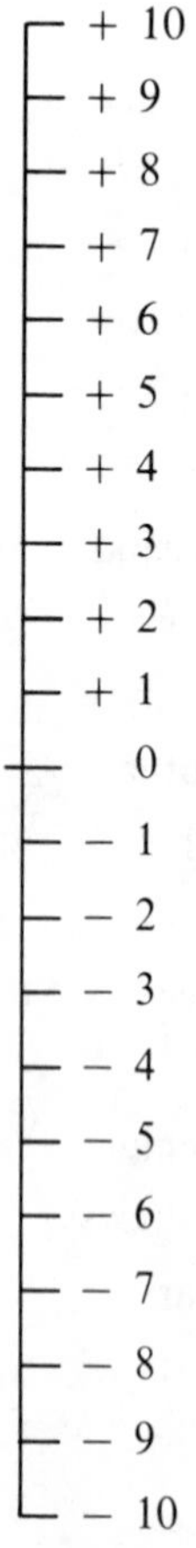
+ 10
+ 9
+ 8
+ 7
+ 6
+ 5
+ 4
+ 3
+ 2
+ 1
0
− 1
− 2
− 3
− 4
− 5
− 6
− 7
− 8
− 9
− 10

Part 3 The number ladder

Start each problem from 0.

A positive sign (+) tells you to go *up* the ladder.
A negative sign (−) tells you to go *down* the ladder.

For + 2 − 5, start at 0, go up 2 and then down 5 to reach − 3.
We write + 2 − 5 = − 3

Work the following.

1 + 2 − 6
2 + 1 − 4
3 + 4 − 5
4 + 2 − 4
5 + 5 − 4
6 + 8 − 3
7 + 4 − 2
8 + 4 − 7
9 + 3 − 12
10 + 4 − 4
11 − 1 + 5
12 − 2 + 6
13 − 3 + 7
14 − 6 + 9
15 − 7 + 3
16 − 8 + 3
17 − 3 + 3
18 − 6 + 6
19 − 9 + 7
20 − 2 − 4
21 − 1 − 3
22 − 6 − 1
23 − 3 − 4
24 − 1 − 7
25 − 5 − 5
26 + 2 + 3

These have at least three steps to them.

27 + 2 + 4 − 8
28 + 4 + 5 − 12
29 + 6 − 4 + 2
30 + 2 − 4 + 2
31 + 3 − 5 + 6 − 1
32 + 4 − 4 + 5 − 7
33 + 2 + 5 − 8 − 13
34 − 1 + 2 − 3 + 4 − 5 + 6 − 7 + 8

Number lines

Find the missing number (with its sign).

35   $+5$? $= +7$ 39 $-1-3+6$? $= -1$
36   -6 ? $= -1$ 40 $+5+3-9$? $= -5$
37   $+3$? $= -3$ 41 $-6+7-8$? $= +5$
38   $-4-2$? $= 0$ 42 $-8+7-6+5-4+3-2+1$? $= 0$

The sign $>$ means 'is greater than'.
The sign $<$ means 'is less than'.

43   Are the following statements **true** or **false**?

a $+5 > +3$ b $+6 > +1$ c $+4 < 0$
d $+1 < +7$ e $0 < +8$ f $0 > -8$
g $+3 > -1$ h $+1 > -5$ i $-6 < +3$
j $-4 < -2$ k $-2 > -3$ l $+5 > -1$
m $-6 > +2$ n $-4 > 0$ o $-2 < -7$

44   Insert $>$ or $<$ between the pairs of numbers to make a true statement.

a $+5$ $+3$ b $+1$ $+7$ c $+2$ 0
d 0 $+6$ e 0 -6 f $+3$ -3
g -3 $+3$ h -1 $+2$ i -1 -2
j $+1$ -6 k -1 $+6$ l -6 -1
m $+3$ -4 n -7 -8 o -3 -2

45   Write the numbers which are represented by the letters a to k on these number lines.

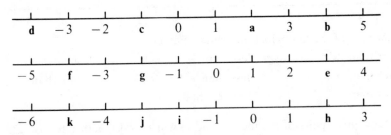

46   Write the numbers which the arrows a to k indicate on this number line. Note that the line is marked in halves.

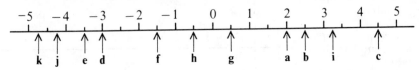

47   This number line is divided into tenths. Write the decimal numbers indicated by the arrows.

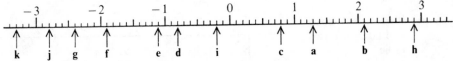

11

Number lines

48 These number lines show x values from -5 to 5.

Use the signs $>$ and $<$ to describe the coloured parts of these lines.
For example, diagram **a** indicates $x > 3$.

a
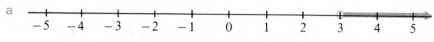

b
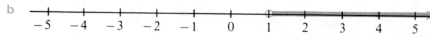

c

d
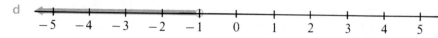

e
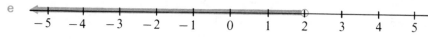

f
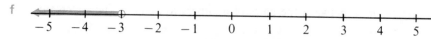

g

h

49 Copy this number line eight times.

```
 +----+----+----+----+----+----+----+----+----+----+
-5   -4   -3   -2   -1    0    1    2    3    4    5
```

Shade that part of the line which indicates numbers

a	greater than 2	b	less than 2	c greater than 0
d	greater than -1	e	less than -1	f less than -3
g	greater than 1	h	greater than -3.	

50 **a** This table gives pairs of numbers x and y, which add together to give a total of 6.
That is, $x + y = 6$.
Copy and complete the table.

x	4	3	2	1	0	-1	-2	-3	-4
y	2	3							

b If $p + q = 4$, copy and complete this table.

p	4	3	2	1	0	-1	-2	-3	-4
q	0								

c If $m + n = 2$, copy and complete this table.

m	4	3	2	1	0	-1	-2	-3	-4
n	-2								

d If $u + v = 1$, copy and complete this table.

u	4	3	2	1	0	-1	-2	-3	-4
v									

Directed numbers

Part 1 Addition

Copy this table.

Complete the top left-hand quarter of the table, by adding together the positive X and Y values.

Use the number ladder to follow the pattern of your answers across the rows of your table, and so complete the top right-hand quarter.

Now, use the number ladder to follow the patterns down the columns to complete the rest of the table.

Number ladder (left margin): +8 +7 +6 +5 +4 +3 +2 +1 0 −1 −2 −3 −4 −5 −6 −7 −8

						Y				
X + Y	+4	+3	+2	+1	0	−1	−2	−3	−4
+4									
+3									
+2									
+1									
X 0									
−1									
−2									
−3									
−4									

1 Use the results in your table to find the answers to these additions.

a $+3 + {}^+2 =$ b $+4 + {}^+3 =$ c $+4 + {}^-2 =$

d $+3 + {}^-3 =$ e $+2 + {}^-3 =$ f $+1 + {}^-3 =$

g $-1 + {}^+4 =$ h $-3 + {}^+4 =$ i $-2 + {}^+3 =$

j $-2 + {}^+1 =$ k $-1 + {}^-2 =$ l $-3 + {}^-1 =$

m $-2 + \ 0 =$ n $+4 + {}^+2 =$ o $+4 + {}^-3 =$

p $-4 + {}^+3 =$ q $-4 + {}^-3 =$ r $0 + {}^-2 =$

s $-1 + {}^-4 =$ t $+1 + {}^-4 =$

2 Find the missing number in each of the following.

a $+4 + \ldots = +6$ b $+2 + \ldots = +3$ c $+1 + \ldots = \ 0$

d $+3 + \ldots = \ 0$ e $\ldots + {}^+2 = \ 0$ f $\ldots + {}^+1 = -2$

g $\ldots + {}^+2 = -2$ h $-3 + \ldots = +1$ i $-1 + \ldots = +2$

j $-2 + \ldots = +1$ k $+1 + \ldots = -3$ l $+3 + \ldots = \ 0$

m $+4 + \ldots = +1$ n $\ldots + {}^-2 = +2$ o $\ldots + {}^+1 = -1$

p $\ldots + {}^+4 = +7$ q $\ldots + {}^-3 = -6$ r $\ldots + {}^-4 = -5$

s $+4 + \ldots = +8$ t $+3 + \ldots = +5$

3 Find the answers to these by using your table twice.

a $+2 + {}^+1 + {}^-4 =$ b $-3 + {}^+4 + {}^+2 =$ c $+1 + {}^-3 + {}^-2 =$

d $-4 + {}^+2 + {}^-1 =$ e $-2 + {}^-1 + {}^+5 =$ f $+3 + {}^+1 + {}^-4 =$

g $-4 + {}^-1 + {}^+3 =$ h $-3 + {}^-3 + {}^+2 =$

4 Use your table to find which numbers must be placed in these boxes to make true statements.

a $+2 + \square = +4$ b $-3 + \square = +1$ c $\square + {}^-1 = +2$

d $\square + {}^+2 = \ 0$ e $\square + {}^+3 = +1$ f $\square + {}^+4 = +2$

g $-1 + \square = -1$ h $-3 + \square = +2$ i $+3 + \square = \ 0$

j $-1 + \square = -3$ k $\square + \ 0 = -2$ l $\square + {}^-1 = \ 0$

m $+3 + \square = -2$ n $\square + {}^-2 = -5$

Directed numbers

5 Solve these equations.

a $x + {}^+2 = {}^+3$ b $x + {}^-1 = {}^-3$ c $x + {}^+3 = {}^+4$

d $x + {}^-2 = {}^+1$ e $x + {}^-2 = 0$ f $x + {}^+1 = {}^-2$

g $x + {}^-1 = {}^+3$ h $x + {}^+1 = {}^+1$ i $x + {}^-2 = {}^+2$

j $x + {}^-2 = {}^-4$

Part 2 Subtraction

Copy this table.

Complete the top left-hand quarter of the table, by subtracting the Y values from the X values.

Use the number ladder to follow the pattern of your answers across the rows of your table, and so complete the top right-hand quarter.

Now, use the number ladder to follow the patterns down the columns to complete the rest of the table.

Number ladder (vertical scale): +8, +7, +6, +5, +4, +3, +2, +1, 0, -1, -2, -3, -4, -5, -6, -7, -8

X − Y	+4	+3	+2	+1	0	−1	−2	−3	−4
+4									
+3									
+2									
+1									
0									
−1									
−2									
−3									
−4									

(X down the left, Y across the top)

1 Use the results in your table to find the answers to these subtractions.

a $^+3 - {}^+2 =$ b $^+4 - {}^+1 =$ c $^+2 - {}^+3 =$

d $^+1 - {}^+4 =$ e $^+3 - {}^+4 =$ f $^-1 - {}^+2 =$

g $^-2 - {}^+4 =$ h $^-3 - {}^+1 =$ i $0 - {}^+2 =$

j $0 - {}^+3 =$ k $^+2 - {}^+2 =$ l $^-3 - {}^+4 =$

m $^-1 - {}^+3 =$ n $^-2 - {}^-4 =$ o $^-1 - {}^-3 =$

p $^+3 - {}^-2 =$ q $^+1 - {}^-4 =$ r $^-3 - {}^-3 =$

s $0 - {}^-2 =$ t $^+1 - {}^+3 =$

2 Find the missing number in each of these.

a $^+4 - \ldots = {}^+2$ b $^+3 - \ldots = {}^+1$ c $^+1 - \ldots = 0$

d $^+2 - \ldots = {}^-2$ e $^+3 - \ldots = {}^+5$ f $^+2 - \ldots = {}^+1$

g $0 - \ldots = {}^+3$ h $^-1 - \ldots = {}^+3$ i $^-3 - \ldots = {}^+1$

j $^-4 - \ldots = {}^-3$ k $\ldots - {}^-2 = {}^+2$ l $\ldots - {}^-2 = {}^+3$

m $\ldots - {}^+3 = {}^+1$ n $\ldots - {}^+1 = {}^-2$ o $^-2 - \ldots = {}^+1$

p $^+3 - \ldots = {}^+4$ q $^-2 - \ldots = {}^-2$ r $^+1 - \ldots = {}^+3$

s $\ldots - {}^-4 = {}^+7$ t $\ldots - {}^-3 = {}^+6$

3 Use your table to find which numbers must be placed in these boxes to make true statements.

a $^+3 - \square = {}^+2$ b $^+4 - \square = {}^+1$ c $^+1 - \square = {}^-2$

d $^+2 - \square = 0$ e $0 - \square = {}^+1$ f $^-1 - \square = {}^-4$

g $^-1 - \square = 0$ h $^-1 - \square = {}^+2$ i $\square - {}^-1 = {}^+3$

14

Directed numbers

j $\square - {}^-3 = {}^+4$ k $\square - {}^-4 = {}^+4$ l $\square - {}^-2 = {}^+1$

m $\square - {}^+2 = {}^-3$ n $\square - {}^+4 = {}^-3$

4 Solve these equations.

a $x - {}^+2 = {}^+1$ b $x - {}^+1 = {}^+3$ c $x - {}^+4 = {}^-4$

d $x - {}^+2 = {}^-3$ e $x - \ 0 = {}^-2$ f $x - {}^-1 = {}^+2$

g $x - {}^-2 = {}^+4$ h $x - {}^-3 = {}^+3$ i $x - {}^-2 = {}^-2$

j $x - {}^-4 = {}^+2$

5 Use your addition and subtraction tables to find the values of these.

a ${}^+2 + {}^+1 - {}^-1 =$ b ${}^-3 + {}^+4 - {}^-2 =$ c ${}^+2 - {}^+4 + {}^-1 =$

d ${}^-1 + {}^-3 - {}^-2 =$ e ${}^-3 + {}^+4 - {}^-3 =$ f ${}^+3 - {}^-1 - {}^+4 =$

g ${}^-2 + {}^+4 - {}^+3 =$ h ${}^-1 - {}^-3 - {}^+4 =$ i ${}^+2 - {}^-1 + {}^-3 =$

j ${}^-3 + {}^-1 - {}^-4 =$

Part 3   Nomograms

1 This nomogram will add numbers on scale A to numbers on scale B.

Place your ruler across the scales, lining it up with your numbers on scale A and scale B. Read off your answer on the coloured scale $A + B$.

Find the answers to these additions.

a ${}^+3 + {}^+1$ b ${}^+2 + {}^+4$

c ${}^+1 + {}^+2$ d ${}^+3 + \ 0$

e ${}^-1 + {}^+1$ f ${}^-2 + {}^+2$

g ${}^+3 + {}^-3$ h ${}^+4 + {}^-4$

i ${}^-1 + {}^-2$ j ${}^-3 + {}^-4$

k ${}^-2 + \ 0$ l ${}^-4 + {}^-1$

m ${}^-3 + {}^-2$ n ${}^-3 + {}^+4$

o ${}^-1 + {}^+3$ p $0 + {}^+2$

q ${}^+1 + {}^-4$ r ${}^+3 + {}^-2$

s ${}^+4 + {}^-1$ t ${}^-2 + {}^-2$

2 Use the addition nomogram to find the missing numbers in each of these statements.

a ${}^+2 + \square = {}^+3$ b ${}^+1 + \square = {}^+5$ c ${}^+4 + \square = {}^+3$

d ${}^+4 + \square = \ 0$ e ${}^+1 + \square = {}^-2$ f ${}^+2 + \square = {}^-2$

g $\ 0 + \square = {}^+1$ h ${}^-2 + \square = {}^-3$ i ${}^-2 + \square = {}^+1$

j ${}^-4 + \square = {}^-2$ k $\square + {}^+2 = {}^+6$ l $\square + {}^+4 = {}^+7$

m $\square + \ 0 = {}^+3$ n $\square + {}^-1 = {}^+2$ o $\square + {}^-3 = {}^+1$

p $\square + {}^-1 = {}^-2$ q $\square + {}^-3 = {}^-7$ r $\square + {}^-4 = {}^-4$

s $\square + {}^+1 = {}^-3$ t $\square + {}^-4 = {}^-6$

15

Directed numbers

3 This nomogram will subtract a number on scale Y from a number on scale X.

Place your ruler to line up your numbers on scales X and Y, and then read off your answer on the coloured scale $X - Y$.

Find the answers to these subtractions.

a	$+6 - +3$	b	$+7 - +3$
c	$+5 - +1$	d	$+3 - \ 0$
e	$+2 - -1$	f	$+2 - -2$
g	$+1 - -3$	h	$0 - -1$
i	$0 - -3$	j	$0 - -2$
k	$-1 - -3$	l	$-2 - -2$
m	$-4 - -4$	n	$-3 - -1$
o	$-3 - -4$	p	$+1 - -2$
q	$+2 - +2$	r	$-5 - -3$
s	$-3 - -3$	t	$-1 - +1$

4 Use the subtraction nomogram to find the missing numbers in each of these statements.

a	$+7 - \Box = +3$	b	$+5 - \Box = +1$	c	$+3 - \Box = \ 0$
d	$+2 - \Box = -1$	e	$+1 - \Box = -3$	f	$+1 - \Box = +3$
g	$+3 - \Box = +4$	h	$-1 - \Box = +2$	i	$-2 - \Box = +1$
j	$-7 - \Box = -3$	k	$\Box - +2 = +4$	l	$\Box - +3 = +1$
m	$\Box - +4 = \ 0$	n	$\Box - +4 = +4$	o	$\Box - \ 0 = +2$
p	$\Box - -1 = +3$	q	$\Box - -2 = \ 0$	r	$\Box - -4 = \ 0$
s	$\Box - -3 = -2$	t	$\Box - -1 = -4$		

Part 4   Yin and Yang

The two halves of a circle divided as shown are the Chinese symbols, called Yin and Yang, for all pairs of opposites which occur in nature. Yin is dark, calm and negative; Yang is bright, lively and positive. Together they combine to form a perfect whole.

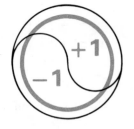

Copy this diagram onto card eight times and cut each card into two pieces.

Each card shows that +1 and −1 add together to give 0.

1 The cards can be used to add positive and negative numbers.
For example,

$+3 + +2$
needs these cards  and  to give a total of +5.

So you write
$+3 + +2 = +5.$

16

Directed numbers

Do these in the same way.

a +1 + +4	b +4 + +2	c +2 + +3
d −1 + −2	e −3 + −4	f −2 + −2
g +1 + +5	h −1 + −2	i +3 + +1

Here is another example.

−3 + +2
needs these cards   to give a total of −1.

So you write
−3 + +2 = −1.

Do these in the same way.

j −4 + +2	k −5 + +1	l −2 + +3
m −1 + +4	n −3 + +3	o −2 + +1
p +3 + −2	q +1 + −4	r +2 + −2
s +3 + −4	t −2 + +5	u −5 + +2
v +2 + −4	w −1 + +6	x +5 + −3

2 The cards can also be used to subtract positive and negative numbers.
For example,

−5 − −3
needs these cards 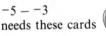 and when
−3 is taken away,
−2 is left.

So you write
−5 − −3 = −2.

Do these in the same way.

a −4 − −2	b −3 − −1	c −6 − −5
d +3 − +2	e +4 − +1	f +5 − +4
g −3 − −3	h +2 − +2	i −5 − −2

Here is another example.

0 − −2 needs some more cards before the −2 can be taken away.

So we think of the 0 as and taking away −2 leaves +2.

You then write
0 − −2 = +2.

Do these in the same way.

j 0 − −3	k 0 − −1	l 0 − +2
m 0 − +3	n 0 − +4	o 0 − −4
p 0 − −5	q 0 − +1	r 0 − +5
s 0 − +6	t 0 − −7	u 0 − −6

Directed numbers

3 Harder subtractions can be done as in this example.

+2 − −1 starts with  but there are no −1's to take away.

You can provide a −1 by introducing a 0.

+2 − −1 now has and taking away the −1 leaves +3.

So you write
+2 − −1 = +3.

Do these in the same way.

a	+3 − −1	b	+3 − −2	c	+1 − −3
d	+4 − −1	e	+2 − −2	f	+1 − +1
g	+2 − −4	h	−2 − +1	i	−3 − +1
j	−1 − +2	k	−4 − +1	l	−2 − +3
m	−2 − +2	n	−3 − +4	o	−1 − −2
p	−1 − −3	q	−2 − −3	r	−3 − −4
s	+1 − +2	t	+2 − +4	u	+3 − +4

4 Here is a mixture of additions and subtractions to work out using your cards.

a	+3 + +1	b	+3 − +1	c	+2 + +4
d	−2 + +4	e	−3 − −2	f	+3 − +2
g	+1 + −2	h	+3 + −2	i	−2 + −3
j	−4 + +1	k	+2 + −3	l	+5 + −2
m	0 − −2	n	0 − −1	o	0 − +3
p	+1 − +3	q	+1 − −2	r	+2 − −1
s	+3 − −1	t	−2 − +1	u	−4 − +2
v	−3 + +1	w	+2 + −2	x	−3 + +3
y	−1 − +3	z	−2 − +2		

Part 5
Multiplication and division

Copy this table.

Complete the top left-hand quarter of the table by multiplying two numbers together.

Imagine a long number ladder and follow the pattern of your answers across the rows of your table to complete the top right-hand corner.

Follow the number patterns down the columns of your table to complete the bottom half.

								Y						
X×Y	+6	+5	+4	+3	+2	+1	0	−1	−2	−3	−4	−5	−6
+6													
+5													
+4													
+3													
+2													
+1													
X 0													
−1													
−2													
−3													
−4													
−5													
−6													

Directed numbers

1 Use the results in your table to find the answers to these.

a $+2 \times +5 =$ b $+4 \times +3 =$ c $+6 \times +2 =$
d $-5 \times +4 =$ e $-3 \times +6 =$ f $-2 \times -4 =$
g $-5 \times -1 =$ h $+4 \times -3 =$ i $+6 \times -2 =$
j $0 \times -3 =$ k $-3 \times -5 =$ l $-1 \times -6 =$
m $+5 \times -2 =$ n $+4 \times 0 =$ o $-2 \times -5 =$
p $-4 \times +2 =$ q $0 \times +6 =$ r $-3 \times -2 =$
s $+5 \times -1 =$ t $-6 \times +5 =$

2 Find the missing number in each of these by using your table.

a $-2 \times \ldots = -6$ b $+4 \times \ldots = -20$ c $-5 \times \ldots = +15$
d $-2 \times \ldots = +12$ e $+5 \times \ldots = -30$ f $\ldots \times +4 = -24$
g $\ldots \times -5 = -20$ h $\ldots \times +3 = +15$ i $\ldots \times -5 = -30$
j $+5 \times \ldots = -25$ k $-6 \times \ldots = -24$ l $+4 \times \ldots = 0$
m $\ldots \times -6 = +18$ n $\ldots \times +4 = -12$ o $\ldots \times -2 = -2$
p $\ldots \times +1 = -1$ q $-5 \times \ldots = -10$ r $-4 \times \ldots = -24$
s $+3 \times \ldots = -3$ t $-3 \times \ldots = +9$

Look at the patterns of the signs in your multiplication table.
The pattern is shown alongside in this diagram.
So, for example,
because $3 \times 7 = 21$, then $+3 \times -7 = -21$.

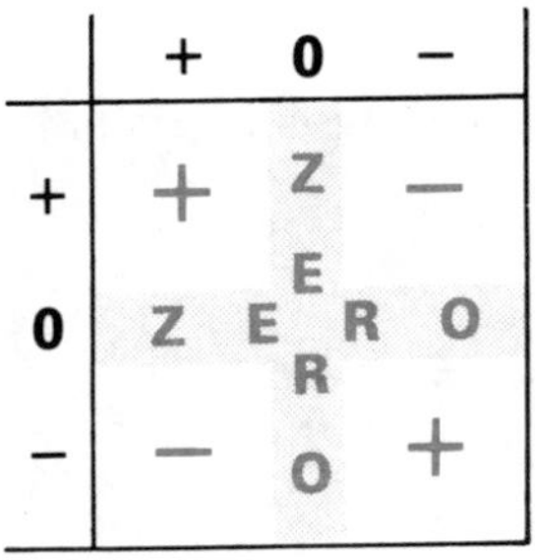

3 Write the answers to these multiplications.

a $+2 \times +6 =$ b $+4 \times +5 =$ c $-3 \times +7 =$
d $-2 \times +8 =$ e $-4 \times +6 =$ f $+3 \times +8 =$
g $-5 \times +3 =$ h $+3 \times -5 =$ i $-8 \times +4 =$
j $+8 \times -4 =$ k $-7 \times +5 =$ l $+7 \times -5 =$
m $-8 \times -3 =$ n $+8 \times +3 =$ o $-8 \times +3 =$
p $+8 \times -3 =$ q $-4 \times -7 =$ r $-6 \times -5 =$
s $+6 \times -4 =$ t $-6 \times -4 =$

4 Find the missing number in each of these.

a $+3 \times \ldots = +12$ b $+5 \times \ldots = +15$ c $+7 \times \ldots = +21$
d $+7 \times \ldots = -21$ e $+3 \times \ldots = -12$ f $+8 \times \ldots = -64$
g $+9 \times \ldots = -18$ h $\ldots \times -3 = +27$ i $\ldots \times -5 = -40$
j $\ldots \times -6 = -30$ k $\ldots \times -3 = +9$ l $-4 \times \ldots = +16$
m $+2 \times \ldots = -12$ n $\ldots \times -7 = -35$ o $\ldots \times -10 = +20$
p $\ldots \times -7 = +63$ q $\ldots \times +6 = 0$ r $\ldots \times -9 = 0$
s $+3 \times \ldots = 0$ t $\ldots \times -7 = -91$

Directed numbers

5   What are the values of these squares?

   a $(+2)^2$ b $(+4)^2$ c $(-3)^2$ d $(-5)^2$ e $(-7)^2$

   f $(+3)^2$ g $(+8)^2$ h $(-9)^2$ i $(-10)^2$ j $(+12)^2$

6   Write the answers to these divisions.

  a $\dfrac{+24}{+6}$ b $\dfrac{+36}{-6}$ c $\dfrac{-32}{+8}$ d $\dfrac{-64}{-8}$ e $\dfrac{+28}{-7}$

  f $\dfrac{+80}{-10}$ g $\dfrac{-49}{-7}$ h $\dfrac{-48}{+6}$ i $\dfrac{+16}{-2}$ j $\dfrac{-42}{-6}$

  k $\dfrac{-14}{+2}$ l $\dfrac{+18}{-9}$ m $\dfrac{-25}{-5}$ n $\dfrac{-45}{-9}$ o $\dfrac{+99}{+11}$

  p $\dfrac{-27}{-9}$ q $\dfrac{+55}{-11}$ r $\dfrac{0}{+3}$ s $\dfrac{-40}{+10}$ t $\dfrac{+56}{-7}$

  u $\dfrac{+12}{-12}$ v $\dfrac{-14}{-14}$ w $\dfrac{-7}{+7}$ x $\dfrac{0}{-3}$ y $\dfrac{-81}{-9}$

  z $\dfrac{+4}{+4}$

7   Find the missing numbers in these divisions.

  a $\dfrac{-16}{\ldots} = +2$ b $\dfrac{+24}{\ldots} = -6$ c $\dfrac{-55}{\ldots} = -11$

  d $\dfrac{+28}{\ldots} = -4$ e $\dfrac{-63}{\ldots} = +9$ f $\dfrac{-144}{\ldots} = -12$

  g $\dfrac{\ldots}{-6} = -2$ h $\dfrac{\ldots}{+4} = -12$ i $\dfrac{\ldots}{+3} = +5$

  j $\dfrac{\ldots}{-2} = +4$ k $\dfrac{\ldots}{+6} = -10$ l $\dfrac{\ldots}{-4} = +9$

8   Find which numbers must be placed in these boxes to make true statements.

  a $\square \times +5 = +20$ b $\square \times +4 = +12$ c $\square \times -3 = -15$

  d $\square \times -2 = -10$ e $\square \times -3 = -12$ f $\square \times +6 = -18$

  g $\square \times +5 = -20$ h $\square \times +6 = -24$ i $\square \times -4 = +20$

  j $-3 \times \square = +12$ k $-7 \times \square = +14$ l $+7 \times \square = +14$

  m $+5 \times \square = +30$ n $-4 \times \square = -8$ o $-9 \times \square = -27$

  p $+7 \times \square = -28$ q $-8 \times \square = -32$ r $+9 \times \square = -45$

9   Find which numbers must be placed in these boxes to make true statements.

  a $\dfrac{\square}{+2} = +4$ b $\dfrac{\square}{+5} = +3$ c $\dfrac{\square}{+4} = -2$ d $\dfrac{\square}{+3} = -4$

  e $\dfrac{\square}{+6} = -5$ f $\dfrac{\square}{-2} = +6$ g $\dfrac{\square}{-3} = +5$ h $\dfrac{\square}{-4} = -9$

Directed numbers

i $\dfrac{\square}{-7} = -4$ j $\dfrac{\square}{-6} = -5$ k $\dfrac{+32}{\square} = +8$ l $\dfrac{+35}{\square} = +5$

m $\dfrac{-30}{\square} = +10$ n $\dfrac{+16}{\square} = -8$ o $\dfrac{+49}{\square} = -7$ p $\dfrac{+27}{\square} = +3$

q $\dfrac{-48}{\square} = -12$ r $\dfrac{-32}{\square} = +16$ s $\dfrac{+64}{\square} = -8$ t $\dfrac{-36}{\square} = -6$

10 Solve these equations.

a $+4x = +8$ b $+3x = +15$ c $+6x = +30$ d $+3x = -12$
e $+7x = -14$ f $-4x = +8$ g $-5x = +20$ h $-6x = +60$
i $+4x = -20$ j $+8x = -40$ k $-5x = -25$ l $-7x = -35$

m $\dfrac{x}{+2} = +3$ n $\dfrac{x}{+6} = +5$ o $\dfrac{x}{+3} = -5$ p $\dfrac{x}{+5} = -2$

q $\dfrac{x}{-4} = -5$ r $\dfrac{x}{-8} = -4$ s $\dfrac{x}{+9} = -3$ t $\dfrac{x}{+10} = -4$

11 Work out these multiplications.

a $+2 \times +4 \times +5 =$ b $+3 \times +2 \times +4 =$ c $+5 \times -2 \times -4 =$

d $+3 \times -5 \times +2 =$ e $-4 \times +3 \times -2 =$ f $-5 \times -2 \times +5 =$

g $-7 \times +1 \times +4 =$ h $-9 \times -1 \times +6 =$ i $+2 \times -2 \times +4 =$

j $+6 \times -7 \times -1 =$ k $-5 \times +3 \times -4 =$ l $-5 \times -6 \times -2 =$

12 Find the values of each of these.

a $\dfrac{-2 \times +6}{-3}$ b $\dfrac{-5 \times +8}{+4}$ c $\dfrac{-7 \times -4}{+2}$ d $\dfrac{+8 \times +4}{-16}$

e $\dfrac{+7 \times -9}{-3}$ f $\dfrac{-8 \times -5}{+20}$ g $\dfrac{+60}{-4 \times +3}$ h $\dfrac{-48}{-2 \times -6}$

i $\dfrac{-32}{+4 \times -2}$ j $\dfrac{-2 \times -20}{+4 \times -5}$ k $\dfrac{+6 \times +12}{-4 \times -9}$ l $\dfrac{-8 \times +5}{-5 \times +2}$

m $\dfrac{-12 \times -5}{-2 \times -10}$ n $\dfrac{-8 \times -7}{+2 \times +2}$ o $\dfrac{+16 \times -3}{-8 \times -6}$ p $\dfrac{0 \times -4}{-2 \times +7}$

q $\dfrac{-6 \times +8}{+1 \times -16}$ r $\dfrac{-7 \times 0}{+9 \times -3}$

Combining numbers

You can combine numbers
on a number ladder   *OR*   using the multiplication table.

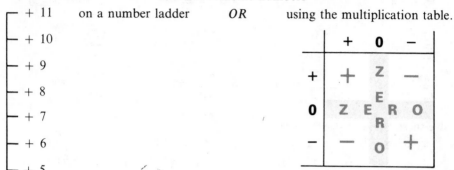

```
  + 11
  + 10
  + 9
  + 8
  + 7
  + 6
  + 5
  + 4
  + 3
  + 2
  + 1
    0
  - 1
  - 2
  - 3
  - 4
  - 5
  - 6
  - 7
  - 8
  - 9
  - 10
  - 11
```

1 Use *either* a number ladder *or* a multiplication table to find answers to these.

a $+5-4=$	b $+5\times-4=$	c $+6-2=$
d $+6\times-2=$	e $+7-5=$	f $+7\times-5=$
g $+2-5=$	h $+2\times-5=$	i $+6-8=$
j $+6\times-8=$	k $+2+4=$	l $+2\times+4=$
m $+3+7=$	n $-2\times-6=$	o $-5+5=$
p $-4\times-6=$	q $0\times-3=$	r $-2\times+8=$
s $-4+5=$	t $-1-3=$	u $-1\times-3=$
v $+2\times+9=$	w $-9-1=$	x $-7+9=$
y $+2-8=$	z $+2\times-8=$	

2 Find the answers to these.

a $-9+7=$	b $0-4=$	c $-3\times-6=$
d $-8\times+7=$	e $-8+7=$	f $+6\times-5=$
g $-6-4=$	h $-8\times-9=$	i $-8-5=$
j $+5\times-12=$	k $-7\times+7=$	l $+14\times+2=$
m $\dfrac{-28}{+7}=$	n $\dfrac{+36}{+4}=$	o $-6-8=$
p $+5-12=$	q $-9\times+11=$	r $-12-8=$
s $\dfrac{-42}{-7}=$	t $\dfrac{-45}{+9}=$	u $-6\times+5=$
v $+13-16=$	w $\dfrac{+60}{-12}=$	x $-12\times+7=$
y $\dfrac{-64}{-16}=$	z $-64+16=$	

```
        0   1   2   3   4   5   6
        ├───┼───┼───┼───┼───┼───┼───   Counting numbers
Negative numbers ├──┼──┼──┼──┼──┼──┼──┼──┼──┼──┼──┼──┼──┤ Positive numbers
        -6  -5  -4  -3  -2  -1   0  +1  +2  +3  +4  +5  +6
```

Positive numbers and counting numbers behave in the same way, and so the +sign is often left out when writing a positive number.

The −sign is *never* left out when writing a negative number.

22

Combining numbers

3   Use *either* a number ladder *or* a multiplication table to find answers to these.

a $8 - 5$ b $3 - 5$ c 4×-2 d -6×3
e $2 - 4$ f $-2 + 7$ g $2 + 8$ h $-3 + 6$
i 5×-3 j -4×-5 k 6×-2 l -7×-3
m $-5 + 3$ n $6 - 9$ o $3 - 8$ p $-1 + 4$
q -5×3 r -2×-8 s $7 - 5$ t $1 - 6$
u $-2 + 4$ v $-2 - 4$ w -2×-4 x 3×-2
y -8×5 z -7×0

4   Say whether these statements are **true** or **false**.

a $7 - 4 = 3$ b $5 - 6 = -1$ c $2 \times -3 = -6$
d $4 \times -1 = 3$ e $3 - 5 = -2$ f $-3 - 5 = 8$
g $-6 \times 2 = -12$ h $-8 \times 3 = -5$ i $-7 + 9 = 2$
j $-3 \times 0 = -3$ k $2 - 8 = -16$ l $-4 \times -2 = 8$
m $-9 \times -2 = -18$ n $-1 - 7 = -8$ o $3 - 5 = 2$
p $-8 + 9 = 1$ q $-4 \times 6 = 24$ r $3 \times -7 = 21$
s $-5 \times 6 = -30$ t $-5 \times -6 = 30$ u $5 - 6 = 30$
v $0 - 3 = -3$ w $0 + 5 = 0$ x $0 \times -4 = 0$
y $6 - 8 = 2$ z $-6 + 8 = 2$

5   Find the values of these.

a $\dfrac{-6}{3}$ b $\dfrac{-8}{-2}$ c $\dfrac{10}{-5}$ d $\dfrac{20}{4}$

e $\dfrac{3 + 9}{2}$ f $\dfrac{5 + 3}{4}$ g $\dfrac{13 - 7}{-2}$ h $\dfrac{1 - 7}{3}$

i $\dfrac{2 - 8}{-3}$ j $\dfrac{-1 + 9}{2}$ k $\dfrac{-7 + 3}{-2}$ l $\dfrac{-10 - 8}{9}$

6   Work the brackets first, to find the values of each of these.

a $(8 - 2) \times 3$ b $(3 - 5) \times 4$ c $(1 - 4) \times -2$
d $(6 - 2) \times 5$ e $-6 \times (3 - 5)$ f $2 \times (0 - 7)$
g $3 \times (-1 + 5)$ h $2 \times (7 - 1)$ i $(3 - 5) \times -5$
j $(9 - 3) \times -2$ k $-4 \times (12 - 3)$ l $-6 \times (7 - 9)$

7   Solve these equations.

a $x + 3 = 1$ b $x + 5 = 2$ c $x - 1 = 3$
d $x - 2 = 5$ e $x + 7 = 8$ f $x + 4 = 1$
g $x - 1 = 0$ h $x - 5 = -2$ i $3x = 12$
j $5x = -15$ k $8x = -40$ l $2x = 14$

m $\dfrac{x}{3} = 4$ n $\dfrac{x}{5} = -2$ o $\dfrac{x}{-2} = 3$

p $\dfrac{x}{-4} = -6$ q $-6x = -24$ r $-3x = -18$

s $\dfrac{x}{-5} = -2$ t $\dfrac{x}{8} = 2$

23

Points and Axes

Introduction

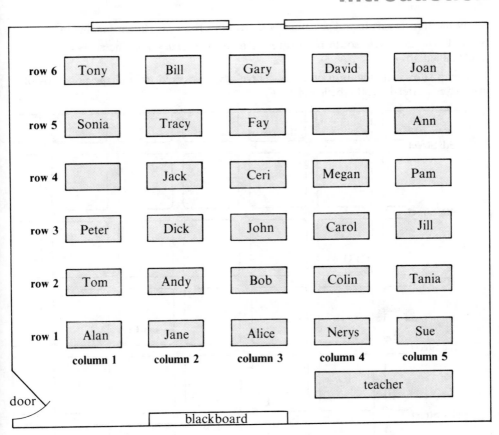

This is a plan of a class-room where pupils sit in five columns making six rows across the room.

1   Give the name of the pupil sitting at the desk in

    a   column 3 and row 2   b   column 5 and row 4

    c   column 1 and row 3   d   column 3 and row 1

    e   column 4 and row 3   f   column 1 and row 6.

2   Write the column number and row number for the position of

    a   Jack   b   Colin   c   Tom

    d   Jill   e   Megan   f   Tracy.

3   Which boy is sitting nearest the door?

4   Which boy is sitting nearest the teacher?

5   Which girl is sitting in the back row?

6   Who is sitting between Tom and Bob?

7   Who is sitting between Pam and Joan?

8   What are the positions of the two empty desks?

25

Introduction

Many modern towns have been built with straight roads as shown on this map.
In the USA the north–south roads are often called *avenues*, and the east–west roads called *streets*.

This map shows the location of a city-centre's two post offices, and the positions of mailboxes (letter-boxes) labelled *A* to *F*.

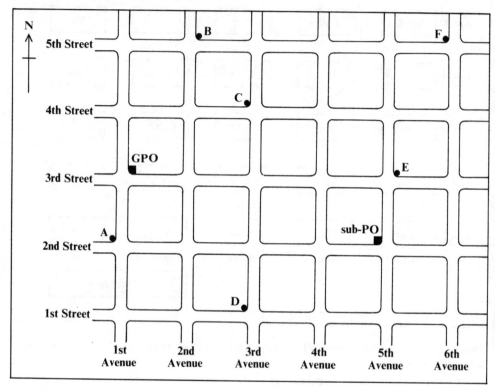

9 What would you find at the intersection of
   a 1st Avenue and 3rd Street   b 3rd Avenue and 4th Street
   c 6th Avenue and 5th Street   d 5th Avenue and 2nd Street?

10 Which avenue and street intersect at
   a mailbox *A*   b mailbox *B*
   c the sub-post-office   d mailbox *D*?

11 Which mailbox is nearest to the General Post Office?

12 Which mailbox is nearest to the sub-post-office?

13 Which post office is nearest to mailbox *D*?

14 Which post office is nearest to mailbox *C*?

15 Which post office is furthest from mailbox *B*?

16 Which two mailboxes are closest together?

17 a You are standing outside the GPO when a stranger asks directions to get
      to the sub-post-office. What directions would you give?
   b How would you direct someone to the GPO from mailbox *D*?

18 You are standing by mailbox *F*. What directions would you give to someone
   who wants to visit the sub-post-office and the GPO by the shortest route?

26

Introduction

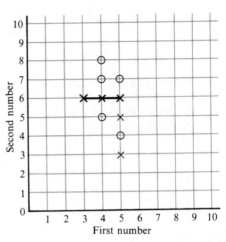

Game 1

This game needs two players and a marker.

Each player in turn says two numbers. The marker takes them as co-ordinates of a point and marks the point with a *nought* or a *cross*. One point is scored when three noughts or three crosses are in line on the grid. The game continues until the grid is filled, when the player with most points is the winner. (The diagram shows the crosses scoring their first point.)

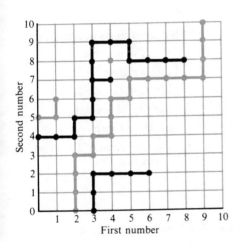

Game 2

This game needs two teams and a marker.

The grid can be any size, but 10 by 10 is useful.

The members of each team in turn say two numbers. The marker takes them as co-ordinates of a point and marks the point in the team's colour. Adjacent points of the same colour are joined along the grid to form a coloured route.

The object is for one team to find a route *across* the grid, as the other finds a route *up* the grid.

The diagram shows a winning route for the mauve team.

The four quadrants

Part 1 First quadrant

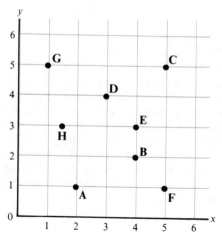

1 Write down the co-ordinates
(or ordered pairs) for
the points labelled *A* to *H*
in this diagram.

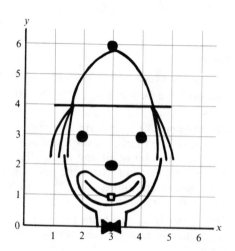

2 What are the co-ordinates of
   a the clown's nose
   b his two eyes
   c his bow-tie
   d the top of his hat
   e his only tooth
   f the two ends of the brim
     of his hat?

3 Draw and label both axes from 0 to 10 for each of these sets of points.
Plot the points and join them *in order* with straight lines.

First shape	Second shape	Third shape	Fourth shape	Fifth shape
(1, 1)	(8, 0)	(0, 0)	(7, 0)	(4, 6)
(4, 1)	(8, 2)	(1, 1)	(7, 1)	(5, 4)
(4, 4)	(9, 8)	(3, 1)	(8, 1)	(6, 4)
(5, 4)	(5, 8)	(4, 0)	(7, 3)	(6, 3)
(5, 1)	(6, 3)	(4, 2)	(8, 3)	(7, 3)
(7, 1)	(5, 2)	(3, 3)	(7, 5)	(7, 4)
(7, 5)	(2, 2)	(3, 7)	(8, 5)	(8, 4)
(4, 7)	(2, 0)	(2, 9)	$(6\frac{1}{2}, 8)$	(10, 8)
(1, 5)	(5, 0)	(1, 7)	(5, 5)	(7, 6)
(1, 1)	(7, 2)	(1, 3)	(6, 5)	(5, 8)
	(7, 0)	(0, 2)	(5, 3)	(4, 8)
	(8, 0)	(0, 0)	(6, 3)	(4, 7)
			(5, 1)	(3, 6)
			(6, 1)	(4, 6)
			(6, 0)	
			(7, 0)	

28

The four quadrants

4   Use this map to write down the co-ordinates of

a   Bridgetown
b   Crown Flatts
c   Whitsea
d   Gildercove
e   Sandy Bay
f   Finterre Point
g   Sundown
h   Aireton.

Which places have these co-ordinates?

i   (1, 5)   j   (5, 2)
k   (4, 5)   l   (6, 7)
m   (1, 8)   n   (3, 2)
o   (5, 9)   p   (7, 8)

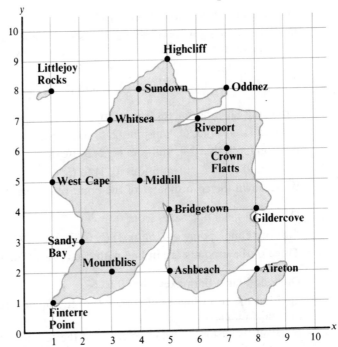

5   Draw and label both axes from 0 to 10.
These points are all on the coastline of an island. Plot them on your axes, and join them *in order* to draw the island.
(2, 8) (2, 6) (1, 5) (1, 3) (2, 2) (4, 2) (6, 4) (6, 3) (5, 2) (6, 1) ...
... (8, 1) (9, 2) (8, 5) (9, 7) (9, 9) (8, 9) (7, 8) (5, 7) (4, 8) (2, 8)
Label the positions of these places on the island:

Lighthouse *L* (3, 2)   Village *V* (5, 4)   Wood *W* (7, 3)
Hill-top *H* (3, 7)   Airstrip *A* (5, 6)   Water tower *T* (2, 4)
Farm house *F* (7, 7)   Caves *C* (7, 1).

6   Draw and label both axes from 0 to 10.
Draw part of the coast of Scotland on your diagram by joining these points in order:
(10, 2) (8, 3) (7, 3) (5, 2) (1, 3) ($\frac{1}{2}$, 4) (1$\frac{1}{2}$, 3) (3, 3) (5, 4) (6, 5) (7, 5) ...
... (8, 6) (7, 7) (7, 8) (6, 8) (4, 7) (3, 7) (5, 8) (7, 8$\frac{1}{2}$) (8, 10).
Label the positions of these places on your map:

Edinburgh (4, 2)   Dundee (6, 8$\frac{1}{2}$)   Glenrothes (4, 5)
Perth (2, 8)   Alloa (1, 4)   St. Andrews (7, 7)
Dunfermline (3, 4)   Bathgate (1, 1)   Bass Rock (8, 3$\frac{1}{2}$).

7   Draw and label both axes from 0 to 6.
Follow these instructions to draw three capital letters.

a   Join (2, 3) to (2, 6), and (1, 6) to (3, 6).
b   Join (4, 3) to (4, 6), and (4, 6) to (6, 3), and (6, 3) to (6, 6).
c   Join (1, 3) to (2, 0) to (3, 2) to (4, 0) to (5, 3).

29

The four quadrants

8 Draw and label both axes from 0 to 8.

Join the following pairs of points with straight lines, and write down the co-ordinates for the *midpoints* of the lines you draw.

a (1, 4) and (3, 8)   b (2, 4) and (8, 8)   c (4, 4) and (8, 6)
d (7, 4) and (7, 0)   e (0, 2) and (6, 0)   f (0, 3) and (5, 3)

9 Draw and label both axes from 0 to 6.
a Join (1, 4) to (5, 6), and join (2, 6) to (5, 3).
b Join (3, 0) to (6, 3), and join (2, 2) to (6, 0).
c Join (0, 4) to (2, 0), and join (0, 1) to (3, 4).
Write down the co-ordinates of the point of intersection of these pairs of lines.

10 Draw and label both axes from 0 to 6.
Plot these nine points: (6, 5) (6, 1) (5, 0) (3, 3) (2, 3) (2, 1) (1, 2) (1, 5) (0, 2).
Three of these points are in line with each other. Draw the line on which they lie.

11 Draw and label both axes from 0 to 6.
a Find the co-ordinates of corner D of the square ABCD, given A(1, 1), B(1, 3) and C(3, 3).
b Find the co-ordinates of corner S of the square PQRS, given P(0, 5), Q(1, 6) and R(2, 5).
c Find the co-ordinates of corner N of the square KLMN, given K(3, 4), L(4, 6) and M(6, 5).

12 Draw and label the x-axis from 0 to 10 and the y-axis from 0 to 4.
a Join (1, 2) to (1, 4) to (2, 3) to (3, 4) to (3, 2) to (4, 4) to (5, 2).
b Join (6, 2) to (6, 4).
c Join (5, 4) to (7, 4) to (7, 2).
d Join (7, 3) to (8, 3).
e Join (8, 2) to (8, 4).
f Join (10, 4) to (9, 4) to (9, 3) to (10, 3) to (10, 2) to (9, 2).
g Join $(3\frac{1}{2}, 3)$ to $(4\frac{1}{2}, 3)$.

Part 2
Two quadrants

1 Write down the co-ordinates (or ordered pairs) for the points lettered from A to I in this diagram.

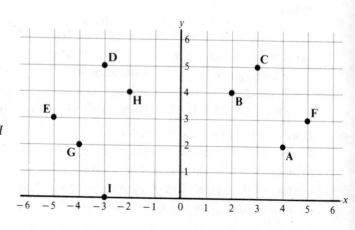

The four quadrants

2 For each of the following three shapes draw and label the axes as shown here.
Plot the points and join them *in order* by straight lines.

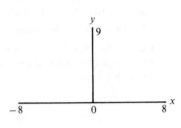

First shape	*Second shape*	*Third shape*
(1, 8)	(2, 6)	(5, 0)
(1, 7)	(4, 8)	(6, 3)
(3, 7)	(5, 6)	(−3, 6)
(3, 6)	(4, 5)	(−2, 9)
(6, 6)	(3, 5)	(−8, 6)
(4, 4)	(3, 2)	(−5, 0)
(−2, 4)	(2, 4)	(−4, 3)
(−3, 6)	(−2, 4)	(5, 0)
(−2, 6)	(−4, 2)	
(−1, 7)	(−3, 5)	
(0, 7)	(−4, 7)	
(0, 8)	(−3, 6)	
(1, 8)	(2, 6)	

3 Write down the co-ordinates (or ordered pairs) for the points lettered *R* to *Z* in this diagram.

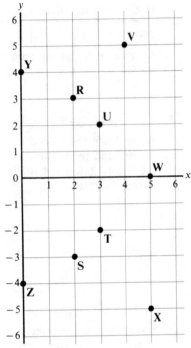

4 For each shape below, draw and label axes as shown below right.

Plot the points and join them *in order*.

First shape	*Second shape*	*Third shape*
(2, 3)	(1, 3)	(1½, 1)
(1, 3)	(2, 3)	(6, 2)
(3, 5)	(5, −3)	(3½, −1)
(5, 3)	(5, 3)	(3½, −5)
(4, 3)	(6, 3)	(2, −6)
(4, 1)	(6, −5)	(3, −5)
(6, 1)	(5, −5)	(4½, −6)
(6, 2)	(2, 1)	(3½, −5)
(8, 0)	(2, −5)	(3, −5)
(6, −2)	(1, −5)	(3, −1)
(6, −1)	(1, 3)	(1, 1)
(4, −1)		(1, 4)
(4, −3)		(0, 4)
(5, −3)		(1½, 5)
(3, −5)		(1½, 1)
(1, −3)		
(2, −3)		
(2, 3)		

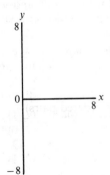

31

The four quadrants

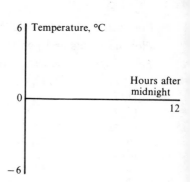

5   A record is kept every hour of the outside
temperature from midnight to midday.

This table gives the results.

Draw and label axes as shown, use the results
to plot twelve points, and join them with a
smooth curve.

Hours after midnight	0	1	2	3	4	5	6	7	8	9	10	11	12
Temperature, °C	2	1	−2	−3	−4	−4	−3½	−3	−2	−1	1	4	6

At what time did the temperature
a   fall below zero   b   rise above zero?

Part 3   Four quadrants

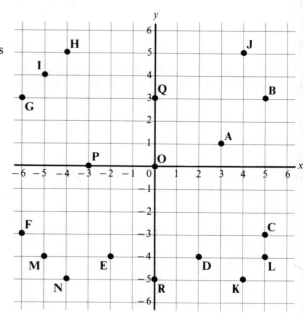

1   Write down the co-ordinates
(or ordered pairs) for
the points lettered A to R
in this diagram.

2   For each of these three sets
of points, draw and label
both axes from −8 to 8.

Plot the points and join
them *in order* with straight
lines.

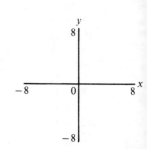

First shape   (4, 6) (1, 1) (6, 4) (4, 0) (6, −4) (1, −1)
(4, −6) (0, −4) (−4, −6) (−1, −1)
(−6, −4) (−4, 0) (−6, 4) (−1, 1) (−4, 6)
(0, 4) (4, 6)

Second shape   (2, 1) (3, −2) (5, −2) (4, −3) (3, −3)
(2, 0) (0, −4) (0, −5) (−4, −5) (−4, −4)
(−3, −4) (−3, −2) (−1, −2) (−1, −3)
(2, 1)

Third shape   (2, −6) (1, −6) (0, −4) (−3, −4) (−8, −7)
(−3, 0) (−2, 4) (0, 6) (2, 4) (4, 5) (2, 3)
(4, 2) (2, 2) (2, 0) (0, −4)

The four quadrants

3 This map shows the two islands Eilean Mor and Eilean Beg.

Write down the co-ordinates of

a Rubha
b Kirkton
c Clachmor
d Sgeirdubh
e Airdmor
f Gormgeodh.

Which places have these co-ordinates?

g (1, 3)
h (−2, 1)
i (3, −2)
j (0, −4)
k (−1, −1)
l (−4, −2)

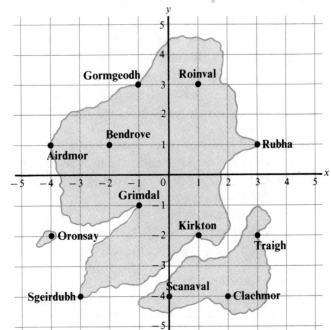

4 Draw and label both your axes from −5 to 5.
Draw part of the coast of eastern England by joining these points in order:
(−3, 5) (0, 3) (1, 1) (1, −1) (−1, −3) (2, −4) (3, −2) (5, −2).
Label the positions of these places on your map:

Spalding (−2, −4)	Grimsby (−2, 4)	Skegness (1, 0)
Lincoln (−5, 1)	Grantham (−5, −3)	King's Lynn (2, −5)
Sleaford (−4, −2)	Louth (−1, 2)	Boston (−1, −2).

5 Draw and label both axes from −6 to 6 as shown here.
Join each set of four points in order to make a square. Write down the co-ordinates of the point at the centre of each square.

a (2, 2) (6, 2) (6, 6) (2, 6)
b (0, 2) (2, 4) (0, 6) (−2, 4)
c (−6, 3) (−3, 4) (−2, 1) (−5, 0)
d (2, 0) (6, −2) (4, −6) (0, −4)
e (−6, −2) (−2, −1) (−1, −5) (−5, −6)

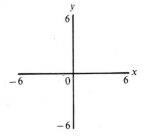

6 Draw and label both axes from −5 to 5.

a Find the co-ordinates of the corner *D* of the square *ABCD*, given *A*(−1, 1), *B*(−1, 5) and *C*(3, 5).
b Find the co-ordinates of the corner *S* of the square *PQRS*, given *P*(−5, −1), *Q*(−3, 1) and *R*(−1, −1).
c Find the co-ordinates of the corner *L* of the square *IJKL*, given *I*(0, −5), *J*(−1, −2) and *K*(2, −1).

33

The four quadrants

7   Draw and label your axes from -5 to 5.
   a   Join (0, 2) to (4, 4) and join (1, 4) to (4, 1).
   b   Join $(-3, -3)$ to (2, 0) and join $(-3, 1)$ to $(1, -3)$.
   c   Join (1, 0) to $(4, -1)$ and join $(1, -2)$ to (3, 0).
   d   Join $(-4, 0)$ to $(-1, 3)$ and join $(-4, 4)$ to $(-1, 1)$.
   Write down the co-ordinates of the points of intersection of these pairs of lines.

8   Draw and label both axes from -6 to 6.
   Draw five rectangles given by the five sets of points below.
   For each rectangle, draw its two diagonals and write down the co-ordinates of the centre.
   a   (6, 2) (6, 6) (4, 6) (4, 2)   b $(-2, 3) (-2, 5) (-6, 5) (-6, 3)$
   c   (4, 0) (0, 4) $(-2, 2)$ $(2, -2)$ d $(5, -2) (6, -4) (2, -6) (1, -4)$
   e $(-6, 1) (-3, 2) (-1, -4) (-4, -5)$

9   Draw and label both axes from -6 to 6.
   a   The points (2, 6) (3, 6) and (3, 2) are three corners of a rectangle. Plot the points, draw the rectangle and write down the co-ordinates of the missing corner.
   b   The points $(-6, 5) (-6, 2)$ and $(-2, 2)$ are the three corners of another rectangle. Plot the points, draw the rectangle and write down the co-ordinates of the missing corner.
   c   Repeat the instructions for the rectangle with three of its corners at $(-6, -4) (-4, -6)$ and $(-1, -3)$.
   d   Repeat again for the rectangle with corners (2, 0) $(0, -2)$ and $(4, -6)$.

10   For each of these sets of points, draw and label your axes from -8 to 8. Plot the points and join them *in order* with straight lines.

   First shape $(-3, 4) (-8, 3) (-3, 5) (-2, 6)$ (0, 6) $(-2, 1)$ (1, 3) (5, 2) $(6, -1)$
   $(6, -2) (3, -2) (2, -3) (2, -4) (-1, -4) (1, -3) (1, -2)$
   $(-1, -1) (-3, -2) (-4, 0) (-3, 3) (-6, 1) (-8, 3)$

   Second shape   (2, 0) $(6, -2) (7, -4) (2, -4) (4, -2) (5, -3) (4, -4) (0, -5)$
   $(-3, -5) (2, -4) (-1, -4) (-7, -5) (-6, -4) (-4, -4)$
   $(-3, -2) (-4, 2) (-6, 1) (-7, 2) (-5, 3) (-7, 3) (-6, 4) (-4, 3)$
   $(-2, 5)$ (0, 4) $(-2, -2)$ (2, 0)

   Third shape   (1, 3) $(1, -1) (-2, -1) (-2, 1) (-4, 1) (-4, -1) (-2, -1)$
   $(-4, -2) (-6, -2) (-4, -1) (-6, -1) (-6, 3) (-5, 3) (-5, 2)$
   $(-4, 2) (-4, 3) (-3, 3) (-3, 2) (-2, 2) (-2, 3) (-1, 3) (-1, 2)$
   (0, 2) (0, 3) (1, 3)

Distorted axes

The grid on which points are plotted and shapes drawn need not always be a square grid.

Earlier this century, Sir D'Arcy Thompson showed in his book *On Growth and Form* that if the shape of certain fish or the skeleton of some animal is drawn on a rectangular grid which is then deformed mathematically, the shape or skeleton on the new grid is that of a different fish or animal.

For example, this rectangular grid has the shape of a porcupine fish (*Diodon*) drawn on it. When the grid is distorted, the shape becomes that of the sunfish (*Mola mola*).

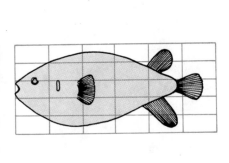
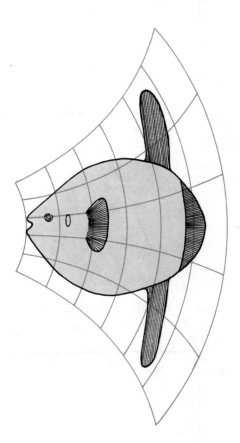

Overleaf are several different grids. Trace them, or perhaps your teacher could provide some for you.

Join these points *in order* to draw some simple pictures, and see how the shape is altered by using different grids.

1st object   (2, 5) (2, 7) (4, 7) (4, 9) (6, 9) (6, 7) (8, 7) (8, 5) (6, 5) (6, 1) (4, 1) (4, 5) (2, 5)

2nd object   (2, 3) (2, 9) (8, 9) (6, 7) (10, 3) (8, 1) (4, 5) (2, 3)

3rd object   (2, 2) (2, 6) (1, 6) (3, 8) (8, 8) (10, 6) (9, 6) (9, 2) (6, 2) (6, 5) (4, 5) (4, 2) (2, 2)

4th object   (1, 1) (1, 9) (8, 9) (8, 7) (3, 7) (3, 6) (6, 6) (6, 4) (3, 4) (3, 3) (8, 3) (8, 1) (1, 1)

35

Distorted axes

Grid A

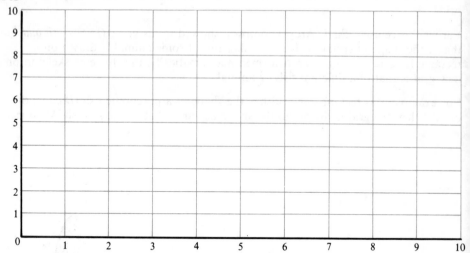

Grid B

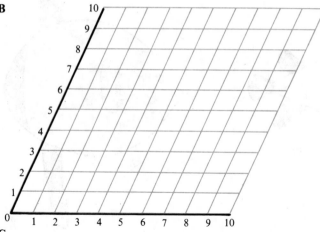

Grid C

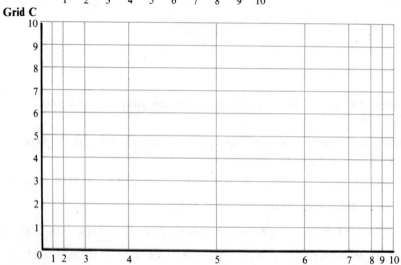

Distorted axes

Grid D

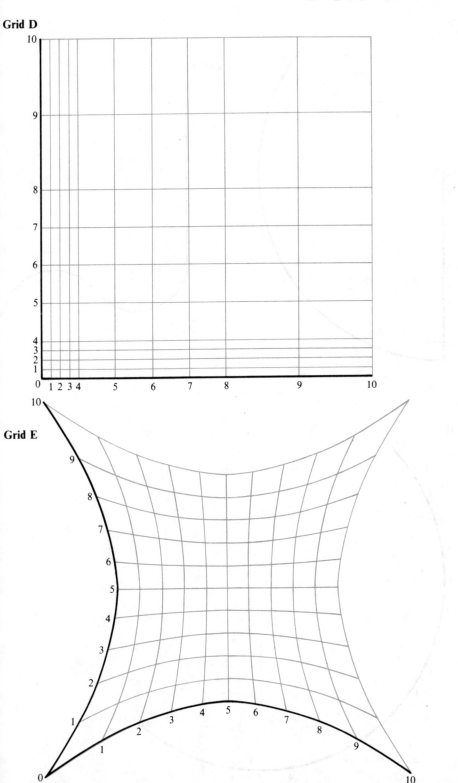

Grid E

Distorted axes

Grid F

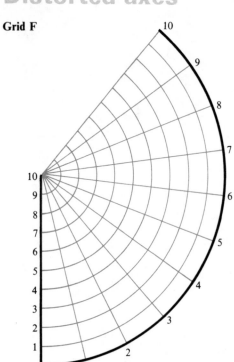

Grid G

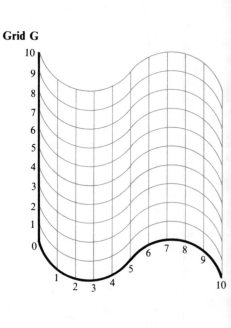

Grid H

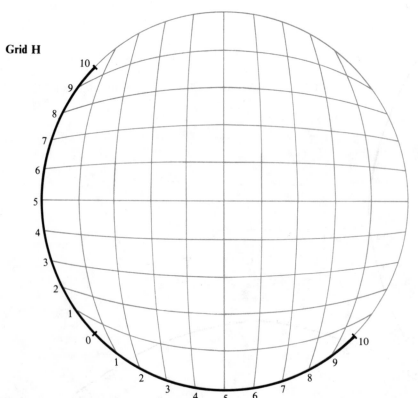

Three dimensions

1 This sketch of part of a town shows various high buildings.

To give the co-ordinates of a point above ground level, a third co-ordinate is required.

The three co-ordinates are then called an *ordered triple*.

Write the ordered triples (x, y, z) for these points.

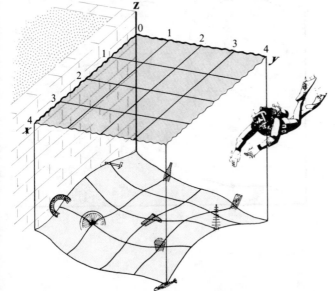

a Point A at the top of a clock tower 30 metres high
b Point B at the top of an office block 50 metres high
c Point C at the top of a building site 60 metres high
d Point D at the top of a church spire 20 metres high
e Point E at the top of a factory chimney 75 metres high
f Point F at the top of a cooling tower 80 metres high
g Point G at the top of a power station chimney 90 metres high
h Point H at the top of a radio transmitter 25 metres high
i Point I at the top of a war memorial 10 metres high

2 A diver swimming off the edge of a jetty notes various objects lying on the bottom of the lake.

Give the ordered triples (x, y, z) for these objects, remembering that as all the objects are *below* the level of the lake, therefore all the z values will be *negative*.

a A bicycle wheel at a depth of 4 metres
b A wellington boot at a depth of $3\frac{1}{2}$ metres
c Fish bones at a depth of 6 metres
d A car tyre at a depth of $3\frac{1}{2}$ metres
e An old bottle at a depth of 4 metres
f A bucket at a depth of 5 metres
g An old hammer at a depth of 3 metres
h A plank of wood at a depth of 6 metres
i A TV aerial at a depth of 3 metres

39

Three dimensions

3   This map shows a coastline, and the contours on the land are at 10-metre intervals.

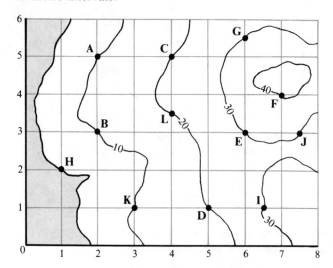

Give the co-ordinates for the lettered points *A* to *L* as ordered triples.

For example, point *A* is (2, 5, 10).

4   This map also shows a coastline. Its contours are at 50-metre intervals, both above and below sea-level.

a   Write the co-ordinates for the lettered points *A* to *J* as ordered triples.

b   Copy and complete these ordered triples for the unlettered points on the map.

(40, 50, …)

(80, 20, …)

(20, …, 100)

(5, …, 150)

(…, 5, 0)

(…, 50, 50)

(75, …, −50)

(50, 5, …)

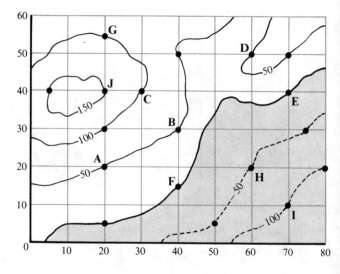

Three dimensions

5

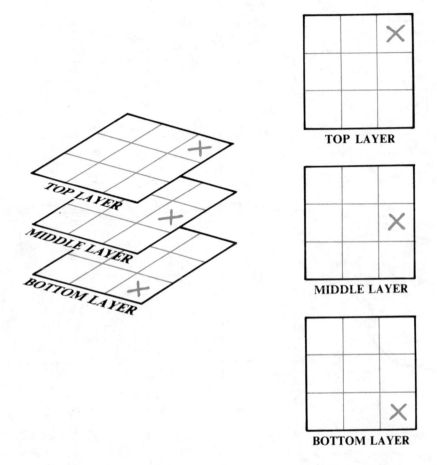

TOP LAYER

MIDDLE LAYER

BOTTOM LAYER

Here is a more complicated version of the traditional game of Noughts and Crosses.

In this three-dimensional game, the object is as usual to get a line of three noughts or three crosses: but the line can now be horizontal, vertical or diagonal.

The winner is the player who first gets three in a line, and the diagram here shows a line of three crosses on a side diagonal.

(A longer game continues until all the spaces are filled, and the winner is now the player with the most lines of three.)

Three dimensions

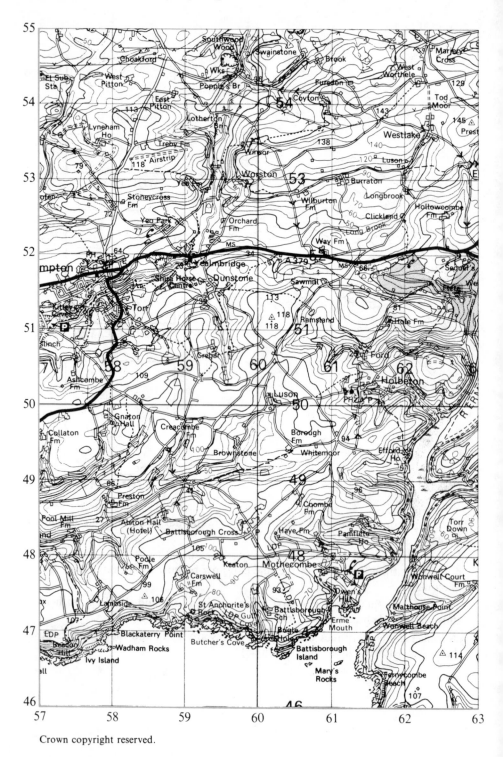

Three dimensions

6   On the facing page is an extract from an Ordnance Survey map of Devon.
    A six-figure number is used to fix the position of a point on the map.

Eastings   These run from left to right across the bottom of the map.
             Two numbers are printed there; the third you must estimate to the
             nearest tenth of a square.

Northings These run from bottom to top up the side of the map.
             Two numbers are printed; the third is again estimated to the nearest
             tenth.

For example, *Ivy Island* on the coast has an easting of 577 and a northing of
467; so its grid reference is 577 467.

What places have these grid references?

a	598 469	b	611 465	c	620 494	d	618 511
e	582 543	f	609 516	g	571 496	h	623 548
i	592 516	j	574 513	k	582 513	l	598 543

7   Write the six-figure grid references for these places.

a   Erme Mouth, on the coast
b   Preston Farm, near the south-west corner of the map
c   Way Farm, on the main A379 road running across the centre of the map
d   the milestone (MS) on the road nearly opposite Way Farm
e   the church (☩) in the village of Holbeton
f   East Pitton, in the north-west corner of the map
g   the village of Luson, in the centre of the map
h   Wonwell Beach, on the coast
i   Alston Hall (Hotel), near the coast
j   the telephone box (☏) in the car park at Mothecombe

8   The map shows heights as contour lines 10 metres apart, and also spot heights
    using a dot (•) or a triangulation point (△).

Find the heights of the points with these grid references.

a	625 467	b	629 538	c	585 474	d	591 482
e	602 512	f	602 514	g	622 462	h	590 490
i	583 538	j	599 521	k	579 485	l	620 493
m	584 524	n	600 543	o	614 507		

Estimate the heights of the places with these grid references, by looking at the
contour lines.

p	Keaton at 596 480	q	Burraton at 612 530
r	the crossroads at 603 532	s	the crossroads at 595 498
t	Torr Down at 626 483	u	Whitemoor at 607 495
v	Clickland at 619 525	w	the wind pump (⚒) at 593 504
x	Ashcombe Farm at 574 503	y	Stoneycross Farm at 582 527
z	Orchard Farm at 595 524		

Lines parallel to the axes

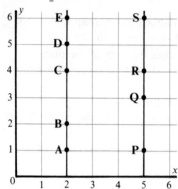
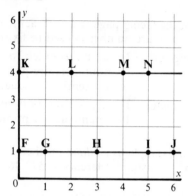

1 a Write the co-ordinates of the lettered points *A* to *E*. What have these co-ordinates in common?

   b Write the co-ordinates of the lettered points *P* to *S*. What have these in common?

   c Repeat for the points *F* to *J*. What have they in common?

   d Repeat for the points *K* to *N*. What have they in common?

2 Draw axes and label them both from −6 to 6.

   a Plot the points (4, 2) (4, 5) (4, 1) (4, −3) (4, −5).
      Draw the line through them, and write its equation on it.

   b Plot the points (2, 4) (2, 6) (2, 1) (2, −3) (2, −5).
      Draw the line through them, and write its equation on it.

   c Plot the points (5, 5) (5, 3) (5, 0) (5, −4) (5, −5).
      Draw the line through them, and write its equation on it.

   d Plot the points (1, 3) (6, 3) (4, 3) (−4, 3) (−3, 3).
      Draw the line through them, and write its equation on it.

   e Plot the points (6, 6) (4, 6) (1, 6) (−3, 6) (−5, 6).
      Draw the line through them, and write its equation on it.

   f Plot the points (5, −4) (3, −4) (0, −4) (−3, −4) (−5, −4).
      Draw the line through them, and write its equation on it.

3 Write the equations of the lines *A* to *H* drawn on this diagram.

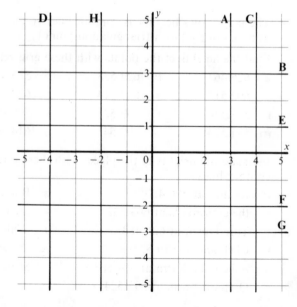

Lines parallel to the axes

4 For each part, draw and label both axes from -6 to 6.
Draw the four lines whose equations are given.
Write the equations on the lines.
Shade the rectangle bounded by the four lines, and find its area.

a $x = 3$ $\quad$ $x = 5$ $\qquad$ b $\;x = 4$ $\quad$ $x = 5$
$\quad$ $y = 4$ $\quad$ $y = 6$ $\qquad\quad$ $y = 2$ $\quad$ $y = 5$

c $\;x = 1$ $\quad$ $x = 6$ $\qquad$ d $\;x = 3$ $\quad$ $x = 4$
$\quad$ $y = 3$ $\quad$ $y = 5$ $\qquad\quad$ $y = -4$ $\quad$ $y = -3$

e $\;x = 1$ $\quad$ $x = 5$ $\qquad$ f $\;x = -3$ $\quad$ $x = -6$
$\quad$ $y = -5$ $\quad$ $y = -2$ $\qquad\;\;$ $y = -3$ $\quad$ $y = -6$

g $\;x = -2$ $\quad$ $x = 3$ $\qquad$ h $\;x = -4$ $\quad$ $x = -2$
$\quad$ $y = 2$ $\quad$ $y = 5$ $\qquad\quad$ $y = -4$ $\quad$ $y = 2$

i $\;x = 2\frac{1}{2}$ $\quad$ $x = 4\frac{1}{2}$ $\qquad$ j $\;x = 4$ $\quad$ $x = 4\frac{1}{2}$
$\quad$ $y = 3$ $\quad$ $y = 2\frac{1}{2}$ $\qquad\quad$ $y = 5$ $\quad$ $y = 5\frac{1}{2}$

k $\;x = -4\frac{1}{2}$ $\quad$ $x = -6$ $\qquad$ l $\;x = 1\frac{1}{2}$ $\quad$ $x = 3\frac{1}{2}$
$\quad$ $y = 3$ $\quad$ $y = 4\frac{1}{2}$ $\qquad\quad$ $y = 0$ $\quad$ $y = 2\frac{1}{2}$

5 Draw and label both axes from -6 to 6.
These sets of points are the corners of four squares.
Draw each square and both its diagonals.
On each diagonal, write its equation.

a (3, 2) (5, 4) (3, 6) (1, 4)

b (2, -2) (4, -4) (6, -2) (4, 0)

c (-5, -3) (-2, -6) (1, -3) (-2, 0)

d (-5, 3) (-4, 4) (-3, 3) (-4, 2)

6 Draw and label both axes from -6 to 6.
These sets of points are the corners of four rhombi.
Draw each rhombus and its two diagonals.
Label each diagonal with its equation.

a (3, 2) (4, 4) (3, 6) (2, 4)

b (4, 1) (6, -2) (4, -5) (2, -2)

c (-3, -4) (-5, -5) (-3, -6) (-1, -5)

d (-5, 3) (-2, 4) (1, 3) (-2, 2)

7 Draw and label both axes from -6 to 6.
Draw four shapes by joining these sets of points in order.
Draw their lines of symmetry: the first three shapes have one, and the fourth
shape has two.
On each line of symmetry, write its equation.

a (4, 1) (3, 4) (4, 5) (5, 4)

b (2, -1) (1, -3) (2, -5) (5, -4) (4, -3) (5, -2)

c (-5, -1) (-5, -2) (-6, -2) (-4, -4) (-2, -2) (-3, -2) (-3, -1)

d (-4, 6) (-4, 5) (-6, 4) (-4, 3) (-4, 2) (-2, 2) (-2, 3) (0, 4) (-2, 5) (-2, 6)

Lines parallel to the axes

8   Draw and label both axes from -6 to 6.
Draw these four triangles and reflect them in the given line.
   a   Reflect triangle (2, 2) (2, 5) (1, 5) in the line $x = 3$.
   b   Reflect triangle $(-1, -2)$ (4, -2) (1, -4) in the line $y = -4$.
   c   Reflect triangle $(-3, -2)$ $(-2, -3)$ $(-4, -5)$ in the line $x = -4$.
   d   Reflect triangle $(-1, 5)$ $(-5, 4)$ $(-4, 3)$ in the line $y = 2$.

9   Draw and label both axes from -6 to 6.
   a   Draw the four shapes whose corners are given here.
   Shape A $(3\frac{1}{2}, \frac{1}{2})$ $(4, \frac{1}{2})$ $(4, -1)$ $(3\frac{1}{2}, -1)$
   Shape B $(1, -3)$ $(1, -5)$ $(-2, -5)$ $(-2, -3)$
   Shape C $(-5, \frac{1}{2})$ $(-5, -\frac{1}{2})$ $(-4\frac{1}{2}, -\frac{1}{2})$ $(-4\frac{1}{2}, \frac{1}{2})$
   Shape D $(-1, 4)$ $(-3, 5)$ (2, 5) (0, 4) $(-\frac{1}{2}, 4)$ $(-\frac{1}{2}, 3\frac{1}{2})$ $(-1, 3\frac{1}{2})$
   b   Reflect shape A in the line $x = 2$.
Reflect shape B in the line $y = -2$.
Reflect shape C in the line $x = -3$.
Reflect shape D in the line $y = 3$.
   c   What picture do these reflections make?

Relations

Arrow diagrams

Mappings and functions

Graphical applications

Arrow diagrams

Part 1   Family relations

1   This diagram shows the relation
    "*... is the father of ...*".

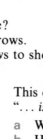

   a   Who is the father?
   b   How many children has he?
   c   How many sons has he?
   d   What relation is Mary to Ken?
   e   What relation is Mary to George?
   f   Copy the diagram without its arrows.
       Onto your copy, draw new arrows to show the relation
       "*... is the son of ...*".

2

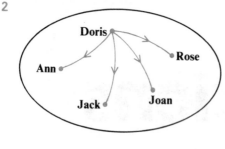

This diagram shows the relation
"*... is the mother of ...*".

   a   Who is the mother?
   b   How many daughters has she?
   c   What relation is Jack to Doris?
   d   What relation is Ann to Joan?
   e   Copy the diagram without its arrows.
       Onto your copy, draw new arrows to
       show the relation
       "*... is the sister of ...*".

3   This diagram shows the relation
    "*... is the mother of ...*".

   a   How many daughters has Sarah?
   b   Which of these daughters has no children?
   c   How many children has Sheila?
   d   What relation is Julie to Sheila?
   e   What relation is Sheila to Alice?
   f   What relation is Sarah to Alice?
   g   What relation is Stephen to Sarah?
   h   Who is Tony's aunt?
   i   Who are Freda's two nieces?
   j   Copy the diagram without its arrows.
       Onto your copy, draw new arrows to show the relation
       "*... is the grandmother of ...*".

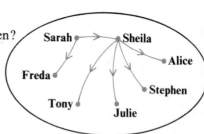

4   This diagram shows
    part of a family tree.

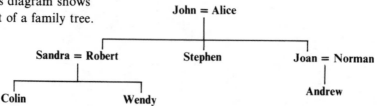

   a   Who is John's wife?   b   Who is Sandra's husband?
   c   How many children have John and Alice?
   d   Have Joan and Norman a son or a daughter?
   e   How many grandchildren have John and Alice?
   f   Who is Wendy's brother?   g   Who is Colin's unmarried uncle?

Arrow diagrams

Write down the missing word or words for each of these sentences:
h   Joan is the ... of Norman.
i   Colin is the ... of Alice.
j   Robert is the ... of Norman.
k   Joan is the ... of Wendy.
l   Andrew is the ... of Robert.
m   Sandra is the daughter-in-law of ...
n   Robert is the uncle of ...

o   Copy this diagram and complete it
    to show the relation
    "... *is the son of* ...".

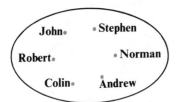

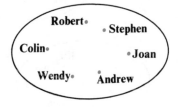

p   Copy this diagram and complete it
    to show the relation
    "... *is the brother of* ...".

Part 2   Other relations

1   Copy these diagrams and draw arrows for the given relations.

a
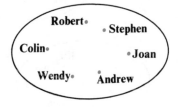
"... *is the initial letter of* ..."

b
"... *is part of* ..."

c
"... *grow(s) on* ..."

d

"... *eat* ..."

e

"... *is 1 more than* ..."

f

"...*divides into 12 to give*..."

2   Use this diagram for each of these
    relations.
    Copy the diagram each time, and draw
    your arrows on it.
    a   "... *is 2 less than* ..."
    b   "... *is 3 more than* ..."
    c   "... *is a half of* ..."
    d   "... *is a factor of* ..."
    e   "... *subtracts from 9 to give* ..."
    f   "... *is less than* ..."

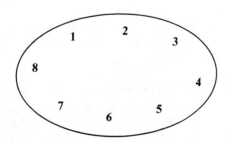

49

Arrow diagrams

3 For each of these arrow diagrams, suggest a suitable relation.

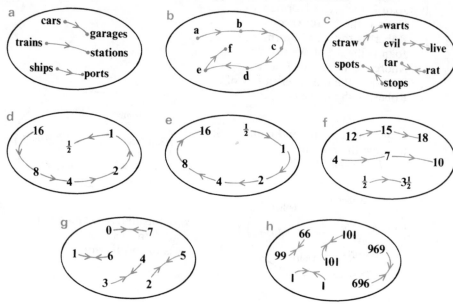

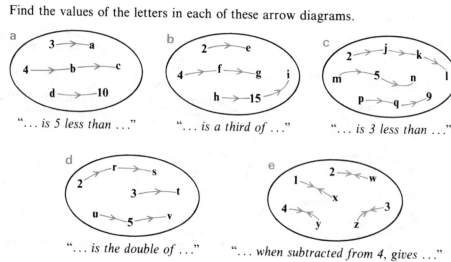

4 Find the values of the letters in each of these arrow diagrams.

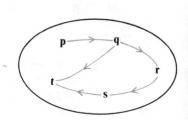

5 This arrow diagram shows five numbers
represented by letters and connected by
the relation
"... is less than ...".

Not all possible arrows are shown.

a Which letter represents the smallest number?
b Which letter represents the largest number?
c Write the letters in order of size with the
smallest first.

Arrow diagrams

6   This arrow diagram shows five numbers
    represented by letters and connected by
    the relation
    "... *is 6 less than* ...". 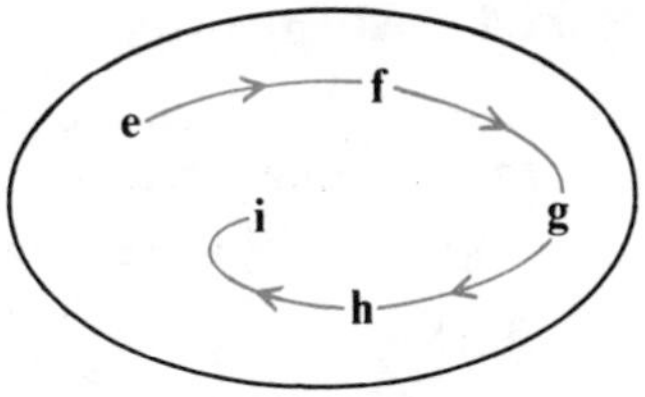
    a   Which letter represents the smallest number?
    b   Which letter represents the largest number?
    c   Which letter has a value 12 more than *g*?

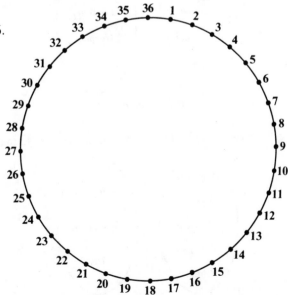

7   Draw an arrow diagram for these seven words.
    {pant, line, pint, last, pine, past, list}
    Complete the diagram by drawing arrows for the relation
    "... *changes one letter to become* ...".

8   Draw an arrow diagram for these six words.
    {ball, pile, bile, tell, time, pale}
    Complete the diagram by drawing arrows for the relation
    "... *changes two letters to become* ...".

9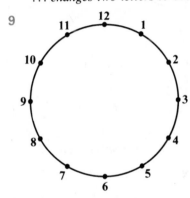

This circle has twelve points numbered
from 1 to 12.

Copy the circle six times.

Use straight arrows to join points for
these relations where *n* takes all values
from 1 to 12.

For values greater than 12, keep counting
clockwise round the circle.
    a   *n is joined to n + 1*   b   *n is joined to n + 2*
    c   *n is joined to n + 3*   d   *n is joined to n + 4*
    e   *n is joined to n + 5*   f   *n is joined to n + 6*

What different patterns would you make if the
circle had more than twelve numbered points?

10 Copy this circle which has
    points numbered from 1 to 36.

    Use straight arrows to join
    points for the relation
    "*n is joined to 2n*"
    where *n* takes all values
    from 1 to 36.

    For values greater than 36,
    keep counting clockwise
    round the circle.

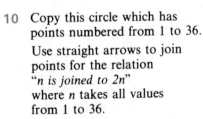

51

Mappings and functions

Part 1 Mappings

1 One set, X (called the *domain*), can be mapped onto another set, Y (called the *range*), using a relation.

Copy each of these diagrams, and draw arrows to map set X onto set Y.

a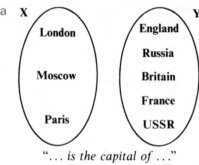

"... is the capital of ..."

b

"... is 2 less than ..."

c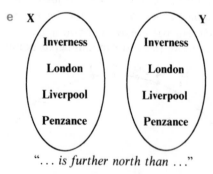

"... is greater than ..."

d

"... is smaller than ..."

e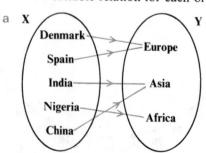

"... is further north than ..."

f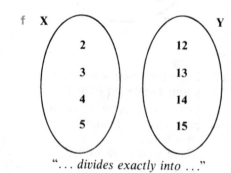

"... divides exactly into ..."

2 Invent a suitable relation for each of these mappings.

a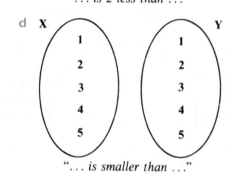

b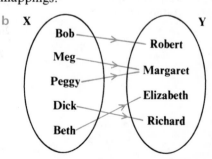

Mappings and functions

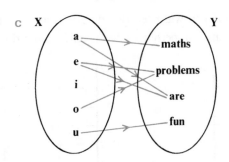

c X ... Y

a — maths
e — problems
i — are
o
u — fun

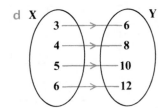 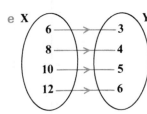 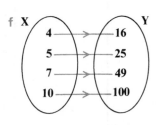

d X ... Y

3 → 6
4 → 8
5 → 10
6 → 12

e X ... Y

6 → 3
8 → 4
10 → 5
12 → 6

f X ... Y

4 → 16
5 → 25
7 → 49
10 → 100

3 Find the values of the letters in these mappings.

a

7 → a
9 → b
12 → c
d → 10

"... is 5 more than ..."

b

2 → e
4 → f
g → 15
h → 20

"... is 4 less than ..."

c

2 → i
5 → j
k → 40
l → 48

"... is a quarter of ..."

d

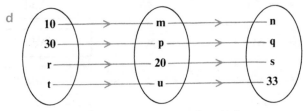

10 → m → n
30 → p → q
r → 20 → s
t → u → 33

"... is the double of ..."   "... is 3 less than ..."

e

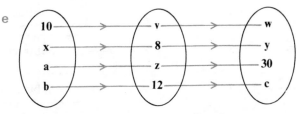

10 → v → w
x → 8 → y
a → z → 30
b → 12 → c

"... is 4 more than ..."   "... is a third of ..."

53

Mappings and functions

4   For these problems you will need two diagrams as shown here.
    Copy these diagrams, or perhaps your teacher could duplicate some for you.

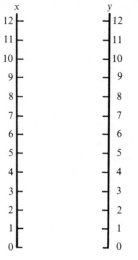

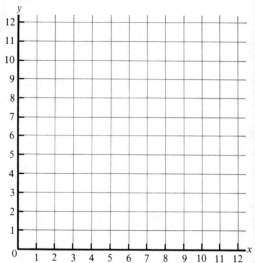

Use each flow diagram to map the domain X onto the range Y.
Draw two diagrams in each case—draw *arrows* on your mapping diagram
                            —plot *points* on your axes.

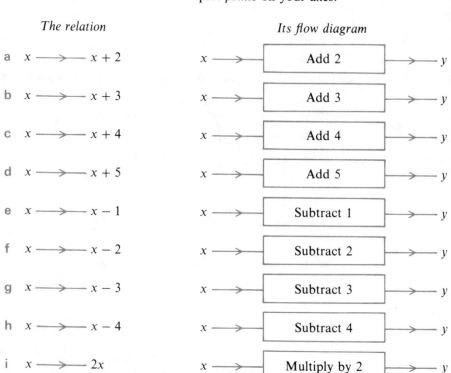

	The relation		*Its flow diagram*
a	$x \longrightarrow x + 2$	$x \longrightarrow$	Add 2 $\longrightarrow y$
b	$x \longrightarrow x + 3$	$x \longrightarrow$	Add 3 $\longrightarrow y$
c	$x \longrightarrow x + 4$	$x \longrightarrow$	Add 4 $\longrightarrow y$
d	$x \longrightarrow x + 5$	$x \longrightarrow$	Add 5 $\longrightarrow y$
e	$x \longrightarrow x - 1$	$x \longrightarrow$	Subtract 1 $\longrightarrow y$
f	$x \longrightarrow x - 2$	$x \longrightarrow$	Subtract 2 $\longrightarrow y$
g	$x \longrightarrow x - 3$	$x \longrightarrow$	Subtract 3 $\longrightarrow y$
h	$x \longrightarrow x - 4$	$x \longrightarrow$	Subtract 4 $\longrightarrow y$
i	$x \longrightarrow 2x$	$x \longrightarrow$	Multiply by 2 $\longrightarrow y$

Mappings and functions

j $x \longrightarrow 3x$ $x \longrightarrow$ | Multiply by 3 | $\longrightarrow y$

k $x \longrightarrow \dfrac{x}{2}$ $x \longrightarrow$ | Divide by 2 | $\longrightarrow y$

l $x \longrightarrow \dfrac{x}{3}$ $x \longrightarrow$ | Divide by 3 | $\longrightarrow y$

m $x \longrightarrow \dfrac{x}{4}$ $x \longrightarrow$ | Divide by 4 | $\longrightarrow y$

n $x \longrightarrow 12 - x$ $x \longrightarrow$ | Subtract *from* 12 | $\longrightarrow y$

o $x \longrightarrow 10 - x$ $x \longrightarrow$ | Subtract *from* 10 | $\longrightarrow y$

p $x \longrightarrow 8 - x$ $x \longrightarrow$ | Subtract *from* 8 | $\longrightarrow y$

q $x \longrightarrow 6 - x$ $x \longrightarrow$ | Subtract *from* 6 | $\longrightarrow y$

r $x \longrightarrow \dfrac{12}{x}$ $x \longrightarrow$ | Divide into 12 | $\longrightarrow y$

s $x \longrightarrow \dfrac{24}{x}$ $x \longrightarrow$ | Divide into 24 | $\longrightarrow y$

t $x \longrightarrow x^2$ $x \longrightarrow$ | Multiply by itself | $\longrightarrow y$

5 Complete the relation $x \longrightarrow$ ▭ for each of these mappings.

a

x	y
4	12
3	11
2	10
1	9
0	8

b

x	y
4	16
3	15
2	14
1	13
0	12

c

x	y
8	$9\frac{1}{2}$
7	$8\frac{1}{2}$
6	$7\frac{1}{2}$
5	$6\frac{1}{2}$

d

x	y
8	4
6	2
4	0
2	-2
0	-4

e

x	y
9	3
7	1
5	-1
3	-3
1	-5

f

x	y
3	6
$2\frac{1}{2}$	5
2	4
$1\frac{1}{2}$	3
1	2

Mappings and functions

g

x		y
8	→	40
6	→	30
4	→	20
2	→	10
0	→	0

h

x		y
2.5	→	25
2	→	20
1.5	→	15
1	→	10
0.5	→	5

i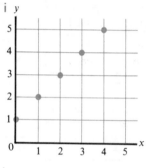

j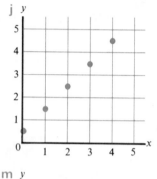

k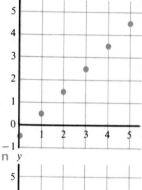

l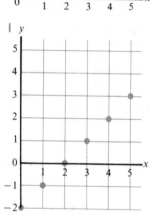

m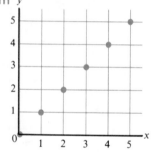

n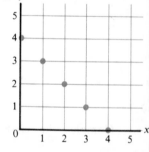

6   For each mapping below, copy this table and complete it using the flow diagram.

x	0	1	2	3	4	5	6
y							

Draw axes with the x-axis labelled from 0 to 6 and the y-axis from 0 to 15.

Plot points onto the axes and write the equation on the line through the points.

Plot **a** to **d** on the same diagram.

a   Equation $y = 2x + 1$

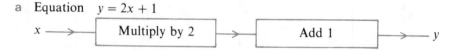

b   Equation $y = 2x + 3$

Mappings and functions

c Equation $y = 2x - 1$

$x \longrightarrow$ | Multiply by 2 | $\longrightarrow$ | Subtract 1 | $\longrightarrow y$

d Equation $y = 2x - 3$

$x \longrightarrow$ | Multiply by 2 | $\longrightarrow$ | Subtract 3 | $\longrightarrow y$

Draw new axes as before, and plot **e** to **h** on the same diagram.

e Equation $y = \frac{1}{2}x + 3$

$x \longrightarrow$ | Halve | $\longrightarrow$ | Add 3 | $\longrightarrow y$

f Equation $y = \dfrac{x + 3}{2}$

$x \longrightarrow$ | Add 3 | $\longrightarrow$ | Halve | $\longrightarrow y$

g Equation $y = \frac{1}{2}x - 1$

$x \longrightarrow$ | Halve | $\longrightarrow$ | Subtract 1 | $\longrightarrow y$

h Equation $y = \dfrac{x - 1}{2}$

$x \longrightarrow$ | Subtract 1 | $\longrightarrow$ | Halve | $\longrightarrow y$

Draw new axes as before, and plot **i** to **l** on the same diagram.

i Equation $y = 2(6 - x)$

$x \longrightarrow$ | Take from 6 | $\longrightarrow$ | Double | $\longrightarrow y$

j Equation $y = 6 - 2x$

$x \longrightarrow$ | Double | $\longrightarrow$ | Take from 6 | $\longrightarrow y$

k Equation $y = 3(5 - x)$

$x \longrightarrow$ | Take from 5 | $\longrightarrow$ | Treble | $\longrightarrow y$

l Equation $y = 14 - 3x$

$x \longrightarrow$ | Treble | $\longrightarrow$ | Take from 14 | $\longrightarrow y$

Mappings and functions

Draw new axes as before, and plot these on the same diagram.

m Equation $y = \dfrac{2x + 3}{2}$

$x \longrightarrow$ | Double | $\longrightarrow$ | Add 3 | $\longrightarrow$ | Halve | $\longrightarrow y$

n Equation $y = \dfrac{3x - 2}{2}$

$x \longrightarrow$ | Treble | $\longrightarrow$ | Subtract 2 | $\longrightarrow$ | Halve | $\longrightarrow y$

o Equation $y = \left(\dfrac{x}{2}\right)^2 - 4$

$x \longrightarrow$ | Halve | $\longrightarrow$ | Square | $\longrightarrow$ | Subtract 4 | $\longrightarrow y$

p Equation $y = \dfrac{x^2}{2} - 4$

$x \longrightarrow$ | Square | $\longrightarrow$ | Halve | $\longrightarrow$ | Subtract 4 | $\longrightarrow y$

Part 2 Introducing functions

Draw a diagram to map each set X onto set Y using the given relation.

1 One–many mappings
   a X = {Asia, America, Europe}
      Y = {China, Canada, India, France, Italy}
      "... *contains the country called* ...".

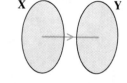

   b X = {1, 2, 3}
      Y = {$1\frac{1}{4}$, $1\frac{1}{2}$, $1\frac{3}{4}$, $2\frac{1}{2}$, $2\frac{3}{4}$, $3\frac{1}{4}$, $3\frac{1}{2}$}
      "... *is the whole number part of* ...".

2 One–one mappings
   a X = {cat, dog, cow, hare}
      Y = {kitten, pup, calf, leveret}
      "... *has its young called* ...".

   b X = {4, 18, 32, 56}
      Y = {9, 2, 16, 28}
      "... *is the double of* ...".

3 Many–many mappings
   a X = {a, g, t}
      Y = {gutter, tarmac, spout}
      "... *is a letter of* ...".

   b X = {1, 2, 3, 4}
      Y = {1, 2, 3, 4}
      "... *is less than* ...".

4 Many–one mappings
   a X = {Paris, Bordeaux, York, Leeds, London}
      Y = {France, Britain}
      "... *is a city of* ...".

   b X = {1, 2, 3, 4, 5, 6}
      Y = {odd, even}
      "... *is* ...".

Mappings and functions

5 A mapping in which each member of set X maps onto *just one* member of set Y is called a *function*.

Which of the four types of mappings above are *functions*?

6 Which of these mappings are *functions*?

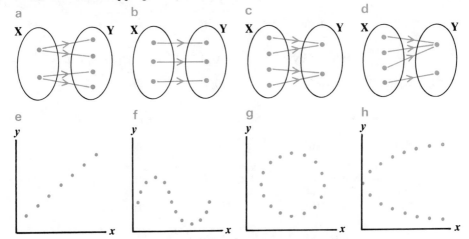

7 The function $x \longrightarrow x + 2$ can be written as $f(x) = x + 2$.

Write these functions in the same way.

a $x \longrightarrow x - 3$ b $x \longrightarrow 4x - 1$ c $x \longrightarrow \frac{1}{2}x + 6$

d $x \longrightarrow x^2$ e $x \longrightarrow x^2 + 4$ f $x \longrightarrow (x + 1)^2$

8 Find the values of the letters **a** to **l** for these functions.

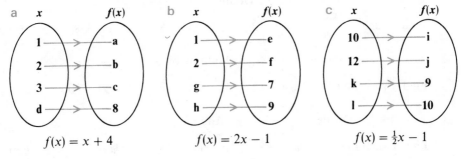

Part 3 Functions as flow diagrams

Use the flow diagrams to find the values required.

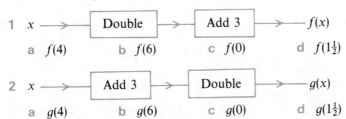

1 $x \longrightarrow$ | Double | $\longrightarrow$ | Add 3 | $\longrightarrow f(x)$

a $f(4)$ b $f(6)$ c $f(0)$ d $f(1\frac{1}{2})$

2 $x \longrightarrow$ | Add 3 | $\longrightarrow$ | Double | $\longrightarrow g(x)$

a $g(4)$ b $g(6)$ c $g(0)$ d $g(1\frac{1}{2})$

59

Mappings and functions

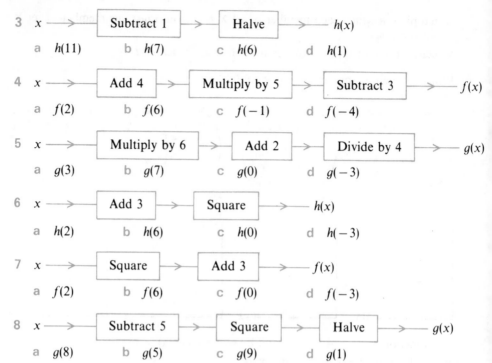

3 x ⟶ | Subtract 1 | ⟶ | Halve | ⟶ $h(x)$

    a $h(11)$ b $h(7)$ c $h(6)$ d $h(1)$

4 x ⟶ | Add 4 | ⟶ | Multiply by 5 | ⟶ | Subtract 3 | ⟶ $f(x)$

    a $f(2)$ b $f(6)$ c $f(-1)$ d $f(-4)$

5 x ⟶ | Multiply by 6 | ⟶ | Add 2 | ⟶ | Divide by 4 | ⟶ $g(x)$

    a $g(3)$ b $g(7)$ c $g(0)$ d $g(-3)$

6 x ⟶ | Add 3 | ⟶ | Square | ⟶ $h(x)$

    a $h(2)$ b $h(6)$ c $h(0)$ d $h(-3)$

7 x ⟶ | Square | ⟶ | Add 3 | ⟶ $f(x)$

    a $f(2)$ b $f(6)$ c $f(0)$ d $f(-3)$

8 x ⟶ | Subtract 5 | ⟶ | Square | ⟶ | Halve | ⟶ $g(x)$

    a $g(8)$ b $g(5)$ c $g(9)$ d $g(1)$

Use the next flow diagrams *in reverse* to find the values of x required.

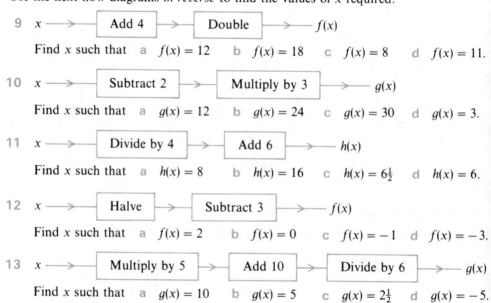

9 x ⟶ | Add 4 | ⟶ | Double | ⟶ $f(x)$

    Find x such that   a $f(x) = 12$ b $f(x) = 18$ c $f(x) = 8$ d $f(x) = 11.$

10 x ⟶ | Subtract 2 | ⟶ | Multiply by 3 | ⟶ $g(x)$

    Find x such that   a $g(x) = 12$ b $g(x) = 24$ c $g(x) = 30$ d $g(x) = 3.$

11 x ⟶ | Divide by 4 | ⟶ | Add 6 | ⟶ $h(x)$

    Find x such that   a $h(x) = 8$ b $h(x) = 16$ c $h(x) = 6\frac{1}{2}$ d $h(x) = 6.$

12 x ⟶ | Halve | ⟶ | Subtract 3 | ⟶ $f(x)$

    Find x such that   a $f(x) = 2$ b $f(x) = 0$ c $f(x) = -1$ d $f(x) = -3.$

13 x ⟶ | Multiply by 5 | ⟶ | Add 10 | ⟶ | Divide by 6 | ⟶ $g(x)$

    Find x such that   a $g(x) = 10$ b $g(x) = 5$ c $g(x) = 2\frac{1}{2}$ d $g(x) = -5.$

14 x ⟶ | Subtract 2 | ⟶ | Treble | ⟶ | Add 8 | ⟶ $h(x)$

    Find x such that   a $h(x) = 32$ b $h(x) = 23$ c $h(x) = 8$ d $h(x) = -1.$

Mappings and functions

Use each pair of flow diagrams, one after the other (in the correct order), to find the values required.

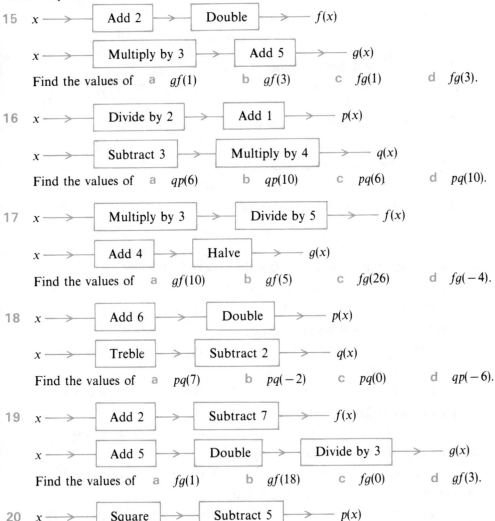

15 $x \longrightarrow$ | Add 2 | $\longrightarrow$ | Double | $\longrightarrow$ $f(x)$

$x \longrightarrow$ | Multiply by 3 | $\longrightarrow$ | Add 5 | $\longrightarrow$ $g(x)$

Find the values of   a $gf(1)$ b $gf(3)$ c $fg(1)$ d $fg(3)$.

16 $x \longrightarrow$ | Divide by 2 | $\longrightarrow$ | Add 1 | $\longrightarrow$ $p(x)$

$x \longrightarrow$ | Subtract 3 | $\longrightarrow$ | Multiply by 4 | $\longrightarrow$ $q(x)$

Find the values of   a $qp(6)$ b $qp(10)$ c $pq(6)$ d $pq(10)$.

17 $x \longrightarrow$ | Multiply by 3 | $\longrightarrow$ | Divide by 5 | $\longrightarrow$ $f(x)$

$x \longrightarrow$ | Add 4 | $\longrightarrow$ | Halve | $\longrightarrow$ $g(x)$

Find the values of   a $gf(10)$ b $gf(5)$ c $fg(26)$ d $fg(-4)$.

18 $x \longrightarrow$ | Add 6 | $\longrightarrow$ | Double | $\longrightarrow$ $p(x)$

$x \longrightarrow$ | Treble | $\longrightarrow$ | Subtract 2 | $\longrightarrow$ $q(x)$

Find the values of   a $pq(7)$ b $pq(-2)$ c $pq(0)$ d $qp(-6)$.

19 $x \longrightarrow$ | Add 2 | $\longrightarrow$ | Subtract 7 | $\longrightarrow$ $f(x)$

$x \longrightarrow$ | Add 5 | $\longrightarrow$ | Double | $\longrightarrow$ | Divide by 3 | $\longrightarrow$ $g(x)$

Find the values of   a $fg(1)$ b $gf(18)$ c $fg(0)$ d $gf(3)$.

20 $x \longrightarrow$ | Square | $\longrightarrow$ | Subtract 5 | $\longrightarrow$ $p(x)$

$x \longrightarrow$ | Treble | $\longrightarrow$ | Subtract 5 | $\longrightarrow$ $q(x)$

Find the values of   a $qp(4)$ b $pq(4)$ c $pq(1)$ d $qp(2)$.

Part 4 Functions as equations

1 If $f(x) = x + 6$, find the values of
  a $f(3)$ b $f(0)$ c $f(-1)$ d $f(-6)$.

2 If $g(x) = x - 7$, find the values of
  a $g(9)$ b $g(7)$ c $g(2)$ d $g(-1)$.

Mappings and functions

3   If $p(x) = 2x + 3$, find the values of
a $p(4)$ b $p(1\frac{1}{2})$ c $p(0)$ d $p(-1)$.

4   If $q(x) = 2(x - 5)$, find the values of
a $q(9)$ b $q(6\frac{1}{2})$ c $q(5)$ d $q(2)$.

5   If $f(x) = \dfrac{3x - 8}{2}$, find the values of
a $f(6)$ b $f(3)$ c $f(2)$ d $f(0)$.

6   If $g(x) = \dfrac{x^2 - 9}{3}$, find the values of
a $g(6)$ b $g(4)$ c $g(3)$ d $g(2)$.

7   If $p(x) = 2x^2 + 4$, find the values of
a $p(3)$ b $p(2)$ c $p(0)$ d $p(-3)$.

8   If $q(x) = (2x)^2 - 8$, find the values of
a $q(3)$ b $q(2)$ c $q(1)$ d $q(0)$.

Use the next equations *in reverse* to find the values of x required.

9   Given $f(x) = x - 3$, find x such that
a $f(x) = 7$ b $f(x) = 1$ c $f(x) = 0$ d $f(x) = -1$.

10   Given $g(x) = x + 5$, find x such that
a $g(x) = 9$ b $g(x) = 5$ c $g(x) = 3$ d $g(x) = 0$.

11   Given $p(x) = 3x$, find x such that
a $p(x) = 6$ b $p(x) = 30$ c $p(x) = -9$ d $p(x) = 1\frac{1}{2}$.

12   Given $q(x) = 2x - 4$, find x such that
a $q(x) = 12$ b $q(x) = 1$ c $q(x) = 0$ d $q(x) = -2$.

13   Given $f(x) = 5x + 7$, find x such that
a $f(x) = 22$ b $f(x) = 7$ c $f(x) = 9\frac{1}{2}$ d $f(x) = 2$.

14   Given $g(x) = 3(x - 4)$, find x such that
a $g(x) = 6$ b $g(x) = 0$ c $g(x) = -9$ d $g(x) = -15$.

15   Given $p(x) = 5(2x - 8)$, find x such that
a $p(x) = 20$ b $p(x) = 0$ c $p(x) = -30$ d $p(x) = -35$.

16   Given $q(x) = \dfrac{3x - 5}{2}$, find x such that
a $q(x) = 2$ b $q(x) = 8$ c $q(x) = -1$ d $q(x) = -7$.

17   Given $f(x) = \dfrac{4x + 1}{3}$, find x such that
a $f(x) = 7$ b $f(x) = 11$ c $f(x) = -1$ d $f(x) = \frac{1}{3}$.

18   Given $g(x) = \dfrac{3(x - 4)}{2}$, find x such that
a $g(x) = 9$ b $g(x) = 0$ c $g(x) = -6$ d $g(x) = -3$.

Mappings and functions

In each of these, two functions are given. Use one function and then the other (in the correct order).

$x \longrightarrow \boxed{f} \xrightarrow{f(x)} \boxed{g} \longrightarrow gf(x)$

$x \longrightarrow \boxed{g} \xrightarrow{g(x)} \boxed{f} \longrightarrow fg(x)$

19 If $p(x) = x - 2$ and $q(x) = 3x$, find the values of
   a $pq(4)$ b $qp(4)$ c $qp(7)$ d $pq(7)$.

20 If $f(x) = \frac{1}{2}x$ and $g(x) = 3x + 2$, find the values of
   a $fg(4)$ b $gf(8)$ c $fg(6)$ d $gf(10)$.

21 If $p(x) = 2x - 4$ and $q(x) = \dfrac{x+1}{2}$, find the values of
   a $pq(7)$ b $pq(1)$ c $qp(3)$ d $qp(0)$.

22 If $f(x) = x^2 - 6$ and $g(x) = \frac{1}{2}x - 3$, find the values of
   a $fg(14)$ b $gf(4)$ c $gf(2)$ d $fg(4)$.

23 If $p(x) = \frac{1}{2}x^2$ and $q(x) = (\frac{1}{2}x)^2$, find the values of
   a $qp(4)$ b $qp(2)$ c $pq(6)$ d $pq(-8)$.

This flow diagram will give you the square of a function.

24   $x \longrightarrow \boxed{f} \xrightarrow{f(x)} \boxed{f} \longrightarrow f^2(x)$

   a Find $f(6)$ and $f^2(6)$ when $f(x) = 2x - 1$.
   b Find $f(2)$ and $f^2(2)$ when $f(x) = 3x + 1$.
   c Find $f(4)$ and $f^2(4)$ when $f(x) = x^2 - 7$.
   d Find $f(-1)$ and $f^2(-1)$ when $f(x) = 4(x + 2)$.
   e Find $f(6)$ and $f^2(6)$ when $f(x) = \frac{1}{2}x - 3$.
   f Find $f(7)$ and $f^2(7)$ when $f(x) = \dfrac{x+2}{3}$.

Part 5   Inverse functions

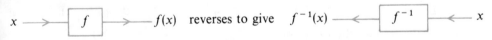

$x \longrightarrow \boxed{f} \longrightarrow f(x)$ reverses to give $f^{-1}(x) \longleftarrow \boxed{f^{-1}} \longleftarrow x$

Use these flow diagrams in reverse to find the required inverses.

1   $x \longrightarrow \boxed{\text{Add } 3} \longrightarrow f(x)$
  Find the values of
   a $f^{-1}(7)$ b $f^{-1}(10)$ c $f^{-1}(3)$ d $f^{-1}(3\frac{1}{2})$.

2   $x \longrightarrow \boxed{\text{Subtract } 5} \longrightarrow g(x)$
  Find the values of
   a $g^{-1}(1)$ b $g^{-1}(3)$ c $g^{-1}(0)$ d $g^{-1}(-1)$.

Mappings and functions

3 $x \longrightarrow$ | Multiply by 3 | $\longrightarrow h(x)$

Find the values of
   a $h^{-1}(12)$ b $h^{-1}(6)$ c $h^{-1}(3)$ d $h^{-1}(1\frac{1}{2})$.

4 $x \longrightarrow$ | Add 3 | $\longrightarrow$ | Double | $\longrightarrow f(x)$

Find the values of
   a $f^{-1}(14)$ b $f^{-1}(10)$ c $f^{-1}(7)$ d $f^{-1}(11)$.

5 $x \longrightarrow$ | Divide by 4 | $\longrightarrow$ | Subtract 1 | $\longrightarrow g(x)$

Find the values of
   a $g^{-1}(2)$ b $g^{-1}(9)$ c $g^{-1}(0)$ d $g^{-1}(\frac{1}{4})$.

6 $x \longrightarrow$ | Add 3 | $\longrightarrow$ | Multiply by 10 | $\longrightarrow h(x)$

Find the values of
   a $h^{-1}(40)$ b $h^{-1}(0)$ c $h^{-1}(35)$ d $h^{-1}(20)$.

7 $x \longrightarrow$ | Halve | $\longrightarrow$ | Treble | $\longrightarrow f(x)$

Find the values of
   a $f^{-1}(15)$ b $f^{-1}(30)$ c $f^{-1}(3)$ d $f^{-1}(1\frac{1}{2})$.

8 $x \longrightarrow$ | Divide by 5 | $\longrightarrow$ | Add 7 | $\longrightarrow$ | Multiply by 3 | $\longrightarrow g(x)$

Find the values of
   a $g^{-1}(33)$ b $g^{-1}(24)$ c $g^{-1}(21)$ d $g^{-1}(15)$.

Use these equations in reverse to find the required inverses.

9 If $f(x) = x + 6$, find the values of
   a $f^{-1}(10)$ b $f^{-1}(7)$ c $f^{-1}(6)$ d $f^{-1}(4)$.

10 If $g(x) = x - 4$, find the values of
   a $g^{-1}(2)$ b $g^{-1}(1)$ c $g^{-1}(0)$ d $g^{-1}(-1)$.

11 If $h(x) = 2x$, find the values of
   a $h^{-1}(10)$ b $h^{-1}(1)$ c $h^{-1}(0)$ d $h^{-1}(-4)$.

12 If $f(x) = 3x - 1$, find the values of
   a $f^{-1}(5)$ b $f^{-1}(20)$ c $f^{-1}(-1)$ d $f^{-1}(-7)$.

13 If $g(x) = \frac{1}{2}x + 5$, find the values of
   a $g^{-1}(9)$ b $g^{-1}(7)$ c $g^{-1}(5)$ d $g^{-1}(2)$.

14 If $h(x) = \dfrac{x - 4}{2}$, find the values of
   a $h^{-1}(3)$ b $h^{-1}(8)$ c $h^{-1}(0)$ d $h^{-1}(-2)$.

Mappings and functions

15 If $f(x) = \dfrac{x + 7}{3}$, find the values of

   a $f^{-1}(4)$ b $f^{-1}(12)$ c $f^{-1}(2)$ d $f^{-1}(0)$.

16 If $g(x) = 2(x - 3)$, find the values of

   a $g^{-1}(8)$ b $g^{-1}(1)$ c $g^{-1}(0)$ d $g^{-1}(-6)$.

17 If $h(x) = 3(2x + 5)$, find the values of

   a $h^{-1}(39)$ b $h^{-1}(15)$ c $h^{-1}(18)$ d $h^{-1}(9)$.

18 If $f(x) = \dfrac{2x - 7}{3}$, find the values of

   a $f^{-1}(1)$ b $f^{-1}(0)$ c $f^{-1}(-2)$ d $f^{-1}(-5)$.

Graphical applications

Part 1 Flow diagrams

1 During a storm you can find how far away the thunder is by counting the number of seconds between the lightning flash and the roll of thunder, and dividing by 5.

Number of seconds ⟶ | Divide by 5 | ⟶ Number of miles away

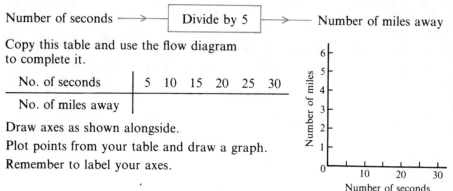

Copy this table and use the flow diagram to complete it.

No. of seconds	5	10	15	20	25	30
No. of miles away						

Draw axes as shown alongside.

Plot points from your table and draw a graph.

Remember to label your axes.

2 A glass marble bouncing on a concrete floor will rebound $\frac{3}{4}$ of the height that it falls from.

Height dropped, cm ⟶ | Divide by 4 | ⟶ | Multiply by 3 | ⟶ Height of rebound, cm

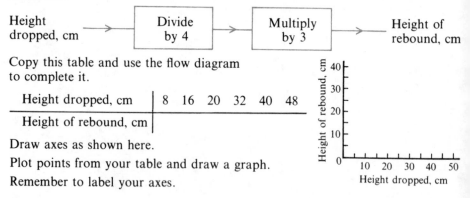

Copy this table and use the flow diagram to complete it.

Height dropped, cm	8	16	20	32	40	48
Height of rebound, cm						

Draw axes as shown here.

Plot points from your table and draw a graph.

Remember to label your axes.

3 You go on a holiday to France or Spain where distances are measured in kilometres. You can use this flow diagram to change kilometres into miles.

Kilometres ⟶ | Divide by 8 | ⟶ | Multiply by 5 | ⟶ Miles

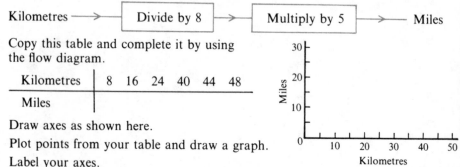

Copy this table and complete it by using the flow diagram.

Kilometres	8	16	24	40	44	48
Miles						

Draw axes as shown here.

Plot points from your table and draw a graph.

Label your axes.

Graphical applications

4 To hire a car, a car firm charges you £20 basic and then 2 pence for every mile which you travel.

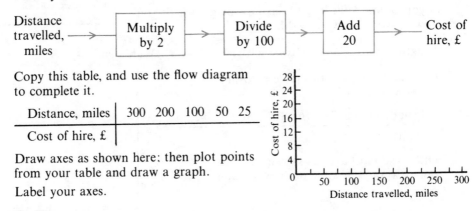

Copy this table, and use the flow diagram to complete it.

Distance, miles	300	200	100	50	25
Cost of hire, £					

Draw axes as shown here; then plot points from your table and draw a graph.
Label your axes.

5 As a child grows up, it needs less and less sleep. This flow diagram gives you a rough guide to the number of hours of sleep needed at different ages.

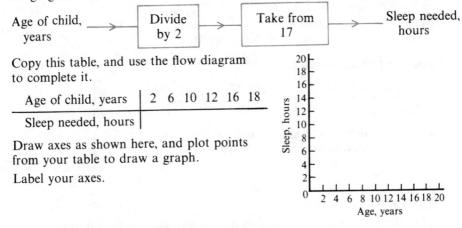

Copy this table, and use the flow diagram to complete it.

Age of child, years	2	6	10	12	16	18
Sleep needed, hours						

Draw axes as shown here, and plot points from your table to draw a graph.
Label your axes.

6 Preston to London is 200 miles. How long it takes you for this journey depends on how fast you go.

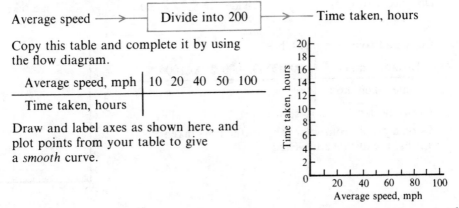

Copy this table and complete it by using the flow diagram.

Average speed, mph	10	20	40	50	100
Time taken, hours					

Draw and label axes as shown here, and plot points from your table to give a *smooth* curve.

Graphical applications

7 If you have to draw a rectangle with an area of 48 cm², you can choose many different lengths and widths.

If you choose your length, this flow diagram tells you how to work out your width.

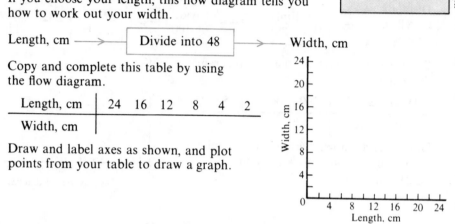

Length, cm ⟶ | Divide into 48 | ⟶ Width, cm

Copy and complete this table by using the flow diagram.

Length, cm	24	16	12	8	4	2
Width, cm						

Draw and label axes as shown, and plot points from your table to draw a graph.

8 The mass of the average man can be found if you know his height, by using this flow diagram.

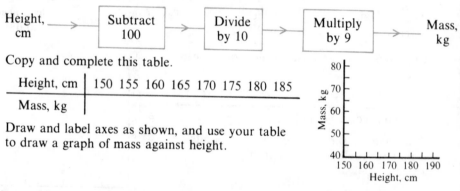

Height, cm ⟶ | Subtract 100 | ⟶ | Divide by 10 | ⟶ | Multiply by 9 | ⟶ Mass, kg

Copy and complete this table.

Height, cm	150	155	160	165	170	175	180	185
Mass, kg								

Draw and label axes as shown, and use your table to draw a graph of mass against height.

9 When you fly, you have to arrive at the airport one hour before your flight.
The time you spend in the air depends on how far you have to go.
The total time for the whole journey can be found from this flow diagram.

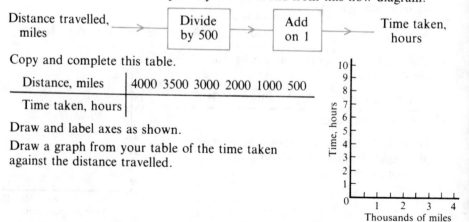

Distance travelled, miles ⟶ | Divide by 500 | ⟶ | Add on 1 | ⟶ Time taken, hours

Copy and complete this table.

Distance, miles	4000	3500	3000	2000	1000	500
Time taken, hours						

Draw and label axes as shown.

Draw a graph from your table of the time taken against the distance travelled.

Graphical applications

10   If you drop a stone from a tall building, this flow diagram tells you how to
      calculate how far it drops after a time given in seconds.

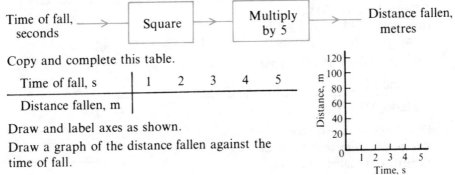

Copy and complete this table.

Time of fall, s	1	2	3	4	5
Distance fallen, m					

Draw and label axes as shown.

Draw a graph of the distance fallen against the
time of fall.

11   If a car has good brakes and it has to stop quickly on a dry road, then the
      distance needed to stop can be calculated using this flow diagram.

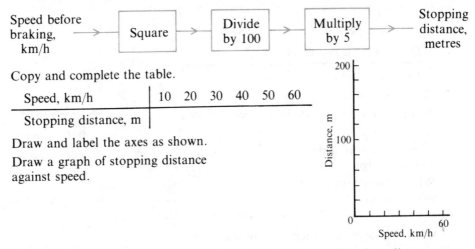

Copy and complete the table.

Speed, km/h	10	20	30	40	50	60
Stopping distance, m						

Draw and label the axes as shown.

Draw a graph of stopping distance
against speed.

12   To find the area of a circle, you need to know its radius. This flow diagram
      gives instructions for calculating the area.

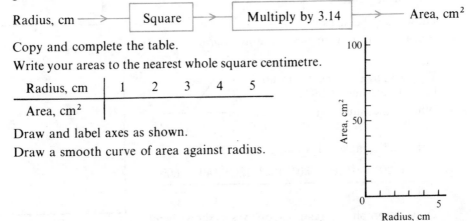

Copy and complete the table.

Write your areas to the nearest whole square centimetre.

Radius, cm	1	2	3	4	5
Area, cm^2					

Draw and label axes as shown.

Draw a smooth curve of area against radius.

Graphical applications

Part 2 Without flow diagrams

1 You go on holiday to Germany, and for every £1 you change, you receive
4 Deutschmarks (DM).
How many DM do you get for
a £2   b £3   c £4   d £5?

Copy this table and enter your answers.

Pounds, £	1	2	3	4	5
Marks, DM	4				

Draw axes as shown here.
Plot points from your table and draw a graph.
Remember to label your axes.

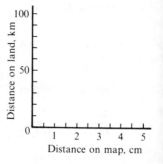

2 On a map of England, each centimetre stands for 20 km.
How many km are given by
a 2 cm   b 3 cm   c 4 cm   d 5 cm?

Copy this table and enter your answers.

Distance on map, cm	1	2	3	4	5
Distance on land, km	20				

Draw and label axes as shown.
Plot points from your table to draw a graph.

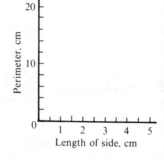

3 The perimeter of a shape is the distance
round its edge.

What is the perimeter of a square with
sides of length
a 1 cm   b 2 cm   c 3 cm   d 4 cm?

Copy this table and enter your answers.

Length of sides, cm	1	2	3	4	5
Perimeter, cm					

Draw and label axes.
Plot points from your table to draw a graph.

4 The two angles x and y add up
to a straight line of 180°.

What is the value of y when x is
a 20°   b 40°   c 80°   d 120°?

Copy and complete this table.

x	20°	40°	60°	80°	100°	120°	140°	160°
y								

Draw the graph of y against x, on axes as shown here.

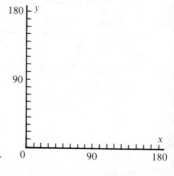

Graphical applications

5  How many degrees does the minute-hand of a clock turn through in

   a 1 hour   **b** 30 min

   c 15 min   **d** 5 min

   e 10 min?

Copy and complete this table.

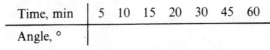

Time, min	5	10	15	20	30	45	60
Angle, °							

Draw the graph of angle against time on axes as shown here.

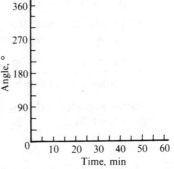

6 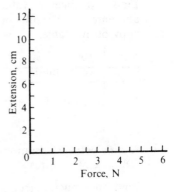 A spring extends 2 cm for every 1 newton force hung on its end.

How far will it extend when you apply a force of

   a 2 newtons   **b** 3 newtons

   c 4 newtons   **d** 5 newtons?

Copy and complete this table.

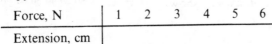

Force, N	1	2	3	4	5	6
Extension, cm						

Draw the graph of force against extension on axes as shown here.

7 A tap is left running into a water tank.

Every minute the water level rises $1\frac{1}{2}$ cm.

How high does it rise after

   a 2 min   **b** 4 min   **c** 6 min   **d** 7 min?

Copy and complete this table.

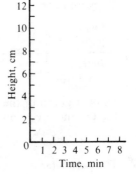

Time, min	1	2	3	4	5	6	7	8
Height risen, cm								

Draw the graph of height against time on axes as shown here.

8 Mr Jackson works an 8-hour shift and his lathe is either running or not running over the 8-hour period.

Copy and complete this table.

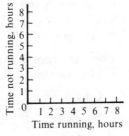

Time running, hours	1	2	3	4	5	6	7	8
Time not running, hours								

Draw a graph of these times on axes as shown.

Graphical applications

9 Bob Reynolds drives his lorry the 400 miles from Leeds to Inverness at a steady speed of 40 mph.

Copy and complete this table to show how far he has gone at various times.

Time from Leeds, hours	2	4	6	8	10
Distance from Leeds, miles					

Draw a graph of distance against time on axes as shown here.

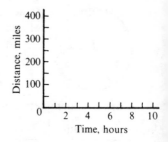

10 Triangle ABC is isosceles with angles B and C equal to x and angle A equal to y.

Find y for different values of x and enter your results in a copy of this table.

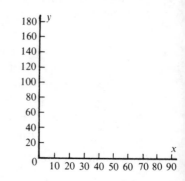

x	10	20	30	40	60	80	90
y							

Draw a graph of y against x on axes as shown.

11 A car's petrol consumption is 20 km per litre, and the car starts a journey with a full tank of 40 litres.

Find how much petrol is left in the tank after travelling the distances given in this table.

Copy and complete the table.

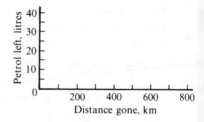

Distance gone, km	0	20	40	100	200	400	600	800
Petrol left, litres								

Draw a graph of the petrol left against the distance gone on axes as shown.

12 The perimeter of a rectangle is always 24 cm, but its width and length vary.

What is its width if its length is
a 11 cm   b 10 cm?

Copy and complete this table and draw a graph of length against width on axes of your choice.

Length, cm	11	10	9	8	6	4	2	1
Width, cm								

Graphical applications

Part 3   Discrete variables

1   The number of spoonfuls of tea you put into the pot depends on the number of persons who are to drink the tea.
The rule is: "One spoonful per person, plus one for the pot".

How many spoonfuls are needed for
a   1 person   b   2 persons
c   3 persons   d   4 persons?

Copy and complete this table.

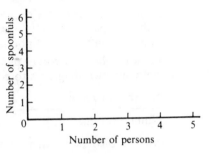

Persons	1	2	3	4	5
Spoonfuls					

Draw a graph of spoonfuls against persons on axes as shown.

2   Two brothers, Malcolm and Tony, share 8 marbles between themselves.

Copy and complete this table to show all the possible ways this sharing can be done.

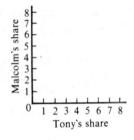

Tony's share	0	1	2	3	4	5	6	7	8
Malcolm's share									

Draw a graph of Tony's share against Malcolm's share.

3   A builder employs one man for 12 hours to do a job.
How long would the same job take
a   2 men   b   3 men?

Copy and complete this table.

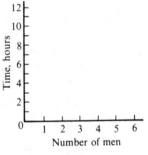

Number of men	1	2	3	4	5	6
Time taken, hours						

Draw a graph of the number of men against the time taken, on axes as shown.

4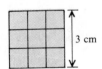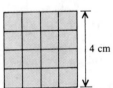

2 cm   3 cm   4 cm

Small squares (of side 1 cm) can be made into large squares as shown above.

Find how many small squares are needed to make the large ones and enter your results in a copy of this table.

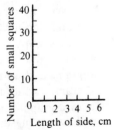

Length of sides of large squares, cm	2	3	4	5	6
Number of small squares needed					

Use axes as shown to draw a graph of your results.

Graphical applications

5

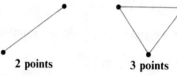

2 points   3 points   4 points   5 points

How many straight lines do you need to join together all pairs of points when you have
a   just 2 points   b   3 points   c   4 points?
Copy this table and enter your results.
Draw your own diagrams to complete the table.

Number of points	2	3	4	5	6	7
Number of lines						

Draw a graph of points against lines using these axes.

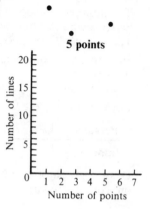

6   A car-ferry's charges depend on the length of the vehicle.
Up to and including 3 m, the charge is £1.
From 3 m up to (and including) 4 m, the charge is £2.
From 4 m up to (and including) 5 m, the charge is £3.
From 5 m up to (and including) 6 m, the charge is £4.
The ferry cannot take vehicles over 6 metres.

Using axes as shown here, draw the above information as a graph.

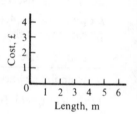

7   The charge for making a long-distance call on the telephone via the operator, is:
     66p for the first 3 minutes
then 22p for each minute (or less) after the first three minutes.
How much will it cost to make a call lasting:
a   2 min   b $3\frac{1}{2}$ min   c   4 min   d $4\frac{1}{2}$ min   e   5 min?
Copy and complete this table.

Length of call, min	0 to 3	from 3 to 4	from 4 to 5	from 5 to 6	from 6 to 7
Cost of call, pence					

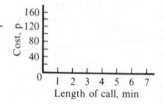

Draw a graph from this table of length of call against cost, on axes as shown here.

8   The Post Office charges the following rates for certain letters sent overseas.

Not over 10 grams 30p
10 grams and up to 20 grams.....45p
20 grams and up to 30 grams.....60p
30 grams and up to 40 grams.....75p
40 grams and up to 50 grams.....90p
50 grams and up to 60 grams 105p

Draw a graph of this information on axes as shown alongside.

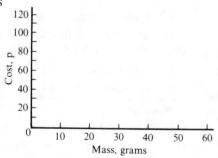

Lines and Curves

Straight lines

Parabolas

Other curves

Points of intersection

Straight lines

Part 1   Flow diagrams

1   x ⟶ ▢ **Double** ▢ ⟶ ▢ **Add 3** ▢ ⟶ y

    a Copy and complete these ordered pairs (or co-ordinates) by using this flow diagram to find the y values.

        $(4, \ldots)\ (3, \ldots)\ (2, \ldots)\ (1, \ldots)\ (\frac{1}{2}, \ldots)\ (0, \ldots)\ (-1, \ldots)\ (-2, \ldots)$

    b Draw axes, labelling the x-axis from -2 to 4 and the y-axis from -6 to 16. Plot the ordered pairs onto your axes.

    c Draw a straight line through the points, and use the flow diagram to write its equation.

2   x ⟶ ▢ **Treble** ▢ ⟶ ▢ **Add 1** ▢ ⟶ y

    a Copy and complete these ordered pairs by using the flow diagram to find the y values.

        $(4, \ldots)\ (3, \ldots)\ (2, \ldots)\ (1, \ldots)\ (\frac{1}{2}, \ldots)\ (0, \ldots)\ (-1, \ldots)\ (-2, \ldots)$

    b Plot the ordered pairs onto the same axes as question **1**.

    c Draw a straight line through the points, and use the flow diagram to write its equation.

3   x ⟶ ▢ **Halve** ▢ ⟶ ▢ **Add 2** ▢ ⟶ y

    a Use this flow diagram to complete these ordered pairs.

        $(4, \ldots)\ (3, \ldots)\ (2, \ldots)\ (1, \ldots)\ (\frac{1}{2}, \ldots)\ (0, \ldots)\ (-1, \ldots)\ (-2, \ldots)$

    b Plot the ordered pairs onto the same axes as question **1**.

    c Draw a straight line through the points, and use the flow diagram to write its equation.

Draw new axes, labelling the x-axis from -2 to 4 and the y-axis from -14 to 14.

For each of these flow diagrams,

    a copy and complete this table

    b plot the ordered pairs onto your axes

    c draw a straight line through the points

    d write on it the equation of the line.

x	-2	-1	0	1	2	3	4
y							

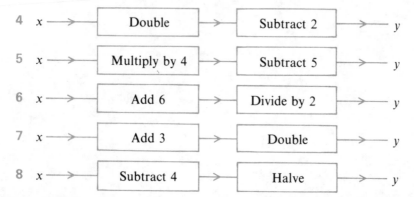

4   x ⟶ ▢ **Double** ▢ ⟶ ▢ **Subtract 2** ▢ ⟶ y

5   x ⟶ ▢ **Multiply by 4** ▢ ⟶ ▢ **Subtract 5** ▢ ⟶ y

6   x ⟶ ▢ **Add 6** ▢ ⟶ ▢ **Divide by 2** ▢ ⟶ y

7   x ⟶ ▢ **Add 3** ▢ ⟶ ▢ **Double** ▢ ⟶ y

8   x ⟶ ▢ **Subtract 4** ▢ ⟶ ▢ **Halve** ▢ ⟶ y

Straight lines

9 For each of these flow diagrams, write the equation connecting x and y.

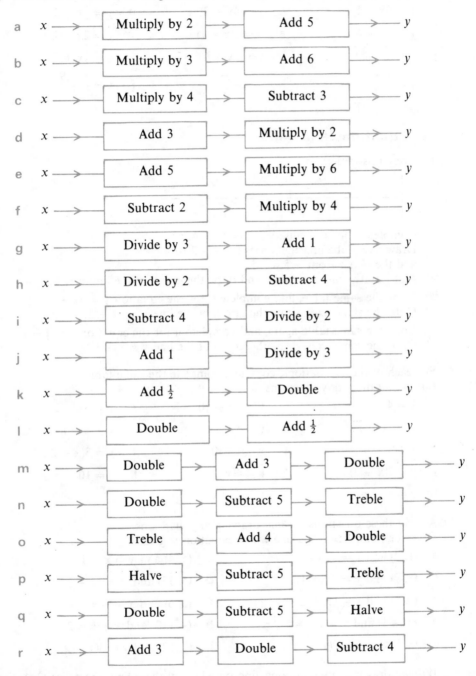

a $x \longrightarrow$ | Multiply by 2 | $\longrightarrow$ | Add 5 | $\longrightarrow y$

b $x \longrightarrow$ | Multiply by 3 | $\longrightarrow$ | Add 6 | $\longrightarrow y$

c $x \longrightarrow$ | Multiply by 4 | $\longrightarrow$ | Subtract 3 | $\longrightarrow y$

d $x \longrightarrow$ | Add 3 | $\longrightarrow$ | Multiply by 2 | $\longrightarrow y$

e $x \longrightarrow$ | Add 5 | $\longrightarrow$ | Multiply by 6 | $\longrightarrow y$

f $x \longrightarrow$ | Subtract 2 | $\longrightarrow$ | Multiply by 4 | $\longrightarrow y$

g $x \longrightarrow$ | Divide by 3 | $\longrightarrow$ | Add 1 | $\longrightarrow y$

h $x \longrightarrow$ | Divide by 2 | $\longrightarrow$ | Subtract 4 | $\longrightarrow y$

i $x \longrightarrow$ | Subtract 4 | $\longrightarrow$ | Divide by 2 | $\longrightarrow y$

j $x \longrightarrow$ | Add 1 | $\longrightarrow$ | Divide by 3 | $\longrightarrow y$

k $x \longrightarrow$ | Add $\frac{1}{2}$ | $\longrightarrow$ | Double | $\longrightarrow y$

l $x \longrightarrow$ | Double | $\longrightarrow$ | Add $\frac{1}{2}$ | $\longrightarrow y$

m $x \longrightarrow$ | Double | $\longrightarrow$ | Add 3 | $\longrightarrow$ | Double | $\longrightarrow y$

n $x \longrightarrow$ | Double | $\longrightarrow$ | Subtract 5 | $\longrightarrow$ | Treble | $\longrightarrow y$

o $x \longrightarrow$ | Treble | $\longrightarrow$ | Add 4 | $\longrightarrow$ | Double | $\longrightarrow y$

p $x \longrightarrow$ | Halve | $\longrightarrow$ | Subtract 5 | $\longrightarrow$ | Treble | $\longrightarrow y$

q $x \longrightarrow$ | Double | $\longrightarrow$ | Subtract 5 | $\longrightarrow$ | Halve | $\longrightarrow y$

r $x \longrightarrow$ | Add 3 | $\longrightarrow$ | Double | $\longrightarrow$ | Subtract 4 | $\longrightarrow y$

10 Use each of the flow diagrams in question **9** to find the y value for the point where $x = 6$.

11 Use each of the flow diagrams in question **9** *in reverse* to find the x value for the point where $y = 12$.

Straight lines

12 Draw your own flow diagrams for these equations.

    a $y = 6x + 5$ b $y = 4x + 2$ c $y = \frac{1}{2}x + 3$

    d $y = \frac{1}{2}x - 4$ e $y = 2(x - 1)$ f $y = 2x - 1$

    g $y = 4(x + 6)$ h $y = 4x + 6$ i $y = \frac{1}{2}x + 7$

    j $y = \dfrac{x + 7}{2}$ k $y = \dfrac{x - 5}{3}$ l $y = \dfrac{x + 9}{4}$

Part 2   Equations and points

1 a Copy this table.

x	−2	−1	0	1	2	3	4
y							

    Complete it for the equation $y = 2x + 4$.
    Draw axes, labelling the x-axis from -2 to 4
    and the y-axis from -5 to 15.
    Plot points using the table, and draw the graph of the line $y = 2x + 4$.

  b Copy the same table, and complete it for the equation $y = 3x + 2$.
    Onto the same axes, draw the graph of the line $y = 3x + 2$.

  c Copy the same table again, and complete it for the equation $y = x - 1$.
    Onto the same axes, draw the graph of the line $y = x - 1$.

2 For each of these equations, copy and complete the same table.
   But do *not* draw any diagrams.

    a $y = 4x + 8$ b $y = 5x + 10$ c $y = 3x - 2$

    d $y = \frac{1}{2}x + 1$ e $y = \frac{1}{2}x - 1$ f $x + y = 8$

    g $x + y = 4$ h $x + y = 0$ i $y = 3(x + 2)$

    j $y = 2(x + 3)$ k $y = 4(x + 1)$ l $y = 10 - x$

    m $y = 7 - x$ n $y = 4 - x$

3 Answer these questions *without* drawing any diagrams.
   Does the point lie on the line whose equation is given?

    a (1, 3) and $y = x + 4$ b (5, 4) and $y = x - 1$

    c (3, 7) and $y = 2x + 1$ d (5, 13) and $y = 2x - 3$

    e (0, 8) and $y = 6x + 2$ f (3, 6) and $x + y = 9$

    g (5, −1) and $x + y = 4$ h (−1, 3) and $x + y = 2$

    i (3, 8) and $y = 2(x + 1)$ j (2, 12) and $y = 3(x - 2)$

4 *Without* drawing any diagrams, find on which of these lines the point (3, 1) lies.

    a $y = x - 2$ b $y = 2x - 5$ c $y = 3x - 10$

    d $x + y = 4$ e $x - y = 4$ f $y = \frac{1}{2}x$

    g $y = \frac{1}{2}(x - 1)$ h $y = 2(4 - x)$

Straight lines

5 On which of these lines does the point $(-2, 1)$ lie?

    a $y = x + 3$ b $y = 2x + 5$ c $x + y = 1$

    d $x + y + 1 = 0$ e $x + 2y = 0$ f $y = \frac{1}{2}x - 2$

    g $y = 3(x + 1)$ h $y = \frac{1}{2}(x + 4)$

6 Which of these points do *not* lie on the line $y = 2x - 3$?
  $(2, 1)$ $(5, 7)$ $(4, 1)$ $(1, 1)$ $(0, -3)$ $(2\frac{1}{2}, 2)$ $(\frac{1}{2}, -2)$ $(1\frac{1}{2}, 0)$ $(\frac{1}{4}, \frac{1}{2})$

7 Which of these points do *not* lie on the line $y = 3x - 5$?
  $(3, 4)$ $(1, -2)$ $(2\frac{1}{2}, 2\frac{1}{2})$ $(0, 5)$ $(-1, -8)$ $(-2, -1)$ $(\frac{1}{2}, 3\frac{1}{2})$ $(4, 7)$ $(3\frac{1}{2}, -\frac{1}{2})$

8 Only *one* of these points does *not* lie on the line $y = 2x + 1$.
  Find which point this is.
  $(0, 1)$ $(3, 7)$ $(-2, -3)$ $(-1, -1)$ $(1, 1)$ $(\frac{1}{2}, 2)$

9 Which *one* of these points does *not* lie on the line $y = 5 - 2x$?
  $(0, 5)$ $(1, 3)$ $(\frac{1}{2}, 4)$ $(-1, 7)$ $(2\frac{1}{2}, 0)$ $(-2\frac{1}{2}, 0)$

10 Which *one* of these points lies on both the line $y = x + 5$ and the line $y = 4x - 1$?
  $(1, 6)$ $(3, 8)$ $(1, 3)$ $(2, 7)$ $(3, 11)$

11 Which one of these points is where the two lines $y = x - 2$ and $x + y = 8$ cross?
  $(7, 5)$ $(2, 0)$ $(5, 3)$ $(6, 2)$ $(9, -1)$

12 Which one of these points is the point of intersection of the lines $x + y = 5$ and $y = 2x - 1$?
  $(1, 4)$ $(3, 2)$ $(-1, 4)$ $(2, 3)$ $(4, -1)$

13 If the point $(x, 7)$ lies on the line $y = 3x + 1$, what is the value of x?

14 These points all lie on the line $y = 4x - 3$. Find the x value of each point.

    a $(x, 1)$ b $(x, 9)$ c $(x, -3)$ d $(x, -1)$

Part 3 Gradients of lines

1 The steepness of a line can be measured by its gradient.

Lines which have the same gradient are parallel.

Which of these lines have the same gradient as

    a line Q

    b line R

    c line T

    d line S?

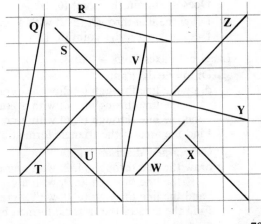

Straight lines

2　Find the gradients of the lettered lines in this diagram.

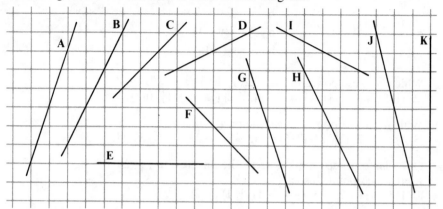

3　Draw and label both axes from 0 to 8.
Join together the following pairs of points with straight lines, and write down the gradient of each line.

a　(1, 4) and (3, 8)　　　b　(1, 4) and (7, 7)　　　c　(1, 4) and (6, 4)

d　(1, 4) and (5, 0)　　　e　(1, 4) and (3, 0)　　　f　(1, 4) and (1, 0)

4　Draw axes labelled from 0 to 8.
Find the gradient of the lines through each of these pairs of points.

a　(2, 1) (3, 3)　　　b　(1, 3) (2, 6)　　　c　(1, 2) (4, 5)

d　(1, 1) (3, 1)　　　e　(4, 5) (6, 1)　　　f　(4, 6) (6, 4)

g　(4, 0) (6, 1)　　　h　(3, 0) (5, 3)　　　i　(0, 6) (1, 0)

j　(4, 2) (4, 3)

5　a　Draw the line through (0, 2) with a gradient of +2.
Does it contain the point (2, 6)?

　b　Draw the line through (2, 4) with a gradient of +1.
Does it contain the point (5, 6)?

　c　Draw the line through (4, 5) with a gradient of 0.
Does it contain the point (0, 5)?

　d　Draw the line through (4, 4) with a gradient of −2.
Does it contain the point (6, 1)?

　e　Draw the line through (2, 2) with a gradient of −$\frac{1}{2}$.
Does it contain the point (5, 1)?

6　Label both axes from −1 to 8.

　a　Onto one diagram,
draw the line through (1, 2) with a gradient of 0
　　　the line through (3, 0) with a gradient of ∞
and the line through (4, 6) with a gradient of −1.
Find the area of the triangle formed by these three lines.

　b　Onto a new diagram,
draw the line through (4, 2) with a gradient of 0
　　　the line through (0, 0) with a gradient of +1
and the line through (6, 0) with a gradient of −1.
Find the area of the triangle formed by these three lines.

Straight lines

c   Onto a new diagram,
    draw the line through (4, 1) with a gradient of $+\frac{1}{2}$
        the line through (2, 5) with a gradient of ∞
    and the line through (6, 2) with a gradient of -1.
    Find the area of the triangle formed by these three lines.

d   Onto a new diagram,
    draw the line through (1, 2) with a gradient of $+2$
        the line through (3, 6) with a gradient of -1
    and the line through (2, 2) with a gradient of 0.
    Find the area of the triangle formed by these three lines.

e   Onto a new diagram,
    draw the line through $(-1, 6)$ with a gradient of -2
        the line through (5, 6) with a gradient of -2
        the line through (4, 2) with a gradient of 0
    and the line through (4, 6) with a gradient of 0.
    Find the area of the parallelogram formed by these four lines.

7   Draw and label the x-axis from 0 to 12 and the y-axis from 0 to 9.
    Copy this table.

	a	b	c	d	e	f
Gradient of line						
Angle with x-axis						
Tangent of angle						

a   Draw the line through (1, 0) and (1, 9).
    Find the gradient of the line and enter your answer in the table.
    Use a protractor to find the angle between this line and the x-axis. Enter
    your angle in the table.
    Use tangent tables to find the tangent of this angle, and enter your result in
    the table.

b   Draw the line through (2, 0) and (4, 8).
    Find the gradient of the line.
    Use a protractor to measure the angle between the line and the x-axis.
    Use tables to find the tangent of this angle.
    Enter your results in the table.

c   Draw the line through (3, 0) and (6, 9).
    Find the gradient of this line, the angle it makes with the x-axis, and the
    tangent of this angle.
    Enter your results as before.

d   Repeat for the line through (4, 0) and (8, 8).

e   Repeat for the line through (5, 0) and (11, 6).

f   Repeat for the line through (6, 0) and (12, 3).

g   What do you notice about your results?

8   On squared paper, draw any line with each of these gradients.
    Use your protractor to measure the angle each makes with the x direction.
    Find the tangent of each angle from tables; and construct your own table for
    your results like that in question **7**.
    a   Gradient of $4\frac{1}{2}$ b   Gradient of $3\frac{1}{2}$ c   Gradient of $2\frac{1}{2}$
    d   Gradient of $1\frac{1}{2}$ e   Gradient of $\frac{1}{4}$

Straight lines

9   Use your tangent tables only (do *not* draw any diagrams) to answer these
    questions.

What is the gradient of a line which makes an angle with the x-axis of:

a   78°   b   58°   c   56.3°   d   11.3°
e   5.7°   f   32°   g   84.3°   h   89.4°?

What is the angle between a line and the x-axis when the gradient of the line is:

i   1.60   j   2.90   k   1.02   l   0.875
m   0.501   n   0.400   o   4.44   p   11.0?

10 a   This road sign means that a steep hill has
        a gradient of 1 in 10 or $\frac{1}{10}$.

        Change $\frac{1}{10}$ to a decimal and then use
        tangent tables to find the angle α at which
        the road is climbing up the hill.

        Find the angles of slope for hills which have these signs.*

b   c   d   e   f

11 The scale of this map is 1 cm for
    10 metres, and the contours are
    drawn at 5-metre intervals.

    Three paths leave point A for the
    points X, Y and Z.

    For each path,
    a   use a ruler to find the horizontal
        distance covered
    b   find the vertical height risen
    c   calculate the gradient of the path
    d   use tables to find the angle at
        which each path is rising.

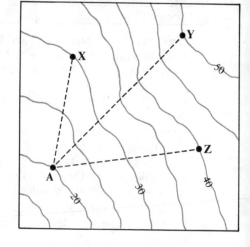

12 Label both axes from 0 to 10.
    Copy this table.

	a	b	c	d	e	f
Gradient of one line						
Gradient of other line						
Angle between lines						

a   Join (1, 5) to (3, 9) and then join (1, 5) to (5, 3).
    Find the gradient of both these lines.
    Measure the angle between the lines with a protractor.
    Enter your results in the table.

*Footnote: You will find that other road signs give this information as a percentage. If 1:10 is
10%, what would 1:5 be?

Straight lines

b   Join (2, 3) to (4, 9) and then join (2, 3) to (5, 2).
Find the gradient of both these lines.
Measure the angle between them with a protractor.
Enter your results in the table.

c   Join (8, 10) to (10, 6) and join (6, 4) to (10, 6).
Find the gradient and angle as before, and enter your results in the table.

d   Join (9, 0) to (10, 4) and join (6, 5) to (10, 4).
Repeat as before.

e   Join (3, 1) to (4, 7) and join (4, 7) to (10, 6).
Repeat as before.

f   Join (5, 10) to (8, 7) and join (6, 10) to (3, 7).
Repeat as before.

g   What do you notice about your results?

13   Write, without drawing a diagram, the gradient of any line which is at right angles to a line with a gradient of

a -5 b -3 c $+\frac{1}{4}$ d $-\frac{1}{3}$ e $+8$
f $+10$ g -7 h $+1$ i $-\frac{3}{4}$ j 0.

14   Say (without drawing any diagrams) whether the two lines with these gradients are perpendicular or not.

a $+2$ and $-\frac{1}{2}$ b $+6$ and $-\frac{1}{6}$ c -4 and $+\frac{1}{4}$
d -3 and $-\frac{1}{3}$ e $+5$ and $+\frac{1}{5}$ f $-\frac{1}{10}$ and -10
g $-\frac{1}{9}$ and $+9$ h $+\frac{3}{4}$ and $-1\frac{1}{3}$ i $+\frac{2}{3}$ and $-1\frac{1}{2}$
j $-\frac{7}{8}$ and $+1\frac{1}{8}$ k $-\frac{3}{5}$ and $+1\frac{2}{5}$ l 0 and ∞

15   a   Answer this problem by drawing and labelling both axes from 0 to 8.

Draw the line through (2, 0) with a gradient of $+3$.

Draw the line through (2, 0) with a gradient of $+\frac{1}{2}$.

Use a protractor to measure
  (i)   the angle between the first line and the x-axis
  (ii) the angle between the second line and the x-axis
  (iii) the angle between the two lines.

b   Answer this problem *without* any diagrams.

One line has a gradient of $+5$.

Another line has a gradient of $+2$.

Use tangent tables to find
  (i)   the angle between the first line and the x-axis
  (ii) the angle between the second line and the x-axis
  (iii) the angle between the two lines.

16   Find the angles between the pairs of lines with these gradients
          (i)   by drawing them on squared paper and using your protractor
and then (ii)   by calculation using your tangent tables.

a $+2$ and $+1$ b $+3$ and $+1$ c $+4$ and $+1$
d $+2$ and $+\frac{1}{2}$ e $+5$ and $+1$ f $+5$ and $+\frac{1}{2}$

Straight lines

Part 4 Gradient and intercept

1 Copy this table four times.

x	-1	0	1	2	3	4
y						

Complete a table for each
of these four equations:

$y = 2x + 4$ and $y = 2x + 1$ and $y = 2x - 1$ and $y = 2x - 3$.

Draw and label the x-axis from -1 to 4 and the y-axis from -8 to 12.

Use your four tables to draw four straight lines on your axes.

Write down the gradient of all the lines.

What has this gradient in common with the equations of the lines?

2 Copy this table four times.

x	-2	-1	0	1	2	3	4
y							

Complete a table for each
of these four equations:

$y = 2x + 4$ and $y = x + 4$ and $y = 0x + 4$ and $y = -x + 4$.

Draw and label the x-axis from -2 to 4 and the y-axis from 0 to 12.

Use your four tables to draw four straight lines on your axes.

Write down the intercept on the y-axis for each line.

What has this y-intercept in common with the equations of the lines?

3 Copy and complete this table for the five straight lines on this diagram.

	a	b	c	d	e
Gradient					
y-intercept					
Equation	$y =$	$y =$	$y =$	$y =$	$y =$

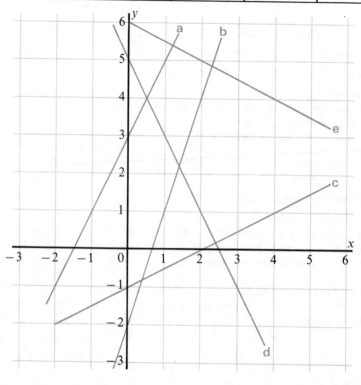

Straight lines

4   By looking at the
    gradients and
    y-intercepts of
    the lettered lines
    on this diagram,
    write their
    equations.

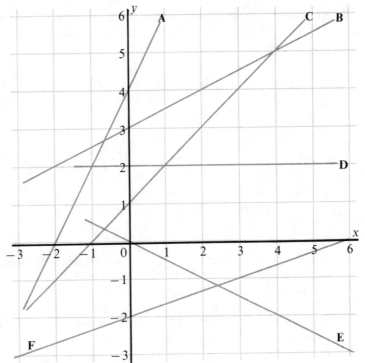

5   Draw and label both axes from -6 to 6.
    Find the gradient, the y-intercept, and hence the equations of the straight lines
    through these pairs of points.
    a   (1, 3) and (2, 5)   b $(-2, 3)$ and (4, 6)   c $(-2, -4)$ and (4, 2)
    d   (0, -1) and (3, -4)   e $(-2, -3)$ and (4, -6)

6   Draw axes, labelling the x-axis from -2 to 10 and the y-axis from -10 to 10.
    Find the gradient, the y-intercept, and hence the equations of the straight lines
    through these pairs of points.
    a   (1, 5) and (2, 7)   b   (1, 3) and (4, 6)   c   (1, -6) and (5, 6)
    d   (2, -1) and (8, 2)   e   (1, -2) and (7, -8)   f   (1, -5) and (3, -9)
    g $(-2, -5)$ and (4, -8)   h $(-2, 9)$ and (5, 2)

7   Write the gradient and y-intercept for each of these lines, *without* drawing their
    graphs.
    a $y = 4x + 2$ b $y = 2x + 4$ c $y = 4x - 2$
    d $y = 3x + 6$ e $y = x - 3$ f $y = 5x - 1$
    g $y = 10 - 2x$ h $y = 7 - 3x$ i $y = \frac{1}{2}x - 1$
    j $y = 3 - \frac{1}{4}x$ k $y = \frac{1}{2} - 3x$ l $y = -5x + 4$
    m $y = 2 - x$ n $y = -x + 8$ o $y = 1 - x$
    p $y = 3x$ q $y = \frac{1}{2}x$ r $y = -4x$
    s $y = 2$ t $y = -3$ u $y = 0$

85

Straight lines

8 Rearrange these equations to make y the subject (i.e. so that the equation reads $y = \ldots$); and hence write the gradient and y-intercept of each line. Do *not* draw any diagrams.

a $2y = 6x + 5$

b $2y = 3x + 8$

c $3y = 6x - 7$

d $4y = 2x - 5$

e $5y = x + 2$

f $\frac{1}{2}y = x - 3$

g $\frac{1}{3}y = 2x + 1$

h $\frac{1}{4}y = x - 1$

i $\frac{1}{4}y = 3x + 1$

j $\frac{1}{3}y = 4x - 3$

k $\frac{1}{5}y = x + 2$

l $y - 3x = 4$

m $y - 2x = 1$

n $y - 5x = 0$

o $y + 2x = 3$

p $2y - 4x = 3$

q $3y - 12x = 5$

r $2y + x = 0$

s $4y + 2x = 1$

t $\frac{1}{2}y - x = 3$

u $\frac{1}{4}y - 2x = 1$

v $\frac{1}{3}y + 3x = 5$

w $2(y + 3x) = 5$

x $3(y - 1) = 4x$

y $\frac{1}{2}(y - 2x) = 4$

z $4(y + 3) = 5x$

9 On axes labelled from -1 to 6, draw the line $y = 2x - 1$.
   Also draw the line parallel to $y = 2x - 1$ through the point (1, 5). Find
   a the gradient   b the y-intercept
   c the equation of this parallel line.

10 Onto axes labelled from 0 to 6, join point $A(0, 6)$ to point $B(4, 4)$.
    Label M, the midpoint of AB.
    Draw the line through M at right angles to AB. Find
    a the gradient   b the y-intercept   c the equation of this line.

11 Onto axes labelled from 0 to 6, join point $P(0, 4)$ to point $Q(4, 0)$.
    Label the point $A(3, 5)$.
    Draw a line through A perpendicular to PQ, and write down its equation by finding its gradient and y-intercept.

12 Onto axes labelled from 0 to 6, draw a square with corners $A(3, 2)$, $B(4, 4)$, $C(6, 3)$, $D(5, 1)$.
    Draw the diagonal AC and find the equation of this diagonal.

13 Draw and label both axes from -2 to 5.
    Draw the rectangle with corners $W(1, 1)$, $X(3, 1)$, $Y(3, 5)$, $Z(1, 5)$.
    Find the equation of the diagonal WY.

14 Draw and label both axes from -2 to 6.
    The points $P(2, -1)$, $Q(6, 1)$, $R(4, 5)$ and S are the four corners of a square.
    a Plot P, Q and R. Draw the square and write the co-ordinates of S.
    b Find the equation of the side SR.
    c Find the equation of the side SP.
    d Find the equation of the diagonal SQ.

15 Draw and label both axes from 0 to 6.
    Join point $A(1, 4)$ to point $B(1, 1)$, and also $A(1, 4)$ to $C(5, 4)$.
    Draw the straight line which bisects the angle BAC and find its equation.

Straight lines

16 Draw and label both axes from -6 to 6.
   a   Join point $A(-3, 1)$ to point $B(-6, 1)$, and also $A(-3, 1)$ to $C(-3, 5)$.
       Draw the straight line which bisects angle BAC and find its equation.
   b   Join point $M(1, 2)$ to point $L(-1, 6)$, and also $M(1, 2)$ to $N(5, 4)$.
       Draw the straight line which bisects the angle LMN and find its equation.

17 The lines $y = 1$ and $x = 3$ are two sides of a right-angled triangle.
   Draw axes labelled from 0 to 6 and draw the lines.
   If the points $(1, 1)$ and $(3, 5)$ are two corners of the triangle, find:
   a   the co-ordinates of the other corner
   b   the equation of the third side of the triangle
   c   the area of the triangle.

18 Draw and label both axes from -4 to 8.
   a   Draw a kite with corners $A(4, 8)$, $B(6, 4)$, $C(1, -1)$, $D(0, 6)$.
   b   Label the point of intersection of the diagonals with the letter M and write
       its co-ordinates.
   c   What size is the angle between DM and AM?
   d   Find the equations of these lines:
       (i) DA (ii) DB (iii) DC (iv) CB (v) CA.

19 The points $(1, 1)$ and $(5, 3)$ are the two corners of a square at the opposite ends
   of one of its diagonals. By drawing a suitable diagram, find:
   a   the co-ordinates of the other two corners of the square
   b   the equations of its two diagonals
   c   the area of the square.

20 A square has a centre $(-1, 1)$ and two corners $(-4, 0)$ and $(-2, 4)$. Find:
   a   the co-ordinates of the other two corners
   b   the equations of the four sides of the square
   c   its area.

Part 5   The three methods

Method 1   Point by point

1 Draw axes, labelling the x-axis from 0 to 6 and the y-axis from 0 to 12.
   Copy and complete the co-ordinates of the three points for each of the equations.
   Plot the points and draw the lines, labelling each line with its equation.
   a   Points $(3, \ldots)$, $(5, \ldots)$, $(0, \ldots)$ on the line $y = 2x + 1$
   b   Points $(3, \ldots)$, $(4, \ldots)$, $(1, \ldots)$ on the line $y = 3x - 2$
   c   Points $(4, \ldots)$, $(2, \ldots)$, $(0, \ldots)$ on the line $y = \frac{1}{2}x + 4$
   d   Points $(4, \ldots)$, $(2, \ldots)$, $(0, \ldots)$ on the line $x + y = 5$

2 Draw new axes, labelling the x-axis from 0 to 6 and the y-axis from -3 to 6.
   Repeat the above instructions for these points and lines.
   a   Points $(4, \ldots)$, $(2, \ldots)$, $(1, \ldots)$ on the line $y = 2x - 3$
   b   Points $(4, \ldots)$, $(2, \ldots)$, $(0, \ldots)$ on the line $y = \frac{1}{2}x - 1$
   c   Points $(1, \ldots)$, $(2, \ldots)$, $(4, \ldots)$ on the line $x + y = 2$
   d   Points $(1, \ldots)$, $(3, \ldots)$, $(5, \ldots)$ on the line $x + y = 3$

Straight lines

3 Draw new axes, labelling the x-axis from 0 to 6 and the y-axis from -5 to 5.
Repeat the same instructions for these points and lines.
   a   Points $(5, \ldots), (2, \ldots), (0, \ldots)$ on the line $y = x - 4$
   b   Points $(5, \ldots), (2, \ldots), (0, \ldots)$ on the line $y = x - 2$
   c   Points $(6, \ldots), (3, \ldots), (0, \ldots)$ on the line $y = \frac{1}{3}x - 5$
   d   Points $(1, \ldots), (3, \ldots), (6, \ldots)$ on the line $x + y = 4$

4 Draw new axes, labelling the x-axis from -3 to 3 and the y-axis from -5 to 10.
Repeat for these points and lines.
   a   Points $(3, \ldots), (0, \ldots), (-1, \ldots)$ on the line $y = x + 2$
   b   Points $(1, \ldots), (-1, \ldots), (-3, \ldots)$ on the line $y = x + 4$
   c   Points $(2, \ldots), (-1, \ldots), (-3, \ldots)$ on the line $y = 2x + 5$
   d   Points $(2, \ldots), (-1, \ldots), (-2, \ldots)$ on the line $y = 2x - 1$

5 Repeat on new axes where both are labelled from -5 to 5.
   a   Points $(4, \ldots), (2, \ldots), (-2, \ldots)$ on the line $y = \frac{1}{2}x - 3$
   b   Points $(3, \ldots), (-1, \ldots), (-3, \ldots)$ on the line $y = \frac{1}{2}x - \frac{1}{2}$
   c   Points $(4, \ldots), (-2, \ldots), (-5, \ldots)$ on the line $y = \frac{1}{3}x + \frac{2}{3}$
   d   Points $(1, \ldots), (-2, \ldots), (-4, \ldots)$ on the line $x + y = 1$

6 Draw and label both axes from 0 to 6.
Choose your own values of x to plot points and draw both these lines onto your axes: $y = 2x - 3$ and $y = x - \frac{1}{2}$.
Write down their point of intersection.

7 Draw and label both axes from -5 to 5.
Choose your own values of x to plot points and draw all these lines onto the same axes: $x + y = 2$, $y = x - 4$ and $y = 5 - 2x$.
Show that these three lines intersect at the same point, and write down its co-ordinates.

8 Draw axes, labelling the x-axis from -3 to 5 and the y-axis from 0 to 8.
Draw both these lines $y = 2x + 4$ and $y = 8 - 2x$, and say what type of triangle is formed by the two lines and the x-axis. Shade this triangle and calculate its area.

9 Draw and label the x-axis from -4 to 4 and the y-axis from -4 to 6.
Draw the lines $x + y = 0$ and $y = 6 - 2x$.
Find the area of the triangle formed by
   a   these lines and the x-axis   b   these lines and the y-axis.

Method 2   Gradient and intercept

10 Draw and label both axes from -4 to 8.
Use the y-intercept and gradient of each of these lines, to draw the four lines on your axes.
   a $y = 2x + 1$ b $y = 2x - 3$ c $y = x + 4$ d $y = x - 1$

11 Draw new axes labelled as before and on them draw these lines.
   a $y = \frac{1}{2}x + 1$ b $y = -2x + 6$ c $y = -x + 2$ d $y = -\frac{1}{2}x - 2$

Straight lines

12 Draw new axes labelled as before and on them draw these lines.
   a $y = x + 1$ b $y = \frac{1}{2}x + 3$ c $y = -\frac{1}{2}x - 1$ d $y = -2x$

13 Draw new axes, labelled as before. Before drawing these next lines, you will need to rearrange the equations to make y the subject (i.e. to make the equation read $y = \ldots$).
   a $2y = 3x - 1$ b $2y = -x + 11$ c $2y + x = -4$ d $4y - 16 = x$

14 Draw axes with the x-axis labelled from 0 to 5 and the y-axis from -2 to 6.
   Use the gradient and y-intercept to draw the two lines $y = 2x - 1$ and $y = -\frac{1}{2}x + 4$.
   Write
   a their point of intersection   b the angle between them
   c the area of the triangle made by the two lines and the y-axis.

15 Label both axes from -8 to 8, and draw the lines $y = \frac{1}{2}x + 6$ and $y = -2x - 4$.
   Write
   a their point of intersection   b the angle between them
   c the area of the quadrilateral made by the two lines and the two axes.

16 Label the x-axis from -4 to 4 and the y-axis from 0 to 8.
   Draw the lines $y = 3x$ and $y = x + 4$. Find
   a their point of intersection
   b the area of the triangle made by the two lines and the y-axis
   c the area of the triangle made by the two lines and the x-axis.

17 Label both axes from 0 to 8.
   Draw the lines $y = 2x$ and $y = \frac{1}{2}x$ and $y = 8 - x$.
   a What kind of triangle is made by these three lines?
   b Calculate, without any measuring, the area of this triangle.

Method 3   Using both intercepts

18 Draw and label both axes from -6 to 6.
   For each line, plot two points, one on each axis.
   Using $x = 0$, find a point on the y-axis; and then using $y = 0$, find a point on the x-axis.
   Hence, draw these four straight lines on your axes.
   a $2x + 3y = 12$ b $6x + 5y = 30$ c $2x + y = 4$ d $5x + 3y = 15$

19 Draw axes as before and on them draw these four lines.
   a $2x + 4y = 8$ b $5x + y = 5$ c $3x - 4y = 12$ d $5x + 3y = -15$

20 Draw axes as before for these four lines.
   a $2x - 3y = 12$ b $3x - 5y = 15$ c $-3x + y = 6$ d $-x + 5y = 5$

21 Repeat for these lines on similar axes.
   a $4x + 5y = 10$ b $2x + 3y = -9$ c $7x + 12y = 42$ d $6x + 14y = -21$

22 Repeat for these lines on similar axes.
   a $4x - 9y = 18$ b $22x - 6y = 33$
   c $10x - 14y = -35$ d $9x - 26y = -39$

Straight lines

23 Label both axes from 0 to 12. Draw the lines $2x + y = 12$ and $x + 2y = 12$.
Shade the smallest quadrilateral made by these two lines and the two axes, and
calculate its area.

24 Label both axes from -8 to 8. Draw these four lines:
$3x + 2y = -12$ and $5x + 5y = 40$ and $3x - 4y = 24$ and $x - 2y = -4$.
Find the area of the quadrilateral made by these four lines.

Part 6 Simultaneous equations

1 These simultaneous equations have been plotted as straight lines.
Write down the solutions of the equations by looking at the diagrams.
Then check your answers by substituting them into the equations.

a $y = 2x - 1$
$y = x + 3$

b $y = 3x - 2$
$y = x + 2$

c $y = \frac{1}{2}x + 3$
$y = 2x - 1\frac{1}{2}$.

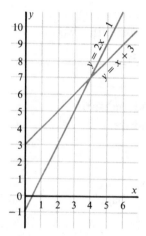   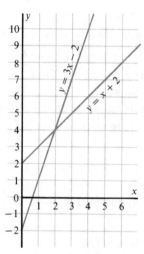   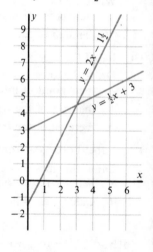

d $x + y = 4$
$2x + y = 6$

e $3x + 8y = 24$
$x + y = 3$

f $3x + 2y = 12$
$2x - y = 1$

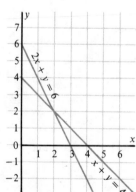   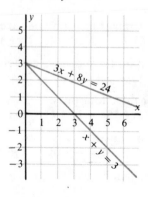   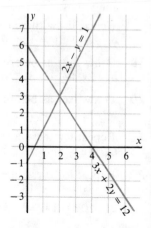

Straight lines

2 **Point by point**

For each pair of simultaneous equations

(i)   draw and label both axes from -2 to 8

(ii) copy and complete the table

(iii) draw two straight lines on your axes

(iv) find the solution.

a $y = x + 1$
$y = 2x$

x	0	1	2	3	4
$y = x + 1$					
$y = 2x$					

b $y = x + 3$
$y = 2x + 1$

x	0	1	2	3
$y = x + 3$				
$y = 2x + 1$				

c $y = \frac{1}{2}x + 4$
$y = x + 2$

x	0	1	2	3	4	5	6
$y = \frac{1}{2}x + 4$							
$y = x + 2$							

d $y = x + 2\frac{1}{2}$
$y = \frac{1}{2}x + 3$

x	0	1	2	3	4	5
$y = x + 2\frac{1}{2}$						
$y = \frac{1}{2}x + 3$						

e $y = x - 1$
$y = \frac{1}{2}x + 2$

x	0	1	2	3	4	5	6	7	8
$y = x - 1$									
$y = \frac{1}{2}x + 2$									

f $y = x + \frac{1}{2}$
$y = 2x - 1$

x	0	1	2	3	4	5
$y = x + \frac{1}{2}$						
$y = 2x - 1$						

g $y = x - 1$
$y = 8 - x$

x	0	1	2	3	4	5	6
$y = x - 1$							
$y = 8 - x$							

h $y = x + 1$
$y = 6 - x$

x	0	1	2	3	4	5	6
$y = x + 1$							
$y = 6 - x$							

Straight lines

3 Using gradient and y-intercept

For each pair of equations, draw and label the x-axis from -3 to 6 and the y-axis from -6 to 6. Using their gradient and y-intercept, draw two straight lines on these axes and find any solutions.

(Note that some simultaneous equations have only *one* solution; some have *no* solutions; and some have an *infinite* number of solutions.)

a $y = x + 4$
$\quad y = 2x + 2$

b $y = 2x - 1$
$\quad y = x + 2$

c $y = 3x - 2$
$\quad y = x + 2$

d $y = 2x + 3$
$\quad y = x + 1$

e $y = x + 1$
$\quad y = x + 3$

f $y = 2x$
$\quad y = x - 3$

g $y = 2x - 1$
$\quad y = 2x + 1$

h $y = \frac{1}{2}x + 4$
$\quad y = 2x - 2$

i $y = 3x + 4$
$\quad y = x + 2$

j $y = \frac{1}{2}x + 1$
$\quad y = x - 2$

k $y = \frac{1}{2}x + 2$
$\quad y = \frac{1}{2}x + 4$

l $y = -2x + 5$
$\quad y = x - 4$

m $y = -3x + 6$
$\quad y = \frac{1}{2}x - 1$

n $y = x + 1$
$\quad y = -2x + 3$

o $y = -x + 6$
$\quad y = -x + 4$

These equations should be rearranged into the form $y = mx + c$ to find the gradients and y-intercepts of the straight lines. Draw and label axes as before. Draw the lines and find any solutions.

p $y - 4x = -6$
$\quad y - x = 3$

q $y - 2x = 1$
$\quad y - 3x = -2$

r $y - 2x = 1$
$\quad y - 2x = 3$

s $y + 4 = 2x$
$\quad y + 3 = x$

t $y - 3 = 2x$
$\quad y + 1 = x$

u $y - x = 2$
$\quad y - 2 = x$

v $y + 1 = \frac{1}{2}x$
$\quad 2y = x - 2$

w $2y = 2x - 4$
$\quad 2y = x + 2$

x $3y = 6x + 9$
$\quad 2y = 4x + 2$

4 Using both intercepts

Using $x = 0$ and then $y = 0$, find the y-intercept and x-intercept for each of these lines. Draw the lines on suitable axes. The values of the intercepts will indicate how far you need to label the axes.

Find any solutions of each pair of simultaneous equations, remembering that there may be only *one* solution, or *no* solutions or an *infinite* number of solutions.

a $x + y = 6$
$\quad 2x + y = 10$

b $x + y = 5$
$\quad x + 2y = 8$

c $3x + 2y = 12$
$\quad x + 6y = 12$

d $4x + y = 8$
$\quad 2x + y = 6$

e $2x + y = 8$
$\quad x + 3y = 9$

f $2y + x = 10$
$\quad 3y + 2x = 18$

g $2x + y = 14$
$\quad x + 3y = 12$

h $2x + y = 10$
$\quad 3x + 4y = 30$

i $x + y = 2$
$\quad x + 3y = 6$

j $2y + x = 6$
$\quad 2y - x = 2$

k $x + 2y = 4$
$\quad 2x + 4y = 15$

l $3y - 8x = 24$
$\quad 3y + 2x = 9$

m $2y + 3x = 3$
$\quad 4y - 3x = -12$

n $3x + 2y = 12$
$\quad 6x + 4y = 24$

o $x - y = 6$
$\quad 2x - 2y = 7$

Straight lines

Part 7 Applications

1 This straight-line graph can be used to convert British pounds (£) to Spanish pesetas (ptas).

Use the graph to change these prices into pesetas.
a £2   b £5
c £4·50   d £1·50

Change these prices into pounds.
e 600 ptas   f 800 ptas
g 500 ptas   h 700 ptas

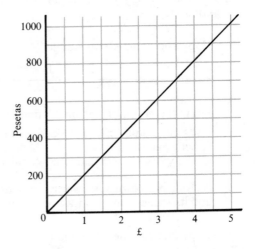

2 This graph shows how the cost of a taxi ride depends on the length of the journey.

Use the graph to find the cost of
a 10 miles   b 4 miles
c 1 mile   d 9 miles.

How far is a journey which costs
e £5   f £2
g £4   h £3·50?

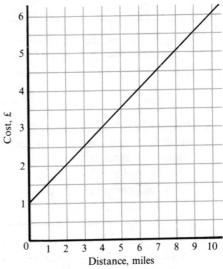

3 Mrs Banks has a certain sum of money to share between her two sons, but she may not give them equal amounts.

This graph shows the different possibilities.

What will David's share be if Stephen gets
a £30   b £40
c £15   d £25?

What will be Stephen's share if David gets
e £10   f £50
g £5   h £0?

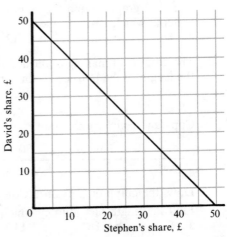

Straight lines

4 A father's age, f years, and his son's age, s years, are connected by
$$f = s + 25.$$
Copy and complete this table:

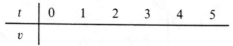

s	0	10	20	30	40	50
f						

Draw the graph of f against s on axes as shown.

Use your graph to find the age of the son when the father's age is
a   80 years   b   60 years   c   40 years   d   30 years.

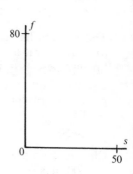

5 A stone is thrown downwards from the top of a tall tower and its speed, v (m/s), at a time t (seconds), is given by
$$v = 10t + 5.$$
Copy and complete this table.

t	0	1	2	3	4	5
v						

Draw the graph of v against t on axes as shown.

Use your graph to find how long it takes to reach a speed of
a   20 m/s   b   40 m/s   c   50 m/s   d   10 m/s.

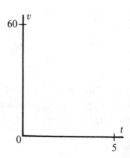

6 Pieces of cloth can be bought by post from a mail-order firm, and their cost £C depends on the length, x metres, where
$$C = 4x + 2.$$
Copy and complete this table.

x	1	2	3	4	5
C					

Draw the graph of C against x on axes as shown.

Use your graph to find the length of a piece of material which costs
a   £8   b   £20   c   £12   d   £16.

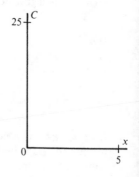

7 The cost £C of making a journey by car depends on the length of the journey, x km, where
$$C = 1 + \frac{x}{10}.$$
Copy and complete this table.

x	20	40	60	80	100
C					

Draw the graph of C against x on axes as shown.

Find the length of a journey which costs
a   £2   b   £6   c   £10   d   £4.

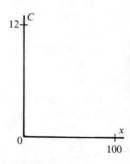

Straight lines

8 A man who is x years old now, might be expected to live for another y years, where
$$y = 70 - x.$$
Copy and complete this table.

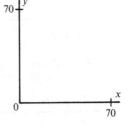

x	20	30	40	50	60
y					

Draw the graph of y against x, and find how much longer you would expect a man to live if his age is now
a 10 years b 25 years c 45 years d 65 years.

9 The amount of sleep, h hours, which a child needs depends on its age, A years, where
$$h = 16 - \tfrac{1}{2}A.$$
Copy and complete this table.

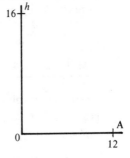

A	2	4	6	8	10	12
h						

Draw the graph of h against A, and find how old you would expect a child to be if it needed to sleep for
a $11\tfrac{1}{2}$ hours   b $14\tfrac{1}{2}$ hours.

10 A car starts a journey with a full tank of petrol.

After it has used p litres of petrol, it can travel a further d km before it needs more petrol.

If $d = 800 - 20p$, copy and complete this table.

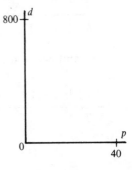

p	0	10	20	30	40
d					

Draw the graph of d against p.
a What is the furthest distance the car can go on a full tank?
b How many litres of petrol will a full tank hold?

For each of these situations, copy and complete the table using the information given; and then draw a straight line graph of your results.
The values in the table will indicate how far you need to label your axes.

11 The length, L cm, of a spring depends on the weight, W newtons, hanging on its end, where
$$L = 5 + \frac{W}{10}.$$

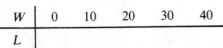

W	0	10	20	30	40
L					

95

Straight lines

12 The total charge, C pence, of an electricity bill depends on the number n of units used, where
$$C = 5n + 600.$$

n	10	50	100	150	200
C					

13 If a gardener plants V m² of vegetables, he will have F m² left for flowers, where
$$F = 50 - V.$$

V	0	10	20	30	40	50
F						

14 The length of time, T hours, which a turkey should be cooked for, depends on its mass, M kg, where
$$T = \frac{M + 10}{4}.$$

M	2	4	6	8	10	12
T						

15 The length, L mm, of the mercury column in a thermometer depends on the temperature, T °C, where
$$L = 20 + \frac{T}{10}.$$

T	0	20	40	60	80	100
L						

16 The amount of tax £T which an employee pays on an income of £I is given by
$$T = \tfrac{3}{10}I - 750.$$

I	4000	6000	8000	10000	12000
T					

Parabolas

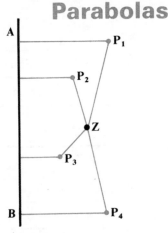

Introduction

1 Draw a straight line AB and mark a point Z
about 2 cm from AB as shown.

The points P_1, P_2, P_3, P_4 are equidistant
from the line AB and the fixed point Z.

Mark these points P_1, P_2, P_3, P_4, and mark
others like them as far from the line as
from Z.

Join all these points with a smooth curve.

This curve is called a **parabola**.

2

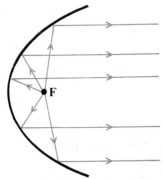

The parabola is a special curve because,
if you place a small light bulb at a
central point F (called the **focus**), the
light reflects from the parabola to form
a beam of light with parallel rays.

In which of these appliances do you think
a parabolic reflector is used?

a	car headlights	b	a radar aerial
c	a lamp-shade	d	a radio telescope
e	a gas ring	f	some electric fires
g	a pocket torch	h	a searchlight

Part 1 Using flow diagrams

1 Copy each table and use the flow diagram to complete it.

Use your table to plot points and so draw the four
parabolas onto one diagram with axes labelled as shown.

Label each parabola with its equation.

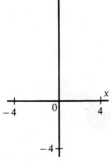

a $y = x^2$

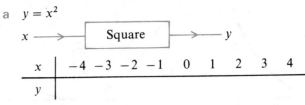

x	-4	-3	-2	-1	0	1	2	3	4
y									

b $y = x^2 + 4$

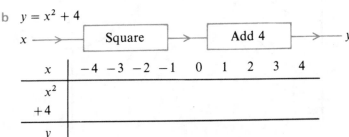

x	-4	-3	-2	-1	0	1	2	3	4
x^2									
$+4$									
y									

Parabolas

c $y = x^2 - 2$

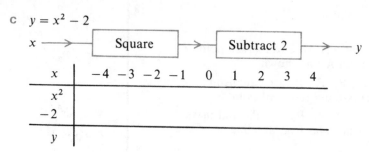

x	-4	-3	-2	-1	0	1	2	3	4
x^2									
-2									
y									

d $y = x^2 - 5$

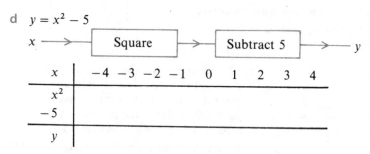

x	-4	-3	-2	-1	0	1	2	3	4
x^2									
-5									
y									

2 This diagram shows the parabola
$y = x^2$ labelled with its equation.

Match the other five curves, labelled
a to **e**, with these five equations.

$y = x^2 + 3$ $y = x^2 - 1$

$y = x^2 - 4$ $y = x^2 + 2$

$y = x^2 - 3$

3 This diagram also shows the
parabola $y = x^2$.

Write down the equations of the
other five curves which are labelled
f to **j**.

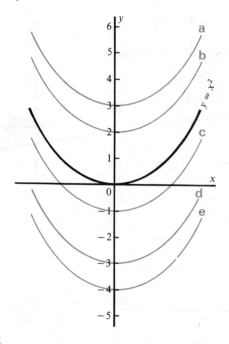

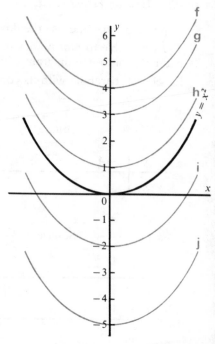

Parabolas

4 Copy each table and use the flow diagram to complete it.
Draw axes with the x-axis labelled from 0 to 6 and the y-axis from 0 to 25.
Use your tables to plot points and so draw the three parabolas on the one diagram.
Label each parabola with its equation.

a $y = (x - 3)^2$

$x \longrightarrow$ [Subtract 3] $\longrightarrow$ [Square] $\longrightarrow y$

x	0	1	2	3	4	5	6
$x - 3$							
y							

b $y = (x - 2)^2$

$x \longrightarrow$ [Subtract 2] $\longrightarrow$ [Square] $\longrightarrow y$

x	0	1	2	3	4	5	6
$x - 2$							
y							

c $y = (x - 5)^2$

$x \longrightarrow$ [Subtract 5] $\longrightarrow$ [Square] $\longrightarrow y$

x	0	1	2	3	4	5	6
$x - 5$							
y							

5 Copy and complete each table using the equation given.
Draw axes with the x-axis labelled from −4 to 4 and the y-axis from −20 to 5.
Use your tables to plot points and so draw the four parabolas on the one diagram.
Label each parabola with its equation.

a $y = -x^2$

x	−4	−3	−2	−1	0	1	2	3	4
y									

b $y = -x^2 + 4$

x	−4	−3	−2	−1	0	1	2	3	4
$-x^2$									
$+4$									
y									

99

Parabolas

c $y = -x^2 + 2$

x	-4	-3	-2	-1	0	1	2	3	4
$-x^2$									
$+2$									
y									

d $y = -x^2 - 3$

x	-4	-3	-2	-1	0	1	2	3	4
$-x^2$									
-3									
y									

6 This diagram shows the parabola $y = -x^2$ labelled with its equation.

Match the other four curves, labelled **a** to **d**, with these four equations.

$y = -x^2 + 1$ $y = -x^2 - 2$
$y = -x^2 - 4$ $y = -x^2 + 3$

7 This diagram also shows the parabola $y = -x^2$.

Write down the equations of the other four parabolas which are labelled **e** to **h**.

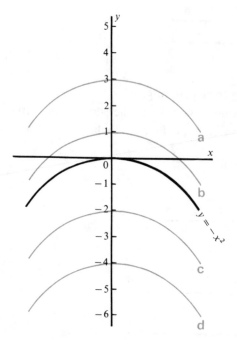

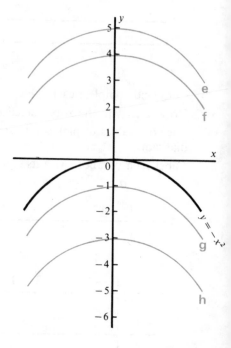

Parabolas

Part 2   Tables of values

1   Draw axes, labelling the x-axis from 0 to 6 and the y-axis from 0 to 25.

Copy and complete each of these tables, and use them to draw three curves on the same diagram.

a $y = x^2 - 6x + 9$

x	0	1	2	3	4	5	6
x^2							
$-6x$							
$+9$							
y							

b $y = x^2 - 4x + 4$

x	0	1	2	3	4	5	6
x^2							
$-4x$							
$+4$							
y							

c $y = x^2 - 10x + 25$

x	0	1	2	3	4	5	6
x^2							
$-10x$							
$+25$							
y							

2   Draw axes, labelling the x-axis from 0 to 6 and the y-axis from -4 to 15.

Copy and complete these tables, and so draw two curves on the same diagram.

a $y = x^2 - 8x + 15$

x	0	1	2	3	4	5	6
x^2							
$-8x$							
$+15$							
y							

b $y = x^2 - 8x + 12$

x	0	1	2	3	4	5	6
x^2							
$-8x$							
$+12$							
y							

3   Draw axes, labelling the x-axis from 0 to 6 and the y-axis from -10 to 20.

Copy and complete these tables and draw both curves on the one diagram.

a $y = x^2 - 3x - 4$

x	0	1	2	3	4	5	6
x^2							
$-3x$							
-4							
y							

b $y = x^2 - 3x - 1$

x	0	1	2	3	4	5	6
x^2							
$-3x$							
-1							
y							

Parabolas

4 Draw axes with the x-axis labelled from 0 to 6 and the y-axis from 0 to 12.
   Copy and complete these two tables and draw both curves on one diagram.

a $y = 6x - x^2$

x	0	1	2	3	4	5	6
$6x$							
$-x^2$							
y							

b $y = 3 + 6x - x^2$

x	0	1	2	3	4	5	6
3							
$+6x$							
$-x^2$							
y							

5 On a new diagram, label the x-axis from 0 to 6 and the y-axis from -12 to 6.
   Copy and complete these two tables and draw both curves on one diagram.

a $y = 4x - x^2$

x	0	1	2	3	4	5	6
$4x$							
$-x^2$							
y							

b $y = 2 + 4x - x^2$

x	0	1	2	3	4	5	6
2							
$+4x$							
$-x^2$							
y							

Part 3 Further tables

1 Draw and label the x-axis from -2 to 4 and the y-axis from -4 to 12.
   Copy and complete these two tables for the equations given, and use them to
   draw two curves on the same diagram.

a $y = x^2 - 3x$

x	-2	-1	0	1	2	3	4
x^2							
$-3x$							
y							

b $y = x^2 - 2x$

x	-2	-1	0	1	2	3	4
x^2							
$-2x$							
y							

Parabolas

2   Draw and label the x-axis from -5 to 2 and the y-axis from -4 to 16.
Copy and complete these two tables for the equations given, and use them to
draw two curves on the same diagram.

a $y = x^2 + 4x$

x	-5	-4	-3	-2	-1	0	1	2
x^2								
$+4x$								
y								

b $y = x^2 + 2x$

x	-5	-4	-3	-2	-1	0	1	2
x^2								
$+2x$								
y								

3   Draw axes, labelling the x-axis from -1 to 5 and the y-axis from -6 to 15.
Copy and complete both these tables for the two equations given.
Draw two curves on the same axes.

a $y = x^2 - 4x + 3$

x	-1	0	1	2	3	4	5
x^2							
$-4x$							
$+3$							
y							

b $y = x^2 - 7x + 7$

x	-1	0	1	2	3	4	5
x^2							
$-7x$							
$+7$							
y							

4   Draw axes, labelling the x-axis from -4 to 3 and the y-axis from -4 to 14.
Copy and complete these two tables, and draw two curves on your axes.

a $y = x^2 + 2x - 3$

x	-4	-3	-2	-1	0	1	2	3
x^2								
$+2x$								
-3								
y								

b $y = x^2 + 3x - 4$

x	-4	-3	-2	-1	0	1	2	3
x^2								
$+3x$								
-4								
y								

Parabolas

5   Draw axes, labelling the x-axis from -3 to 5 and the y-axis from -12 to 12.
    Copy and complete both tables and draw two curves on your axes.

a $y = x^2 - 2x - 3$

x	-3	-2	-1	0	1	2	3	4	5
x^2									
$-2x$									
-3									
y									

b $y = x^2 - 3x - 10$

x	-3	-2	-1	0	1	2	3	4	5
x^2									
$-3x$									
-10									
y									

6   Label the x-axis from -5 to 1 and the y-axis from -6 to 10.
    Copy and complete both tables and draw two curves on your axes.

a $y = x^2 + 5x + 4$

x	-5	-4	-3	-2	-1	0	1
x^2							
$+5x$							
$+4$							
y							

b $y = x^2 + 6x + 3$

x	-5	-4	-3	-2	-1	0	1
x^2							
$+6x$							
$+3$							
y							

7   Label the x-axis from -2 to 4 and the y-axis from -12 to 4.
    Copy and complete both tables to draw two curves on your axes.

a $y = 4 - x^2$

x	-2	-1	0	1	2	3	4
4							
$-x^2$							
y							

b $y = 4x - x^2$

x	-2	-1	0	1	2	3	4
$4x$							
$-x^2$							
y							

Parabolas

8   Label the x-axis from -2 to 4 and the y-axis from -8 to 10.

Copy and complete these tables to draw two curves on your axes.

a $y = 8 + 2x - x^2$

x	-2	-1	0	1	2	3	4
8							
$+2x$							
$-x^2$							
y							

b $y = 6 + x - x^2$

x	-2	-1	0	1	2	3	4
6							
$+x$							
$-x^2$							
y							

9   Construct a table to draw the graph of each of these equations over the range of x values given.

Draw each graph and use it to solve the quadratic equation.

a $y = x^2 - 4x + 3$ for x values from 0 to 4
Hence solve the equation $x^2 - 4x + 3 = 0$.

b $y = x^2 - 8x + 12$ for x values from 0 to 6
Hence solve the equation $x^2 - 8x + 12 = 0$.

c $y = x^2 - 3x - 4$ for x values from -2 to 4
Hence solve the equation $x^2 - 3x - 4 = 0$.

d $y = x^2 + 2x + 1$ for x values from -3 to 1
Hence solve the equation $x^2 + 2x + 1 = 0$.

e $y = x^2 - 2x + 3$ for x values from -1 to 3
Hence solve the equation $x^2 - 2x + 3 = 0$.

10   Construct a table to draw the graph of each of these equations over the range of x values given.

Draw each graph and use it to find the solutions of the quadratic equation as decimals.

a $y = x^2 - 3x - 3$ for $-1 \leqslant x \leqslant 4$
Hence solve the equation $x^2 - 3x - 3 = 0$.

b $y = x^2 - 2x - 5$ for $-2 \leqslant x \leqslant 4$
Hence solve the equation $x^2 - 2x - 5 = 0$.

c $y = x^2 + x - 4$ for $-3 \leqslant x \leqslant 2$
Hence solve the equation $x^2 + x - 4 = 0$.

d $y = 2x^2 + 3x - 4$ for $-3 \leqslant x \leqslant 2$
Hence solve the equation $2x^2 + 3x - 4 = 0$.

e $y = 5 + 2x - x^2$ for $-2 \leqslant x \leqslant 4$
Hence solve the equation $5 + 2x - x^2 = 0$.

Parabolas

Part 4   Applications

1   a   A field gun fires a shell so that its height, y metres, is given by $y = 7x - x^2$,
where x is the horizontal distance travelled (in hundreds of metres).
Copy and complete this table. Draw axes as
shown here, and on them draw the path of the shell.

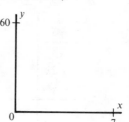

x	0	1	2	3	4	5	6	7
$7x$								
$-x^2$								
y								

b   A mortar gun fires its shell so that $y = 12(4x - x^2)$.
Copy and complete this table.
Draw the path of the shell on the same diagram.

x	0	1	2	3	4
$4x$					
$-x^2$					
$4x - x^2$					
y					

c   How high does the field gun fire its shell?
d   How high does the mortar gun fire its shell?
e   How far can the field gun fire on level ground?
f   How far can the mortar gun fire on level ground?
g   Which type of gun would you use to fire over nearby buildings?

2   a   Another field gun fires its shell so that its height, y metres, is given by
$y = 9x - x^2$, where x is the horizontal distance travelled (in hundreds of metres).
Copy and complete this table. Draw axes as
shown here, and on them draw the path of the shell.

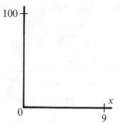

x	0	1	2	3	4	5	6	7	8	9
$9x$										
$-x^2$										
y										

b   Another mortar gun fires its shell so that $y = 10(6x - x^2)$.
Copy and complete this table, and draw the path of the shell on the same diagram.

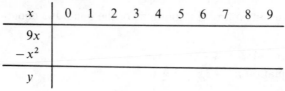

x	0	1	2	3	4	5	6
$6x$							
$-x^2$							
$6x - x^2$							
y							

c   Answer the same five questions as in problem **1** above.

Parabolas

3 a A science experiment lowers the temperature in °C of an object from room temperature to below freezing over a period of 6 hours. If t is the time from the start of the experiment in hours, then the temperature, θ °C, is given by $\theta = t^2 - 9t + 10$.

Copy and complete this table.

t	0	1	2	3	4	5	6
t^2							
$-9t$							
$+10$							
θ							

Plot θ against t, choosing your own scales on the axes.

b What was the room temperature at the start of the experiment?

c What was the object's temperature after $3\frac{1}{2}$ hours?

d How long did it take for the temperature to fall to freezing-point?

4 a An aircraft flying at a height of 10 km above ground level goes into a dive and then pulls out of the dive. Its height, y km, is given by $y = \frac{1}{4}x^2 - 3x + 10$ where x is the horizontal distance (in km) which it travels.

Copy and complete this table, and use it to draw the path of the aircraft. Choose your own scales on the axes.

x	0	2	4	6	8	10
$\frac{1}{4}x^2$						
$-3x$						
$+10$						
y						

b At what height was the aircraft flying before the dive?

c How close did it get to ground level before climbing again?

d How far did it travel horizontally in the descent?

e How high above the ground was it after pulling out of the dive?

5 a A ski-jump is built at the top of a slope and the height, y metres, at a point on the jump depends on the horizontal distance, x metres, where $y = \frac{1}{4}x^2 - 2x + 9$.

Copy and complete this table, and use it to draw the shape of the jump. Choose your own scales on the axes.

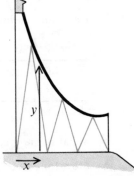

x	0	1	2	3	4	5
$\frac{1}{4}x^2$						
$-2x$						
$+9$						
y						

b How high is the start of the jump above the ground?

c How high is the end of the jump above the ground?

d What is the closest distance between the bottom of the jump and the ground?

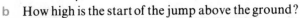

107

Parabolas

6 A 10-metre length of rope, tied at its ends to make a loop, is laid on the ground in the shape of a rectangle of width x metres.

The area, A m^2, of the rectangle is given by $A = 5x - x^2$.

a Copy and complete this table, and use it to draw the graph of A against x.

x	0	1	2	3	4	5
$5x$						
$-x^2$						
A						

b What is the largest possible area of the rectangle?

c What is the value of x in this case?

7 A gardener has 12 metres of fencing which he uses to make a rectangular plot alongside a brick wall.

The area, A m^2, inside the fence depends on the width, x m, of the plot, and is given by $A = 12x - 2x^2$.

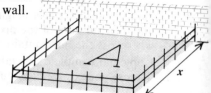

a Copy and complete this table, and use it to draw the graph of A against x.

x	0	1	2	3	4	5	6
$12x$							
$-2x^2$							
A							

b What is the largest possible area of garden which he can fence off?

c What will be the value of x in this case?

8 A cricket ball is thrown over level ground so that after t seconds its height, h metres, is given by $h = 20t - 5t^2$.

a Copy and complete this table, and draw the graph of h against t.

t	0	1	2	3	4
$20t$					
$-5t^2$					
h					

b What is the greatest height reached by the ball?

c How long does it take to reach this greatest height?

d How long does it take before it hits the ground?

9   A boy throws a stone from a cliff top into the sea below, so that its height, h metres, above the sea after t seconds is given by $h = 40 + 10t - 5t^2$.

a   Copy and complete this table, and use it to draw the graph of h against t.

t	0	1	2	3	4
40					
$+10t$					
$-5t^2$					
h					

b   What is the height of the cliff?
c   What is the greatest height of the stone above sea-level?
d   How long does it take to reach this greatest height?
e   How long does it take until it splashes into the sea?

10   A ball is thrown from a point O at the bottom of a slope OH which rises gradually, so that it hits the slope at the point P.

The height, y metres, of the ball is given by the equation
$$y = 8x - x^2$$
where x is the horizontal distance (in metres) which it has travelled.

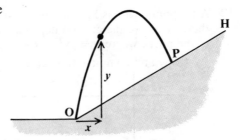

a   Draw and label the x-axis from 0 to 10 and the y-axis from 0 to 20.

Copy and complete these tables, and use them to draw the slope OH and the path of the ball on one diagram.

For the ball, $y = 8x - x^2$.

x	0	1	2	3	4	5	6	7	8
$8x$									
$-x^2$									
y									

For the slope, $y = \frac{1}{2}x$.

x	0	1	2	3	4	5	6	7	8
y									

b   What is the greatest height of the ball above O?
c   How much higher is P than O?
d   What is the horizontal distance between P and O?

11   A girl throws a rounders ball so that it rises to a height of y metres after travelling horizontally a distance of x metres, where $y = 2x - \frac{1}{10}x^2$.

a   Copy and complete this table, and draw the path of the ball.

x	0	2	4	6	8	10	12	14	16	18	20
$2x$											
$-\frac{1}{10}x^2$											
y											

b   What is the greatest height which the ball reaches?
c   If it is thrown over level ground, how far away does it hit the ground?

Parabolas

12 Coastguards on the edge of a cliff fire a rocket out to sea. The height, y metres, of the rocket above the sea is given by $y = 60 + 24x - 4x^2$ where x is the horizontal distance of the rocket from the cliff, in tens of metres.

   a Copy and complete this table, and draw the path of the rocket.

x	0	1	2	3	4	5	6	7	8
60									
$+24x$									
$-4x^2$									
y									

   b How high is the cliff?

   c How far out from the foot of the cliff does the rocket hit the sea?

   d What was the greatest height that the rocket reached?

13 A telephone wire is held by two posts 80 metres apart. The height, y metres, of the wire above the ground depends on the distance x (tens of metres) from one of the posts, where $y = \frac{1}{8}x^2 - x + 10$.

   a Copy and complete this table, and draw the shape which the wire hangs in.

x	0	1	2	3	4	5	6	7	8
$\frac{1}{8}x^2$									
$-x$									
$+10$									
y									

   b How high are the two poles?

   c How high is the middle of the wire above the ground?

   d How much does the wire sag in the middle?

14 A suspension bridge carries a road over a 50-metre span. The shape of the suspending chain is given by $h = \frac{1}{50}x^2 - x + 20$ where h is the height of the chain above the road, in metres, and x is the distance across the bridge, in metres.

   a Copy and complete this table.

x	0	10	20	30	40	50
$\frac{1}{50}x^2$						
$-x$						
$+20$						
h						

Draw the shape of the bridge onto axes of your own choice. The road itself is along the x-axis of your diagram.

   b How high are the towers at each end of the bridge?

   c How high is the chain above the road 15 metres from either end of the bridge?

   d What is the smallest distance between the chain and the road?

Parabolas

15 A rounders ball is thrown so that its height, h metres, above level ground, is given by $h = 1 + \frac{7}{10}x - \frac{3}{100}x^2$ where x is the horizontal distance (in metres) from the thrower.

   a Copy and complete this table and draw the path which the ball takes.

x	0	5	10	15	20	25
1						
$+\frac{7}{10}x$						
$-\frac{3}{100}x^2$						
h						

   b What is the greatest height of the ball?
   c How far from the thrower does the ball strike the ground?
   d At what height above the ground did the thrower let go of the ball?
   e How high was the ball when 8 m horizontally from the thrower?

16 Between 10 o'clock in the morning (10.00 h) and 3 o'clock in the afternoon (15.00 h), the outside temperature, θ °C, in the garden is given by $\theta = -80 + 14t - \frac{1}{2}t^2$ where t is the time of day given on the 24-hour clock.

   a Copy and complete this table.

t	10	11	12	13	14	15
-80						
$+14t$						
$-\frac{1}{2}t^2$						
θ						

   Plot the variation in temperature with time, using axes with a false origin and your choice of scales.
   b What is the maximum temperature during the day?
   c At what time does this maximum temperature occur?
   d What is the temperature at 10.30 a.m.?
   e At what time is the temperature 15°C?

17 a The number of articles which a manufacturing company produces each hour can be varied; and the cost £C of producing them depends on how many are made. If x is the number of hundreds produced, then $C = 3x^2 - 25x + 100$. Copy and complete this table, and draw the graph of C against x.

x	0	2	4	6	8	10	12
$3x^2$							
$-25x$							
$+100$							
C							

   (i) What is the cost of production even when no articles are made?
   (ii) What is the cost of production when 900 articles are made?
   (iii) What number of articles are to be made for the cost to be a minimum?

Parabolas

b The income £I made by selling these articles is given by $I = 15x$ where x is the number of hundreds of articles sold.

Copy and complete this table.

x	0	2	4	6	8	10	12
I							

Draw the graph of I against x, on the *same* diagram as part **a**.

c When 400 articles are made, what is   (i)   the cost of production
  (ii)   the income on their sale
  (iii)   the profit made?

d When 600 articles are made, what is   (i)   the cost of production
  (ii)   the income on their sale
  (iii)   the profit made?

e When 1000 articles are made, what is   (i)   the cost of production
  (ii)   the income on their sale
  (iii)   the profit made?

f What is the profit when 333 articles are made?

g Between what values of x does the income I exceed the cost of production C?

h Copy the table below and use your two graphs to complete it for the profit P where $P = I - C$.

x	0	2	4	6	8	10	12
C							
I							
P							

Draw a graph of P against x using your own choice of scales.

i What values of x make P zero?

j How many articles should be produced to give maximum profit?

Part 5 Harder problems

1 **a** Draw axes, labelling the x-axis from -4 to 3 and the y-axis from -4 to 10.
Copy and complete this table, and draw the graph of $y = x^2 + 3x$.

x	-4	-3	-2	-1	0	1	2
x^2							
$+3x$							
y							

b Use your graph to write down the solutions of the equation $x^2 + 3x = 0$.

c On the same diagram, draw the straight line $y = x + 3$.
Write down the points of intersection of this line with the curve.

d Also draw the straight line $y = x - 1$ on the diagram.
Write down the point where this line and the curve meet.
Copy and complete this sentence by filling in the missing word.
    "The line $y = x - 1$ is a t ... to the curve $y = x^2 + 3x$."

Parabolas

2 a Draw axes, labelling the x-axis from -2 to 5 and the y-axis from -7 to 12.
Copy and complete this table, and draw the graph of $y = x^2 - 2x - 3$.

x	-2	-1	0	1	2	3	4	5
x^2								
$-2x$								
-3								
y								

b Use your graph to write down the solutions of the equation $x^2 - 2x - 3 = 0$.

c On the same diagram, draw the straight line $y = 2x + 2$.
Write down the points of intersection of this line and the curve.

d Draw the straight line which is parallel to the line $y = 2x + 2$ and which is also a tangent to the curve. Find
(i) the point at which this tangent touches the curve
(ii) the gradient of the tangent   (iii) its y-intercept   (iv) its equation.

3 a Draw axes, labelling the x-axis from -3 to 4 and the y-axis from -6 to 12.
Copy and complete this table and draw the graph of $y = 6 + x - x^2$.

x	-3	-2	-1	0	1	2	3	4
6								
$+x$								
$-x^2$								
y								

b Solve the equation $6 + x - x^2 = 0$.

c From the point (0, 10), draw *two different* tangents to the curve.
For each tangent, find
(i) the point at which it touches the curve
(ii) the gradient of the tangent   (iii) its y-intercept   (iv) its equation.

4 a Draw axes, labelling the x-axis from -2 to 6 and the y-axis from -7 to 14.
Copy and complete both these tables, and draw the graphs of
$y = x^2 - 2x + 6$ and $y = 6x - x^2$ onto the same diagram.

x	-2	-1	0	1	2	3	4
x^2							
$-2x$							
$+6$							
y							

x	-1	0	1	2	3	4	5	6
$6x$								
$-x^2$								
y								

b Write down the two solutions of the equation $6x - x^2 = 0$.

c Say why the equation $x^2 - 2x + 6 = 0$ has no solutions.

d Write down the points of intersection of the two curves.

e Draw a straight line through these points of intersection and find
(i) the gradient, (ii) the y-intercept, and (iii) the equation, of this line.

Parabolas

5 a Draw axes labelled from -4 to 5 on the x-axis and from -6 to 14 on the y-axis. Copy and complete these two tables and draw the graphs of $y = x^2 - 5x + 8$ and $y = 6 - x - x^2$ on the same diagram.

x	-1	0	1	2	3	4	5
x^2							
$-5x$							
$+8$							
y							

x	-4	-3	-2	-1	0	1	2	3
6								
$-x$								
$-x^2$								
y								

b Write down the point at which the two curves touch.

c Draw a straight line at this point so that it is a tangent to both curves. Find
(i) the gradient of this tangent   (ii) its y-intercept   (iii) its equation.

6 a Copy and complete this table and draw the graph of $y = x^2 - 2x + 3$ using axes labelled from -2 to 4 on the x-axis and -4 to 11 on the y-axis.

x	-2	-1	0	1	2	3	4
x^2							
$-2x$							
$+3$							
y							

b Explain in words why the equation $x^2 - 2x + 3 = 0$ has no solution.

c Draw the straight line $y = 2x$ on the same diagram, and write down both solutions of the equation $x^2 - 2x + 3 = 2x$.

d Draw the straight line $y = 2x - 1$, and write down the solution of the equation $x^2 - 2x + 3 = 2x - 1$.

e Draw the straight line $y = 2x - 4$ and say in words why the equation $x^2 - 2x + 3 = 2x - 4$ has no solutions.

7 a Copy and complete this table and draw the graph of $y = 4 + 3x - x^2$ onto axes where both are labelled from -1 to 10.

x	-1	0	1	2	3	4
4						
$+3x$						
$-x^2$						
y						

b Write down the solutions of $4 + 3x - x^2 = 0$.

c Draw the line $y = 7 - x$ on the same diagram and write down the solutions of the equation $4 + 3x - x^2 = 7 - x$.

d Draw the line $y = 8 - x$ and write down the solution of $4 + 3x - x^2 = 8 - x$.

e Draw the line $y = 9 - x$ and say in words why there are no solutions of $4 + 3x - x^2 = 9 - x$.

Other curves

Part 1

For each equation,
  a copy and complete the table
  b draw axes, *either* labelled as shown *or* using suitable scales of your own choice
  c plot points and draw the curve
  d draw any asymptotes as dotted lines.

1 $y = \dfrac{12}{x}$

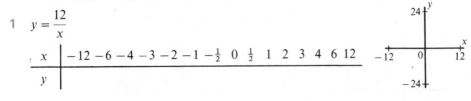

x	−12	−6	−4	−3	−2	−1	−½	0	½	1	2	3	4	6	12
y															

2 $y = \dfrac{24}{x}$

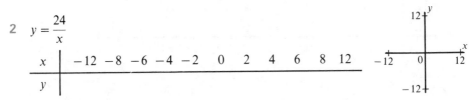

x	−12	−8	−6	−4	−2	0	2	4	6	8	12
y											

3 $y = \dfrac{16}{x}$

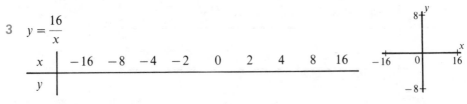

x	−16	−8	−4	−2	0	2	4	8	16
y									

4 $y = \dfrac{12}{x - 3}$

x	−9	−3	−1	0	1	2	3	4	5	6	7	9	15
x − 3													
y													

5 $y = \dfrac{24}{x - 4}$

x	−8	−4	−2	0	2	4	6	8	10	12	16
x − 4											
y											

6 $y = \dfrac{16}{x + 2}$

x	−18	−10	−6	−4	−2	0	2	6	14
x + 2									
y									

115

Other curves

7 $y = \dfrac{12}{x} + 4$

x	-12	-6	-4	-3	-2	-1	0	1	2	3	4	6	12
$\dfrac{12}{x}$													
y													

8 $y = \dfrac{24}{x} + 2$

x	-12	-8	-6	-4	-2	0	2	4	6	8	12
$\dfrac{24}{x}$											
y											

9 $y = \dfrac{16}{x} - 3$

x	-16	-8	-4	-2	0	2	4	8
$\dfrac{16}{x}$								
y								

10 $y = \dfrac{16}{x} + x$

x	-16	-8	-4	-2	0	2	4	8
$\dfrac{16}{x}$								
y								

11 $y = \dfrac{36}{x^2}$

x	-4	-3	-2	-1	0	1	2	3	4	6
x^2										
y										

12 $y = \dfrac{36}{x^2} + x$

x	-4	-3	-2	-1	0	1	2	3	4	6
$\dfrac{36}{x^2}$										
y										

116

Other curves

The curves you have just drawn in numbers **1** to **10** all belong to a family of curves called **hyperbolas**.

The curves in numbers **11** and **12** have no special name.

Those in the remainder of this exercise belong to a family of curves called **cubics**.

13 $y = x^3 - 9x$

x	-4	-3	-2	-1	0	1	2	3	4
x^3									
$-9x$									
y									

14 $y = x^3 - 4x$

x	-3	-2	-1	0	1	2	3
x^3							
$-4x$							
y							

15 $y = x^3 - 6x + 1$

x	-3	-2	-1	0	1	2	3
x^3							
$-6x$							
$+1$							
y							

16 $y = x^3 + 2x^2$

x	-3	-2	-1	0	1
x^3					
$+2x^2$					
y					

17 $y = x^3 - 3x^2$

x	-1	0	1	2	3	4
x^3						
$-3x^2$						
y						

18 $y = x^3 - 4x^2 + 6$

x	-1	0	1	2	3	4
x^3						
$-4x^2$						
$+6$						
y						

Construct your own tables for these equations to help you draw the curves. Use the range of x values given.

19 $y = x^3 - 6x^2 + 9x$ for x values from -1 to 4

20 $y = x^3 - 8x^2 + 16x$ for x values from -1 to 5

21 $y = x^3 - 3x^2 - 6x + 8$ for x values from -3 to 5

22 $y = x^3 - 5x^2 + 2x + 8$ for x values from -2 to 5

Other curves

Part 2 Curves and lines

1 **a** Copy and complete this table for the equation $y = \dfrac{4}{x}$.

x	-4	-2	-1	0	1	2	4
y							

Label both axes from -4 to 4 and draw the curve $y = \dfrac{4}{x}$.

b Join the points $(0, 4)$ and $(4, 0)$ with a straight line.
Copy and complete this sentence.
"This line is a t ... to the curve at the point $(\ldots, \ldots)$."

c Draw another straight line, parallel to the other one, which is also a tangent to the curve.

2 **a** Copy and complete this table for the equation $y = \dfrac{8}{x - 4}$.

x	0	2	3	4	5	6	8
$x - 4$							
y							

Label the x-axis from 0 to 8 and the y-axis from -8 to 16; and draw the curve.

b Join the points $(0, 16)$ and $(8, 0)$ with a straight line.
Copy and complete this sentence.
"This line is a t ... to the curve at the point $(\ldots, \ldots)$."

c Draw another tangent to the curve, which is parallel to the first line.

3 **a** Copy and complete this table for the equation $y = x^3 - 9x + 2$.

x	-3	-2	-1	0	1	2	3
x^3							
$-9x$							
$+2$							
y							

Label the x-axis from -4 to 3 and the y-axis from -8 to 12, and draw the curve.

b Use your graph to write down the three solutions of $x^3 - 9x + 2 = 0$ as decimals.

c Join the points $(0, 4)$ and $(2, -8)$ with a straight line.
Copy and complete this sentence.
"The line is a t ... to the curve at the point $(\ldots, \ldots)$."

4 **a** Copy and complete this table for the equation $y = x^3 - 4x - 2$.

x	-2	-1	0	1	2	3
x^3						
$-4x$						
-2						
y						

Label the x-axis from -2 to 3 and the y-axis from -5 to 13, and draw the curve.

b   Use your graph to write down the three solutions of $x^3 - 4x - 2 = 0$ as decimals.

c   On the same diagram, draw the straight line $y = x$, and write down as decimals the points of intersection of the line with the curve.

d   Also draw the straight line $y = x + 6$, and write down the one point of intersection.

e   Draw two more straight lines, parallel to the two you have already drawn, so that both of them are tangents to the curve.

5   a   Copy and complete this table for the equation $y = (\frac{1}{2}x)^3 - x^2$.

x	-2	0	2	4	6	8
$(\frac{1}{2}x)^3$						
$-x^2$						
y						

Choose scales for your axes and draw the curve.

b   The x-axis itself is a tangent to this curve. Draw another tangent which is parallel to the x-axis, and write its equation.

c   Copy and complete this table for the equation $y = \frac{1}{2}x - 4$, and draw the line on the same diagram.

x	-2	0	2	4	6	8
y						

d   Write down the x values of the points which give the solutions of the equation $(\frac{1}{2}x)^3 - x^2 = \frac{1}{2}x - 4$.

6   a   Construct your own table to help you draw the graph of
$y = x^3 - x^2 - 6x + 6$ for x values from -3 to 3.

b   Use your graph to write down the solutions of $x^3 - x^2 - 6x + 6 = 0$.

c   Draw the straight line $y = 2x - 6$ on the same diagram, and use it to find the solutions of the equation $x^3 - x^2 - 6x + 6 = 2x - 6$.

d   Draw the straight line $y = 2x$, and use it to find the solutions of the equation $x^3 - x^2 - 6x + 6 = 2x$.

e   Draw another straight line which is parallel to the other two lines and is also a tangent to the curve.

7   a   Construct your own table to help you draw the graph of
$y = 5 + 9x - x^2 - x^3$ for x values from -3 to 3.

b   Use your graph to find the solutions of $5 + 9x - x^2 - x^3 = 0$.

c   On the same diagram, draw the straight line $y = 4x$, and use it to find the solutions of the equation $5 + 9x - x^2 - x^3 = 4x$.

d   Draw the straight line $y = 4x + 8$ and use it to find the solutions of the equation $5 + 9x - x^2 - x^3 = 4x + 8$.

119

Other curves

8   a   Construct your own table for the equation $y = 1 + x + 4x^2 - x^3$ for x values from -1 to 4, and use it to draw the graph.

    b   Explain in words why the equation $1 + x + 4x^2 - x^3 = 0$ has no solution between $x = -1$ and $x = 4$. Explain further why there will be only one solution, and say whether it will be where $x < -1$ or $x > 4$.

    c   Draw a straight line through the points $(-1, -4)$ and $(1, 6)$.
      At which point is this line a tangent to the curve?
      Find   (i)   the y-intercept
             (ii)   the gradient
     and (iii)   the equation of this line.

    d   Draw another straight line through the points $(-1, 0)$ and $(3, 4)$.
      At which point is this line a tangent to the curve?
      Find   (i)   the y-intercept
             (ii)   the gradient
     and (iii)   the equation of this line.

9   a   Draw the graph of $y = 4x + 4x^2 - x^3$ for x values from -2 to 4.

    b   Find the negative solution of the equation $4x + 4x^2 - x^3 = 0$.

    c   Draw the line $y = 4x$ and find its points of intersection with the curve.

    d   Draw the straight line through $(-1, 10)$ and $(3, 18)$, and find its y-intercept, its gradient and its equation.

    e   Use your diagram to find the solutions of the equation
    . $4x + 4x^2 - x^3 = 2x + 12$.

Points of intersection

1 a Copy and complete these two tables.

For $y = x^2 - 4x + 5$

x	0	1	2	3	4	5
x^2						
$-4x$						
$+5$						
y						

For $y = x + 1$

x	0	1	2	3	4	5
y						

   b Label the x-axis from 0 to 5 and the y-axis from 0 to 10 and draw the graphs of these equations. Write down their points of intersection.

   c Use your diagram to write the solutions of the equation $x^2 - 4x + 5 = x + 1$.

   d Check your answers by solving this equation algebraically.

2 a Copy and complete these two tables for the equations given, and draw the graphs of the equations on one diagram. Write down their points of intersection.

For $y = x^2 - 5x + 7$

x	0	1	2	3	4	5
x^2						
$-5x$						
$+7$						
y						

For $y = x - 1$

x	0	1	2	3	4	5
y						

   b Use your diagram to write the solutions of the equation $x^2 - 5x + 7 = x - 1$, and check your answers by solving this equation algebraically.

3 a Copy and complete these two tables for the equations given, and draw their graphs on the same diagram. Write down their points of intersection.

For $y = x^2 - 6x + 8$

x	0	1	2	3	4	5	6
x^2							
$-6x$							
$+8$							
y							

For $y = x - 2$

x	0	1	2	3	4	5	6
y							

   b Use your diagram to write the solutions of the equation $x^2 - 6x + 8 = x - 2$ and check your answers by solving the equation algebraically.

Points of intersection

4   a   Copy and complete these two tables for the equations given, and draw their graphs on the same diagram. Write down their points of intersection.

For $y = x^2 + x - 2$

x	-3	-2	-1	0	1	2	3
x^2							
$+x$							
-2							
y							

For $y = x + 2$

x	-3	-2	-1	0	1	2	3
y							

   b   Use your diagram to write the solutions of the equation $x^2 + x - 2 = x + 2$ and check your answers by solving the equation algebraically.

5   a   Construct your own tables of values for the equations $y = x^2 - 5x + 4$ and $y = 1 - x$ for the range of x values from 0 to 5.
Draw their graphs on the same diagram, and write down their points of intersection.

   b   Solve the equation $x^2 - 5x + 4 = 1 - x$ from your diagram, and check your answers algebraically.

6   a   Construct your own tables of values for the equations $y = x^2 - 4x$ and $y = 4 - x$ for the range of x values from -2 to 5.
Draw their graphs on the same diagram, and write down their points of intersection.

   b   Solve the equation $x^2 - 4x = 4 - x$ from your diagram, and check your answers algebraically.

7   a   Construct your own tables of values for the equations $y = x^2 - 7x + 10$ and $y = 2x - 4$ for $0 \leqslant x \leqslant 8$.
Draw their graphs on the same diagram, and write down their points of intersection.

   b   Solve the equation $x^2 - 7x + 10 = 2x - 4$ from your diagram, and check your answers algebraically.

8   a   Copy this table twice, and complete it for the equations $y = \dfrac{12}{x}$ and $y = x - 1$.

x	-4	-3	-2	-1	0	1	2	3	4
y									

Draw the graphs of these equations on the same diagram, and write down their points of intersection.

   b   Use your diagram to write the solutions of the equation $\dfrac{12}{x} = x - 1$, and then check your answers algebraically.

9   a   Copy this table twice, and complete it for the equations $y = \dfrac{6}{x}$ and $y = x + 1$.

x	-6	-3	-2	-1	0	1	2	3	6
y									

Draw the graphs of these equations on the same diagram, and write down their points of intersection.

   b   Use your diagram to write the solutions of the equation $\dfrac{6}{x} = x + 1$, and then check your answers algebraically.

122

Points of intersection

10 a Copy this table twice, and complete it for the equations

$y = \dfrac{6}{x-2}$ and $y = x - 1$.

x	-4	-1	0	1	2	3	4	5	8
y									

Draw their graphs on the same diagram and write down their points of intersection.

b Write the solutions of $\dfrac{6}{x-2} = x - 1$ from your diagram, and check your answers algebraically.

11 a Copy and complete this table twice for the equations

$y = 2x - 1$ and $y = \dfrac{12}{x-3}$,

x	-3	-1	0	1	2	3	4	5	6
y									

and draw their graphs on the same diagram. Write down their points of intersection.

b Write the solutions of $\dfrac{12}{x-3} = 2x - 1$, and check your answers algebraically.

12 a Copy and complete these two tables for the equations given. Draw their graphs on the same diagram, and write down their points of intersection.

For $y = x^3 - 4x^2 + 6$

x	0	1	2	3	4
x^3					
$-4x^2$					
$+6$					
y					

For $y = 6 - 3x$

x	0	1	2	3	4
y					

b Use your diagram to write the solutions of the equation $x^3 - 4x^2 + 6 = 6 - 3x$.

13 a Copy and complete these two tables for the equations given. Draw their graphs on the same diagram, and write down their points of intersection.

For $y = x^3 - x^2 + 1$

x	-2	-1	0	1	2	3
x^3						
$-x^2$						
$+1$						
y						

For $y = 2x + 1$

x	-2	-1	0	1	2	3
y						

b Use your diagram to solve the equation $x^3 - x^2 + 1 = 2x + 1$.

14 a Construct your own tables of values for the equations $y = x^3 - 3x^2 + 1$ and $y = x - 2$ for x values in the range from -2 to 4. Draw their graphs on the same diagram, and write down their points of intersection.

b Solve the equation $x^3 - 3x^2 + 1 = x - 2$.

Points of intersection

15 a Construct your own tables of values for the equations $y = x^3 - 2x^2 - 1$ and $y = 3x - 1$ for $-1 \leqslant x \leqslant 4$.

Draw their graphs on the same diagram, and write down their points of intersection.

b Solve the equation $x^3 - 2x^2 - 1 = 3x - 1$.

16 a Construct your own tables of values for the equations $y = x^2 - 4x + 3$ and $y = x^2 - 2x$ for $-1 \leqslant x \leqslant 4$.

Draw their graphs on the same diagram and hence write down the solution of the equation $x^2 - 4x + 3 = x^2 - 2x$.

b Check your answer algebraically.

Inequalities

Introduction

1 Write down an inequality for each coloured section of the x-axis.
A coloured dot includes the end value, but an empty dot does not.

Examples

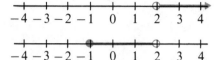 gives the inequality $x > 2$.

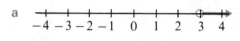 gives the inequality $-1 \leqslant x < 2$.

a 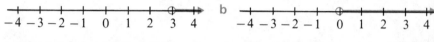 b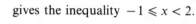

c 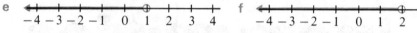 d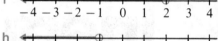

e 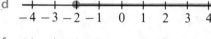 f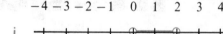

g 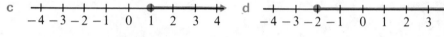 h

i 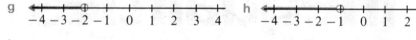 j

k 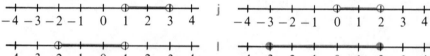 l

m 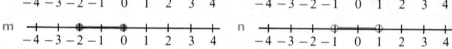 n

2 Draw and label the x-axis from -4 to 4, and for each of these inequalities colour in that part of the x-axis indicated by the inequalities.
Remember when to use coloured dots and empty dots.

a $x > 1$ b $x < 1$ c $x < 0$ d $x \leqslant 3$

e $x \leqslant -2$ f $x \geqslant -1$ g $0 < x < 1$ h $-1 < x < 0$

i $1 \leqslant x \leqslant 2$ j $-1 \leqslant x \leqslant 2$ k $-3 \leqslant x \leqslant 0$ l $-1\frac{1}{2} < x < \frac{1}{2}$

3 Match the statements below with these four expressions.

$x \geqslant 6$ $x < 6$ $x > 6$ $x \leqslant 6$

a x is less than 6.   b x is less than or equal to 6.

c x is greater than or equal to 6.   d x is greater than 6.

4 Match the statements below with these four expressions.

$y < 4$ $y \geqslant 4$ $y > 4$ $y \leqslant 4$

a y is greater than 4.   b y is less than 4.

c y is not more than 4.   d y is not less than 4.

Introduction

5   Write down all possible *integer* (whole number) values of x if
    a $6 < x < 10$ b $14 < x < 18$ c $0 < x \leqslant 5$ d $8 \leqslant x \leqslant 12$
    e $-2 < x \leqslant 3$ f $-3 \leqslant x < 1$.

6   Write down all possible *odd* values of x if
    a $4 < x < 12$ b $8 < x < 14$ c $0 < x < 6$ d $-2 < x < 2$
    e $-4 < x \leqslant 5$ f $4 < x \leqslant 11$.

7   Write down all possible *even* values of y if
    a $7 < y < 13$ b $19 < y \leqslant 24$ c $2 \leqslant y \leqslant 8$ d $4 \leqslant y < 11$
    e $-3 < y \leqslant 6$ f $0 \leqslant y < 9$.

8   Write down *two* possible integer values of y if
    a $y > 2$ b $y > 10$ c $y < 8$ d $y \leqslant 26$.

Regions

Part 1

1 a Write down the co-ordinates of the eight points marked on the coloured line.
What have they in common?
What is the equation of the line?

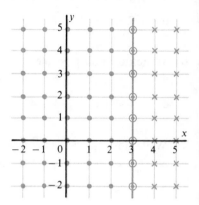

b What can you say about the x values of the points to the *right* of the coloured line?
What inequality describes these points?

c What can you say about the x values of the points to the *left* of the coloured line?
What inequality describes these points?

2

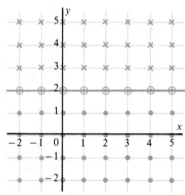

a Write down the co-ordinates of the eight points marked on the coloured line.
What have they in common?
What is the equation of the line?

b What can you say about the y values of the points *above* the coloured line?
What inequality describes these points?

c What can you say about the y values of the points *below* the coloured line?
What inequality describes these points?

3 Write inequalities to describe the regions of these diagrams which are *not* shaded.

A *solid* boundary line means the boundary is included as part of the region and so you must use either ≤ or ≥.

A *dotted* boundary line means the boundary is *not* included as part of the region and so you must use either < or >.

a 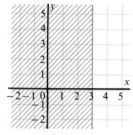   b 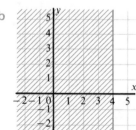   c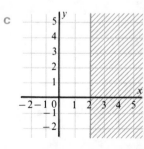

Regions

d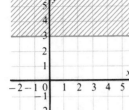

e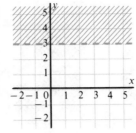

f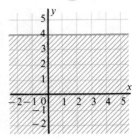

g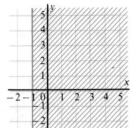

h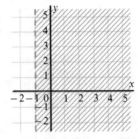

i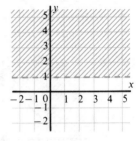

4   Write inequalities to describe the regions of these diagrams which are *not* shaded. Remember the difference between solid boundaries and dotted boundaries.

a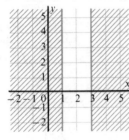

b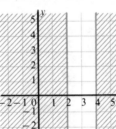

c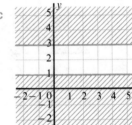

d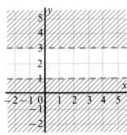

e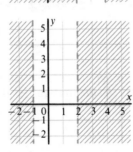

f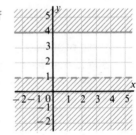

5   Write *two* inequalities to describe the unshaded regions of these diagrams.

a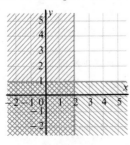

b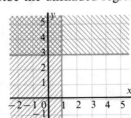

c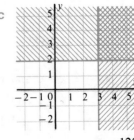

129

Regions

d 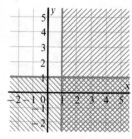 e 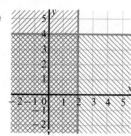 f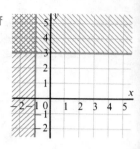

6 Write down an inequality for each boundary of the unshaded regions of these diagrams. Where there is a slanting boundary line, its equation is given.

a 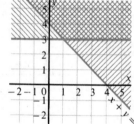 b 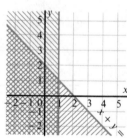 c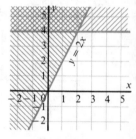

d 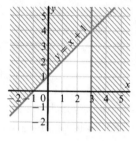 e 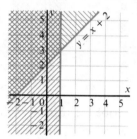 f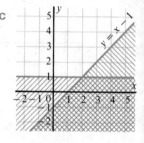

7 Draw and label both axes from -2 to 4 and draw the boundaries of each of these regions.

Shade that part of your diagram which is *not* described by the inequalities. (This is sometimes called *shading out*, rather than *shading in*.)

a $x \geqslant 2$ and $y \geqslant 1$ b $x \leqslant 3$ and $y \leqslant 2$

c $x \geqslant 1$ and $y \leqslant 3$ d $1 \leqslant x \leqslant 3$ and $y \geqslant 2$

e $2 \leqslant x \leqslant 4$ and $y \geqslant -1$ f $x \leqslant 2$ and $2 \leqslant y \leqslant 3$

g $x \geqslant -1$ and $0 \leqslant y \leqslant 2$ h $0 \leqslant x \leqslant 3$ and $1 \leqslant y \leqslant 2$

These next boundaries include some slanting lines. You will need to plot a few points in order to draw them.

i $y \leqslant x + 1$ and $x \geqslant 2$ j $y \geqslant x - 1$ and $x \leqslant 3$

k $y \leqslant x + 2$ and $y \leqslant 3$ l $y \geqslant x$ and $y \geqslant 1$

m $x + y \leqslant 3$ and $x \geqslant 1$ n $x + y \leqslant 4$ and $1 \leqslant x \leqslant 3$

o $x + y \geqslant 2$ and $2 \leqslant y \leqslant 3$ p $x + y \leqslant 4$ and $0 \leqslant x \leqslant 1$

130

8   For each part, draw and label both axes from -6 to 6.
    Shade that part of the diagram which is *not* described by the given inequalities,
    and calculate the area of the unshaded region.

a $1 \leqslant x \leqslant 4$
    $2 \leqslant y \leqslant 6$

b $2 \leqslant x \leqslant 5$
    $-3 \leqslant y \leqslant 2$

c $-2 \leqslant x \leqslant 1$
    $-4 \leqslant y \leqslant -1$

d $-3 \leqslant x \leqslant 0$
    $-2 \leqslant y \leqslant 3$

e $1 \leqslant x \leqslant 4$
    $y \leqslant x + 1$
    $y \geqslant x - 4$

f $0 \leqslant x \leqslant 3$
    $y \leqslant x$
    $y \geqslant x - 5$

g $-2 \leqslant y \leqslant 4$
    $y \leqslant x + 2$
    $y \geqslant x - 2$

h $y \geqslant 1$
    $x + y \leqslant 5$
    $y \leqslant x + 1$

i $x \geqslant -2$
    $y \leqslant 4$
    $y \geqslant x - 1$

j $x \leqslant 1$
    $y \geqslant -2$
    $y \leqslant x + 4$

k $y \geqslant 0$
    $y \leqslant 2x + 2$
    $x + y \leqslant 5$

l $y \geqslant 1$
    $y \leqslant 2x - 1$
    $y \leqslant 4 - \frac{1}{2}x$

9   For each part, draw and label both axes from 0 to 12.
    Shade that part of the diagram which is *not* described by the given inequalities.

a $4x + y \geqslant 12$
    $x + 2y \geqslant 12$
    $x \geqslant 0, y \geqslant 0$

b $5x + 3y \geqslant 30$
    $x + 4y \geqslant 8$
    $x \geqslant 0, y \geqslant 0$

c $3x + y \geqslant 12$
    $2x + 3y \geqslant 18$
    $x \geqslant 0, y \geqslant 0$

d $6x + y \geqslant 12$
    $x + y \geqslant 8$
    $2x + 5y \geqslant 20$
    $x \geqslant 0, y \geqslant 0$

e $4x + 5y \leqslant 40$
    $y \leqslant 3x$
    $y \geqslant 0$

f $2x + y \leqslant 10$
    $4x + 9y \leqslant 36$
    $y \leqslant 2x$
    $y \geqslant 0$

g $3x + 5y \leqslant 30$
    $y \leqslant 2x$
    $y \geqslant \frac{1}{2}x$

h $3x + 4y \leqslant 36$
    $9x + 4y \geqslant 36$
    $y \geqslant \frac{1}{3}x$

10   Draw and label both axes from 0 to 8 for each part.
     Shade that part of the diagram which is *not* given by the inequalities.
     Use a *solid* line when the boundary is *included*
     but a *dotted* line when the boundary is *excluded*.

a $x + y < 6$
    $x + 2y < 8$

b $x + y \leqslant 5$
    $3x + 8y > 24$

c $x + 3y \geqslant 6$
    $2x + y \geqslant 8$

d $3x + 2y > 12$
    $y < 2x$

e $y < x + 1$
    $y > x - 1$
    $x + y > 4$

f $y \leqslant 4$
    $y \geqslant \frac{1}{2}x$
    $6x + 5y > 30$

11   Draw and label both axes from 0 to 6, and shade out the region given by the
     inequalities, using solid and dotted boundary lines as required.
     Use your unshaded regions to write down all possible points which have *integer*
     values of x and y.

a $2x + 3y > 12$
    $y < 3$
    $x < 5$

b $x + y < 6$
    $y > 1$
    $x \geqslant 1$

c $y < x + 2$
    $y > 2$
    $x \leqslant 4$

d $y \leqslant 2x$
    $y \geqslant \frac{1}{2}x$
    $x + y < 5$

e $2x + y > 6$
    $y > x$
    $y < 5$

f $3x + y > 6$
    $x + 3y > 6$
    $x + y < 6$

g $y < 2x + 1$
    $y > x + 1$
    $x \leqslant 2$

h $y \leqslant \frac{1}{2}x + 3$
    $y \geqslant x$
    $x \geqslant 1$

i $y < \frac{1}{2}x + 2$
    $y > \frac{1}{2}x - 1$
    $2 < x < 4$

Regions

Part 2 Maximum and minimum values

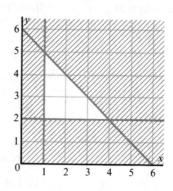

1 Which point in this unshaded region has
  a the largest x value
  b the largest y value?

2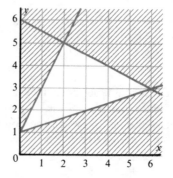

Which point in this unshaded region has
  a the largest x value
  b the largest y value
  c the smallest x value?

3 Which point in this unshaded region has
  a the largest x value
  b the largest y value
  c the smallest x value
  d the smallest y value?

4 Draw and label both axes from 0 to 10.
Shade that part of your diagrams *not* described by these inequalities.

  a $x \geqslant 2$ Which point of the unshaded region has
      $y \geqslant 3$ (i) the largest x value
      $x + y \leqslant 8$ (ii) the largest y value?

  b $x + y \leqslant 9$ Which point of the unshaded region has
      $y \leqslant 2x$ (i) the largest x value
      $y \geqslant 2$ (ii) the smallest x value
                 (iii) the largest y value?

  c $y \leqslant x + 4$ Which point of the unshaded region has
      $y \geqslant x - 4$ (i) the largest x value
      $x + y \leqslant 10$ (ii) the smallest x value
      $x + y \geqslant 4$ (iii) the largest y value
                 (iv) the smallest y value?

d $y \leqslant 2x$ Which point of the unshaded region has
  $y \geqslant \frac{1}{2}x$ (i)   the smallest y value
  $y \leqslant 9$ (ii) the smallest x value?
  $x \leqslant 8$

e $y \leqslant \frac{1}{2}x + 4$ Which point of the unshaded region has
  $x + y \geqslant 7$ (i)   the largest y value
  $2 \leqslant x \leqslant 6$ (ii) the smallest y value
  (iii) the smallest x value?

f $x + y \leqslant 9$ Which point of the unshaded region has
  $y \geqslant \frac{1}{2}x$ (i)   the largest y value
  $y \leqslant x - 2$ (ii) the smallest y value
  (iii) the largest x value
  (iv) the smallest x value?

5 a Copy and complete this table by writing in the three extreme corners of the unshaded region. Then calculate the value of $2x + y$ at each corner.

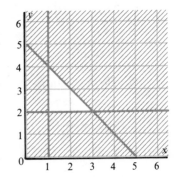

Corner	(,)	(,)	(,)
Value of $2x + y$			

b At which corner has $2x + y$ its maximum value?
c At which corner has $2x + y$ its minimum value?

6

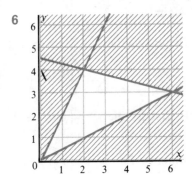

a Copy and complete this table.

Corner	(,)	(,)	(,)
Value of $x + y$			

b At which corner has $x + y$ its maximum value?
c At which corner has $x + y$ its minimum value?

7 a Copy and complete this table.

Corner	(,)	(,)	(,)
Value of $x + y$			

b At which corner has $x + y$ its minimum value?
c Why is there no maximum value of $x + y$?

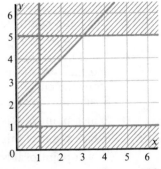

133

Regions

8 a Copy and complete this table.

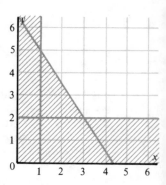

Corner	(,)	(,)
Value of $x + 3y$		

b At which corner has $x + 3y$ its minimum value?

c Why is there no maximum value of $x + 3y$?

9 For each part, draw and label both axes from 0 to 8.

Shade the region *not* described by the inequalities.

Find the point of the permitted region which gives the maximum or minimum value required.

a The inequalities $\begin{cases} y \leqslant x + 3 \\ x \leqslant 4 \\ y \geqslant 4 \end{cases}$

Maximise $x + y$

b The inequalities $\begin{cases} y \geqslant x + 1 \\ x \geqslant 2 \\ y \leqslant 7 \end{cases}$

Maximise $x + y$

c The inequalities $\begin{cases} y \geqslant x + 1 \\ y \leqslant 2x - 2 \\ y \leqslant 6 \end{cases}$

Maximise $x + 2y$

d The inequalities $\begin{cases} x + y \leqslant 7 \\ x \geqslant 1 \\ y \geqslant 2 \end{cases}$

Maximise $4x + y$

e The inequalities $\begin{cases} x + y \geqslant 6 \\ x + 2y \geqslant 8 \\ x \geqslant 2 \\ y \geqslant 1 \end{cases}$

Minimise $2x + y$

f The inequalities $\begin{cases} 2x + y \geqslant 6 \\ x + y \geqslant 5 \\ y \geqslant 2 \\ x \geqslant 0 \end{cases}$

Minimise $x + 3y$

g The inequalities $\begin{cases} 2x + y \geqslant 8 \\ y \leqslant 2x \\ y \geqslant 1 \end{cases}$

Minimise $4x - y$

h The inequalities $\begin{cases} y \geqslant \frac{1}{2}x + 2 \\ x + y \geqslant 5 \\ y \leqslant 5 \end{cases}$

Maximise $3x - y$

i The inequalities $\begin{cases} y \leqslant 3x \\ y \geqslant \frac{1}{2}x \\ y \leqslant 6 \\ x \leqslant 6 \end{cases}$

Maximise $y - 2x$

j The inequalities $\begin{cases} y \leqslant x + 2\frac{1}{2} \\ y \leqslant 2x \\ y \geqslant x \\ y \leqslant 7 \end{cases}$

Minimise $2x + y$

10 a Copy and complete this table for the equation $y = x^2$.

x	-3	-2	-1	0	1	2	3
y							

b Label the x-axis from -3 to 3 and the y-axis from 0 to 10.

Draw the curve $y = x^2$ and the line $y = 2x + 3$ on your axes.

Shade out the region given by $y \geqslant x^2$ and $y \leqslant 2x + 3$.

c Which point of this region has the maximum value of y?

d Which point of this region has the minimum value of x?

e Which point of this region has the maximum value of $x + y$?

Regions

11 a Copy and complete this table for the equation $y = x^2 + 3$.

x	-3	-2	-1	0	1	2	3
x^2							
$+3$							
y							

b Draw axes, labelling the x-axis from -3 to 3 and the y-axis from 0 to 12.

Draw the curve $y = x^2 + 3$ and the line $y = x + 9$ on your axes.

Shade out the region given by $y \geqslant x^2 + 3$ and $y \leqslant x + 9$.

c Which point of this region has
(i) the minimum value of x (ii) the minimum value of y?

d What is the maximum possible value of $x + y$ in this region?

12 a Copy and complete this table for the equation $y = x^2 - 4x + 3$.

x	0	1	2	3	4
x^2					
$-4x$					
$+3$					
y					

b Draw axes, labelling the x-axis from 0 to 4 and the y-axis from -1 to 4.

On your axes, shade out the region given by
$$y \geqslant x^2 - 4x + 3, \qquad y \leqslant \tfrac{1}{2}x + 1, \qquad x \leqslant 3.$$

c Which point in this region has the maximum value of y?

d Which point in this region has
(i) the minimum value of y (ii) the minimum value of x?

e What is the maximum value of $x + y$ and at which point does it occur?

Part 3   True or false

State whether each of these inequalities is *true* or *false*.

1 Region A is where $\begin{cases} y > x + 1 \\ x > 2 \end{cases}$ a
b

Region B is where $\begin{cases} y < x + 1 \\ x > 2 \end{cases}$ c
d

Region C is where $\begin{cases} y > x + 1 \\ x < 2 \end{cases}$ e
f

Region D is where $\begin{cases} y > x + 1 \\ x > 2 \end{cases}$ g
h

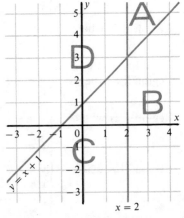

135

Regions

2 Region E is where $\begin{cases} y > x - 1 \\ y > -3 \end{cases}$ a b

Region F is where $\begin{cases} y > x - 1 \\ y < -3 \end{cases}$ c d

Region G is where $\begin{cases} y > x - 1 \\ y > -3 \end{cases}$ e f

Region H is where $\begin{cases} y < x - 1 \\ y < -3 \end{cases}$ g h

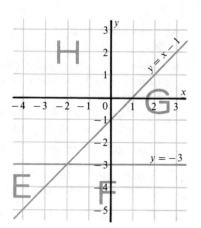

3 Region J is where $\begin{cases} y > 2x \\ y > -x + 2 \end{cases}$ a b

Region K is where $\begin{cases} y > 2x \\ y > -x + 2 \end{cases}$ c d

Region L is where $\begin{cases} y > 2x \\ y > -x + 2 \end{cases}$ e f

Region M is where $\begin{cases} y > 2x \\ y > -x + 2 \end{cases}$ g h

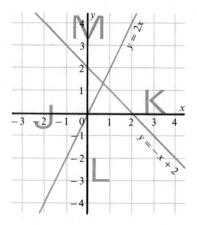

4 Region N is where $\begin{cases} y > x \\ x > 3 \end{cases}$ a b

Region P is where $\begin{cases} y < x \\ y > -2 \\ x > 3 \end{cases}$ c d e

Region Q is where $\begin{cases} y > -2 \\ x > 3 \end{cases}$ f g

Region R is where $\begin{cases} y > x \\ y < -2 \\ x > 3 \end{cases}$ h i j

Region S is where $\begin{cases} y < -2 \\ y < x \end{cases}$ k l

Region T is where $\begin{cases} y > -2 \\ x < 3 \\ y < x \end{cases}$ m n o

Region U is where $\begin{cases} y < x \\ y < -2 \\ x < 3 \end{cases}$ p q r

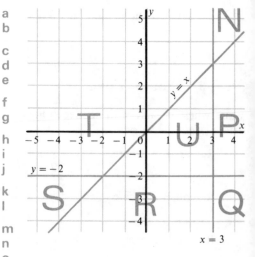

136

5   Region V is where $\begin{cases} y < -1 \\ y > x + 3 \end{cases}$ a
                                                                          b

    Region W is where $\begin{cases} y < -1 \\ y < x + 3 \\ y < -x + 1 \end{cases}$ c
                                                                                        d
                                                                                        e

    Region Z is where $\begin{cases} y > -x + 1 \\ y > x + 3 \end{cases}$ f
                                                                              g

    Region A is where $\begin{cases} y < -1 \\ y > -x + 1 \\ y < x + 3 \end{cases}$ h
                                                                                        i
                                                                                        j

    Region B is where $\begin{cases} y > -1 \\ y > -x + 1 \end{cases}$ k
                                                                           l

    Region C is where $\begin{cases} y < x + 3 \\ y < -x + 1 \\ y > -1 \end{cases}$ m
                                                                                        n
                                                                                        o

    Region D is where $\begin{cases} y < x + 3 \\ y < -1 \\ y < -x + 1 \end{cases}$ p
                                                                                        q
                                                                                        r

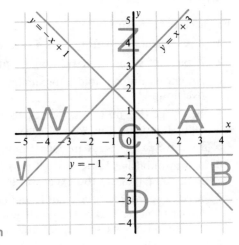

137

Forming inequalities

Part 1

For each of these statements, write the information in symbols using an inequality.

1   n passengers are sitting on a 40-seater bus.

2   A piece of string x metres long is cut off a 10-metre ball.

3   An empty tin can hold a maximum of 5 litres; but when I pour in x litres, some overflows.

4   Before getting on a bus, I check that I have enough to pay the 40 pence fare, and I board the bus with x pence in my pocket.

5   I receive £x per week in pocket-money, but I am never given more than £2.

6   A firm publishes books only if they have at least 50 pages; but books of more than 300 pages are too expensive to publish. Their latest book has x pages.

7   A passenger-ferry to a small island can take at most 20 passengers. But the ferryman never makes the journey with less than 5 passengers. Today he made the trip with x passengers on board.

8   A firm builds several types of house, though all of them have at least 2 bedrooms. The biggest house they build has 5 bedrooms. Mr and Mrs Naylor bought one of their houses with n bedrooms.

9   Mrs Cook never bakes a cake unless she bakes at least two at the same time; but she has storage space for at most six cakes. Yesterday she baked x cakes.

10   A teacher has x boys and y girls in his class, and the school never allows a class to have more than 30 pupils.

11   I drive x km and then walk y km to get to work depending on the route I take. The longest possible route is 20 km long.

12   The local police station has space to keep no more than 5 stray pets overnight. Last night they accepted x stray dogs and y stray cats.

13   A farmer has x hectares of arable land and y hectares of pasture, in addition to some woodland and some waste land. His farm has a total of 900 hectares.

14   Mrs Fletcher buys x metres of cotton material at £3 per metre and also y metres of wool material at £4 per metre. She receives some change from a £20 note.

15   When Jimmy Adams goes to watch a cricket match, he always spends at least £1 on things to eat. Last Saturday, he bought x ice-creams at 20 pence each and y bars of chocolate at 15 pence each.

16   A lorry has a maximum possible load of 8000 kg. Mr Field loads it with x sacks of potatoes at 100 kg each and y sacks of turnips at 80 kg each.

17   Yesterday I had x helpings of breakfast cereal and y slices of brown bread. Each helping of cereal has 5 units of vitamin B, and each slice of bread has 8 units of vitamin B. My intake of vitamin B at breakfast is always more than 40 units.

18   In a 2-hour exam, Amanda did x short questions taking 2 minutes each and then y long questions taking 15 minutes each. She finished inside the 2 hours before the exam ended.

19   Miss Preston must earn at least £90 a week to cover all her living expenses, and she does this by having two part-time jobs. She earns £x per hour for 15 hours on one job, and then £y per hour for 18 hours on the other job.

20   A gardener plants an area of y m^2 with potatoes and another x m^2 with cabbages. The area of potatoes is more than twice the area with cabbages.

Forming inequalities

21 A school concert has y seats at £2 each and x seats at £1 each, and the income from the sale of tickets must exceed £100 for each performance.

22 There are y expensive seats and x cheaper seats in the school hall which can hold no more than 300 seats altogether.

23 Mrs Staines knows that the number y of fancy cakes she has to make for her son's birthday party will be no more than three times the number x of ice-creams which she has to buy.

24 The number n_1 in the congregation at church for the evening service is always at least 30 more than the number n_2 who attend the morning service.

25 The number n_1 of miles which a hiker can walk in a day is always at least 60 miles less than the number n_2 of miles which he could have cycled in the same time.

Part 2

For each of these situations, write the information in symbols using one (or more) inequalities.

1 The distance x km from my home to school is more than 5 km.

2 The number n of people who came to my birthday party was less than 25.

3 The egg-box holds a maximum of six eggs and there are n eggs in it at the moment.

4 In one week, a woman buys a number n of loaves of bread. She buys more than two loaves but less than six loaves.

5 You go to a garage to buy a number n of litres of petrol. You must buy at least five litres, and your car has a 40-litre tank.

6 It always takes me between 20 minutes and 25 minutes to walk to school. Today it took me t minutes.

7 An opening batsman has a lowest score of 12 and a highest score of 87 so far this season. Yesterday he scored x runs.

8 I throw one dice and the score is x.

9 An obtuse angle is more than a right angle but less than a straight line.
This diagram shows an obtuse angle of $x°$.

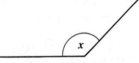

10 My neighbour's car can seat 5 people. It passed me today with n people in it.

11 Pencils cost 5p each; and you buy a certain number n of them, receiving some change from a £1 coin.

12 Records cost £4 each and I bought n of them, receiving change from a £20 note.

13 One bar of chocolate costs 18p and I receive change from two £1 coins after buying n bars.

14 Daffodil bulbs are 3p each and tulip bulbs 10p each. You have £2 at the most to spend, and you buy x daffodil and y tulip bulbs.

15 You purchase x four-pence stamps and y five-pence stamps, and receive change from a £1 coin.

16 My dog eats x tins of food each day, and my bitch eats y tins of food each day. In one week they eat a total of less than 40 tins.

17 A tradesman has 450 boxes to transport in a lorry and a van. The lorry can take 50 boxes at a time, and the van 15 at a time. The lorry makes x trips and the van y trips.

Forming inequalities

18 The same tradesman as above finds each trip in the lorry costs 50p and each trip in the van costs 30p. He wants the total cost to be less than £7.

19 A supermarket has a display of soap powder. There are x packets of Aza (each 12 cm wide) and y packets of Zopy (each 10 cm wide), standing on a shelf side by side. The shelf is 4 metres long.

20 An automatic packing machine takes 3 seconds for a box of type X and 5 seconds for a box of type Y. In 5 minutes, the machine must deal with at least x of type X and y of type Y.

21 A man on a production line takes 8 seconds to fix a bolt onto a product and 4 seconds to fix a nail. He must fix at least x bolts and y nails each minute.

22 A cyclist travels at an average speed of x km/h for 5 hours, but he covers less than 100 km.

23 A motorist averages a speed of x km/h for 2 hours on the motorway and y km/h for 3 hours on ordinary roads. His total journey is less than 250 km.

24 An examination takes 2 hours, and has two sections A and B. Section A has ten questions and section B six questions. A candidate attempts all the questions and finishes before the allotted time. He averages x minutes for each section A question, and y minutes for each in section B.

25 A ferry has enough room to hold 12 cars. But a lorry would take up the space of three cars. On one particular trip, there are x lorries and y cars on board.

26 a There must be at least 2000 books in a school library, of which x are fiction and y are non-fiction.
    b There must also be more non-fiction than fiction.

27 a A shop stocks more than 250 yoghurt cartons of which y are "Derwent Vale" and x are "Shee".
    b There must be more "Derwent Vale" than "Shee".

28 a A school has 200 pupils in its 5th form of which x are taking O-level and y are taking CSE exams in maths, and some of them take both exams.
    b The number taking CSE is more than twice the number taking O-level.

29 A rectangular table top is x metres long and y metres wide. The length must be more than double the width; the area must exceed 1 m^2; and the diagonal must be more than 3 metres long. Write inequalities to show
    a that x and y must be positive
    b the restriction on length and width
    c the restriction on the area
    d the restriction on the diagonal.

30 You have birthday money to spend on x books and y records. The books you decide on are £1 each and the records £4 each. Give inequalities for each of the following.
    a You cannot buy a negative number of either.
    b There are no more than 3 books which you would buy.
    c There are no more than 10 records which you would buy.
    d Your birthday money amounts to £20.
    e You decide to spend more on records than on books.

31 Some fruit squash is made from oranges and lemons. Each tin of squash requires y oranges and x lemons. Write inequalities for these statements.
    a There cannot be a negative number of either fruit.
    b Each tin of squash requires at least 12 pieces of fruit.
    c For a good flavour, there must be more than twice as many oranges as lemons.
    d If each orange costs 15p and each lemon 10p, the total cost per tin must be less than 90 pence.

Forming inequalities

32 You visit the school's tuck-shop to buy x bars of chocolate at 15 pence each and y tubes of mints at 10 pence each. Write inequalities for these statements.
   a You cannot buy a negative number of either.
   b You have a total of only 50 pence to spend.
   c You must buy at least two tubes of mints.
   d The tuck-shop restricts you to buying no more than 3 bars of chocolate.

33 A girl has £2·40 to spend on make-up. She decides to spend some or all of it on x lipsticks and y boxes of talc. Give inequalities for these statements.
   a She cannot buy a negative number of articles.
   b She needs not more than 3 lipsticks.
   c She also needs at least two boxes of talc.
   d Each lipstick costs 30 pence and each box of talc 60 pence.

34 A transport firm has two kinds of lorries, x Juggers and y Nauts. They get a contract to carry 720 trays of fruit and 400 tonnes of vegetables. Write inequalities for the following.
   a They cannot use a negative number of either type of lorry.
   b One full Jugger holds 90 trays; and one full Naut holds 48 trays.
   c One full Jugger holds 30 tonnes of vegetables; and one full Naut holds 50 tonnes of vegetables.

35 The table shows the number of units of vitamin A and vitamin B in one kilogram of foods X and Y.

	Units of vitamin A	Units of vitamin B
1 kg of food X	4	9
1 kg of food Y	8	6

For one person, the minimum daily intake required is 20 units of vitamin A and 15 units of vitamin B, consumed in x kg of food X and y kg of food Y. Write inequalities for
   a the fact that no negative quantities of food can be eaten
   b the required intake of vitamin A
   c the required intake of vitamin B.

36 A greengrocer sells two sizes of boxes of flowers and fruit as Christmas presents. This table shows the mass of fruit and number of flowers in the two sizes.

	Mass of fruit (kg)	Number of flowers
Each large box	6	15
Each small box	2	10

The total mass of fruit available is 50 kg and the total number of flowers is 300. In the week before Christmas, the shopkeeper prepares x large boxes and y small boxes. Write inequalities for the following:
   a x and y must be positive numbers
   b the mass of fruit used
   c the number of flowers used.

Linear programming

Part 1 Listing possibilities

1 A lady wants to plant her garden with both apple trees and pear trees.

There are various restrictions placed on how many of each type she can have, and these are shown in the diagram by the shading.

The *unshaded* region (including its solid boundaries) gives the permitted numbers of trees.

Write down the nine possibilities.

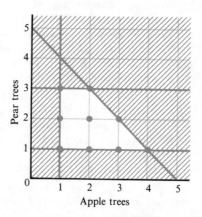

2

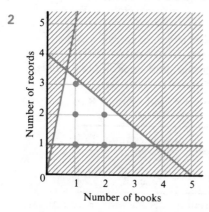

David Johnson will spend his birthday money on records and books.

The *unshaded* region (including its solid boundaries) shows the possible choices which he can buy.

Write down these possibilities.

3 A firm is to buy two types of new machines, one made in Britain and the other in Germany, to modernise its factory.

Use the unshaded region to write down the different possible combinations which could be bought.

(Remember that a dotted boundary is *not* included in the unshaded region.)

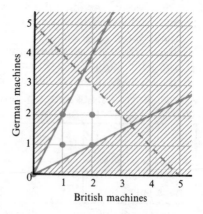

4

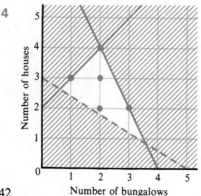

A builder has a plot of land on which he intends to put up some houses and bungalows.

Use the unshaded region to write down the possible combinations which are allowed.

Linear programming

In each of these problems,
 a draw both axes labelled from 0 to 10
 b write an inequality for each of the numbered statements
 c draw solid or dotted boundary lines on your diagram
 d shade the diagram, leaving the permitted region *unshaded*
 e write down a list of the possibilities as requested.

5 Mrs Ingham goes shopping for loaves of bread and some cakes.
   She carries home in her bag x loaves and y cakes.
      (i)   She must buy at least 4 loaves of bread.
      (ii) She must buy at least 3 cakes.
      (iii) Her shopping bag can hold no more than a total of 10 items.

   a List the different possible numbers of loaves and cakes which she could buy.
   b What is the largest number of loaves she could buy?
   c What is the largest number of cakes she could buy?

6 Alan Parker breeds rabbits and he decides to buy x bucks and y does.
      (i)   He wants at least 2 bucks.
      (ii) He wants at least 4 does.
      (iii) He only has space for at most 8 animals.

   a List the different possible numbers of bucks and does which he could buy.
   b What is the largest number of bucks allowed?
   c What is the largest number of does allowed?

7 Anna Lister buys her lunch at school where she decides to have x sandwiches
   and y pieces of fruit.
      (i)   She will need at least 3 sandwiches.
      (ii) She will want at least 1 piece of fruit.
      (iii) She will not want to buy more than 6 items altogether.

   a List the different numbers of sandwiches and pieces of fruit which are possible.
   b What is the largest number of sandwiches which she could buy?
   c What is the largest number of pieces of fruit allowed?

8 A handyman needs to buy y large electric plugs and x small ones to complete a
   job he is doing.
      (i)   He needs at least 2 large plugs.
      (ii) The number of large plugs must be less than (or equal to) twice the
            number of small plugs.
      (iii) The total number of plugs will be less than or equal to 7.

   a List the possible numbers of large and small plugs which could be bought.
   b What is the largest number of the small size allowed?
   c What is the smallest number of the small size allowed?

9 A shop sells two types of cassette tapes. Mr Lee wants to buy y cheap tapes and
   x expensive ones.
      (i)   He will need at least 5, but no more than 8, of the cheap tapes.
      (ii) He will need no more than 4 expensive ones.
      (iii) The number of cheap tapes must be less than three times the number of
            expensive tapes.

   a List the different possibilities of cheap and expensive tapes which he could buy.
   b What is the smallest number of expensive tapes allowed?
   c What is the largest number of cheap tapes allowed?

Linear programming

10 A warehouse stocks crates of two types of garden peat. They have y crates of sphagnum peat and x crates of brown peat.
   (i)   They never have more than 5 crates of sphagnum in stock.
   (ii) They always have at least 4, but never more than 7, crates of brown peat in stock.
   (iii) The number of crates of sphagnum is always more than half the number of crates of brown peat.

   a List the possible combinations of crates which they could have in store.
   b What is the smallest number of crates of brown peat allowed?
   c What is the largest number of crates of sphagnum peat allowed?

11 A small firm runs a van and a lorry. A particular job will need x trips with the van and y trips with the lorry.
   (i)   There will certainly have to be at least 2 trips with the van.
   (ii) The lorry will make at least 3, but no more than 6, trips.
   (iii) The total number of trips of van and lorry will be at least 6.
   (iv) The total number of trips will be no more than 9.

   a List the possible numbers of trips which they could make.
   b What is the greatest number of trips which the van could make?
   c What is the least number of trips which the lorry could make?

12 A doctor prescribes two types of pills for a patient. There are y red pills and x white pills to be taken daily.
   (i)   No more than 6 red pills must be taken each day.
   (ii) No more than 3 white pills must be taken each day.
   (iii) The total number of pills must be at least 5 a day.
   (iv) The number of red ones must be at least 2 more than the number of white ones.

   a List the possible numbers of pills which would be allowed.
   b What is the least number of red ones allowed each day?
   c What is the largest number of white ones allowed each day?

Part 2 Maximising

1 A farmer is to buy x cows and y sheep.
   Write an inequality for each of these statements.
   (i)   He must buy at least 3 cows.
   (ii) He must buy at least 4 sheep.
   (iii) He can accommodate a total of no more than 12 animals.
   Draw and label both axes from 0 to 15.
   Show, by shading, the region given by your inequalities.

   Profit He hopes to make a profit of £200 on each cow and £100 on each sheep.

   Copy and complete this table for the extreme corners of the permitted region.

Corner	(,)	(,)	(,)
Profit, £			

   Find the maximum possible profit; and give the number of cows and sheep he will have to buy to make this profit.

Linear programming

2 A school buys two new types of chocolate bar for its tuck-shop.
It decides to buy x boxes of Soggichoc and y boxes of Gungibars.

Write an inequality for each of these statements.
  (i) The tuck-shop must have at least 5 boxes of Soggichocs.
  (ii) It must have at least 2 boxes of Gungibars.
  (iii) It has storage space for a total of at most 14 boxes.

Draw and label both axes from 0 to 15.
Show, by shading, the region given by your inequalities.

Profit It is hoped to make a profit of £5 on each box of Soggichocs and £8 on each box of Gungibars.

Copy and complete this table for the extreme corners of the permitted region.

Corner	(,)	(,)	(,)
Profit, £			

Find the maximum possible profit; and say how many boxes of each type must be bought.

3 A gardener has land on which he wants to plant x apple trees and y plum trees.

Write an inequality for each of these statements.
  (i) He wants to plant at least 3 apple trees.
  (ii) He must also plant at least 3 plum trees.
  (iii) He has land for a total of no more than 10 trees.

Draw and label both your axes from 0 to 12; and indicate, by shading, the region given by your inequalities.

Profit The gardener will sell the fruit in the autumn, and he hopes to make a profit of £10 on each apple tree and £6 on each plum tree.

Copy and complete this table for the extreme corners of the permitted region.

Corner	(,)	(,)	(,)
Profit, £			

Find his maximum possible profit; and give the number of apple trees and the number of plum trees which he must plant.

4 A builder has a site on which he intends to build x houses and y bungalows.
The council restrict the numbers of each which he is allowed to build.

Write inequalities for these statements.
  (i) There must be at least 4 and at most 10 houses.
  (ii) There must be at least 2 and at most 8 bungalows.
  (iii) The maximum number of dwellings allowed is 15.

Draw and label both axes from 0 to 16; and indicate, by shading, the region given by your inequalities.

Profit He intends charging prices so that there is a profit of £5000 on each house and £8000 on each bungalow.
Construct a table for the extreme corners of the permitted region; and so find the maximum possible profit he can make.
How many houses and bungalows are needed to give this profit?

Linear programming

5 The keeper of a public park designs a floral display using two kinds of plants. He will use x bundiflora and y gloriosus.

Write inequalities for these statements.
  (i)   He must use at least 60 but at most 90 bundiflora.
  (ii) He must use at least 40 but at most 100 gloriosus.
  (iii) The display area can take a maximum of 180 plants.

Draw and label both axes from 0 to 200; and show the region given by your inequalities.

Cost Each bundiflora costs 10 pence and each gloriosus costs 20 pence. Construct a table for the extreme corners of the region; and so find the maximum possible cost of the display. How many of each type of flower are needed for this maximum cost?

6 A TV repairer mends x black-and-white and y colour sets each day.

Write inequalities for these statements.
  (i)   He always mends at least 4 black-and-white sets every day.
  (ii) He always mends at least 3 colour sets every day.
  (iii) The firm he works for says he must mend a total of at least 10 sets every day.
  (iv) He never has time to mend more than a total of 15 sets daily.

Draw and label both axes from 0 to 16; and indicate the region given by your inequalities.

Earnings Each black-and-white set earns the repairer £8 and each colour set earns him £12.
Construct a table for the extreme corners of the region, and find his maximum possible earnings for one day. How many sets of each type does he need to repair in this case?

7 A doctor recommends two courses of tablets for a patient. The daily dosage is y white tablets and x green ones.

Write these four statements as inequalities, and find the region which they represent on axes labelled from 0 to 12.
  (i)   At least 2 white tablets must be taken each day.
  (ii) No more than 7 green tablets must be taken daily.
  (iii) The total number of tablets taken each day must be no more than 12.
  (iv) The number of white tablets must be less than (or equal to) twice the number of green ones.

Each white tablet contains 5 units of a certain drug, and each green tablet contains 4 units of the same drug. Construct a table for the extreme corners of the permitted region to find the maximum number of units of this drug which can be taken in one day. How many tablets of each colour will be taken in this case?

8 A farmer sows x hectares of barley and y hectares of wheat.

Write these statements as inequalities, and find the region which they represent on axes labelled from 0 to 12.
  (i)   He must sow at least 2 hectares of wheat.
  (ii) The number of hectares of wheat must be less than (or equal to) twice the number of hectares of barley.
  (iii) Each hectare of barley costs £200 to sow, and each hectare of wheat costs £100; but the farmer has no more than £1200 to spend.

146

Linear programming

Each hectare of barley can be sold for £800 and each hectare of wheat for £500. Investigate the extreme corners of the permitted region to find the maximum income from the sale. How many hectares of each crop should he sow for this maximum income?

9   The school play is staged in the hall where x rows of expensive seats and y rows of cheaper seats are to be arranged.

Write inequalities for these statements and find the region they represent on axes labelled from 0 to 12.
(i)   There must be at least 4 rows of the cheaper seats.
(ii) The number of rows of cheap seats should be no more than twice the number of rows of the expensive ones.
(iii) Each row of expensive seats has 16 chairs, and each row of the cheap seats has 24 chairs; but the hall can accommodate a total of no more than 192 seats.

If a full row of expensive seats brings in £60 and a full row of cheap seats brings in £72, find the number of rows of both types of seat which will produce the maximum income.

10 Two men earn their living making tables and chairs; and each week they make x tables and y chairs.

Write inequalities for these statements and find the region they represent on axes labelled from 0 to 12.
(i)   They must make at least 2 tables each week.
(ii) The number of chairs made must be less than (or equal to) twice the number of tables made.
(iii) Each table takes 12 hours to make, and each chair 6 hours to make; but the two men together work for only 72 hours each week.

If each table produces a profit of £80 and each chair a profit of £30, find how many of each they should make for the greatest weekly profit.

Part 3   Minimising

1   A firm manufactures two soap powders, Wyto and Zopee, which are packed into containers ready for transporting by rail. Each day they pack x loads of Wyto and y loads of Zopee.

Write down an inequality for each of these three statements.
(i)   There is an order for at least 4 loads of Wyto each day.
(ii) At least 3 loads of Zopee must also be loaded each day.
(iii) There must be a total of at least ten loads each day for the train provided.

Draw axes labelled from 0 to 10, and show, by shading, the region of the diagram given by the inequalities.

Cost   Each container of Wyto costs £30 to load, and each container of Zopee costs £20.

Copy and complete this table for the two extreme corners of the permitted region.

Corner	(,)	(,)
Cost, £		

What is the minimum cost of loading the whole train, and how many loads of each powder will then be needed?

147

Linear programming

2 Mr Westerton owns a cafe and he wants to buy x small tables and y large tables for it.

Write inequalities for each of these statements.
(i) He will need at least 4 new small tables.
(ii) He will also need at least 2 new large tables.
(iii) There is space for a total of at least 8 tables.

Draw axes labelled from 0 to 10, and show, by shading, the region given by the inequalities.

Cost Each small table will cost £30 and each large one £40.

Copy and complete this table for the two corners of the permitted region.

Corner	(,)	(,)
Cost, £		

Find the least cost of buying the tables and say how many of each size should be bought.

3 A garage orders two new models of car in preparation for the new year.
It is decided to have x Aurora and y Vespera in the showrooms.

Write inequalities for these statements.
(i) There will be an order for at least 3 Auroras.
(ii) An order will also be placed for at least 2, but no more than 8, Vesperas.
(iii) A demand is expected for a total of at least 10 cars.

Draw axes labelled from 0 to 12, and indicate, by shading, the region given by the inequalities.

Cost Each Aurora costs £5000 and each Vespera costs £6000.

Copy and complete this table for the extreme corners of the permitted region.

Corner	(,)	(,)	(,)
Cost, £			

What is the least amount the garage has to spend on new cars, and how many of each model should be ordered in this case?

4 A mother organises her daughter's birthday party and expects to invite x boys and y girls.

Write inequalities for these statements, and find the region they describe on axes labelled from 0 to 10.
(i) There will be at least 5 girls invited.
(ii) She will invite at least 2, but not more than 7, boys.
(iii) The number of girls will be at least 2 more than the number of boys.

If each boy is expected to eat 3 bread rolls and each girl 2 bread rolls, investigate the corners of the permitted region to find the minimum number of rolls which the mother should order. Also find the number of boys and girls invited in this case.

Linear programming

5   A supermarket employs x part-time and y full-time assistants.

Write inequalities for these statements, and indicate the region which they describe on axes labelled from 0 to 10.
  (i)   There must always be at least 6 full-time assistants.
  (ii) The number of full-time assistants will always be less than (or equal to) twice the number of part-time assistants.
  (iii) The number of full-time assistants must always be at least one more than the number of part-time ones.

If each part-time assistant earns £30 per week, and each full-time one earns £80 per week, investigate the corners of the permitted region to find the least amount of money which is needed to employ them for a week. How many part-time and how many full-time assistants will then be needed?

6   A farmer plants x fields of oats and y fields of barley.

Write these statements as inequalities and indicate them on axes labelled from 0 to 12.
  (i)   He must plant at least two fields with oats.
  (ii) He must also plant no more than 7 fields with barley.
  (iii) The total number of fields will be at least eight.
  (iv) Each field of oats needs 10 hours to sow, and each field of barley needs 20 hours to sow; and the farmer will spend at least 120 hours sowing all the fields.

Each field of oats costs £120 to sow, and each field of barley costs £150. Find the minimum cost of the whole operation and the number of fields of each type required.

7   A tour operator has allocated a car and a minibus to transport holiday-makers from the airport to their hotel. He expects the car will have to make x trips and the minibus y trips.

Write these statements as inequalities and indicate them on axes labelled from 0 to 14.
  (i)   The car will always have to make at least 2 trips.
  (ii) The car can take 5 passengers and the minibus 10 passengers. The total number of passengers is never less than 40.
  (iii) The car has space for 3 cases and the minibus 12 cases. The total space for suitcases must exceed (or equal) 36 cases.

Each car journey costs 60 pence, and each minibus journey costs 90 pence. What is the minimum cost possible, and how many trips must each vehicle then make?

8   A holiday airline has to buy its own aircraft, and it decides to purchase x jets and y turbo-props.

Indicate the region on axes labelled from 0 to 10, which these statements describe.
  (i)   There must be at least 4 jets.
  (ii) The airline must have a total of at least eight aircraft.
  (iii) Each jet can hold 80 passengers and each turbo-prop 120 passengers. At any time, there must be places for a total of at least 720 passengers.

If each jet costs £4 million and each turbo-prop £1 million, find the number of each type necessary for a minimum total cost, and state what this total cost will then be.

Linear programming

9   A mother makes her own fruit squash for her children, using x lemons and y oranges.

Draw axes labelled from 0 to 15 and indicate the region which these statements describe.
   (i)   The number of oranges should be no more than three times the number of lemons.
   (ii) She wants to use no more than 12 pieces of fruit altogether.
   (iii) Each lemon weighs 100 grams and each orange 200 grams; and she wants to use at least 1400 grams of fruit.

If a lemon costs 10 pence and an orange 15 pence, find her cheapest method of making the squash, stating how many of each fruit she should use.

10 A dietician prescribes x pills and y capsules to be taken each day by one of his patients.

Draw axes labelled from 0 to 12 and indicate the region which these statements describe.
   (i)   The patient must take at least one pill each day.
   (ii) At least two capsules must also be taken daily.
   (iii) Each pill contains 4 units of vitamin C, and each capsule contains 2 units of vitamin C. The daily intake of this vitamin must exceed (or equal) 16 units.
   (iv) There are 3 units of riboflavin in each pill, and 6 units in each capsule. The daily requirement of riboflavin must be not less than 30 units.

Find the minimum number of items which the patient must take each day to ensure he has the required intake, and state how many pills and capsules are needed in this case.

Further Topics

Areas under lines and curves

Rates of change

Distance, speed and acceleration

Areas under lines and curves

Part 1   Areas under lines

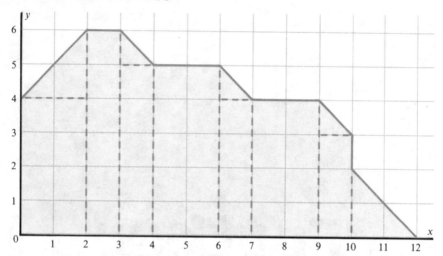

1   This diagram shows an area between a line and the x-axis, which has been divided into strips of rectangles and triangles.

Count the squares in all the strips, and so find the area between the line and the x-axis.

2   Draw axes, labelling the x-axis from 0 to 20 and the y-axis from 0 to 12 for each part.

Plot each set of points and join them with straight sections in the order given here.

Divide the area between the line and the x-axis into strips of rectangles and triangles, and count squares to find the total area between the line and the x-axis.

a   (0, 3) (4, 7) (6, 7) (8, 9) (10, 9) (15, 4) (16, 4) (20, 0)
b   (0, 5) (3, 5) (5, 3) (10, 8) (13, 8) (16, 5) (18, 5) (20, 3) (20, 0)
c   (0, 9) (4, 5) (6, 7) (8, 7) (11, 4) (14, 4) (16, 2) (18, 2) (20, 0)
d   (0, 10) (3, 10) (5, 8) (9, 8) (10, 7) (13, 10) (20, 3) (20, 0)
e   (0, 0) (2, 2) (2, 4) (5, 7) (9, 7) (11, 9) (16, 4) (16, 2) (17, 1) (19, 1) (20, 0)
f   (0, 9) (3, 9) (8, 4) (10, 6) (12, 6) (15, 3) (17, 5) (20, 2) (20, 0)
g   (0, 2) (3, 2) (5, 4) (7, 4) (8, 3) (11, 6) (12, 6) (15, 9) (16, 8) (18, 10) (20, 10) (20, 0)
h   (0, 9) (4, 5) (4, 3) (5, 2) (6, 1) (9, 1) (10, 2) (12, 2) (15, 5) (15, 6) (20, 11) (20, 0)

3   Draw axes, labelling the x-axis from 0 to 20 and the y-axis from 0 to 12 for each part.

Plot each set of points and join them with straight sections in the order given here.

Divide the area between the line and the x-axis into strips of rectangles and triangles, and calculate their areas to find the total area between the line and the x-axis.

a   (0, 6) (3, 6) (5, 8) (8, 8) (10, 11) (12, 9) (14, 9) (16, 5) (20, 5) (20, 0)
b   (0, 0) (2, 6) (5, 9) (7, 9) (10, 12) (12, 12) (16, 10) (18, 6) (20, 4) (20, 0)

Areas under lines and curves

c   (0, 4) (2, 10) (5, 9) (6, 9) (9, 12) (11, 10) (13, 2) (15, 1) (17, 3) (18, 3) (20, 1) (20, 0)

d   (0, 12) (2, 5) (4, 3) (8, 2) (10, 2) (11, 6) (13, 8) (15, 9) (16, 9) (18, 7) (20, 0)

e   (0, 5) (2, 10) (5, 12) (6, 12) (8, 10) (10, 4) (13, 2) (16, 1) (20, 0)

f   (0, 9) (1, 3) (3, 1) (6, 1) (9, 2) (12, 4) (14, 9) (16, 11) (20, 12) (20, 0)

g   (0, 0) (2, 9) (4, 11) (6, 9) (8, 5) (10, 4) (12, 7) (14, 8) (17, 6) (20, 7) (20, 0)

h   (0, 12) (2, 2) (4, 11) (6, 5) (8, 10) (10, 6) (12, 9) (14, 7) (16, 8) (17, 7) (20, 7) (20, 0)

4   Draw axes, labelling the x-axis from 0 to 20 and the y-axis from 0 to 12.
Plot these points and join them in order:
(2, 7) (2, 8) (5, 11) (9, 12) (12, 12) (16, 10) (18, 8) (18, 4) (16, 1) (12, 1) (9, 2) (5, 4) (2, 7).
Divide the area inside the loop into strips of rectangles and triangles, and so find the area of the loop.

5   Draw axes as before and join these points in order to draw a loop.
Divide the area inside the loop into strips of rectangles and triangles and so find the area of the loop.
(1, 6) (3, 12) (6, 12) (10, 11) (13, 9) (15, 5) (15, 3) (13, 1) (10, 1) (6, 2) (3, 4) (1, 6)

6   Draw axes as before and plot each of these sets of points. Join them in order to form a loop, split each loop into strips and so find the area of each loop.
  a   (1, 4) (1, 7) (4, 11) (6, 11) (8, 10) (12, 9) (16, 10) (20, 10) (20, 5) (16, 3) (12, 6) (8, 5) (6, 2) (4, 2) (1, 4)
  b   (20, 7) (17, 5) (11, 4) (5, 3) (2, 5) (0, 8) (2, 11) (5, 12) (11, 9) (17, 8) (20, 7)
  c   (2, 3) (2, 4) (3, 6) (6, 9) (10, 11) (16, 12) (20, 12) (16, 11) (10, 7) (6, 2) (3, 2) (2, 3)

7   A plan of a flower-bed in a park is drawn on axes with a scale of 1 unit for 1 metre. The straight side of the flower-bed is 20 metres along the x-axis. The other side of the flower-bed is found by joining these points in order.
  a   Draw axes with the x-axis from 0 to 20 and the y-axis from 0 to 12. Plot the points, draw the plan of the flower-bed, and find its area in square metres.
(0, 0) (0, 2) (1, 5) (3, 8) (5, 9) (7, 9) (9, 8) (10, 6) (12, 4) (15, 3) (20, 2) (20, 0)
  b   It is filled with plants so that there are 12 plants for every square metre. Find the number of plants needed.
  c   If each plant costs 5 pence, find the total cost of filling the flower-bed.

8   A plan is made of the land in front of a hotel to a scale of 1 unit for each metre. The axes show two straight edges of the land, and the third edge is shown by joining these points in order:
(0, 7) (4, 6) (6, 6) (8, 7) (10, 9) (14, 10) (16, 9) (18, 3) (20, 1) (20, 0).
  a   Draw axes, labelling the x-axis from 0 to 20 and the y-axis from 0 to 12. Calculate the area of the land in square metres.
  b   Three quarters of this land is to be turfed to make a lawn. How much will the turf cost if each square metre is 48 pence?
  c   The other quarter of the land is to be planted with shrubs. If three shrubs take up 5 m^2, how many will be needed?

Areas under lines and curves

9   A map of a builder's yard is made with all lengths in metres. Its edges are straight and its corners are given by these points:
(10, 0) (2, 4) (2, 7) (4, 12) (6, 13) (12, 13) (15, 12) (20, 11) (20, 6) (17, 6) (12, 1) (10, 0).

   a   Draw axes, labelling the x-axis from 0 to 20 and the y-axis from 0 to 14. Plot these points and join them in order to make a map of the yard. Find its area in square metres.

   b   The builder decides to tarmac the yard at a cost of £3·48 per m². How much will it cost him?

10   This diagram shows an area split into three trapezia.

   Use the formula $A = \frac{1}{2}h(a + b)$ to calculate the area of each trapezium, and so find the total area between the line and the x-axis.

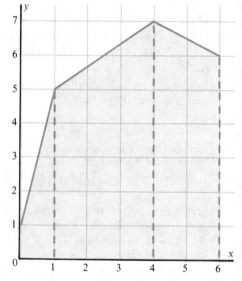

11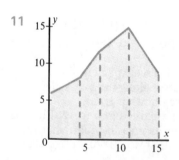

   Draw axes as shown here and copy this diagram using these points in order:
(0, 6) (4, 8) (7, 12) (11, 15) (15, 9).

   Divide the area under the line into four trapezia as shown by the dotted lines. Use the formula $A = \frac{1}{2}h(a + b)$ to calculate the area of each trapezium, and hence find the total area between the line and the x-axis.

12   Draw and label both axes from 0 to 12.

   Plot these points and join them in order:
(0, 12) (2, 10) (5, 6) (7, 8) (11, 4) (12, 2).

   Divide the area under your line into five trapezia. Find
   a   the area of each trapezium by using the formula
   b   the total area between the line and the x-axis.

13   Draw and label both axes from 0 to 16.

   Plot these points and join them in order:
(0, 1) (4, 8) (6, 10) (9, 14) (11, 9) (15, 8) (16, 6).

   Divide the area under your line into six trapezia. Find
   a   the area of each trapezium by using the formula
   b   the total area between the line and the x-axis.

154

Areas under lines and curves

14 For each table, draw and label axes on which points are to be joined in order. Divide the area under the line into trapezia, find the area of each trapezium, and so find the total area between the line and the *x*-axis.

a

x	0	2	4	6	8
y	1	$6\frac{1}{2}$	8	$9\frac{1}{2}$	10

b

x	0	2	4	6	8
y	1	$1\frac{1}{2}$	3	$5\frac{1}{2}$	9

c

x	0	2	4	6	8	10	12
y	7	$6\frac{1}{2}$	6	5	4	$2\frac{1}{2}$	$\frac{1}{2}$

d

x	0	10	20	30	40	50	60
y	30	15	8	7	10	15	23

e

x	0	10	20	30	40	50
y	10	20	25	20	5	10

f

x	0	5	10	15	20	25	30
y	30	25	30	70	75	55	10

g

x	0	20	40	60	80	100
y	60	60	65	75	60	10

h

x	0	3	6	9	12	15
y	12	18	20	14	16	20

Part 2 Areas under curves

Introduction – to estimate the area under the curve *AB*

Split the area *ABCD* into strips of equal width *h*.

Approximate each strip by a rectangle. Judge the height of the rectangle so that the shaded areas indicated are equal.

The area of the strip is then equal to the area of the rectangle.

Calculate the area of the rectangle.

Repeat for other strips and other rectangles and add together the areas of all the rectangles.

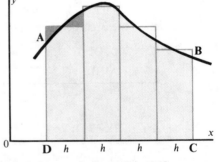

1 Draw axes, labelling the *x*-axis from 0 to 12 and the *y*-axis from 0 to 140.
Plot the points given in each of these tables, and draw a smooth curve through them. Estimate the area under the curve by approximating it with six rectangles.

a

x	0	2	4	6	8	10	12
y	10	20	40	70	100	120	130

b

x	0	2	4	6	8	10	12
y	140	90	60	40	30	20	15

c

x	0	2	4	6	8	10	12
y	70	50	40	50	90	120	140

d

x	0	2	4	6	8	10	12
y	30	80	110	120	110	90	80

Areas under lines and curves

2 Draw axes and label both from 0 to 70.

Plot the points given in each of these tables, and draw a smooth curve through them. Estimate the area between the curve and the x-axis by dividing it into seven strips.

a

x	0	10	20	30	40	50	60	70
y	15	40	50	45	40	45	60	70

b

x	0	10	20	30	40	50	60	70
y	50	60	65	65	50	30	20	35

3 Draw a smooth curve through the points given in each of these tables, and estimate the area between the curve and the x-axis.

a

x	0	50	100	150	200	250	300
y	300	175	125	125	150	150	75

b

x	0	50	100	150	200	250	300
y	75	25	25	100	200	275	275

4 Copy and complete each table below for the given equation.

Draw the graph of y against x.

Estimate the area between each curve and the x-axis.

a $y = x^2 + x + 1$

x	0	1	2	3	4
x^2					
$+x$					
$+1$					
y					

b $y = x^2 + 2x + 1$

x	0	1	2	3	4
x^2					
$+2x$					
$+1$					
y					

c $y = x^2 - 5x + 7$

x	0	1	2	3	4
x^2					
$-5x$					
$+7$					
y					

d $y = x^2 - 4x + 6$

x	0	1	2	3	4	5	6
x^2							
$-4x$							
$+6$							
y							

e $y = x^2 - 2x + 2$

x	0	1	2	3	4	5
x^2						
$-2x$						
$+2$						
y						

f $y = x^2 - 14x + 50$

x	0	1	2	3	4	5	6
x^2							
$-14x$							
$+50$							
y							

Areas under lines and curves

5 Copy and complete the two tables below for the equations given.
   Draw the two graphs of y against x on different diagrams.
   Estimate the areas between the curves and the x-axis.

a $y = 20 - x - x^2$

x	0	1	2	3	4	5
20						
$-x$						
$-x^2$						
y						

b $y = 9 + 2x - x^2$

x	0	1	2	3	4
9					
$+2x$					
$-x^2$					
y					

Part 3   The trapezium rule

Introduction – to estimate the area under the curve AB

Split the area $ABCD$ into strips of equal width, h.

Join $AXYZB$ with straight lines.

Each strip is now approximated by a trapezium.

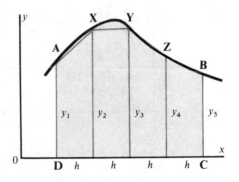

Area of first trapezium $= \frac{1}{2}h(y_1 + y_2)$
Area of second trapezium $= \frac{1}{2}h(y_2 + y_3)$
Area of third trapezium $= \frac{1}{2}h(y_3 + y_4)$
Area of fourth trapezium $= \frac{1}{2}h(y_4 + y_5)$

By addition,
total area of all trapezia $= \frac{1}{2}h[y_1 + y_2 + y_2 + y_3 + y_3 + y_4 + y_4 + y_5]$
$= \frac{1}{2}h[y_1 + y_5 + 2(y_2 + y_3 + y_4)]$.

So, in general,
area under curve $AB \simeq \frac{1}{2} \times$ width $\times$ [first y + last y + 2 $\times$ (middle y's)].

1 Plot the values given in this table
   and draw a curve through them.
   Estimate the area under the curve by
   splitting it into seven trapezia.

x	0	2	4	6	8	10	12	14
y	1	5	7	8	8	4	2	1

2 Plot a curve passing through the
   points given in this table, and
   estimate the area between the curve
   and the x-axis by using six trapezia.

x	0	1	2	3	4	5	6
y	35	20	10	10	15	20	20

3

x	0	25	50	75	100	125	150	200	250	300
y	2	10	14	16	16	12	8	4	2	1

Plot the points and draw the curve using the above table. Use the trapezium
rule to estimate the area between the curve and the x-axis.

157

Areas under lines and curves

4   Use the trapezium rule to estimate the area under each of the curves given by these tables. There is no need to draw any graphs.

a
x	0	10	20	30	40	50
y	6	18	28	36	42	44

b
x	0	4	8	12	16	20	24
y	12	10	9	11	15	18	20

c
x	0	5	10	15	20	25	30
y	12	16	19	20	20	18	15

d
x	0	20	40	60	80	100	120
y	0.3	0.2	0.2	0.5	0.9	1.2	1.3

e
x	20	24	28	32	36	40	44
y	4.8	6.2	7.4	8.2	8.7	8.8	8.6

f
x	15	18	21	24	27	30	33	36
y	114	124	130	132	131	123	107	86

g
x	0	0.1	0.2	0.3	0.4	0.5	0.6
y	1.1	1.1	1.3	1.6	1.7	1.7	1.3

h
x	0	$\frac{1}{2}$	1	$1\frac{1}{2}$	2	$2\frac{1}{2}$	3	$3\frac{1}{2}$
y	2.2	1.7	1.4	1.3	1.3	1.4	1.5	1.6

5   a   Copy and complete this table for the equation $y = x^2 - 5x + 7$.
    b   Draw the graph of y against x.
    c   Estimate the area between the curve and the x-axis for $0 \leqslant x \leqslant 4$.
    d   Can you say if your answer is an overestimate or underestimate of the true value of the area?

x	0	1	2	3	4
x^2					
$-5x$					
$+7$					
y					

6   a   Copy and complete this table for the equation $y = x^2 - 4x + 6$.
    b   Draw the graph of y against x.
    c   Estimate the area between the curve and the x-axis for $0 \leqslant x \leqslant 6$.
    d   Can you say if your answer is an overestimate or underestimate of the true value of the area?

x	0	1	2	3	4	5	6
x^2							
$-4x$							
$+6$							
y							

7
x	0	1	2	3	4	5
2						
$+5x$						
$-x^2$						
y						

Copy and complete this table for the equation $y = 2 + 5x - x^2$ and draw a graph of the values obtained.

Estimate the area between the curve and the x-axis and say if you have over- or underestimated the true value of the area.

Areas under lines and curves

8

x	0	1	2	3	4
8					
$+2x$					
$-x^2$					
y					

Use a copy of this table to draw the graph of $y = 8 + 2x - x^2$ and estimate the area under the curve.

State if your estimate is greater or less than the true value of the area between the curve and the x-axis.

9   Construct your own tables of values for the following equations.

In each case, draw a curve and estimate the area between the curve and the x-axis over the range of x-values given.

a $y = \dfrac{12}{x}$ for $1 \leqslant x \leqslant 6$

b $y = \frac{1}{2}x^2$ for $2 \leqslant x \leqslant 8$

c $y = x^3 - 2x^2 + 4$ for $0 \leqslant x \leqslant 3$

Part 4   The average height of a curve

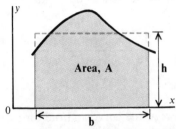

Area, A

h

b

If h is the average height of the curve over the distance b, then

area under the curve $A = b \times h$

so,

average height of curve $h = \dfrac{A}{b}$.

1 a   Draw axes and on them plot the points given in this table. Draw a smooth curve through them.

x	0	2	4	6	8
y	1	6	4	2	1

   b   Divide the area between the curve and the x-axis into four strips. Use the trapezium rule to find this area.

   c   Calculate the average height of the curve and draw this average height on your diagram.

2 a   Draw a curve given by the values in this table.

x	0	5	10	15	20	25
y	20	22	25	25	17	0

   b   Divide the area under the curve into five strips and use the trapezium rule to calculate this area.

   c   Find the average height of the curve and draw a straight line on your diagram to show this average height.

3 a   Use this table to draw a curve and find the area between the curve and the x-axis using the trapezium rule.

x	0	10	20	30	40	50
y	0	0.2	1.0	2.4	2.9	3.0

   b   Calculate the average height of the curve and illustrate it on your diagram.

Areas under lines and curves

4 Without drawing any graphs, calculate for each of these tables
   (i)   the area between the curve and the x-axis
  (ii)   the average height of the curve.

a

x	0	4	8	12	16	20
y	9	16	22	24	24	23

b

x	0	0.2	0.4	0.6	0.8
y	2.7	2.3	2.1	2.0	1.9

c

x	100	110	120	130	140
y	12.5	15.0	17.1	18.8	20.1

d

x	1	$1\frac{1}{2}$	2	$2\frac{1}{2}$	3	$3\frac{1}{2}$	4
y	52	44	40	39	41	49	60

5 A boy measures the temperature every hour during the school day with these
  results.

Time	9 a.m.	10 a.m.	11 a.m.	Noon	1 p.m.	2 p.m.	3 p.m.	4 p.m.
Temperature °C	9.0	12.3	13.6	14.4	14.8	15.0	14.4	13.0

  a   Over how many hours did he take readings?
  b   Draw a graph of temperature against time.
  c   Use the trapezium rule to find the area between the curve and the time-axis.
  d   Calculate the average temperature during the day and illustrate it on your
      graph.

6 The depth of water in a storage tank varies throughout the day as water is being
  used. The depth is measured on the hour as shown in the table.

Time	8 a.m.	10 a.m.	Noon	2 p.m.	4 p.m.	6 p.m.	8 p.m.
Depth, m	3.6	2.8	2.4	3.1	2.6	2.3	3.4

  a   Over how many hours are these readings taken?
  b   Draw a graph of these results and use the trapezium rule to estimate the
      area under the curve.
  c   Calculate the average depth of water during the day, and illustrate your
      answer by a straight line on the graph.

7 A spring is gradually stretched as it is loaded with weights. Its extension is
  measured as the load increases, with these results.

Extension, cm	0	2	4	6	8
Load, newtons	0	17	29	36	40

  a   Draw a graph of load against extension, and estimate the area between the
      curve and the extension-axis.
  b   Calculate the average load and illustrate this on your diagram.

Areas under lines and curves

8 A car is test-driven so that it accelerates from rest as fast as possible and then brakes as hard as possible. Its speed is recorded every second as shown in this table.

Time, s	0	1	2	3	4	5	6	7	8	9	10
Speed, m/s	0	8	14	18	22	24	25	13	6	2	0

a Draw a graph of speed against time.

b What is the top speed of the car, and after how many seconds were the brakes put on?

c Use the trapezium rule to calculate the area under the curve.

d Find the average speed of the car during the test and illustrate this average speed on your diagram.

9 A new town is built over a five-year period. The number of people, y (in thousands), is planned to increase over the five years as given by the equation $y = \frac{1}{2}x^2 + 1$ where x is the number of years.

a Construct a table of your own and draw the graph of y against x for values of x from 0 to 5.

b Calculate the area between the curve and the x-axis.

c Calculate the average population of the town during these five years and draw a line on your graph to illustrate this average value.

10 The temperature, y °C, of a scientific experiment is controlled automatically over a six-hour period so that $y = t^2 - 4t + 10$, where t is the number of hours from the start of the experiment.

a Construct a table of values from $t = 0$ to $t = 6$, and draw the graph of temperature y against time t.

b Estimate the area under the curve over this period.

c Calculate the average temperature during the six hours of the experiment, and illustrate it by a straight line on your diagram.

Part 5 Applications

1 Find the area beneath each of the following graphs and give your answers their correct units.

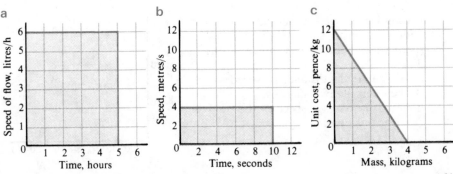

a
Speed of flow, litres/h
Time, hours

b
Speed, metres/s
Time, seconds

c
Unit cost, pence/kg
Mass, kilograms

161

Areas under lines and curves

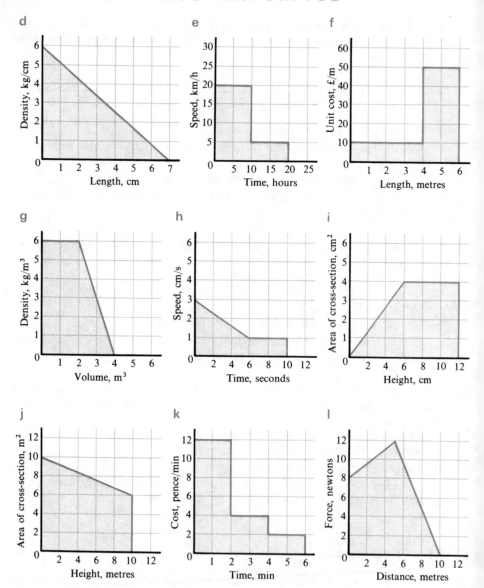

d

e

f

g

h

i

j

k

l

2 A train leaves one station and two
   minutes later stops at the next one. Its
   speed varies with time as shown in this
   diagram.
   a Calculate the distance travelled
      between the two stations.
   b Find the average speed of the train
      over this time.

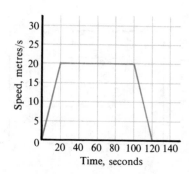

Areas under lines and curves

3   Another train takes 3 minutes to go from one station to the next, with its speed changing with time as shown in this diagram. Calculate
   a   the distance between the two stations
   b   the average speed of the train during its journey.

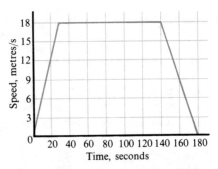

Andrew Shepherd goes on a 16-mile sponsored walk for charity. He is sponsored at 40 pence/mile for the first 6 miles, but after this the amount per mile increases as shown in this diagram.
   a   How much will he collect if he completes the full 16 miles?
   b   How much will he collect if he covers only half of the walk?

4

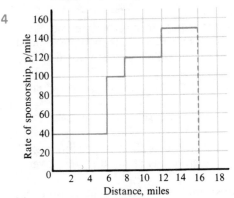

5   An electricity company charges 12 pence/unit for the first 40 units used, then 8 pence/unit for the next 50 units used, and the rate reduces after this as shown in the diagram. How much will you be charged if you use
   a   90 units   b   150 units?

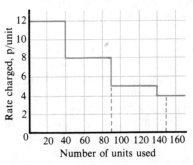

A meter measures the rate at which water is flowing into an empty tank over a period of one hour, and the graph illustrates its readings. Calculate
   a   the volume of water which flows into the tank during this hour
   b   the average rate at which it is flowing in.

6

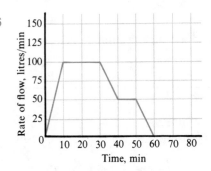

7   This diagram shows how the speed of a car increases as it starts from rest. The four sections of the graph indicate the speeds in the four gears, and after 24 seconds, the car has reached its maximum speed of 14 m/s.
   Calculate the distance it has covered during these 24 seconds.

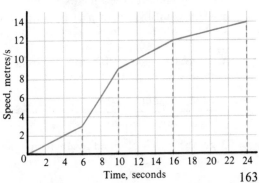

Areas under lines and curves

8 A cyclist takes 2 minutes to travel to the Post Office. His speed is increasing during the first 40 seconds, and then it gradually decreases until he comes to rest.
Calculate
a the distance to the Post Office
b his average speed for the journey.

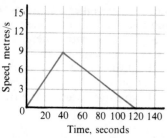

9 Another cyclist takes one minute for a short trip. Starting from rest, he increases his speed steadily for 20 seconds up to 8 m/s. He then keeps a steady speed of 8 m/s for a further 30 seconds before gradually slowing down to rest.
a Draw axes, labelling the time axis in seconds, and draw the graph of speed against time.
b Calculate the distance he travels and his average speed.

10 Water suddenly starts to flow into a tank at a rate of 30 litres per minute. This rate is held steady for 4 minutes, before it is gradually reduced to zero over a further 6 minutes.
Draw the graph of the rate of flow against time and calculate the amount of water which has entered the tank.

11 The shaft of an engine, starting from rest, accelerates steadily until after 2 minutes it has a rotational speed of 2000 rpm. It keeps this speed of rotation constant for a further 4 minutes, before it gradually slows down to rest over a further 10 minutes.
Sketch the graph of rotational speed against time, and calculate
a the number of revolutions which the shaft has turned through
b its average speed of rotation.

12 A meter measures the rate of flow of oil into a central-heating boiler every ten minutes, with these results.

Time, min	0	10	20	30	40	50	60
Rate of flow, litres/min	7	4	4	5	6	5	1

a Draw a graph of the rate of flow against time.
b Estimate the volume of oil which has been used, by finding the area between the graph and the time axis.
c Use your answer to part b to find the *average* rate of flow of oil (in litres/min) and draw a straight line on your graph to illustrate this average.

13 An aeroplane takes off from rest along a runway. Its speed increases with time as in this table, and it takes off at a speed of 80 m/s.

Time, seconds	0	5	10	15	20	25	30
Speed, m/s	0	3	8	16	28	45	80

Draw the graph of speed against time, and estimate the minimum length of the runway.

Areas under lines and curves

14 An engine is running continuously over a period of two hours, and the speed of the engine is read on a meter every 15 minutes.

Time, min		0	15	30	45	60	75	90	105	120
Speed of rotation, revs/min		300	800	900	800	500	300	200	100	100

   a Draw a graph of speed against time, and estimate the area under the graph to find the number of revolutions which the engine turns through in 2 hours.

   b Find the average speed of the engine (in revs/min), and illustrate this on your diagram by a straight line.

15 A tap is fully open with water gushing out at a rate of 2 litres per second. The tap is slowly turned off during the next ten seconds, and the rate of flow of water is given in this table.

Time, seconds		0	2	4	6	8	10
Rate of flow, litres/s		2.0	1.9	1.6	1.2	0.6	0

Draw the graph of rate of flow against time, and estimate the volume of water which has flowed from the tap in this time.

16 It takes Mrs Jones 2 minutes to drive to the shops by car. Her speed every ten seconds is noted.

Time from home, s		0	10	20	30	40	50	60	70	80	90	100	110	120
Speed, m/s		0	9	14	15	15	16	10	2	3	9	11	8	0

   a Draw a graph of speed against time, and hence calculate the distance to the shops.

   b Find the *average* speed of the car and draw a straight line on your graph to illustrate it.

   c During the journey Mrs Johnson has to go round a busy roundabout. At what time do you think this occurs?

17 A cyclist has a speedometer fitted to his machine which records his speed every 20 seconds on his way to school on a morning when he stops to post a letter.

Time from home, s		0	20	40	60	80	100	120	140	160	180	200	220	240
Speed, m/s		0	7	9	8	4	0	0	5	10	13	12	8	0

   a Draw a graph of speed against time.

   b How long did he take to post the letter?

   c Estimate the total distance he travels to school.

   d What is his average speed for the whole journey? Illustrate it by drawing a straight line on your diagram.

Areas under lines and curves

18 The area of cross-section of a 12-metre length of pipe changes as the distance from one end increases.

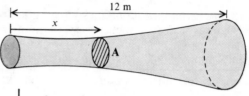

Distance from one end x, m	0	2	4	6	8	10	12
Area of cross-section A, m^2	1.0	0.7	0.6	0.7	1.0	1.4	2.0

a Draw a graph of area against distance and say what the area under the graph represents.
b Estimate the volume of the pipe (in m^3).
c Find the *average* area of cross-section (to 2 significant figures) and mark it on your graph by a straight line.

19 A meter connected to the electricity supply in a house measures the rate at which power is being used. The meter is read at irregular intervals during a full day.

Time	12 midnight	6 a.m.	8 a.m.	12 midday	2 p.m.	4 p.m.	6 p.m.	10 p.m.	12 midnight
Rate of use, kW	0.5	1.0	3.5	2.5	3.0	2.5	4.0	2.5	1.0

a Draw a graph of these readings; and give reasons for the two large peaks on your curve.
b The area under the curve gives the amount of electricity used (in kW-h). Use a method of your choice to calculate the amount of electricity used during the 24-hour period.
c Find the average rate of using electricity (in kW to 2 significant figures) and show it on your graph by a straight line.

20 When a spring is extended a distance x metres by a force F newtons, the strength of the force has to increase as the extension increases. This table gives the force required to extend a spring 0.5 metres. Draw a graph of F against x.

Extension, x m	0	0.1	0.2	0.3	0.4	0.5
Force, F N	0	9	16	22	27	32

a The area under the curve gives the amount of work needed (in joules) to extend the spring. Estimate this area and write down the work required.
b Find the average force during the extension, and draw it on your graph.

21 During the thirty years from 1950 to 1980 the population of the town of Haliford has increased, and the rate of increase is tabulated here in thousands of people per year.

Year	1950	1955	1960	1965	1970	1975	1980
Rate of increase (000's per year)	1.0	1.0	1.5	2.5	4.0	5.0	4.0

Draw the graph of the rate of increase against time and estimate
a the increase in Haliford's population over these 30 years, and
b the average rate of increase. Illustrate this average rate on your graph.

Areas under lines and curves

22 A stone is thrown vertically down from the top of a cliff.
Its speed, v m/s, is given by $v = 10t + 3$ where t is the time of fall in seconds.
It strikes the ground at the bottom of the cliff after 4 seconds.

Copy and complete this table, and draw the graph of v against t.

t	0	1	2	3	4
v					

Find
a   the speed with which it was thrown
b   the height of the cliff
c   the average speed during its fall.

23 An object is travelling at a steady speed of 16 m/s when its brakes are applied.
It then takes 4 seconds for it to stop.
During these 4 seconds, its speed, v m/s, is given by $v = 16 - t^2$ where t is the time measured in seconds from when the brakes were first applied.

Copy and complete this table, and draw the graph of v against t.

t	0	1	2	3	4
16					
$-t^2$					
v					

Hence estimate
a   how far the object travels with its brakes on
b   the average speed of the object during this period.

24 An automatic valve controls the rate of flow of gas, R cm^3/min, in an experiment. Over a period of 8 minutes, the rate of flow varies with the time t (min) as given by the equation $R = t^2 - 10t + 27$.

Copy and complete this table, and draw the graph of R against t.

t	0	2	4	6	8
t^2					
$-10t$					
$+27$					
R					

Estimate the volume of gas used in the experiment during this time interval. Also estimate the average rate of using the gas, and illustrate this average on your graph.

25 Hot water is cooled so that the rate of cooling, R °C/min, at a time t (min) from the start is given by $R = \frac{1}{10}t^2 - 2t + 10$.

Copy and complete this table, and draw the graph of R against t for the time interval given.

t	0	2	4	6	8	10
$\frac{1}{10}t^2$						
$-2t$						
$+10$						
R						

Hence estimate the fall in temperature of the water during this 10-minute period.

Rates of change

Part 1 Constant rates of change

1 In a science experiment the temperature of some water is controlled so that it rises steadily over a period of 5 minutes, as shown in the diagram.
What is the rate of change of the temperature?

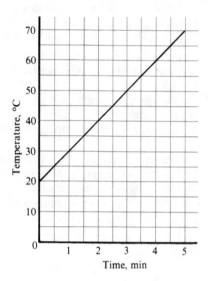

A car starts a motorway journey with a full tank of 40 litres, and it uses this petrol at a steady rate over a period of 5 hours as shown.
What is the rate at which it uses petrol?

2

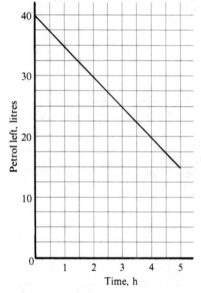

3 A balloon rises steadily after release from ground level. Use the graph to find its rate of change of height.

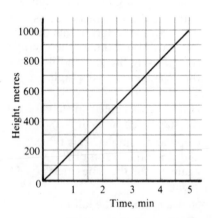

A train travelling at a steady speed covers the distance shown in this diagram. Find its rate of change of distance (or *speed*).

4

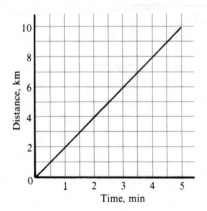

Rates of change

5

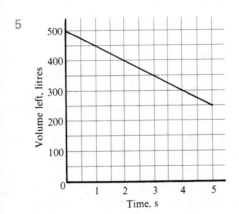

This graph shows that water runs from a tank at a steady rate. Find the rate of flow of the water.

Find the rate of change of the quantities which are varying with time as shown in these four graphs.

6

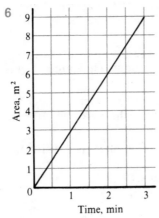

7

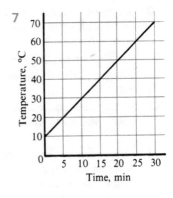

8

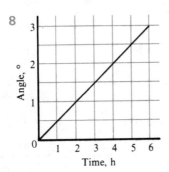

9

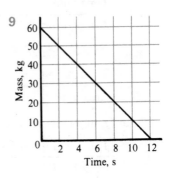

10 A car travels on a motorway at a steady speed of 80 km/h. How far does it go in 3 hours?

11 The temperature of a liquid is rising at a steady rate of 5 °C/min. What is the increase in its temperature over 4 minutes?

12 A gang of workmen dig a trench at a steady rate of 8 metres/hour. How much longer is the trench after 4 hours work?

13 A machine makes plastic cups at a constant rate of 25 cups/second. How many are made in 5 minutes?

14 A central heating system uses fuel at a constant rate of $2\frac{1}{2}$ litres per hour. How much is used over an 8-hour period?

Rates of change

15 A farmer harvests his crop at a steady rate of 500 m²/min. What area does he cover in 20 minutes?

16 The temperature of some water is 5 °C. It is heated so that the temperature rises at a constant rate of 2 °C/min. What will the temperature be after 8 minutes?

17 A petrol storage tank has 800 litres left in it, when a tanker arrives and takes 6 minutes to fill it at a constant rate of 1500 litres/minute. How much is then in the storage tank?

18 A cyclist lives 8 km from the city centre. If he leaves home and rides away from the city at a steady rate of 20 km/h, how far is he from the city centre after $2\frac{1}{2}$ hours?

19 20 m² of fence is already painted when Mr Turnbull starts to paint. If he covers $\frac{1}{2}$ m²/min, what area of fence will be painted after he has worked for 1 hour?

20 An empty beaker has a mass of 150 grams. Water drips into it at a constant rate of 10 grams per minute. What will be the mass of water and beaker together after 1 hour?

21 An aircraft has 3 tonnes of fuel at the start of a flight, and it uses it at a constant rate of $\frac{1}{2}$ tonne per hour. How much fuel is left at the end of a 5-hour flight?

22 A full water tank holds 12 m³ of water. If water is run off at a steady rate of $\frac{1}{2}$ m³/min, how much is left in the tank after 10 minutes?

23 Copy each of these tables. Complete them using the given rate of change which is taken as constant.
Draw graphs of your results.

a Rate of change = 6 °C/min

Time, min	0	1	2	3	4
Temperature, °C	2				

b Rate of change = 8 cm/s

Time, s	0	1	2	3	4
Height, cm	10				

c Rate of change = $\frac{1}{2}$ km²/h

Time, h	0	1	2	3	4
Area, km²	4				

d Rate of change = $2\frac{1}{2}$ m³/day

Time, days	0	1	2	3	4
Volume, m³	6				

e Rate of change = 0.2 m/min

Time, min	0	5	10	15	20
Length, m	1				

f Rate of change = 0.5 amps/s

Time, s	0	4	8	12	16
Current, amps	3.0				

24 The temperature of a gas is 70 °C, and it rises at a constant rate of 5 °C/min. How long will it take to reach a temperature of 100 °C?

25 The tension in a spring is 5 newtons. If it is increased at a constant rate of 2 N/min, how long will it be before the tension is 17 newtons?

26 A salesman is 480 km from Glasgow and travelling towards the city at a steady speed of 80 km/h. How long will he take to reach the half-way point?

27 A bowl of capacity 12 litres is half full of water. A tap starts to drip into the bowl at a constant rate of $\frac{1}{2}$ litre per hour. How long will it take before the bowl starts to overflow?

Rates of change

28 The voltage across a resistor is 4 volts, and it then rises steadily at a rate of $\frac{1}{4}$ volt/second. How long will it take to reach a voltage of 20 volts?

29 A nurse leaves a patient on a saline drip of 500 mℓ. If the drip is used at a steady rate of $\frac{1}{2}$ mℓ/min, how long will it be before half of the solution is used?

30 A ship has already covered 30 nautical miles of a 200-nautical-mile journey, when it increases its speed to a constant 20 knots. How long will the rest of the journey take at this speed?

Part 2   Average rates of change

1 Water is heated in a beaker and its temperature over 10 minutes is given in this table and on the graph below.

Time t, min	0	1	2	3	4	5	6	7	8	9	10
Temperature, °C	15	20	27	36	47	58	69	77	83	87	89

The rate of change of temperature is *not* constant.

Use the table to find the average rate of change of temperature

a from $t = 0$ to $t = 4$

b from $t = 0$ to $t = 6$

c from $t = 4$ to $t = 8$

d from $t = 4$ to $t = 10$.

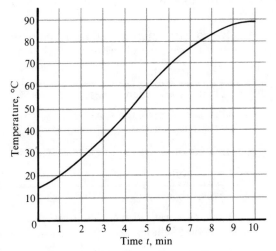

2 The current used in a scientific experiment increases over an 8-second period as shown in this table and on the graph below.

| | A | | B | | C | | D | |
Time, s	0	1	2	3	4	5	6	7	8
Current, amps	4	10	15	19	22	24	27	28	29

Use the values in the table to find the average rate of increase of current

a between A and B

b between A and C

c between B and C

d between B and D.

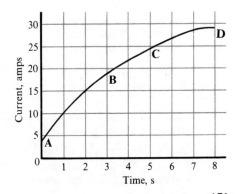

171

Rates of change

3 This table and graph show the depth of water in a tidal river over a 12-hour period.

Time t, hours	0	2	4	6	8	10	12
Depth, metres	3	7	13	15	14	8	3

Use the table to find the average rate of change of the depth over these time intervals.

Note the difference between a rate of *increase* and a rate of *decrease*.

a from $t = 0$ to $t = 4$

b from $t = 0$ to $t = 6$

c from $t = 6$ to $t = 8$

d from $t = 6$ to $t = 12$

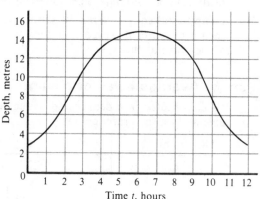

4 Mr and Mrs Robson take their family the 90 miles to the coast by car. Their son makes a note of the distance they have gone every half hour.

Time from start, hours	0	$\frac{1}{2}$	1	$1\frac{1}{2}$	2	$2\frac{1}{2}$	3
Distance travelled, miles	0	8	22	34	66	78	90

What is their average speed during
a the first hour   b the first two hours   c the whole journey?

5 Mrs Watson weighs her new baby regularly, and during its first year the results are:

Age, months	0	2	4	6	8	10	12
Mass, lb	7	10	13	16	18	$18\frac{1}{2}$	19

What is the rate of increase in its mass during
a its first four months   b its first six months   c its first twelve months?

6 A schoolboy is heating a bar of metal in the science lab and measuring its temperature every minute. He then draws a graph labelling his points A to I.

Time, min	0	1	2	3	4	5	6	7	8
Temperature, °C	20	31	39	47	54	59	63	67	68
Point	A	B	C	D	E	F	G	H	I

Without drawing a graph, find the average rate of increase of temperature
a between A and C b between A and D
c between B and H d between E and I.

7 An empty storage tank is filled with water and the volume pumped in is noted every minute.

Time, min	0	1	2	3	4	5	6	7	8	9	10
Volume, litres	0	30	80	130	190	250	290	325	355	380	390

Find the average rate of flow of water
a during the first 2 minutes   b during the first 5 minutes
c during the last 2 minutes   d during the last 5 minutes.

Rates of change

8 An athlete runs the 500-metre race with these times.

Time, s	0	20	40	60	80	100	120	140
Distance covered, m	0	60	100	140	190	250	350	500
Point	A	B	C	D	E	F	G	H

Draw a graph with the points A to H joined by a smooth curve.

Find the average speed of the athlete between

a A and C b A and F c C and D

d B and G e F and G f   the whole race.

9 A schoolgirl, as part of her geography project, measures the outdoor temperature on the hour during the day.

Time	8 a.m.	9 a.m.	10 a.m.	11 a.m.	12 noon	1 p.m.	2 p.m.	3 p.m.	4 p.m.	5 p.m.	6 p.m.
Temperature, °C	4	5	10	15	21	23	25	24	20	18	16

Draw a graph of these results.

Taking care to note when the temperature *increases* and when it *decreases*, find the average rate of change of temperature for these periods:

a   8 a.m. to 10 a.m.   b   9 a.m. to 11 a.m.   c   11 a.m. to 2 p.m.

d   9 a.m. to 2 p.m.   e   8 a.m. to 4 p.m.   f   1 p.m. to 3 p.m.

g   noon to 3 p.m.   h   2 p.m. to 3 p.m.   i   4 p.m. to 6 p.m.

j   11 a.m. to 6 p.m.

10 A car travels 300 km from Bristol to Manchester in 4 hours. Find its average speed.

11 A flight from London to New York takes 7 hours to cover 3150 km. What is the plane's average speed?

12 A slimmer had a mass of 100 kg on January 1st, but by April 1st had reduced it to 73 kg. Find the average rate of loss per month.

13 In one quarter of a year (13 weeks), a family used 559 units of electricity and 7189 cubic feet of gas. What is their average rate of consuming each of these fuels per week?

14 On a cold morning the temperature rises 12 degrees in 3 hours. What is the average rate of rise in temperature?

15 On a frosty morning the temperature rises from -3 °C at 8 a.m. to 6 °C at 11 a.m. Find the average rate of increase of temperature.

16 A baby, born 20 cm long, stands 105 cm high on its fifth birthday. What is its average rate of growth in cm per year?

17 A tape recorder rotates 1500 times during 20 minutes. Find its average rate of rotation
a   in revs per minute   b   in revs per second.

18 An empty 12000-litre tank is filled with water in 50 minutes. What is the average rate of flow of water
a   in litres per minute   b   in litres per second?

Rates of change

19 A family go on holiday by car and travel 1600 km using 80 litres of petrol costing £32. Find the average rate of consuming petrol
   a in km per litre   b in pence per km.

20 A bricklayer lays 900 bricks in 6 hours and in that time earns £27. Find
   a the average rate at which he lays bricks
       (i) in bricks per hour   (ii) in bricks per minute
   b his average rate of earning
       (i) in £ per hour   (ii) in pence per brick.

Part 3   Instantaneous rates of change

1 This graph shows the temperature of a beaker of water which is heated and then allowed to cool.

The rate of change of temperature is *not* constant.

What is this rate of change at the instant when the time *t* is
   a 3 min
   b 7 min
   c 13 min?

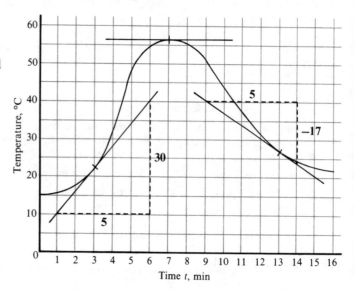

2 A cold water tank supplies a factory, and the volume of water in it is monitored over a period of 12 hours, with the results shown in this graph.

What is the rate of change of volume at the instant when the time *t* is
   a 3 h
   b 6 h
   c 10 h?

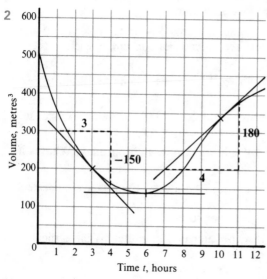

Rates of change

3   Mrs Linton kept a record of her daughter's height every birthday until she was 20 years old.

Age, years	0	2	4	6	8	10	12	14	16	18	20
Height, cm	20	62	88	102	110	120	136	152	159	160	160

Draw a graph of her results and estimate the rate at which her daughter's height was changing
a   on her 4th birthday
b   on her 10th birthday
c   on her 19th birthday.

4   In the village of Skelmanby, a refugee camp was set up in 1970 which gave temporary homes to homeless people. The camp closed down in 1980. The population of the village was recorded on every January 1st.

Year	1970	1971	1972	1973	1974	1975	1976	1977	1978	1979	1980
Population	2500	4700	5700	6000	5800	5400	4600	3800	3400	3000	2800

Use the results in the table to draw a graph and estimate the rate at which the population was changing on
a   January 1st 1972
b   January 1st 1978.

At the start of which year was the rate of change of population
c   zero
d   greatest?

5   The pressure of a gas (in mm of mercury) in an experiment changes over a 10-minute period as shown in this table.

Time, min	0	1	2	3	4	5	6	7	8	9	10
Pressure, mm	65	63	55	37	23	16	14	14	17	22	28

Draw a graph of these readings and find
a   the times when the rate of change of the pressure is zero
b   the instantaneous rate of change of pressure 8 minutes after the start
c   the instant when the pressure is falling fastest, and the rate of change at this instant.

6   The voltage in an electrical component oscillates slowly with a time period of 10 seconds.

Time, s	0	1	2	3	4	5	6	7	8	9	10
Voltage	20	11	6	6	11	20	29	34	34	29	20

Draw the graph of voltage against time, and find
a   the instants when the voltage has zero rate of change
b   the instantaneous rate of change in the voltage 1 second after the start.
c   the instant when the rate of change of voltage is greatest, and the rate of change at this time.

Rates of change

7 The angle through which a narrow beam of light is deflected in an optical experiment is measured.

Time, s	0	5	10	15	20	25	30	35	40	45	50
Angle, °	0	52	71	75	69	50	42	43	54	66	64

Draw the graph of the results in this table, and find
a how long after the start of the experiment the rate of change in the angle is zero
b the rate of change in the angle at the instant 5 seconds after the start of the experiment; and then again 40 seconds after the start
c at what instant the angle is *decreasing* at its fastest; and estimate the rate of change at this point.

8 Copy and complete this table for the equation $y = 8t - t^2$.

Draw the graph of $y = 8t - t^2$ and find the instantaneous rate of change of y when

a $t = 2$ b $t = 4$
c $t = 6$.

t	0	1	2	3	4	5	6	7	8
$8t$									
$-t^2$									
y									

9 Copy and complete this table to help you draw the graph of $y = 5 + 10t - t^2$.

Find the instantaneous rate of change of y when

a $t = 3$ b $t = 5$
c $t = 8$.

t	0	1	2	3	4	5	6	7	8	9	10
5											
$+10t$											
$-t^2$											
y											

10 Construct your own table and draw the graph of $y = t^2 - 12t + 40$ for values of t from 0 to 12.

Find the rate of change of y at the instants when
a $t = 3$ b $t = 6$ c $t = 8$.

11 Construct your own table and draw the graph of $y = t^2 - 4t + 4$ for values of t from 0 to 6.

Find the rate of change of y at the instants when
a $t = 1$ b $t = 2$ c $t = 5$.

12 Draw the graph of $y = 10 + 6t - t^2$ for values of t from 0 to 8, and so find the instantaneous rate of change of y when
a $t = 1$ b $t = 3$ c $t = 5$.

Distance, speed and acceleration

Part 1   Distance—time graphs

1   a   An object is positioned so that for
25 seconds its distance from a fixed
point *A* is always 30 metres, as shown in
this diagram.

What is its speed?

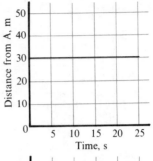

b   Another object starts from the point *A* and
gradually moves so that after 25 seconds it
is 50 metres from *A*.

What is its speed?

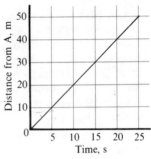

c   A third object also starts from *A* and
moves so that after 10 seconds it is
40 metres from *A*. It then stays in this
position for the remaining 15 seconds.
    (i)   What is its speed during the first
          10 seconds?
    (ii) What is its speed after the first
          10 seconds?

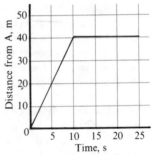

d   This object is positioned 40 metres from *A*,
and then after 5 seconds starts moving
towards *A*. It reaches *A* after travelling for
20 seconds.

What is its speed
    (i)   during the first 5 seconds
    (ii) during the last 20 seconds?

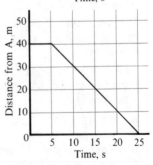

e   Another object starts at *A* and moves so
that after 15 seconds it is 30 metres from *A*.
It then returns to *A* during the next
10 seconds.

What is its speed
    (i)   during the first 15 seconds
    (ii) during the last 10 seconds?

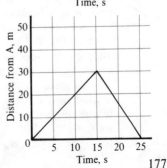

Distance, speed and acceleration

2

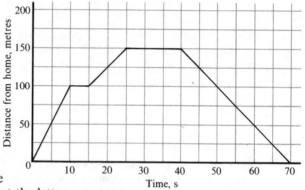

An observer stands at a point where he can see many forms of transport. This diagram shows the distances travelled by

| a light aircraft, *A* | a train, *B* |
| a lorry, *C* | a bicycle, *D* |

and a pedestrian, *E*.

Find the speed of each of them in m/s.

What do you notice about the speeds and the steepness of the lines on the diagram?

3 Adam Briggs goes on an errand for his father by bicycle. He leaves home to post a letter at the Post Office 100 metres away. He then cycles a further 50 metres to collect a newspaper, before returning home.

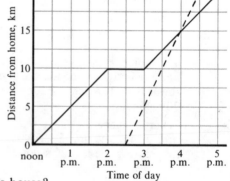

Find

a his speed between his home and the Post Office
b how long he took to post the letter
c his speed between the Post Office and the newsagents
d how long he took to collect the newspaper
e his speed on his way home.

4 One Sunday, Mr Jackson decided to go on a 20 km walk, leaving home at 12 noon. He called on a friend for a while during the walk.

His son travelled the same route by bicycle, leaving home during the afternoon.

This graph shows Mr Jackson's journey in solid lines, and his son's as a broken line.

a What was Mr Jackson's speed of walking between noon and 2 p.m.?
b How long did he spend at his friend's house?
c How far is it between Mr Jackson's home and his friend's?
d What was Mr Jackson's speed of walking after he left his friend's house?
e At what time did he arrive at the end of his 20 km walk?
f When did his son leave home?
g How long did his son take to cycle the 20 km?
h At what speed did his son ride?
i At what time during the afternoon was Mr Jackson overtaken by his son?
j How much further did Mr Jackson have to walk when his son overtook him?
k How long did his son have to wait at the end for his father to arrive?

178

Distance, speed and acceleration

5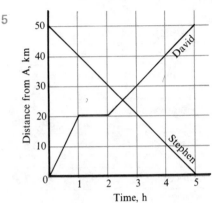

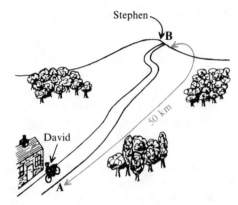

Two villages A and B are 50 km apart. Two cyclists, David and Stephen, one in each village, take 5 hours to travel to the other village, crossing each other on the way. David leaves A and has a rest on the way: Stephen leaves B but takes no rest.

a   What is David's speed in his first hour?

b   How long does David rest for?

c   At what speed does David travel after his rest?

d   What is Stephen's speed in the opposite direction?

e   After how many hours do they pass each other?

f   How far from village A are they when they pass each other?

6   Draw axes, labelling the time axis in minutes from 0 to 8, and the distance axis in kilometres from 0 to 5.

A car leaves its garage and in 2 minutes covers a distance of 4 km at a steady speed. It then stays at rest for another 2 minutes, before taking 4 minutes for the return journey back to the garage.

Draw a graph of its distance from the garage against time, and find its speed
a   during the first 2 minutes   b   during the last 4 minutes.

7   Draw axes, labelling the time axis in minutes from 0 to 20, and the distance axis in metres from 0 to 2000.

A narrow-gauge railway runs alongside the coast at a seaside resort. On its outward journey, it covers a distance of 2000 metres at a steady speed in 5 minutes. It then takes 10 minutes to change its passengers before taking 4 minutes for the return journey.

Draw a graph of distance against time, and find its speed
a   on the outward journey   b   on the return journey.

8   A vehicle on a test bed is made to travel 40 metres in 5 seconds at a steady speed, and then immediately return to its starting-point in 4 seconds.

Draw axes, labelling the time axis in seconds from 0 to 10 and the distance axis in metres from 0 to 40.

Draw a graph of distance against time, and find
a   its speed on the outward journey   b   its speed on the return journey.

179

Distance, speed and acceleration

9 The timetable for the 245 km coach journey from London to Lincoln is shown here, with the arrival and departure times for places on route, and their distances from London.

Draw axes with the time axis labelled from 12 noon to 18.00 (6 p.m.), and the distance axis from 0 to 250 km.

Use the timetable to draw a graph of distance from London against time, and find the speed at which the coach travels between

a London and Scalton
b Scalton and Garchester
c Garchester and Tonfield
d Tonfield and Lincoln.

London–Lincoln			
London	0 km	d	12.00
Scalton	60 km	a	13.00
		d	13.15
Garchester	100 km	a	14.15
		d	14.30
Tonfield	220 km	a	16.30
		d	17.00
Lincoln	245 km	a	17.30

10

Glasgow–Manchester			
Glasgow	0 km	d	8.00
Muirhead	90 km	a	9.30
		d	10.00
Jedburn	120 km	a	10.45
		d	11.00
Hazelrigg	145 km	a	11.30
		d	12.00
Beckmond	265 km	a	13.30
		d	13.45
Manchester	300 km	a	14.15

This is a timetable for the coach journey from Glasgow to Manchester. The distances are measured from Glasgow.

Labelling the time axis from 8.00 (8 a.m.) to 15.00 (3 p.m.) and the distance axis from 0 to 300 km, draw a graph of distance from Glasgow against time.

Find the speed at which the coach travels between

a Glasgow and Muirhead
b Muirhead and Jedburn
c Jedburn and Hazelrigg
d Hazelrigg and Beckmond
e Beckmond and Manchester.

11 The distance, d metres, which an object is from a fixed point A, varies with the time, t seconds, where $d = 5 + 4t$.

Copy and complete this table. Draw axes as shown, and draw the graph of d against t.

a How does the graph tell you that the object has a *steady* speed?
b Find this speed.

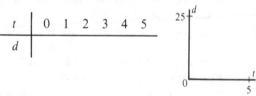

t	0	1	2	3	4	5
d						

12 Another object moves so that its distance, d metres, from a fixed point A depends on the time, t seconds, where $d = 15 - 3t$.

Copy and complete this table and draw the graph of d against t.

a Find the speed of the object.
b How long did it take for the object to reach point A?

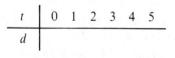

t	0	1	2	3	4	5
d						

Distance, speed and acceleration

13 An automatic machine runs
along a channel so that its
distance from one end of the
channel alters over a 12-second
period.

This graph shows how the
distance changes. Find the speed
of the machine

a   at the instant 2 seconds from
the start

b   at the instant 5 seconds from
the start

c   at the instant 7 seconds from
the start

d   at the end of the 12-second
period.

e   How far is the machine from
the end of the channel when
it finally comes to rest?

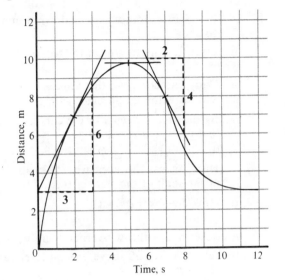

14 A hot-air balloon rises vertically to a height of 800 metres over a 10-minute
period, as shown in this table.

Time, min	0	1	2	3	4	5	6	7	8	9	10
Height, m	0	300	460	520	540	580	680	780	800	800	800

Draw the graph of height against time, and draw tangents to the curve to find
the speed of the balloon at the instant

a   2 minutes after the start   b   5 minutes after the start
c   9 minutes after the start.

15 A bean is planted and the height of the shoot is measured at the same time each
day for a week from the day it first appears.

Day	0	1	2	3	4	5	6	7
Height, mm	4	6	10	20	28	30	32	38

a   Draw the graph of height against time, and draw tangents to the curve to
find the rate of growth of the shoot in mm/day at the time of measuring
(i) on the second day   (ii) on the fourth day.

b   On which day was the shoot growing fastest?

16 A ball is rolled down a slope so that its distance from the bottom of the slope is
as in this table.

Time t, s	0	1	2	3	4	5	6	7	8
Distance x, metres	12.0	11.6	10.5	8.9	7.0	5.1	3.5	2.4	2.0

a   Draw the graph of distance against time and find the speed of the ball
(i) when $t = 3$ (ii) when $t = 6$.

b   At which two times is the speed of the ball zero?

c   At which time is the ball rolling fastest?

Distance, speed and acceleration

17 A stone works loose part-way down a mine shaft and drops to the bottom in 5 seconds.

Its distance, x metres, from the top of the shaft depends on the time, t seconds, where $x = 20 + 5t^2$.

a Copy and complete this table, and draw the graph of x against t.

t	0	1	2	3	4	5
20						
$+5t^2$						
x						

b By drawing tangents to the curve, find the speed of the stone
  (i) when $t = 2$ (ii) when $t = 4$.

c How far was the stone from the top of the shaft at the start of the fall?

d How deep is the shaft?

18 A cricket ball is thrown vertically up with a speed of 30 m/s.

Its height, h metres, above ground level varies with the time, t seconds, such that $h = 2 + 30t - 5t^2$.

a Copy and complete this table and draw the graph of h against t.

t	0	1	2	3	4	5	6
2							
$+30t$							
$-5t^2$							
h							

b Estimate the speed of the ball when
  (i) $t = 1$ (ii) $t = 3$ (iii) $t = 4$.

c What is the greatest height of the ball above ground level?

d How long did it take to reach this greatest height?

e What was the height of the ball above the ground when the thrower let go?

f Extend your curve slightly to find the time taken for the ball to hit the ground.

Part 2 Speed—time graphs

1 An object moves for 3 seconds at a constant speed of 6 m/s as shown in this diagram.

Find
a the distance travelled in this time
b its acceleration.

2
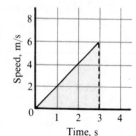

Another object gradually increases its speed from zero to 6 m/s over a period of 3 seconds.

Find
a the distance travelled in this time
b its acceleration.

Distance, speed and acceleration

3 Find (i) the distance travelled
   and (ii) the acceleration, of the four objects whose speeds vary with the time
   as shown in these diagrams.

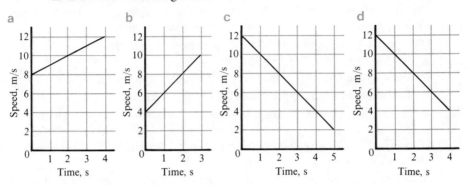

4 These diagrams show how the speeds of various objects vary with time.
   Copy each diagram onto squared paper, and divide the area under each graph
   into rectangles and triangles to find the distance travelled by each object.

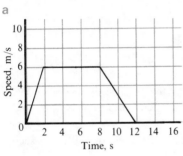

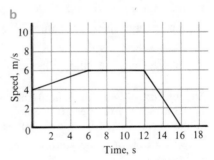

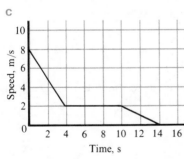

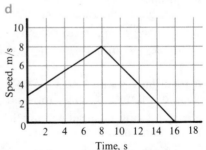

5 Draw axes, labelling the time axis in seconds from 0 to 10 and the speed axis in
   m/s from 0 to 10.

   A bicycle travels at a constant speed of 8 m/s for 6 seconds, before
   slowing down gradually to rest over a further 4 seconds.

   Draw a graph of its speed against time, and find
   a the total distance travelled
   b the average speed of the bicycle over the whole 10 seconds
   c the deceleration (or retardation) over its last 4 seconds.

Distance, speed and acceleration

6 Draw axes, labelling the time axis in minutes from 0 to 10 and the speed axis in km/min from 0 to 2.

A train starts from rest and increases its speed steadily up to 2 km/min over 2 minutes. It then runs for a further 4 minutes at a constant speed of 2 km/min, before gradually slowing down to rest in a final 4 minutes.

Draw a graph of speed against time on your axes, and find
a   the total distance travelled in km

b   the average speed over the whole 10 minutes in km/min

c   the acceleration during the first 2 minutes in km/min^2

d   the deceleration (or retardation) during the last 4 minutes in km/min^2.

7 Draw axes, labelling the time axis in minutes from 0 to 20 and the speed axis in km/min from 0 to 2.

A train travels between two stations A and B. Starting from rest at A, it accelerates steadily for 2 minutes and reaches a speed of 1.5 km/min which it then holds steady for a further 12 minutes. Finally, it decelerates (or retards) at a steady rate until it comes to rest 6 minutes later at station B.

Draw a graph of speed against time on your axes, and find
a   the total distance travelled

b   the average speed over the whole period

c   the acceleration during the first 2 minutes

d   the deceleration during the last 6 minutes.

8 An object moves at a constant speed of 2 m/s for 10 seconds, before it gradually accelerates for a further 10 seconds to reach a speed of 6 m/s. It now holds this higher speed steady for a final 10 seconds.

Draw a graph of speed against time, labelling your axes from 0 to 30 seconds and from 0 to 6 m/s, and find
a   the total distance covered in the 30 seconds

b   the average speed over the whole period

c   the acceleration during the middle 10 seconds.

9 A point moves with a steady speed of 10 m/s for 6 seconds. It then gradually slows down until it comes to rest 4 seconds later.

Sketch a graph of speed against time and calculate
a   the total distance travelled

b   the average speed over the whole 10 seconds

c   the deceleration while slowing down.

10 Starting from rest and moving in a straight line, an object accelerates for 3 minutes until it reaches a speed of 300 metres/min. It holds this speed steady for another 8 minutes, before decelerating gradually for 4 more minutes to rest.

Draw a graph of speed against time, and calculate
a   the total distance it has travelled

b   its average speed for the whole journey

c   its acceleration at the start and deceleration at the end of the journey.

Distance, speed and acceleration

11 A stone is thrown vertically down a mine shaft, so that after t seconds its speed, v m/s, is given by $v = 10t + 5$. After 4 seconds, it hits the bottom of the shaft.

Copy and complete this table, and draw the graph of v against t.

t	0	1	2	3	4
v					

Find
a the speed with which it was thrown
b its acceleration, and explain why the acceleration is constant
c the distance it falls down the shaft
d its average speed.

12 A young child accidentally drops a toy from the top of a tall building. The speed, v m/s, of the toy after a time of t seconds is given by $v = 2 + 10t$ and after 5 seconds it strikes the ground.

Draw axes, labelling the time axis from 0 to 5 and the speed axis from 0 to 60. Draw the graph of v against t, and say why the acceleration of the toy is constant.

Find
a the initial speed of the toy   b its acceleration
c the height of the building.

13 This diagram shows how the speed of a car varies during the 16 seconds of its motion.

Find the acceleration of the car at the instant when the time, t is
a 2 seconds
b 6 seconds
c 12 seconds.

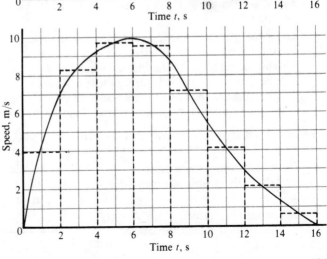

14 This is the same speed–time graph for the same car.

Use the rectangles provided to find an approximate value of the area under the curve.
a Write down the distance travelled by the car.
b Calculate its average speed over the whole 16 seconds.

185

Distance, speed and acceleration

15 A cyclist travels along a road so that in the first 7 seconds of his journey his speed is as given in this table.

Time t, s	0	1	2	3	4	5	6	7
Speed, m/s	0	$\frac{1}{2}$	2	5	$7\frac{1}{2}$	9	10	10

Draw a graph of his speed against time.

Find
a   his acceleration at the instant when $t = 2$
b   his acceleration at the instant when $t = 5$
c   the period of time when the acceleration is zero
d   the instant when the acceleration has its greatest value
e   the total distance travelled in these 7 seconds
f   his average speed over the 7-second period.
Draw a straight line on your graph to illustrate this average speed.

16 A car travels along a road for 14 seconds, with speeds given in this table.

Time t, s	0	1	2	4	6	8	10	12	14
Speed, m/s	0	10	20	26	14	7	3	$\frac{1}{2}$	0

Draw a graph of speed against time.

Find
a   the period of time when the car is accelerating
b   the period of time when the car is decelerating
c   the instant when the car has zero acceleration
d   the instantaneous acceleration when $t = 3$
e   the instantaneous acceleration when $t = 8$
f   the period of time during which the acceleration is constant
g   the total distance travelled during the journey
h   the average speed for the journey.
Draw a straight line on your graph to illustrate this average speed.

17 An object travels from rest for 6 seconds so that its speed, v m/s, after a time t (s) is given by this table.

t	0	1	2	3	4	5	6
v	0	0.6	1.2	1.7	2.0	2.2	2.3

Draw the graph of speed against time and estimate
a   the time when the acceleration is almost zero
b   the acceleration at the instant when $t = 4$
c   the distance travelled during these 6 seconds
d   the average speed over this 6-second period.
Illustrate this average speed on your diagram by a straight line.

18 An object moves in a straight line so that its speed, v m/s, at a time t (s) is given by $v = 12 + 4t - t^2$.

Copy and complete this table, and draw the graph of v against t.

t	0	1	2	3	4	5	6
12							
$+4t$							
$-t^2$							
v							

Find
a   its starting velocity
b   the time at which the object is at rest

Distance, speed and acceleration

   c   the acceleration with which it starts its journey
   d   its acceleration at the instant when $t = 2$
   e   its acceleration at the instant when $t = 4$
   f   the distance it covers during these six seconds
   g   its average speed over this period.

Indicate this average speed on your graph by drawing a straight line.

19   A model car on a test bed starts from rest, accelerates and then decelerates to rest again.

Copy and complete this table, given that its speed, v m/s, varies with the time t (s) from the start, where $v = 6t - t^2$.

t	0	1	2	3	4	5	6
$6t$							
$-t^2$							
v							

Draw the graph of v against t and hence estimate

   a   the distance travelled by the model
   b   its average speed over the 6 seconds
   c   the time when its acceleration is zero
   d   its instantaneous acceleration after 2 seconds.

20   The rotor of an electric motor is rotating at a constant speed of 200 revs/s, when, for a period of 6 seconds, its speed ω changes such that $\omega = 10t^2 - 60t + 200$ where t is the time in seconds.

   a   Construct a table of values to help you calculate ω from $t = 0$ to $t = 6$; and draw the graph of ω against t for this time period.
   b   What is the lowest speed which the rotor reaches?
   c   Over what period is the rotor slowing down?
   d   Over what period is the rotor speeding up?
   e   At what instant is its acceleration zero?
   f   Find its acceleration at the instant when $t = 4$.
   g   How many revolutions does it turn through during these 6 seconds?

Logarithms

	0	1	2	3	4	5	6	7	8	9
1.0	0.000	004	009	013	017	021	025	029	033	037
1.1	0.041	045	049	053	057	061	064	068	072	076
1.2	0.079	083	086	090	093	097	100	104	107	111
1.3	0.114	117	121	124	127	130	134	137	140	143
1.4	0.146	149	152	155	158	161	164	167	170	173
1.5	0.176	179	182	185	188	190	193	196	199	201
1.6	0.204	207	210	212	215	217	220	223	225	228
1.7	0.230	233	236	238	241	243	246	248	250	253
1.8	0.255	258	260	262	265	267	270	272	274	276
1.9	0.279	281	283	286	288	290	292	294	297	299
2.0	0.301	303	305	307	310	312	314	316	318	320
2.1	0.322	324	326	328	330	332	334	336	338	340
2.2	0.342	344	346	348	350	352	354	356	358	360
2.3	0.362	364	365	367	369	371	373	375	377	378
2.4	0.380	382	384	386	387	389	391	393	394	396
2.5	0.398	400	401	403	405	407	408	410	412	413
2.6	0.415	417	418	420	422	423	425	427	428	430
2.7	0.431	433	435	436	438	439	441	442	444	446
2.8	0.447	449	450	452	453	455	456	458	459	461
2.9	0.462	464	465	467	468	470	471	473	474	476
3.0	0.477	479	480	481	483	484	486	487	489	490
3.1	0.491	493	494	496	497	498	500	501	502	504
3.2	0.505	507	508	509	511	512	513	515	516	517
3.3	0.519	520	521	522	524	525	526	528	529	530
3.4	0.531	533	534	535	537	538	539	540	542	543
3.5	0.544	545	547	548	549	550	551	553	554	555
3.6	0.556	558	559	560	561	562	563	565	566	567
3.7	0.568	569	571	572	573	574	575	576	577	579
3.8	0.580	581	582	583	584	585	587	588	589	590
3.9	0.591	592	593	594	595	597	598	599	600	601
4.0	0.602	603	604	605	606	607	609	610	611	612
4.1	0.613	614	615	616	617	618	619	620	621	622
4.2	0.623	624	625	626	627	628	629	630	631	632
4.3	0.633	634	635	636	637	638	639	640	641	642
4.4	0.643	644	645	646	647	648	649	650	651	652
4.5	0.653	654	655	656	657	658	659	660	661	662
4.6	0.663	664	665	666	667	667	668	669	670	671
4.7	0.672	673	674	675	676	677	678	679	679	680
4.8	0.681	682	683	684	685	686	687	688	688	689
4.9	0.690	691	692	693	694	695	695	696	697	698
5.0	0.699	700	701	702	702	703	704	705	706	707
5.1	0.708	708	709	710	711	712	713	713	714	715
5.2	0.716	717	718	719	719	720	721	722	723	723
5.3	0.724	725	726	727	728	728	729	730	731	732
5.4	0.732	733	734	735	736	736	737	738	739	740

Logarithms

	0	1	2	3	4	5	6	7	8	9
5.5	0.740	741	742	743	744	744	745	746	747	747
5.6	0.748	749	750	751	751	752	753	754	754	755
5.7	0.756	757	757	758	759	760	760	761	762	763
5.8	0.763	764	765	766	766	767	768	769	769	770
5.9	0.771	772	772	773	774	775	775	776	777	777
6.0	0.778	779	780	780	781	782	782	783	784	785
6.1	0.785	786	787	787	788	789	790	790	791	792
6.2	0.792	793	794	794	795	796	797	797	798	799
6.3	0.799	800	801	801	802	803	803	804	805	806
6.4	0.806	807	808	808	809	810	810	811	812	812
6.5	0.813	814	814	815	816	816	817	818	818	819
6.6	0.820	820	821	822	822	823	823	824	825	825
6.7	0.826	827	827	828	829	829	830	831	831	832
6.8	0.833	833	834	834	835	836	836	837	838	838
6.9	0.839	839	840	841	841	842	843	843	844	844
7.0	0.845	846	846	847	848	848	849	849	850	851
7.1	0.851	852	852	853	854	854	855	856	856	857
7.2	0.857	858	859	859	860	860	861	862	862	863
7.3	0.863	864	865	865	866	866	867	867	868	869
7.4	0.869	870	870	871	872	872	873	873	874	874
7.5	0.875	876	876	877	877	878	879	879	880	880
7.6	0.881	881	882	883	883	884	884	885	885	886
7.7	0.886	887	888	888	889	889	890	890	891	892
7.8	0.892	893	893	894	894	895	895	896	897	897
7.9	0.898	898	899	899	900	900	901	901	902	903
8.0	0.903	904	904	905	905	906	906	907	907	908
8.1	0.908	909	910	910	911	911	912	912	913	913
8.2	0.914	914	915	915	916	916	917	918	918	919
8.3	0.919	920	920	921	921	922	922	923	923	924
8.4	0.924	925	925	926	926	927	927	928	928	929
8.5	0.929	930	930	931	931	932	932	933	933	934
8.6	0.934	935	936	936	937	937	938	938	939	939
8.7	0.940	940	941	941	942	942	943	943	943	944
8.8	0.944	945	945	946	946	947	947	948	948	949
8.9	0.949	950	950	951	951	952	952	953	953	954
9.0	0.954	955	955	956	956	957	957	958	958	959
9.1	0.959	960	960	960	961	961	962	962	963	963
9.2	0.964	964	965	965	966	966	967	967	968	968
9.3	0.968	969	969	970	970	971	971	972	972	973
9.4	0.973	974	974	975	975	975	976	976	977	977
9.5	0.978	978	979	979	980	980	980	981	981	982
9.6	0.982	983	983	984	984	985	985	985	986	986
9.7	0.987	987	988	988	989	989	989	990	990	991
9.8	0.991	992	992	993	993	993	994	994	995	995
9.9	0.996	996	997	997	997	998	998	999	999	1.000
10.0	1.000									

Tangents

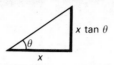

Angle in degrees	0	1	2	3	4	5	6	7	8	9
0	0.000	.002	.003	.005	.007	.009	.010	.012	.014	.016
1	0.017	.019	.021	.023	.024	.026	.028	.030	.031	.033
2	0.035	.037	.038	.040	.042	.044	.045	.047	.049	.051
3	0.052	.054	.056	.058	.059	.061	.063	.065	.066	.068
4	0.070	.072	.073	.075	.077	.079	.080	.082	.084	.086
5	0.087	.089	.091	.093	.095	.096	.098	.100	.102	.103
6	0.105	.107	.109	.110	.112	.114	.116	.117	.119	.121
7	0.123	.125	.126	.128	.130	.133	.133	.135	.137	.139
8	0.141	.142	.144	.146	.148	.149	.151	.153	.155	.157
9	0.158	.160	.162	.164	.166	.167	.169	.171	.173	.175
10	0.176	.178	.180	.182	.184	.185	.187	.189	.191	.193
11	0.194	.196	.198	.200	.202	.203	.205	.207	.209	.211
12	0.213	.214	.216	.218	.220	.222	.224	.225	.227	.229
13	0.231	.233	.235	.236	.238	.240	.242	.244	.246	.247
14	0.249	.251	.253	.255	.257	.259	.260	.262	.264	.266
15	0.268	.270	.272	.274	.275	.277	.279	.281	.283	.285
16	0.287	.289	.291	.292	.294	.296	.298	.300	.302	.304
17	0.306	.308	.310	.311	.313	.315	.317	.319	.321	.323
18	0.325	.327	.329	.331	.333	.335	.337	.338	.340	.342
19	0.344	.346	.348	.350	.352	.354	.356	.358	.360	.362
20	0.364	.366	.368	.370	.372	.374	.376	.378	.380	.382
21	0.384	.386	.388	.390	.392	.394	.396	.398	.400	.402
22	0.404	.406	.408	.410	.412	.414	.416	.418	.420	.422
23	0.424	.427	.429	.431	.433	.435	.437	.439	.441	.443
24	0.445	.447	.449	.452	.454	.456	.458	.460	.462	.464
25	0.466	.468	.471	.473	.475	.477	.479	.481	.483	.486
26	0.488	.490	.492	.494	.496	.499	.501	.503	.505	.507
27	0.510	.512	.514	.516	.518	.521	.523	.525	.527	.529
28	0.532	.534	.536	.538	.541	.543	.545	.547	.550	.552
29	0.554	.557	.559	.561	.563	.566	.568	.570	.573	.575
30	0.577	.580	.582	.584	.587	.589	.591	.594	.596	.598
31	0.601	.603	.606	.608	.610	.613	.615	.618	.620	.622
32	0.625	.627	.630	.632	.635	.637	.640	.642	.644	.647
33	0.649	.652	.654	.657	.659	.662	.664	.667	.669	.672
34	0.675	.677	.680	.682	.685	.687	.690	.692	.695	.698
35	0.700	.703	.705	.708	.711	.713	.716	.719	.721	.724
36	0.727	.729	.732	.735	.737	.740	.743	.745	.748	.751
37	0.754	.756	.759	.762	.765	.767	.770	.773	.776	.778
38	0.781	.784	.787	.790	.793	.795	.798	.801	.804	.807
39	0.810	.813	.816	.818	.821	.824	.827	.830	.833	.836
40	0.839	.842	.845	.848	.851	.854	.857	.860	.863	.866
41	0.869	.872	.875	.879	.882	.885	.888	.891	.894	.897
42	0.900	.904	.907	.910	.913	.916	.920	.923	.926	.929
43	0.933	.936	.939	.942	.946	.949	.952	.956	.959	.962
44	0.966	.969	.972	.976	.979	.983	.986	.990	.993	.997

If, for small values of the angle (up to about 4°), more figures are required than are given in the table, they can be obtained from the formula $\tan(\theta°) \approx 0.01746\theta$.

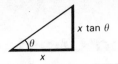

Tangents

Angle in degrees	0	1	2	3	4	5	6	7	8	9
45	1.00	1.00	1.01	1.01	1.01	1.02	1.02	1.02	1.03	1.03
46	1.04	1.04	1.04	1.05	1.05	1.05	1.06	1.06	1.06	1.07
47	1.07	1.08	1.08	1.08	1.09	1.09	1.10	1.10	1.10	1.11
48	1.11	1.11	1.12	1.12	1.13	1.13	1.13	1.14	1.14	1.15
49	1.15	1.15	1.16	1.16	1.17	1.17	1.17	1.18	1.18	1.19
50	1.19	1.20	1.20	1.20	1.21	1.21	1.22	1.22	1.23	1.23
51	1.23	1.24	1.24	1.25	1.25	1.26	1.26	1.27	1.27	1.28
52	1.28	1.28	1.29	1.29	1.30	1.30	1.31	1.31	1.32	1.32
53	1.33	1.33	1.34	1.34	1.35	1.35	1.36	1.36	1.37	1.37
54	1.38	1.38	1.39	1.39	1.40	1.40	1.41	1.41	1.42	1.42
55	1.43	1.43	1.44	1.44	1.45	1.46	1.46	1.47	1.47	1.48
56	1.48	1.49	1.49	1.50	1.51	1.51	1.52	1.52	1.53	1.53
57	1.54	1.55	1.55	1.56	1.56	1.57	1.58	1.58	1.59	1.59
58	1.60	1.61	1.61	1.62	1.63	1.63	1.64	1.64	1.65	1.66
59	1.66	1.67	1.68	1.68	1.69	1.70	1.70	1.71	1.72	1.73
60	1.73	1.74	1.75	1.75	1.76	1.77	1.77	1.78	1.79	1.80
61	1.80	1.81	1.82	1.83	1.83	1.84	1.85	1.86	1.86	1.87
62	1.88	1.89	1.90	1.90	1.91	1.92	1.93	1.94	1.95	1.95
63	1.96	1.97	1.98	1.99	2.00	2.01	2.01	2.02	2.03	2.04
64	2.05	2.06	2.07	2.08	2.09	2.10	2.11	2.12	2.13	2.13
65	2.14	2.15	2.16	2.17	2.18	2.19	2.20	2.21	2.23	2.24
66	2.25	2.26	2.27	2.28	2.29	2.30	2.31	2.32	2.33	2.34
67	2.36	2.37	2.38	2.39	2.40	2.41	2.43	2.44	2.45	2.46
68	2.48	2.49	2.50	2.51	2.53	2.54	2.55	2.56	2.58	2.59
69	2.61	2.62	2.63	2.65	2.66	2.67	2.69	2.70	2.72	2.73
70	2.75	2.76	2.78	2.79	2.81	2.82	2.84	2.86	2.87	2.89
71	2.90	2.92	2.94	2.95	2.97	2.99	3.01	3.02	3.04	3.06
72	3.08	3.10	3.11	3.13	3.15	3.17	3.19	3.21	3.23	3.25
73	3.27	3.29	3.31	3.33	3.35	3.38	3.40	3.42	3.44	3.46
74	3.49	3.51	3.53	3.56	3.58	3.61	3.63	3.66	3.68	3.71
75	3.73	3.76	3.78	3.81	3.84	3.87	3.89	3.92	3.95	3.98
76	4.01	4.04	4.07	4.10	4.13	4.17	4.20	4.23	4.26	4.30
77	4.33	4.37	4.40	4.44	4.47	4.51	4.55	4.59	4.63	4.66
78	4.70	4.75	4.79	4.83	4.87	4.92	4.96	5.00	5.05	5.10
79	5.14	5.19	5.24	5.29	5.34	5.40	5.45	5.50	5.56	5.61
80	5.67	5.73	5.79	5.85	5.91	5.98	6.04	6.11	6.17	6.24
81	6.31	6.39	6.46	6.54	6.61	6.69	6.77	6.85	6.94	7.03
82	7.12	7.21	7.30	7.40	7.49	7.60	7.70	7.81	7.92	8.03
83	8.14	8.26	8.39	8.51	8.64	8.78	8.92	9.06	9.21	9.36
84	9.51	9.68	9.84	10.0	10.2	10.4	10.6	10.8	11.0	11.2
85	11.4	11.7	11.9	12.2	12.4	12.7	13.0	13.3	13.6	14.0
86	14.3	14.7	15.1	15.5	15.9	16.3	16.8	17.3	17.9	18.5
87	19.1	19.7	20.4	21.2	22.0	22.9	23.9	24.9	26.0	27.3
88	28.6	30.1	31.8	33.7	35.8	38.2	40.9	44.1	47.7	52.1
89	57.3	63.7	71.6	81.8	95.5	115	143	191	286	573

Conversions and Constants

Length

$$10 \text{ mm} = 1 \text{ cm}$$
$$100 \text{ cm} = 1 \text{ m}$$
$$1000 \text{ m} = 1 \text{ km}$$

Area

$$100 \text{ mm}^2 = 1 \text{ cm}^2$$
$$10\,000 \text{ cm}^2 = 1 \text{ m}^2$$
$$10\,000 \text{ m}^2 = 1 \text{ hectare (ha)}$$
$$100 \text{ ha} = 1 \text{ km}^2$$

Volume/capacity

$$1000 \text{ cm}^3 = 1 \text{ litre}$$
$$1000 \text{ litres} = 1 \text{ m}^3$$

Mass

$$1000 \text{ grams} = 1 \text{ kg}$$
$$1000 \text{ kg} = 1 \text{ tonne}$$

Imperial–metric conversions

Length

1 inch	= 2.54 cm	1 cm	= 0.394 inches
1 foot (= 12 inches)	= 30.5 cm		
1 yard (= 3 feet)	= 0.914 m	1 m	= 1.09 yards
1 mile (= 1760 yards)	= 1.61 km	1 km	= 0.621 mile
		8 km	= 5 miles

Area

1 sq. inch	= 6.45 cm^2	1 cm^2	= 0.155 sq. inch
1 sq. foot	= 929 cm^2		
1 sq. yard	= 0.836 m^2	1 m^2	= 1.20 sq. yards
1 acre (= 4840 yd^2)	= 0.405 ha	1 ha	= 2.47 acres
1 sq. mile (= 640 acres)	= 2.59 km^2	1 km^2	= 0.386 sq. mile

Volume/capacity

1 cubic inch	= 16.4 cm^3	1 cm^3	= 0.061 cu. inch
1 cubic yard	= 0.765 m^3	1 m^3	= 1.31 cu. yards
1 pint	= 0.568 litres	1 litre	= 1.76 pints
1 gallon (= 8 pints)	= 4.55 litres	1 litre	= 0.22 gallon

Mass

1 ounce	= 28.35 grams	1 gram	= 0.0353 ounce
1 pound (= 16 ounces)	= 0.454 kg	1 kg	= 2.20 pounds
1 ton (= 2240 pounds)	= 1.02 tonnes	1 tonne	= 0.984 ton

The metric prefixes

deca	da	10	deci	d	10^{-1}
hecto	h	10^2	centi	c	10^{-2}
kilo	k	10^3	milli	m	10^{-3}
mega	M	10^6	micro	μ	10^{-6}
giga	G	10^9	nano	n	10^{-9}
tera	T	10^{12}	pico	p	10^{-12}

Constants (to 3 significant figures)

π	= 3.14
$\log \pi$	= 0.497
1 radian	= 57.3°
Radius of the Earth	= 6370 km
Acceleration due to gravity	= 9.81 m/s^2
Velocity of light	= 3×10^8 m/s